CATCHING EPICS

- Halie Fewkes -

May your writing dreams become reality.
Enjoy!!!

—Halie Fewkes

Second Printing, 2018
Tally Ink Publishing

Cover Art by Ginger Anne London

ISBN 978-0-9961699-3-6

www.secretsofthetally.com

CHAPTER ONE

Ratuan-Day came but once a year, and Ebby's wild grin was beginning to hurt her face as Tabriel Vale finally came into sight through the thick cedars. An ancient wooden cart creaked beneath her as she stood on a hay bale to get a better view, grasping the splintering rails as the wheels lurched over a few fallen branches.

"Sit down, Ebby," Sembla warned. "What are we supposed to tell Ratuan if you fall out and break your neck?"

Ebby planted herself on the bale of hay and clasped her hands tightly in her lap, nervous to finally be on her way to see Ratuan. Strange things were happening, and she needed to confide in him just how many whispered conversations she'd interrupted in the past month.

"I can't believe you're so eager to get away from us," said Sembla's aging husband, Reso. Reso had a surprisingly young face when he chose to shave the grey away, but he was already beginning to look wild after two days on the trail.

Ebby switched between four sets of pseudo-parents every year, and Reso and Sembla were always her second-favorites. Sembla knew why, and told Reso, "You know she gets this way every year we take her to live with Margaret and Jelk. That's where Ratuan is."

1

Ebby tried to keep her excitement under wraps by biting her lips together and squeezing the life out of her own hands. Reso laughed, "Ohhhhh, that's right. Ebby, we've warned you about boys, haven't we?"

"He's not that kind of a boy," Ebby said, frowning at Reso to make the point clear. Ratuan was her best friend. The kind good for climbing trees, and catching lizards, and building animal traps that never worked. Ebby didn't need to admit that she had noticed the color of his eyes during their staring contests — a cross between green and brown — or how often she thought about the time he grabbed her hand to keep her from falling into the creek behind his house.

"They're only eleven," Sembla said, setting a hand on her husband's arm.

Ebby couldn't help but clarify, "Ratuan's twelve."

"See? An older man," Reso said to his wife. He leaned toward Ebby and tilted his head to the left, and then to the right before a giant grin broke through his scruffy beard. "Did you... run a comb through your hair?"

Ebby tried to resist blushing, not wanting to give away how much time she'd spent combing out her wispy blonde locks. Her hair hadn't even reached her shoulders in its previous knotted state, but it now cascaded past them, spilling onto the painted tunic she had toiled over for days. What had once been a shapeless piece of linen that sagged to her knees was now a colorful sunset that gained her compliments everywhere she went. Ratuan hadn't seen it yet.

"Alright, we're here!" she exclaimed, jumping from the back of the moving cart and dashing to the front of the caravan before Reso or Sembla could say *hold it, young lady!* Another year older, another step faster!

2

Since everybody was travelling in anticipation of the upcoming Eclipsival, Tabriel Vale had a lively group of merchants and entertainers brightening the already sunny afternoon.

Ebby looked everywhere, finally concluding that Ratuan hadn't reached town yet. The cottage he called home, which Ebby would call home for the next three months, lay miles away. Usually such a distance was frowned upon because of the Escali danger, but Ratuan's family got away with living in the woods because his father was an incredible mage — at least, he had been until very recently.

Ebby lost herself in a moment of sorrow before joyous sounds from the world renowned Travelling Baking Show snapped her out of it. Ebby had seen the troupe of hilarious bakers once before in Dincara, and she edged her way over as they tossed ingredients and clinked their cookware to the tune of a fiddle. The enticing aroma of fresh breads and meats wafted through the crowd, and if Ebby had ever owned a coin in her life, she would be pulling it out of her pocket right now to buy something.

The cook with the curliest hair twirled a plate, a beautiful and breakable plate, on the tip of her smallest finger, and another baker set a roasted rodent on its wobbling surface. Miss curly-hair held it out to the nearest watcher, a tall teenager whose tied back hair reached to her waist, a darker version of blonde than Ebby's and not so thin or wispy.

Ebby froze, thinking for one second that she recognized the girl before she inconveniently turned her head away, laughing at the plate in front of her. "Really, I'm fine," the girl insisted. It had been years since Ebby had heard this voice, and she walked thoughtlessly forward, wondering why this girl kept appearing in her life at significant times. And what would be significant about today?

3

The Baking Show was teasing the older girl while an ancient looking man stepped from the tent to tell her, "We accept many forms of payment! If you don't have coin, we'll take indentured servitude, firstborn children—"

"Come on, Allie," said the curly-haired troupe-member, waving the plate in an enticing circle. "You know we could use you around here."

The girl, Allie, reached sturdy arms out to take the plate. "Alright, sign me up for indentured servitude," she said, grinning until she looked up at just the right angle for her dark eyes to meet Ebby's gaze of blue. Allie froze immediately, wind blowing stray wisps of hair across her face but not breaking their eye contact. This was her.

"Ebby!"

Startled, Ebby whipped around and saw Sembla, finally catching up to her. "You can't run away from us like that. Ever."

"I'm sorry," Ebby said quickly, turning back to the girl — who had vanished.

Ebby darted to look around the tent's corner and found nothing. Nobody. She scanned through every nearby face and ran back to the table where bits of sandwich were landing in a perfect pile, thrown by a cook across the tent.

"Where did she go?" Ebby asked the curly-haired girl, frustrated nearly to the point of tears.

"Who?" The baker replied, eyes on Ebby while she caught a ceramic plate thrown at the back of her head.

"The girl who was just here! You called her Allie."

"Oh, that one… She went… Um, I'm not really sure where she went." Curly-hair leaned over the table to look each way and frowned. "She was just here."

Exasperated, Ebby flipped around to search the crowd one more time.

4

Gone. Ebby had lost her again.

"Ebbs!" Ratuan called from across the market, and she quickly spotted him with his mother and Reso by the caravan. Ebby glanced around one last time, but that Allie girl had vanished like she always did, so Ebby took off toward Ratuan, nervous energy putting an extra spring in each step.

Ratuan threw his hands out to catch her as she crashed into him with a happy squeal, hugging him as tightly as her thin arms could manage while having her own lungs crushed happily in return.

"I missed you," Ebby groaned, her voice flattened.

Ratuan tightened his hold and spun them both in a clumsy circle. "I missed you too."

Aware that Reso and Margaret were watching them, Ebby held back all the things she wanted to say and show him, and instead exclaimed. "You're taller than me now! Not fair."

"I think I'm the tallest of anyone our age," he replied, beaming. His acorn colored hair had also darkened, just a shade since she'd seen him last.

Ratuan's mother turned away and whispered to Reso, "She's *really* getting fast."

Their voices were close to silence, but Ebby still heard Reso reply, "You should have seen her earlier when one of our wheels got stuck in the mud. She just about picked up the entire wagon and threw it back onto the trail."

"Shouldn't we... I mean, are you sure you want her staying with us? Now that Jelk..."

Ebby caught a glimpse of Reso's comforting smile as words failed Margaret. "It's fine, I saw our old friend about a month ago and explained the situation to him," Reso said. "And honestly, we had to bring Ebby or she would have run off to find you. It may be time to start keeping an eye on her and Ratuan."

Ebby looked at the sky, ready to die of embarrassment, hoping Ratuan hadn't heard the exchange. But she *did* want to know if Ratuan could provide any insight about their conversation, now that his mother had apparently joined the secret whisper club.

Ratuan pulled playfully at her painted tunic as she released him and said, "I'll bet you made this yourself?"

"I did," Ebby replied, feeling a smile tug at the nervous knots in her stomach. She stepped between two of the carts and pulled Ratuan with her, not wanting Reso and Margaret to watch them, but not wanting to step into the woods either. Tabriel Vale was practically surrounded by the protection of mages, but sometimes people still went missing.

"Something weird is happening," she told him, grateful that she could finally put the situation into words. "Reso and Sembla are scaring me."

Ratuan frowned and flicked his eyes toward the pair. "What do you mean?"

"I just... They're whispering all the time, and I know it's about me... And they keep giving me things and taking me places like they never think they're going to see me again. I mean, don't you think they would tell me if I was dying or something?"

"You're not dying."

"Well something's happening, and I think your mother knows about it too. And remember that girl, the one I told you about when we were breaking rocks in the creek? I saw her today."

Ratuan blinked and studied her face, knowing this was important. "The one who saved you from that Escali raid—"

"Shhhhhhhhhh!" Ebby glanced around to make sure nobody was near them. She whispered, "Yes. I never catch more than a glimpse of her before she disappears, but she's here today."

She caught Ratuan wondering to himself if the girl might be imagined, and Ebby shook her head to clear it. She had thought for a second she could hear his thoughts.

"We should go look for her," Ratuan said, trying to please Ebby even though he didn't expect to find the girl.

"I don't think we'll find her either," Ebby said. "Let's look though."

Ratuan led the way toward the commotion of Tabriel Vale's marketplace, and turned back around to ask, "Do you still have your friendship rock?"

"Of course," Ebby said, pulling half of an unremarkable grey stone from her pocket. Ratuan withdrew his half to show he still had it, and Ebby smiled, knowing they would always have each other.

Well...

"I... have to show you something," Ebby said, knowing she shouldn't feel guilty, but feeling guilt anyway. She stepped between a stand of knives and a stand of glass figurines, then picked up a pinecone.

Ebby concentrated thousand-degree thoughts on the cone until it began smoking. Ratuan understood what she was doing even if she didn't have it quite right, and even though he smiled, she could feel a wave of sadness hit him. "You have a power?"

"Yes," she replied, looking at the ground. "I was hoping you might have found one too?"

Ratuan only shook his head. "I don't think I'm gifted."

"You're gifted, just... in a different way."

Ebby and Ratuan jumped when his mother, Margaret, found them and asked if they were ready to go. "We're ready," Ebby said, sorry to see creases of exhaustion across Margaret's face. She could remember Margaret's curly hair springing from beneath three

7

headbands back before Jelk died, but now it held less life than her saddened eyes.

"Can we walk ahead if we stay in sight?" Ratuan asked, grabbing Ebby's hand as he shot a pleading look to his mother.

"Alright," Margaret said with a tired smile, "just don't get too far."

Ratuan pulled Ebby toward the wooded trail he knew so well. A hundred thousand tree needles shaded the forest floor making it a paradise for ferns and delicate wildflowers, and their dirt trail wound around both fallen and standing trees to take them home.

Something about Ratuan was strange too. Ebby could feel that he was happy for her, but she could also feel a conflicting jealousy because she would soon leave him for the Dragona. She glanced at their linked hands and wondered if all hand-holders felt this sensation.

"I don't have to tell anybody," she said.

Her hand grew instantly warmer as Ratuan clarified, "About your power?"

"Well, I don't have to tell them right away," Ebby said, smiling as she felt Ratuan's hopeful joy. "We can still have our three months together, and I can tell them I have a power before I leave."

"You would put off going to the Dragona, just for me?" he asked.

A sharp scream cut through the forest ahead of them, followed by the earsplitting shriek of somebody being murdered, and Ebby's reply died in the hush of panic that hit them both.

It had come from that girl, Allie. Ebby could feel it.

Chapter Two

Margaret caught up and frantically grabbed their shoulders as Ratuan said, "That's her, isn't it?"

Ebby nodded while Margaret hissed, "Back to town. Now!"

Ratuan was as afraid as Ebby, but he knew how much this girl meant to her. So instead of fleeing back to town, he ran straight toward the next hideous shriek.

Stunned, Margaret cried, "Ratuan! No, come back!" and Ebby ran after him. Margaret took off at a dead sprint after the kids, but Ebby was ridiculously fast and Ratuan had a head start. Ebby and Ratuan reached Allie in a patch of white ground flowers, writhing and coughing with tears streaming down her face.

"Can we get her back to town?" Ratuan asked as Allie tried to prop herself onto a shaking elbow and speak. Ebby knelt to listen, terrified out of her wits, but needing to know what she would say.

"You!" Allie rasped, pointing at Ebby as she collapsed into more coughing and rolled onto her back again. Grimacing against the pain, she cried, "You've got to run."

Margaret grabbed the kids and yanked them to their feet. "Out of here! Now!"

"But I think she's a mage. We have to help her," Ebby said, sensing strength and power from this girl, now violently thrashing and shuddering.

Margaret threw Ebby and Ratuan behind her, then turned and shoved them both toward town. "Run now," she said, "and we'll send her help from town."

Margaret's forceful push suddenly became a restraint to pull them back to her as an Escali dropped down from a tree limb — a monster with wickedly black hair and spikes of bone jutting from his elbows, now crouched aggressively with his teeth bared at them.

"Oh no," Ebby felt the words tumble from her mouth, "No no no no no no."

Everything that had ever existed, everything that had ever mattered, was about to end, and fear absolutely shut Ebby down. She couldn't move, speak, cry, run, or do anything but throw her hands over her face and lean closer to Margaret and Ratuan.

Margaret fumbled to lift a heavy rock from the ground as their best hope of a defense, and told the kids, "Both of you run, and stay together!"

Ebby wanted to cry and protest, but the Escali darted forward before anybody could act. Ebby squeezed her eyes as an arm wrapped around her shoulders and jerked her off the ground.

She opened them again as the monster stopped to growl at Margaret and Ratuan, their shocked stupor paralyzing them as Ebby's had. Ebby gasped for a few breaths before she realized that the arm spikes from horror stories were a hairs-breadth from her body, and she let loose a terrified shriek, flailing her legs into the air, trying to squirm away. Ratuan launched himself at the Escali, biting and clawing in an attempt to free Ebby as she focused intense amounts of heat into her hands and wrapped them around the Escali's incredibly strong arm.

10

When Ebby looked to Margaret for help, she saw that a second monster with horribly black hair had grabbed Ratuan's mother from behind and was just about to lock his jaws around her throat.

"NO!" Ebby screamed, pulling her chin tight against her body and clamping her eyes shut.

"Gataan!" Ebby's Escali shouted as she heard a faint gurgle and a body drop to the ground. "Not necessary!"

The second monster didn't respond to him, and the first was beginning to notice Ebby's scorching hands searing his flesh. "What the —"

The arm around her shoulders became two hands around her ribs, and then the Escali threw her through the air to the one with blood on his teeth. Ebby managed to conjure a wave of flame that scorched both the monster and surrounding foliage, but when he crushed her hands together in one of his, she could no longer burn anything except herself.

Ebby screamed again and tried to pull her arms free from the brawny Escali with the tied back hair while the spiky-haired brute slammed Ratuan into the dirt. His body only rolled once before settling beneath a massive sword fern, and Ebby gulped down a sob before she used a sudden burst of strength to wrench her hands free from the bigger monster.

Ebby ran straight to her best friend and dropped to her knees beside him with her jaw falling open, unable to express her horror and unable to muster a will to get up and run. Ratuan wasn't moving, neither was Margaret, and so neither was Ebby. If she was going to die, she was going to do it right here.

Even though Allie was still convulsing, she had almost pulled herself to her knees to glare through a tangle of hair. "You'll die for this, Sav," she told the spiky-haired Escali before coughing a dark red substance onto the ground.

11

The monster broke a wicked grin and stooped to tell Allie, "I probably will. But it won't be at your hands."

He swiftly kicked Allie in the stomach and then jerked his head back to pierce Ebby with his cloudy eyes.

Then the Escali ripped her away from Ratuan.

Ebby clawed at the air as he bolted into the trees with her in tow. She screamed as loud as her lungs would allow. She screamed again as leaves and ferns slapped at the bottoms of her feet, then she twisted and kicked and tried to conjure another flame to burn him. The wind she faced from their sheer speed prevented any more fire, but she shrieked and flailed until her cries turned into sobbing coughs.

Twenty minutes ago she had been so happy, torn only by the decision of where to live and how to gain attention. Now she wished she could end her life with a thought so she wouldn't have to see how the Escalis would end it. She nuzzled her face into the neck of her gigantic painted tunic and just tried to detach herself, to let somebody else face the fear, the pain, the grief that overwhelmed her. This somebody was going to die a horrible death, and Ebby wanted to be far away when it happened.

Escalis were built to run, fight, and kill, so they quickly covered ground that would have taken Ebby's caravan three days to cross.

A third brute appeared in the air in front of them, forcing Ebby's attackers to a rough stop, so sudden that it knocked the wind from her lungs. This one had the same aggressive monstrous features, and his hair flowed down his back in the same hue as theirs, three shades darker than black.

His voice was deep and vicious, but Ebby didn't hear what he said because she was shocked to feel herself hit the ground. The Escalis were angry with each other, and she was the reason. This third monster wanted her.

12

Too terrified to get up and run, Ebby crawled away from them and huddled against the large roots of an aging tree, hoping that if a conflict was about to ignite, she wouldn't be hurt.

When she peeked up at them, she found magic in the hands of the new Escali, a deep green glow being held toward her.

No.

Only one Escali could use magic.

This couldn't be him.

But his mastery became undeniable as the entire forest darkened into oppressive cave walls. Ebby was now huddled alone on a grey-stone floor where no one could hear her grief.

She pushed herself into the nearest corner and her cries came out as screams as she pounded small hands onto the rough stone. She tried to release a shriek of denial, or resistance, or *something* helpful. Ebby heaved air out of her body like a poison and could barely choke down a single breath to replenish it. If she had eaten anything during the day, she would have thrown it all up by now.

Ratuan would never climb another tree. He could never beat her in another game of chess, and the magic of holding his hand would never make her feel warm or fuzzy, ever again.

A soul-stifling cloud of despair sapped the strength from her entire body, smothering her will to live as it spread pain through every limb.

Her cries became weaker and hushed as she keeled onto her side and pulled her tunic over her face. The smell of dried berries and flower petals, crushed into the sunset on her clothes, only served to mock her now. How could she ever, in a hundred stupid lifetimes, have cared about a painted tunic?

Her lungs finally gulped in a full breath which she wasted on her next wail of anguish, a sound more pathetic than a wounded and pleading animal. Ebby tried to pull it together, to hold perfectly still and think through a clear string of thoughts. With her sanity

13

on the brink of collapsing, she found herself focusing on stories Reso used to tell her every night.

In his soft bed-time voice, he'd narrated endless legends of the courageous Sir Avery, the only person in the world who could stand up to Prince Avalask. Remembering Reso's soothing voice helped her take a stuttered breath, but she knew the odds of Sir Avery showing up. He wouldn't.

Her existence depended on escaping in a hurry, but when she pulled the collar of her tunic down below her eyes, she found that the stone room didn't contain a single door or even a window. All it held was a table in the middle, shelves along one wall holding up twisted black-glass artwork, and a cold fireplace covered by a metal grate. Ebby brought a small flame to her hands and tried to gather her courage. Surely the fireplace vented to the surface of the world. It was her only way out.

She had nothing left to battle her paralyzing fear, no hope to hold onto except her own continued existence. So getting to her feet was an accomplishment worthy of song and praise, because it was proof that her life was still worth enough to fight for.

She approached the fireplace until she heard a tiny crunch behind the dense metal grate, full of tiny holes she couldn't see through. Ebby stopped in terror and waited… waited… waited until she could finally convince herself the sound had been imagined, then she reached a shaking hand to pull it aside.

The grate snapped back against the fireplace, startling her. "Stay away!" a frightened voice said from inside, perhaps a girl, or a boy no older than she was. Ebby could hardly believe it, and felt a sense of what might be called relief. Here was hope, hope that she might have somebody to hold onto when the Escalis came for her.

"You can… c-come out," Ebby whispered, wiping her eyes. "I'm… not…" her throat constricted around her reassurance.

"I told you to get back!"

Ebby was pretty sure the voice was a boy's. She wanted him to know she wasn't an Escali, so she slipped all ten fingers through small holes in the metal to tug the whole thing away. With her forehead pressed against the mantle, she only needed to crack it open to see inside, but the boy was struggling to hold it closed. As soon as she wedged the grate open and the light of the room reached him, a startling hiss greeted her. Ebby jerked back and fell on her rear as the grate snapped shut again. The Escali hiding inside the fireplace was young, perhaps just a little older than she was, but definitely a vile monster. He might have even had the royally black hair, but she wasn't positive.

Ebby scrambled back to her corner in a heartbeat — which was saying something, considering how fast her heart was beating — and wished she had never left. She hunkered down as fresh tears plagued her eyes, not wanting to think about why he was in the room with her. She knew what Escalis ate to survive, and could only pray she would at least be dead before they started on her.

A pair of Epic's feet landed next to the table, and Ebby tucked her head beneath her arms to sob against her legs.

"Don't be afraid of me. I'm all the way over here," he said. He was trying to speak softly, but the depth of his terrifying voice just couldn't be softened. Ebby had only felt fear like this once before in her life, attacking her with a pain worse than her coming death. She gasped small breaths, not knowing which would be her last, and cringed as she heard him approach.

Death felt like a gentle hand on her shoulder, and her panic evaporated in the next second, leaving her as calm as the sleeping. Magic. It was some sort of calming magic. And the hand on her shoulder was real.

A mere arm's length from her face, the Epic said, "You're ok, Ebby, you're safe here. I just need you to listen. Alright?"

15

Ebby took a steady breath and hiccupped as her core relaxed into less pain. Without her emotions terrorizing her, she was able to wipe the tears from her stinging eyes and lift her chin to see him.

The room's light had visibly dimmed to accommodate the black of Prince Avalask's flowing hair, and he might have been considered handsome if his green eyes didn't have the cloudy quality of a nightmare. "Do you know who I am?" he asked without a trace of a growl in his voice.

She nodded, and he slowly took his hand off her shoulder before kneeling to her level. Ebby hiccupped again and wondered how he could be speaking her language.

"It comes with being an Epic," he told her. "We can speak all languages."

He was reading her thoughts!

He let out a sigh, and said, "*Sorry*. It's a hard habit to break."

Without emotions to plague her, Ebby thought deliberately about Margaret and Ratuan's deaths so the mind reader would have to see them. "I am so truly sorry," he said, his eyes seeming to mean it. "Nobody was supposed to die getting you here. I promise, my brothers are in for more trouble than you know for killing Margaret."

As Prince Avalask spoke, the small Escali edged out of the fireplace and darted behind him. "I see the two of you haven't met. Vack, why don't you say hello to Ebby?"

She heard a desperate whisper from behind the Epic. "Get me out of here."

"Believe me, son, she's more afraid of you than you are of her. But you'll get used to her. You'll both be here for a while."

No no no no no. Prince Avalask's son? His firstborn son?

The kid kept a tight hold on his father as he peaked around to see Ebby, revealing nothing more than a messy burst of royally black hair on his head and thick black gloves on his hands.

"Ebby, I don't have a lot of time to talk, and I don't want to keep any secrets from you," Prince Avalask said. "You've assumed correctly. Vack is the next Escali Epic."

Ebby couldn't feel terror at the moment, but she felt nausea at the realization of *just* who was in front of her.

"I know the Humans haven't announced their new Epic yet, and I want you to know why. Sir Avery had a daughter, Ebby. After five generations of boys for Epics, you're the very first girl, and Sir Avery did absolutely everything in his power to hide you. That's why you never met him, and that's why you move around so often, always staying with families more powerful than you know."

Ebby turned to the side and began retching until Prince Avalask set his hand back on her shoulder and the desire to purge herself receded, leaving only stupefied shock.

But she knew she was dreaming. She was *not* the great Sir Avery's daughter.

"I know this is hard to hear, especially right now, but this is why you're here," Prince Avalask said. "I've been looking for you since the day you were born."

Ebby didn't want to listen further. This was madness. Absolute insanity.

"And I'm..." Prince Avalask looked at his hands as though his words had slipped through them. "I'm... sorry to do this to you, but you're going to grow up to be very powerful, Ebby. If you spend the rest of your life battling Vack, like every Human and Escali Epic before you, then it's all a waste. I brought you here because I want the two of you to meet now, before the world spoils you both. Because if you can somehow manage to get along, the two of you could change everything."

Ebby wasn't stupid. If any of this Epic bogus was true, then she knew exactly why she was here. They were going to hurt her — do things to make her forget who she was. If Prince Avalask could

17

force her to join them, then the Escalis would have three Epics who could topple buildings, set fields ablaze, cause death with a snap of their fingers... And Humanity would only have one.

She promised herself on the spot that she would never let that happen. No amount of brain washing would ever convince her to join the Escalis, not if she kept a tight hold on her memory of Ratuan and Margaret.

"Ratuan isn't dead yet," Prince Avalask said.

Yet?

Oh no. *No.* Her false calm exploded into fear, and she stuttered, "Please help him?" She was stuck. Even if she wasn't stuck, she wasn't an Epic yet. She could barely light a pinecone on fire.

"I will," Prince Avalask said, rising to his full height. "I'll go take care of Ratuan, but please find a way to get along while I'm gone. Just... try. And no more hiding in the fireplace."

The metal grate fused itself to the nook in the wall, destroying its role as a sanctuary. Then Prince Avalask leapt into the air and disappeared from between the two kids.

Ebby caught a full look at Vack before he dashed into the farthest corner of the room and hunkered down. His green eyes weren't as frighteningly cloudy as his father's, but his teeth were still sharp and he still had spikes of bone growing from his elbows. They probably weren't any longer than her fingers, but who cared?

Ebby couldn't imagine why Vack was acting as though he was afraid of *her*. There was nothing in the world she could do to harm him, short of attempting to light him on fire. If he was an Epic though, he would have no problem putting out the small flames she could conjure and proceeding to kill her. She was not going to try to initiate conflict with him. She wasn't about to initiate any form of contact.

She had to get away from the Escalis. The world might actually depend on it.

Without Prince Avalask's presence, she relapsed into bawling, and hot tears ran from her eyes as she scooted carefully toward the fireplace.

Vack stayed exactly opposite her in the room, keeping the greatest distance possible between them, and when Ebby finally reached her only hope of escape, she didn't know what to do. It *had* to vent to the surface. Perhaps she could melt enough of the grate away to get through and crawl out?

Ebby pressed her hands against the cold metal and felt it heat beneath her touch. She had to pull her hands back as it became searing hot, and an orange glow began to creep into the polished shine as she focused. It got hotter and hotter as she felt a mocking scorn from across the room.

Ebby froze, trying to make sure she wasn't imagining the connection with Vack. And now he thought she was stupid for questioning such a thing when she was an Epic.

Ebby didn't want to turn her puffy eyes toward him, and kept them on the metal grate as he said, "You're trying to melt the grate *to a fireplace*. That's what it's there for. To *not melt*."

Nobody had ever spoken to her so scathingly in her life, and she crouched down to slump against the wall. Her situation was hopeless, and her only idea was even foolish to an Escali.

As more tears poured from her eyes, she was also beginning to realize rasping thirst clinging to her dry throat. She hated the fact that something as petty as thirst could bother her now. Nevertheless, now that she faced the middle of the room, she saw two bowls of water and a loaf of bread on the central table. She had no idea how long they'd been sitting.

She didn't want to approach the table or be any closer to Vack than necessary, plus if she really was an Epic, she should be able to easily levitate something across the room, right? She had to figure out if she had any other powers to aid her escape anyway.

Ebby reached her hands toward one of the bowls of water and willed for it to come to her. She saw it twitch feebly, truly shocked to see it react at all. She tried again, concentrating with all her might, and the clay bowl toppled off the table, breaking into three pieces on the floor.

Ebby bit her lip and didn't want to try again with the second bowl. What if she spilled that one too? She was beyond thirsty, so she moved one leg slightly in front of her and slowly shifted her weight onto her feet, watching for a reaction from Vack across the room. He had noticed, but he wasn't doing anything in response.

As Ebby crept forward, she noticed something nagging at her mind. *Hungry. So very hungry.* No, she wasn't hungry, she was thirsty. The idea fluttered around her feelings until she noticed Vack watching her intently, afraid she was going to run off with the bread, but too afraid to stop her.

Ebby decided to extend a gesture of peace. Maybe Escalis could also eat bread along with their… horrific diet. She picked it up with a shaking hand and attempted to levitate it toward him, but the loaf burst into flames in her hands, and Vack gasped in outrage.

She was just about to explain that she hadn't meant to light it on fire when she heard him growl, and the bowl of water in her hands froze into a solid block. Vack must have been able to hear her thirsty thoughts too.

"Fine, you can have it," she said throwing the bowl over to him in defeat. She meant for it to land at his feet and make him feel guilty, but it exploded on the wall behind him instead, thrown with a force she hadn't known she possessed. Vack's wide eyes screamed '*madwoman!*' as Ebby remembered, oh yeah, extreme strength *was* a mage power.

She was about to apologize, but Vack yanked his black gloves off to retaliate. He could actually levitate quite well and sent the shattered ice and bowl shards zooming toward her. Ebby didn't know what power she used to deflect them, but when she stuck her hands out, they slammed into the wall beside her, dislodging the shelf of art.

The twisted glass figurines exploded into sharp shards, skittering to a stop all across the stone floor as the shelf clattered loudly to the ground.

Vack charged toward the middle of the room, and Ebby fled to the fallen shelf, picking it up to shield herself as Vack upended the table to hide behind. The attacks ceased for a moment as Ebby thought quickly. What other mage powers did she know of?

Invisibility. She willed for it to happen, then saw herself flicker a few times. After a little more concentration, she disappeared altogether to her great relief. She set her shelf-shield down, but Vack was perfectly concealed behind his overturned table. Ebby edged slowly around Vack's hideout, positive he couldn't see her, and then felt her stomach drop when she didn't see him on the other side either. Was he invisible too, stalking her at that very moment?

Fear fluttered through her like when she was alone in the dark. She didn't know how to locate people, so she tried to listen for Vack's thoughts instead.

She caught them, drifting in the air, and Vack's feelings were so intriguing that Ebby lost her concentration on staying invisible and reappeared. He was petrified, afraid of more than just her now. He was afraid of falling… Of falling?

Ebby looked up and saw Vack clinging to the ceiling high above her.

"How did you get up there?" She realized she had spoken aloud after it was too late.

21

Vack's terrified voice cracked as he whispered, "*I don't know.*"

Ebby didn't know either, but she preferred that he live on the ceiling as she figured out what she was going to do. Apparently she really was an Epic, and although an Epic had a range of powers to choose from, the ability to jump into the air and reappear in a new location was suddenly her favorite. That was how Prince Avalask was getting in and out of the room, but Ebby knew that jumping could also go horribly wrong. Her best opportunity to figure it out would be while Vack was preoccupied.

Ebby concentrated all of her efforts on a spot across the room and then leapt into the air. Nothing happened. She tried again, this time getting a running start before jumping. Again she landed only a little ahead of where she had leapt, and not due to any magical means.

Really? She could get any power to work except the one she needed most?

Vack figured out how to get off the ceiling and floated to the floor as she tried again. Run and then jump. Run and jump. Run again, and then she glanced off to the side to see Vack hurl the entire table at her as she jumped. Her heart lurched in fear, as did her entire body, reappearing across the room where she had been concentrating. The table smashed against the wall behind her, and she clutched at her core to make sure she hadn't died of fright. Heat began to flood into her face and she turned to glare at Vack.

"That's how you jump," he told her. "Now you can get out of here and quit ruining my life."

"Ruining your — your," Ebby stammered, the events of the day compressing around her. Margaret dead, Ratuan dying, Escali abduction, no Dragona, no future, Sir Avery's daughter... "Ruining *your* life?" she repeated indignantly. Ebby took a furious step forward and Vack skipped back a step in response. She took another as Vack tried to keep his distance and then another until she was marching angrily across the room and had Vack backed into a corner.

Her march of hatred involved no actual plan of action, and so she stopped right in front of him, dangerously close. Vack hissed at her, like a cornered tama cat as he shrank back against the wall. She just couldn't comprehend why. He was taller, faster, stronger, almost impossible to kill, and yet so afraid of Ebby that he couldn't even touch her.

"I'm not afraid to touch you," he scowled. Vack jabbed a finger into her shoulder to prove it, then withdrew his hand quickly and uncertainly.

Ebby pushed him back in retaliation and bit her lip. She didn't like to touch him either.

"Why do you keep acting like I'm the monster in the room? You're the Human here. You're the killer," Vack said, still trying to distance himself.

"I'm the killer?" she asked, astounded. *"I'm the killer?"*

"Quit repeating everything I say! Don't you have any words of your own?"

"Words of my —"

"Quit it! What do you want?"

"I just want to leave," Ebby replied, wondering if anything had ever been more obvious.

"Good, I want you to leave too — and to back up!" Ebby took a step back and Vack's rigid shoulders relaxed a fraction. "You just have to get away from my father, and even a Human should be smart enough to figure out how."

Ebby shook her head with no idea how to escape from a fully powerful Epic.

"Find Sir Avery," Vack told her. "He's the only one who can stop my father from bringing you back here."

Ebby scrunched her eyebrows and studied him. Her response came out so flat that it could barely be considered a question. "You want to help me leave."

"I wish you gone, dead, anywhere but with us. My father wants you and me to train together, but you have no business being here."

"Tell me about it!" Ebby exclaimed, although she couldn't believe Vack would let her escape. Epics were the queens of the chessboard. Once captured, only a fool would give them back. If she couldn't be converted to their side, then she would probably be their next meal so she couldn't grow up to oppose him.

"Will you leave already?" Vack pushed.

"Explain to me, before I do, why you're letting me go," she said. "You're fine letting me turn into the Human's next Epic? You want to give up... dinner as well?" she asked, her stomach in an uncomfortable bind. Death by consumption was probably never a comfortable topic between the consumer and the consumed.

"Dinner?" Vack asked. "You want me to invite you to dinner? You torched all our food!"

Ebby wrapped her arms tightly around her stomach before asking, "Don't you... eat Human flesh to survive?"

Vack's response was a horribly long perplexed stare before his slow and disgusted, *"No."*

Relief swept through Ebby, but her inner self clenched with embarrassment. This was no time to be embarrassed! She took a few short breaths but couldn't shake it.

"Is there something preventing you from leaving?" Vack demanded.

"Let's hope not," she muttered, turning around. She wasn't sure if she had the ability to jump outside the room, and didn't know where to go to find Sir Avery, but she leapt forward and disappeared, ready to land anywhere in the world that didn't have Escalis.

24

CHAPTER THREE

bby crashed headfirst into a thick green bush without any hint of grace and wriggled her way out of the leafy snarl. She got to her feet to see a vast, ancient wilderness all around her. Evergreens as thick as buildings obstructed her view at every angle and mosses dangled from the tallest branches to the ground, looking like they hadn't been disturbed in years.

She hugged her arms around her tummy, trying not to panic in the unfamiliarity. If she was going to find Sir Avery, she needed to find other people, and getting up on a ridge would be her best bet. She wasn't naive enough to expect the sight of friendly chimney smoke rising nearby, but a mountain range or body of water could at least orient her.

Ebby began to climb the needle-ridden, dusty slope as fond old memories danced through her mind, bringing more tears to her eyes. She had loved playing catch with Ratuan, loved curling up with Sembla's ugly grey dog as Reso told her stories, loved braiding her friends' hair when she lived in Dincara...

Not ten steps into her journey, she heard from behind her, "This isn't a problem you can run from." She lost all the breath in her lungs and closed her eyes.

Instinct told Ebby to drop to her knees and beg Prince Avalask to let her go. She was already crying. It would only be a step further.

"Don't... do that," Prince Avalask said, sounding uncomfortable. "It won't help you."

"Why?" She put a hand on a nearby stump to steady herself as she turned to face him. "You don't need me. What do I have to do to get out of this?"

"I want you to grow up and not be an enemy, Ebby. That's all I want. You could be the Epic generation that actually benefits the world."

"I," Ebby said, pausing for courageous effect, "will always be your enemy. And that is *how* I will benefit the world." She then turned around and restarted her journey toward the ridge top, skittishly aware that Prince Avalask was following along behind her, but trying to act brave.

"What good can you do if we remain enemies?" Prince Avalask asked as they walked.

"Well, I can stop Vack from carrying out his evil schemes. That's my job as the Human Epic, isn't it?"

"What if Vack doesn't have any evil schemes?"

"Then something's wrong with him. That's his job as the Escali Epic."

Prince Avalask chuckled behind her. "Just humor me for a second and think about it. What if, by some *impossible* miracle, Vack was born with decent intentions?"

"That couldn't happen." Even if by *some* miracle Vack wasn't evil, he was still an Escali. She wouldn't ever aid an Escali.

"Your thinking is flawed," Prince Avalask said. Ebby wished she knew how to keep him out of her thoughts. "If Vack had exactly the same personality, but was in a Human body, you would have no trouble with him. Escali blood isn't saturated in evil. How different

26

are we really? Isn't it our good and bad intentions that matter in the end?"

Without an adequate response, Ebby stopped and turned around to face him, exactly at eye level due to the hill's steep incline. "I don't want to go back."

"I know you don't, but Ebby, you're one of the four Epics in the world. If you and Vack are raised like the rest of us, you'll spend your entire lives fighting each other." Ebby's knees shook and she turned her eyes to the ground before they could fill with more tears. "I promise, you won't like it that way. You'll take lives when you could be saving them, and someday, you'll be forced to have kids to carry on the legacy too. They'll also fight, suffer, and die... When does it end?"

Ebby hugged herself and repeated softly. "I don't want to go back."

"And I'm sorry you have to," Prince Avalask said, a green glow creeping into his hands. "The future depends on you."

The next time Ebby blinked, she opened her eyes to find herself back in the cave without doors. As soon as Vack saw her with Prince Avalask, he scrunched his face and growled, "Can't you accomplish anything?"

"Don't talk to your guests like that, Vack," Prince Avalask said.

"Guests?" Ebby repeated indignantly.

Prince Avalask mixed a small chuckle with a sigh. "Consider yourself a prisoner if it makes you feel better."

"We're both prisoners," Vack sulked from across the room.

"I suppose you sort of are, since you're both absolutely forbidden from jumping from now on. This is going to be my only warning on the matter. And even though prisoners aren't usually allowed beds, I've decided to make an exception for you two."

A strange Escali version of a bed appeared in each of the room's opposing corners.

27

"We're just going to fight each other as soon as you're gone," Vack said. Ebby clenched her fists in dread.

"I'm sure you will. Just remember what I told you about biting. It's not an acceptable gesture in her culture. Other than that, feel free to settle your differences. There's bread, water, and cooked greyfish on the table, and I'll make sure you get more tomorrow."

Prince Avalask disappeared once again, and the two young Epics remained a room-length apart, observing each other in anticipation. Ebby finally decided to break the silence and say what needed to be said. "I don't want to settle any of our differences."

"Good. Me neither."

Vack approached the table, keeping his eyes fixed dangerously on her. He grabbed his share of everything and retreated to the shallow wooden box he called a bed, elevated two cubits off the ground by four supports with a stiff woven mat lining the bottom. Vack stuffed his half of the bread loaf into his mouth, and Ebby moved hesitantly toward the food and water.

She gulped her water down in a matter of seconds, clinking the clay bowl onto the table and treasuring every drop in her parched throat.

"Thank you," she said to the bowl itself, knowing Vack could have easily poured it out.

Vack barely choked his bread down before retorting, "Don't say thank you. If you say thank you, and I say you're welcome, then we just took the first step toward cooperating. *There will be no cooperating.*"

"Ok," Ebby replied defensively, "Sorry."

"Don't say you're sorry either! Enemies are not sorry."

"Alright, I'm sorry — I mean... No, I'm not. Leave me alone?"

Vack took a deep breath and stared incredulously at the ceiling. When he looked back down at the fish in his hands he muttered, "*Useless.*"

Ebby chewed the inside of her lip bitterly. She was not useless.

"Yes, you are," Vack replied.

She stared at her feet now, angry tears in the corners of her eyes. How had her life turned into this miserable mess, stuck with Vack the monster? Maybe he didn't eat Human beings as she'd originally thought — but he was downright mean.

Ebby squeezed the clay bowl furiously between her hands, wanting it to explode or shatter or something. Instead, a lightning bolt shot from her hands with a deafening crack, ripping the air apart and striking the wall right above Vack's head. Between Ebby and Vack, she would never know whose eyes were wider, and she bolted back to her side of the room to dive beneath her bed, bread and fish in hand.

As soon as she opened her mouth to apologize, Vack shouted, "No! You're not sorry." He pointed to the wall where the lightning had hit. "This is what enemies do!"

Ebby closed her mouth again and simply stared at Vack. He was insane. Mean and insane.

She waited for him to retaliate, but a counterattack never came. He had to know she hadn't shot at him on purpose. She couldn't set off a lightning bolt again if she tried.

Nor did she want to try. That lightning could have just as easily hit her when it went rogue. What would Margaret say if she could see Ebby playing with such danger now?

Vack still wasn't coming after her, so she dedicated another messy round of tears to Margaret and Ratuan before biting into her mini bread loaf. Ebby felt no pleasure at all, chewing and swallowing the food, but she needed to keep her strength up to escape. She also needed to start acting like an Epic.

29

Ebby couldn't help but hear whispers of Vack's thoughts as she made an escape plan. He was still horribly afraid of her, and ashamed of showing such a weakness in her presence. Among his general resentment of her Humanity, Ebby also caught a hint of what tasted like jealousy. He was jealous that she was stealing his father's attention, and angry that she was the reason Vack couldn't be with him.

Ebby tried to block out Vack's bitter feelings with sheer focus, bringing a small flame to her hands. This was how she would defend herself. She brightened the fire and got her fingers to spit brilliant sparks, illuminating her face and the underside of the bed in flickering orange warmth. She even tried snapping her fingers to produce a flame, simply because she thought it would look impressive, but she hadn't yet figured out how to snap. Ratuan had always joked that it was her greatest weakness.

Ebby's blinks became longer as exhaustion finally caught up with her, and every time her head began to droop, she would jerk it back up to make sure Vack was exactly where he was supposed to be. She practiced turning invisible to avoid falling asleep, but drifted off while she was concentrating and quickly startled herself back awake. She tried to levitate what was left of the bread in her hands, but fell into a short doze instead. Her nap ended when a flaming piece of bread dropped into her lap, scorching both Ebby and her tunic as she brushed it hastily away.

Ebby leaned her head back against the wall and promised herself she'd only allow herself five minutes to relieve her itching eyes.

But they glued themselves together the second she closed them, and her last moments with Ratuan plagued her in the form of dreams. She relived the sickening thud of him hitting the ground, and she knelt frantically to shake him as blood began to pool beneath his hair. Ebby cried and wanted to scream, knowing how

30

this would go, knowing the Escalis were about to pick her up and tear her away from him.

"Ratuan, wake up," she pleaded, but as she grabbed his shoulders, his eyes shot open with wicked red irises that would haunt her conscious moments to come.

Panic woke her to the smell of something burning, and Ebby's arm and stomach screamed with searing pain where her fiery hands rested pressed against her. She squirmed desperately to her feet, flinging her burning hands away from her body, and a flash of destructive red light jumped from her palms.

A sound like grinding, colliding boulders shook their entire cave, and Vack woke with a frightened snarl as part of the wall over his bed was severed and fell in a crushing cloud of dust. Several of the larger hunks of rock hit him before he could scramble away from his bed, and Ebby clenched two fists against her mouth, horror struck.

Vack turned to bare his white teeth and hiss at her, blood pouring from his nose, and she immediately forgot about the searing burns on her arm and stomach. Ebby darted back beneath her bed to curl into a ball. "I'm sorry, I'm sorry, I didn't mean to," she pleaded, hoping he wouldn't spring at her with vengeance.

Stinging heat built behind Ebby's eyes, but the tears didn't surge forth until Prince Avalask appeared between her and Vack, and she knew she was truly in trouble. She had damaged his only son, the most important kid in the Escali world. Prince Avalask handed Vack a grey towel, which Vack promptly shoved against his nose to stifle the gruesome bleeding, and then the prince lowered his head to see Ebby beneath her bed.

"I'm sorry. I didn't mean to," she cried, trying to shrink away from his scary, attentive eyes. "I didn't mean to," she repeated weakly as he set a hand on the wooden bedframe and crouched down with something concealed beneath his fingers.

31

Ebby threw her arms over her face and heard Vack run up behind his father to grab him. In the quietest breath possible, Vack whispered, "She didn't mean to," and Ebby felt a reluctant rush of gratitude.

Prince Avalask sighed and said, "Thank you, Vack. And Ebby, you're not in trouble. I brought you something."

She peeked beneath her arms as he set a pair of thick leather gloves at her feet. Ebby's eyes roamed over heavy straps, woven around palms and fingertips, like a jail for her hands. "I don't want to wear them," she cried as she attempted to flatten herself into the corner.

"Look, I'm not shackling them to your wrists," Prince Avalask said. "But we've all had to go through this. I got my first pair when I was four, and your father wore them back when he was training too. You can take them off whenever you want, but you're a danger to yourself if you don't wear them."

Ebby eyed the ugly Escali leather with disgust. She hadn't needed gloves a week ago.

"I think..." Prince Avalask started, but stopped to ponder his words. "I don't think any of us went through the trauma you did yesterday, at least not at such a young age. That's why all your powers are hitting you at once. It's tough to be an Epic in training, but it's alright to burn through a few pairs of gloves. I don't want either of you hurting yourselves."

Ebby glanced at the black gloves on Vack's hands and didn't want to match him.

"Now, I need to go," Prince Avalask said, "but are you alright?"

Ebby didn't like the question. Not one single thing in her life was alright, but she nodded anyway.

"And Vack? You hanging in there, buddy?"

Vack scrunched his nose and eyebrows, less subtle about his hatred of Ebby. "We'll go ahead and call that a yes." Prince Avalask smiled to himself. He stood and disappeared, but Vack didn't retreat to his rock filled bed, and Ebby fixed her eyes on the gloves to avoid his glare.

"You burned yourself." Vack pointed it out like a flaw so Ebby couldn't possibly mistake his words for sympathy.

"I know," she whispered.

"Why aren't you putting the gloves on?"

Ebby felt like she might be sick if she slipped her fingers into the Escali leather. Everything about it would be wrong. "I don't want to."

Vack considered her silently with his eyebrows drawn low. He finally turned around to shovel the rocks off his bed with cupped hands, and Ebby looked down at the burned fabric of her tunic. She had scorched a hole straight through it near her bellybutton.

Ebby touched her fingertips lightly to the hand-shaped blister on her arm and whimpered at the flash of agony, as bad as the initial scorching. She knew Epics could heal injuries, but couldn't figure out how to make it work. She crawled onto her bed and curled into a ball, trying to repair her scorched shirt and blistered skin, unable to accomplish either.

Vack finished clearing his bed and climbed back into it, but Ebby kept herself awake for hours more before sleep brought her another round of nightmares. She thrashed against the rough Escali hands holding her and tried to squirm away before they could sink their teeth into her like they had to Margaret. Desperate to escape, she pulled away from them until an invisible force helped her break free and fly away from their dangerous snarling.

And this time she woke with the ground far beneath her. Ebby realized she had drifted toward the ceiling in her sleep, and she flailed her arms as she tried to find something she could grab for support. She quickly lost all control, wobbled haphazardly, and fell, landing on the bed with a crunch that sounded like she had landed in gravel.

Ebby howled and grabbed her ankle, waking Vack for the second time in what felt like hours. The pain in her elbows and rear couldn't begin to compare to the shattering of her foot. Tears sprang immediately to her eyes and she sobbed as she rolled up her pant leg to see the swelling. If she had ever gotten an injury like this at home, Ratuan would have run for miles to find her help. Margaret and Jelk would have known exactly what to do. All she had now was mind numbing pain shooting through her entire foot, and nobody to rely on but herself.

Vack had crept forward and crouched behind the central table to watch her turmoil. "Don't try it, Tear-salt," he said. "If you don't know what you're doing, you'll make it worse."

"What d-did you call me?"

"Tear-salt," he repeated viciously. "Because all you ever do is cry. You could raze an entire field with the salt from your tears. You could salt a hundred thousand slugs. Stop crying!"

Ebby screamed frustration, took all of the pain from her foot, and threw it across the room at Vack. Ebby's ankle suddenly felt perfect, as though nothing had ever happened, while Vack jumped up and held his own foot in agony. "Knock it off!" he shouted, and the throbbing shot back into Ebby's ankle, making her grimace. "I'm offering to help you, you fool."

Ebby glared at Vack, loathing him. Why would he want to help her?

"Because my father will kill me if he comes back and finds you broken." Vack edged around the table and entered Ebby's territory.

"Leave me alone, please. I don't want your help," Ebby said, wiping tears from her eyes.

Vack grabbed her foot and replied, "Yes, you do."

34

Ebby would have yanked it away from him if it had hurt any less. "You're just going to break it more," she groaned. Her teary eyes couldn't focus on anything other than the spikes on Vack's bent elbows. Ebby suspected she was the first Human to ever see arm spikes at such a close range while not being murdered.

"Da' showed me how to fix injuries like this."

"Your father is a horrible ogre, and he probably showed you wrong!"

"He is for trapping me in here with you," Vack said as the pain in Ebby's foot began to seep away.

"I am trapped in here too, *Vack!* And how dare you make fun of me for crying. My life was fine until your family came in and tore it apart."

"I'm in exactly the same situation, *Tear-salt,* and you don't see me crying."

"No you're not," Ebby said. "You weren't kidnapped. You already lived here! Your mother wasn't killed, and none of your friends were hurt by monsters in order to trap you here."

Vack dropped her healed foot onto the wooden bedframe and shifted his eyes up. "My mother, aunt, grandmother, and every woman in the past three generations of my family have been killed. All by *your* people." He stood tall and walked back to his side of the room.

Ebby didn't want to feel bad for Vack, but she couldn't help having empathy. She wouldn't wish the horrible gut wrenching loss that she felt for Margaret and Ratuan on anybody else. Not even Vack. But he had already been through the same thing. Maybe they weren't so different after all.

"You and I have nothing in common," Vack said in response to her thought. "Don't forget it. My father can't keep us in here forever."

35

Ebby gazed down at her foot and twisted it in a few painless circles. And she knew her gratitude wasn't wanted, but she would feel guilty if she didn't thank him.

"Vack—"

"Tear-salt! No thank yous!"

Ebby watched him carefully, and then asked, "Can you hear every single thought I have?"

"Yes, and it's torture. I would ask Da' to teach me to block them out, but I can't because of you."

"I can't hear the words in your head," Ebby told him.

"I'm not surprised."

"No, I hear more of your feelings. Your emotions."

Vack finally gave Ebby his full attention, as though such an idea had physically harmed him. "What do you mean?" he asked.

"I can't really tell what you're thinking, but I can tell why. Like the way you call me Tear-salt. I can tell that it's the most offensive name you know, and you use it because you think it will keep you from liking me. I can tell when you're afraid, and angry, and jealous—"

"I am *not* jealous of you!" Vack snarled. "Whatever you think you're sensing is wrong. I am not afraid, I am not jealous, and I do not worry about befriending you. You're everything I despise."

"I don't want to be friends with you either, Vack. But you don't have any reason to hate me."

Vack pointed to Ebby's elbows and then to his own — the difference between them. "I have every reason. You Humans kill everything in your path."

"Escalis do exactly the same thing! And I've never killed anybody… Have you?"

Vack stared at the ground, relieved to hear so, before he answered, "No."

36

Ebby was an eleven year old girl. How could Vack think for a minute that she might have killed somebody?

Vack scowled and said, "You're the one who thought I was here to eat you."

Ebby rolled her ankle around a few more times before she admitted, "I guess we've both been a bit misinformed, haven't we?"

"No. Only you. And why are you still here? Is anybody even looking for you?"

Ebby gripped her left hand with her right as she tried to hide how much that question terrified her. "Of course they are. They have to be."

CHAPTER FOUR

Archie was about twenty paces behind me while the sun punched through a breezy forest canopy and danced across our steep slope. I pushed my protesting legs to hike faster in hopes that I could ignore the past three months running through my mind. My calves burned with resentment for hills and my breathing grew ragged, but distraction was difficult to come by when so much was wrong.

I stepped on *one twig* and cringed as it snapped beneath the palm of my foot. I stopped my quick ascent toward the ridgetop to glance back at Archie, whose brows were raised to ask, *Are you happy now?*

The joking smirk on his face didn't prevent me from flicking my eyes up to the sky in irritation, and then I shot a look back that said, *We will never find anything at your pace!*

We usually split up so I could hike in wide arcs and push skittish deer toward him, but today we'd decided to stay together, resulting in the struggle of me trying to drag him along and him trying to pull me to a near stop. It was true, Archie often spotted animals I'd blazed straight past, but I couldn't handle moving ten paces an hour to look for them.

I could smell game in the air, so I turned to face the wind and climbed until I crested the hill to find a herd of fifteen deer far below, picking away at the valley's greenery where a tiny stream snaked back and forth throughout the grass. Archie caught up in silence and jabbed his elbow into my side.

"Will you lighten up?" he breathed as I jerked my gaze toward him. "This is supposed to be the calming part of our lives."

I glanced back to the valley to make sure we hadn't been noticed as Archie crouched from the sight of the herd, and then I narrowed my eyes at him. *Calm* was beyond reach right now, at least for me.

The battle in Dincara had put Humanity in a horrible position. Escalis had overrun the place, killed Dincara's beloved leader Sir Laud when they entered his rigged-to-explode spire, and then they'd shipped the survivors off to Tekada, the continent where Humanity originated.

That left us with fifty-four escapees from the battle who'd now taken refuge at the Dragona, most of them not even mages. Sir Laud's son, Tarace, had stepped up as the closest thing to a leader we could find since both Anna and Sir Darius were killed in Dincara, but leadership was obviously new to him.

Archie and I had immediately volunteered to hunt for the Dragona's food so we could try to find the children who'd fled the battle. They'd been instructed to run to Kellington if Dincara was lost, but they never arrived.

And we still hadn't found them.

Archie grabbed my shoulders to give me a rough shake, then dug his fingers playfully into my hair to mess it up.

"Will you knock it off?" I snarled quietly, ducking away.

"Sure, if we can worry about the Dincaran kids and Sir Avery's daughter later," he said. "The Dragona's going to starve if we lose our minds out here."

I stared down at the undisturbed herd, now distracted by thoughts of Sir Avery's daughter too. I only had one fleeting memory of her — the sight of her screaming while Sav grabbed her and ran. If she wasn't dead, she was certainly locked away in a dungeon somewhere, and knowing Sav's nature, she was probably beaten and starving.

"Can I borrow these?" Archie asked, pulling my bow from my hands and my quiver off my shoulder.

"What are you—" my eyes doubled in size as Archie turned and launched my bow into the branches of the closest pine tree, watching it catch and stick in the needly twigs.

I made a quick snatch to grab his bow off his shoulder in retaliation, but Archie jerked back from reach.

"What do you want me to do now?" I hissed, gesturing at the deer below. "You want me to whistle and hope they come running to me?"

"I never know what you're going to do," he replied, his eyes playful. "If you went running down the hillside and tried to bite them, I'd have to throw my hands up and say *'there she goes.'*"

I grabbed a piece of bark off the nearest trunk and threw it at his knee, watching it rebound off the shimmering barrier that was his power. Archie squinted back, putting a finger to his lips to be quiet.

Now wasn't a good time to mess around, but in fairness, there never was a good time anymore. I could count on my fingers the instances Archie and I had been alone in the past few months, and it was only to exchange a quick joke about sleep deprivation before parting ways to steal a nap.

We'd stayed up *twice* when I had too many Tally-related questions to ignore, and Archie's stories had turned into all-night affairs each time. And twice, we'd paid for it the next day when neither of us had enough energy to locate a single animal.

I dropped my hunting pack on the ground and glanced into the limbs overhead to pretend I was going after my bow, then I spun and rammed into him. Archie barely stumbled back as I collided with his shield. I could only touch him if he touched me first, but

40

he made the mistake of trying to push me away on reflex, which meant his shield didn't stop me from wrapping an arm over his shoulder to grab at his bow as he held it at arm's length. Archie used his free forearm to push me up against a tree, pinning me just long enough to lob the weapon up into the limbs where it settled to rest comfortably next to mine.

I turned my head to the side and ducked forcefully beneath his arm, darting past him so I could leap into the branches. But instead of trying to stop me, Archie snatched my pack off the ground and dashed back. I took a quick second to retrieve both bows, and then leapt back to the ground and pursued.

Archie was already in the process of scattering everything I owned across the ground. He had removed my wool blanket, unrolled it, and wrapped it around a small flower, as though worried it might catch a chill. He had also unfolded my map and stabbed my pocket knife through the top of it to nail it to a tree. He had unwound my entire ball of twine and now sat on the ground, wrapping it at weird angles around his fingers with a piece of *my* jerky between his teeth.

I dropped my jaw and glowered, my eyes demanding *how dare you?*

Archie shrugged and held the crazy pattern of twine out to me with both hands, like it was a game and the next move was mine. I ran at him and he leapt back to his feet, abandoning the twine to grab my dragon skin quiver as I grabbed my satchel. I started to stuff everything back into my pack as Archie began tossing arrows into the air, one after the next, like confetti. I shot him a gaping grin and mouthed, "Knock it off!" I threw a handful of dirt and leaves at him as an entire bundle of my arrows was strewn across the ground.

Archie tilted his head and frowned like he couldn't understand, so I abandoned my repacking and tackled him, taking him down to

41

the ground as silently as we could land, careful not to hit any of the scattered arrows. I grabbed the quiver out of his hands and threw it from reach.

"You don't know how lucky you are that I like you," I said, trying to glare angrily even though a silly smile had taken over.

He grinned and lay his head back against a mossy rock. "Also lucky that half the local wildlife was born deaf."

The deer below had ignored our entire battle, but one doe lifted her head and perked her ears at the word *deaf*, purely for the sake of irony.

We both froze and waited for her to decide she hadn't heard anything, but the longer we stayed still, the harder it was going to be to get up.

I couldn't necessarily say I had Archie pinned, but I did have enough of my upper body on top of him to put a strange longing in my chest and a nervous flutter in my stomach. He chuckled and glanced up, reminding me how heart-stopping the color blue could be on smiling eyes.

"Hey, Archie?" I whispered. His grin faded as I leaned closer, closing what little distance remained between us as a sudden, panicked voice in my mind screamed, *Don't do it!*

Archie rolled out from under me in a forceful hurry, and I had to throw my hands to the ground to keep from eating dirt.

"We're going to lose them," he whispered, eyes fixed on the valley where two more were now wary of us and the first doe stamped her foot nervously. "I'll go down and push them up to you."

"Alright. I'll get this repacked," I said, snatching up a handful of arrows to keep my reddening face hidden.

This was the second time I had tried to make a move. I'd convinced myself that the first one was a fluke, that he truly hadn't noticed my nervous attempt to kiss him when it felt so enticing, and

42

so easy, and so *right*. And I hadn't been hit with an unwanted panic attack the first time. It had been months since my instincts last leapt into my conscious thoughts to save me from danger, and I wasn't sure why they picked now to come back. Although being rejected twice had a certain sting to it, kissing Archie wasn't a threat to my life. He just didn't want the same kind of relationship I did, and I didn't know why.

Alright, yes I did... All our fighting, our sparring, the fun we poked at each other, it was just fun between friends. I wasn't good at taking directions, or listening, or keeping my temper in check when something upset me — to sum it all up, I was missing at least half the feminine traits I should have been born with, and I wasn't the only person who thought so.

Archie took off to circle behind the herd as I moved to grab my bow, and one of my dumber concerns made its way to mind.

"Guys want to be with girls who look and act like girls." That was what Jesse, the ugly coward who'd also escaped Dincara, told me last week when we'd gotten stuck chopping firewood together. I should have kicked him in the shins and told him he was an idiot, but I'd stopped my axe mid-swing instead to consider him over my superior pile of chopped wood. *"I'm just saying, Allie, that you're more of man than I am. Good luck finding somebody who's into that. I can guarantee it's not Archie."*

I smashed a pinecone in my fingers now, angry that such an unimportant comment could be bothering me when I had so many other things to worry about. Jesse and I were decided enemies, and I knew he'd do anything to get under my skin... But his cruel observations were nothing short of truth, and hearing them aloud made them harder to ignore.

The herd of deer below scattered toward me, and I crept closer with my bow now at the ready. I drew the string back with quick precision as two does bounded past, and I sank an arrow through

43

one's heart, pulling another from my quiver before the second doe could flinch. I had my arrow aimed perfectly in the kill zone. All I had to do was release.

Guys want to be with girls who look and act like girls.

I clenched my teeth together, knowing my killer instinct wasn't attractive and my competitive side wasn't really either. I could cover them up. I could pretend I needed more help. *But then I wouldn't be me.*

And so I released my arrow at the last moment, straightening as the doe crashed into the berry bush behind which she'd almost escaped. This one didn't die as quickly as the first, and I had to pull my knife from my side to take care of her. I didn't love this part of hunting, but people have to eat.

The deed was done, and a deep voice said from behind me, "You hesitated with that second shot." I whipped around and withdrew another arrow, finding nothing but empty forest. The laughing tone in Prince Avalask's voice gave him away, but I still knew I would yelp if he reappeared too close.

"Where have you been?" I demanded of the silent trees and leafy undergrowth. "Archie and I have been looking for you!"

"You haven't been looking in the right places," Prince Avalask replied from behind me. I twisted sharply to see him leaning against a fallen cedar, picking off a tiny green sprig off his sweeping black cloak. "You haven't left the Dragona in months to do anything but hunt."

"It's been... complicated," I said as Prince Avalask fixed his icy green gaze on me. I held a great deal of respect for this Epic, who could take anything in the world he wanted, who could end my life with a snap of his fingers, but whom I trusted not to. "Every time we try to leave, some new crisis comes up, and Tarace... means well, and people hold him in high regard, but he doesn't know how to run the Dragona." I folded my arms and grumbled, "So

44

everybody's learned to bring their problems straight to me and Archie."

Prince Avalask grinned and asked, "What? Fame's not to your liking?"

I scowled back and said, "*Attention* makes it difficult to leave, and without leaving, we haven't been able to figure out what happened to kids who fled before the Dincaran battle." I raised my eyebrows at him and added, "There were kids from the Dragona with them too?"

"They're fine. We've got them." Prince Avalask said, twiddling the twig across his fingers. "And your little red-of-head friend is safe with the rest of them. We've put them to work in Dekaron."

My heartbeat stuttered as I repeated, "Put them to work?" Heat crept into my face. "They're children!"

"Unless you have an extreme mortality rate, I wouldn't expect them to die from cooking."

I stared hard at him, looking for any sign of deception, but all I found was a twist in his mouth, as though my skepticism amused him. Something about his nonchalance put me at ease.

"And Sir Avery's daughter?" I asked. "I keep dreaming about her, about the day I woke up and watched Sav steal her away. You know he has her, right?"

"Savaul never had her for more than five minutes. I've got her with my son now, and let me tell you something," he pushed away from the fallen tree with an exasperated grin, "training the two of them is like training snails to jump. Ebby doesn't want to learn from me, Vack is trying to get her back to Sir Avery every time I turn around, and they can barely carry out a conversation without harming one another."

I frowned. "*Why* are you trying to train Sir Avery's daughter?"

He rolled his eyes toward the sky as though I was far from the first to ask. "I have this *insane* idea about raising a generation of

45

Epics who get along. I'm trying to get Ebby and Vack to work together so their powers aren't a waste like every one of their forefathers."

"And how's that working for you?"

"Not well," he replied with a hopeless laugh. "But, you know, I'm getting small victories. They promised to have one conversation per day if I gave them separate rooms, and we're working our way up from there. But if this works, Allie, the two of them could change everything."

I could see in his eyes that he wanted me to believe his cause, and I studied him uncertainly, not sure why my approval would matter. "Why did you wait until now to tell me this? You've had her since the beginning of summer."

"Because I know you, and I know you'll see things my way," he said, glancing toward the valley. "And while I'm up here talking to you, Sir Avery is down speaking with Archie. He's offering Archie anything he wants if Archie can bring Ebby home. And I'm asking you, please, not to let that happen."

"*What?*" I asked, unable to keep incredulity off my face. "If this is as important as you say, Archie's not going to be... bribed out of doing the right thing. If it's better to leave her with you, then we'll leave her with you." Prince Avalask just raised his eyebrows to say *believe what you will,* and I scrunched mine back at him. "What is Sir Avery offering him?"

"Something Archie desperately wants, and something I can't give him."

What had been a perfectly calm conversation suddenly made my blood boil.

"I have no interest in your vague, ambiguous *half-explanations,*" I barked, startling the forest birds into silence. "If Archie needs something from Sir Avery, tell me what it is. Now," I added for angry emphasis, glaring into his smiling, cloudy eyes.

"I wondered where this side of you was hiding," he said, my predictability seeming to comfort him. "Listen, we'll compromise, and I'll tell you part of what's going on. Now wait, hang on," he said, lifting his hands as I bared my teeth to protest. "I really would tell you the whole story, but it's not my place. You need to hear it from Archie."

I bit back an angry retort and listened.

"Here's what I will say," Prince Avalask went on. "No matter how righteous my intentions are, and no matter how much the world could benefit from my plan, Archie is going to take Sir Avery's side."

"And you're trying to say you want me on yours," I finished for him.

He cringed sympathetically. "Driving a wedge right between the two of you, I know. I wouldn't ask if so much wasn't at stake."

I sighed and fixed my eyes on the ground. "What's going to happen to all the kids from Dincara?"

"I honestly don't know," Prince Avalask replied. "Most of them are going to grow up to be mages, so we can't just give them back. They're innocent now, but they'll be Humanity's most dangerous later."

"Sure, but what if… the war was over, and there was no reason to fear them?" I asked. "Returning the kids might be an act big enough to warrant peace."

Prince Avalask broke a hearty laugh and shook his head at my wishful suggestion. "I don't think we're quite as gracious as you're hoping. We have the upper hand as long as we hold those kids. There's no reason to give them back."

"I know you do, but having the upper hand in peace-talks means you get to dictate the terms. And isn't peace something Izfazara wants?"

Prince Avalask considered me for just a moment before releasing a dismissive sigh. "Even *if* I convinced my uncle this was a good idea, making the deal itself would be next to impossible. No Human being on the continent listens to King Kelian, and there's nobody left who they rally around, now that Anna and Sir Darius are gone. There are the city leaders, but they have interaction spells protecting them. I can't find, speak with, or harm a Human leader I haven't met, unless somebody close to them introduces me."

"I've heard of interaction spells," I said. "Tarace is in charge at the Dragona right now, and I know he's got one. But..." I shot Prince Avalask a meaningful look. "Since somebody introduced me to Tarace back in Dincara, that means I can now interact with him however I like. I could even introduce him to you, if the fancy struck."

Prince Avalask cocked a questioning eyebrow. "And you're telling me you'd be willing to do that?"

When he asked so bluntly, it struck me how reckless a plan it was, walking into the Dragona with the Escali Epic at my side to introduce him to Tarace. "It's... not a decision I would make lightly," I admitted, "but Tarace is *from* Dincara. If you gave him the option to bring those kids home safely, I'm pretty sure he'd make a deal with you. And if I helped end the Human-Escali war, how much trouble could I be in, really?"

I had his interest, and he asked, "Do you think Tarace might have a shot at convincing all the other city leaders to go along with it?"

"I think if all those kids' lives are on the line, he'd make a valiant effort."

Prince Avalask stared hard at me before drumming his fingers thoughtfully against the stump beside him. "I think it's an exercise in futility, but I could bring the idea to Izfazara and see what he thinks. Now, Sir Avery just sent Archie back to the Dragona, and I have to be off, so I'll send you to join him. But on a side note, Allie, do you think you could give my brothers their falcon back? They're all sorts of upset about losing him."

I let a laugh escape and said, "Gyr? We tied him up outside and Flak has been taking care of him, bringing him food. I'm sure we could throw him into the deal that ends the war though, if it would help."

Prince Avalask met my grin with an eye-roll before massive shadows spilled across the surrounding foliage, cast by the dragons coming to carry our kills home. Prince Avalask flicked a hand and the world around me morphed into the sparring field back home.

Archie whirled at the sound of my feet hitting the ground and somehow managed to finish his thought to Liz while we exchanged worried expressions.

"You were *both* talking to Sir Avery?" Liz demanded, probably because I'd just appeared in midair. "Oh well, it doesn't matter," she dismissed the idea with a wave. "I was just coming up to the dragon caves to see if you were back yet. The Travelling Baking show is here!" she exclaimed as I moved to join them, her enthusiasm bringing a smile to my face. "And they've brought hunters with them from the north, so you two can stop harping on the rest of us about food for the winter."

"You have no idea how happy I am to hear that," I said, shooting Archie a sideways glance of relief. "That'll free us up to do other things with our time."

I expected him to grin knowingly back at me, but creases of fresh concern had appeared between his eyebrows.

"Do the hunters have a name?" he asked.

"Yeah, Terry jumped out to welcome them," Liz said. "She called them the Shar-something. Shar...ee, I think?"

Archie groaned and muttered, "Zhauri. They're a mercenary brotherhood from up north."

49

"Isn't that what I said?" Liz asked.

"Not Shar, Zhar. The same way you say treasure, or vision. But they're not..." he looked at his hands for a quick second. "They don't go places for the sake of hunting *animals*."

"Are you trying to say they hunt people?" I asked uneasily.

"Pretty exclusively, but they never come south," Archie replied, taking a step closer to us. "They're the five most powerful mages in the world, next to the Epics, of course, and they use deplorable methods to hunt whoever they've been paid to hunt." He shot me a meaningful look, and said, "We *cannot* afford to get mixed up with them."

"I don't know why you're looking at me." I drew a halo over my head. "I have no interest in trouble."

"I'm serious." He lowered his voice. "Until we know who they're after, we're *all* staying as far from them as possible."

"Alright," I said with a dramatic sigh. "I'll be on my best behavior."

Liz grabbed us both by the shoulders with great importance. "Guys, enough of this. I *love* the Travelling Baking Show. Don't make me miss their first performance at the Dragona."

My stomach growled, and Liz addressed it in delight. "Thank you for agreeing! Now let's go. I'm hungry too."

CHAPTER FIVE

We found the Travelling Baking Show outside the entrance to the Wreck, where the seven entertainers and their horse had already amassed a ring of news-hungry watchers.

Archie, Liz, and I joined the crowd just in time for the barrage of, "What happened?"

"Are you guys alright?"

"Which city are you coming from?"

"Is that a bite mark on your arm?"

Their horse hung his head dramatically low and their baking cart bore enough scratches and scorch marks, they could easily claim lightning had struck them.

"I hear Tarace is in charge around here. Do you think we could, you know, talk to him? Or any sort of leader?" Tight curls spiraled to the shoulders of the girl speaking. Corliss, my favorite among the crew. She glanced my direction before recognition lit her face and turned into a wide grin.

"Well if it isn't Allie and Archie!" she exclaimed. "Word has it that you two have been helping run the place. What do you say? Could the Dragona spare a few extra rooms for the daring, hilarious, famous, *and* beloved Travelling Baking Show?"

I caught Jesse on the other side of the room giving a great sneer at Corliss' attention. Jesse hated us, and especially hated when anybody paid us any mind.

I began to say, "Of course—" as Archie flatly replied, "Absolutely not."

Corliss raised her eyebrows at him and then squinted skeptically, her every expression dramatic. There was a reason she was a favorite among the bakers.

"Look at you lot," Archie exclaimed, gesturing to the mud on Corliss' face and the state of their cart. "Nobody wants the Travelling Tragedy staying here."

"How dare you fling such insults," Corliss said, flaring her eyes indignantly. "Sure. The roads here were rough, so we're tattered and stained."

The rest of the Travelling Baking Show sang, "But you'll still get us rooms if you have half a brain!"

A chorus of chuckles and giggles rose from everybody watching as Jesse slunk away from the crowd in irritation, toward the living tunnels. Archie was just barely, *barely* keeping an outburst of laughter under wraps. He took a breath to say something, but had to stop and compose himself again. "Did you honestly force your poor crew to learn that limerick on the way here?"

"Everybody loves my limericks!" Corliss cried indignantly. "And this was too good to pass up, because knowing you, Archie," Corliss gestured to her scratched and stained self, "I knew our sorry state was going to come up."

She shot him a showy, bright-toothed grin before she regally declared, "*Life* is a stage for the actors who know their lines."

Archie finally broke into laughter at the spectacle and said, "It's good to see you," before they grabbed each other with the unreserved kind of hug that comes naturally to close friends.

"It's good to see you're not dead yet, ya brat," she replied into his shoulder, sending a hint of jealousy through me — jealousy and concern that maybe they were closer friends than I knew. "And you too, Allie." She pulled away to give me a hug as well. "I want a full update on everything happening with you."

I mixed laughter with a hopeless sigh and replied, "How many hours do you have?" then felt Liz's heated gaze boring into the back of my head. "And Corliss, this is my sister Liz—"

"Liz, you look like the jealous type. Get over here." Corliss wrapped her arms quickly around Liz, and I held my breath as Liz froze for an unsure moment. Corliss's bold move was apparently the right one though, because I heard Liz giggle to herself, and I knew she would like Corliss from here on out. Everybody did, it seemed.

"Alright then, glad we've got that settled," Corliss addressed the crowd again. "We're going to need a hand getting our stuff put away, and eight rooms — yes the horse gets his own. And I will personally bake a pie for anybody who can bring me a warm meal right now. I think this is what starvation feels like. Yeah..." She clutched at her stomach. "This might be it..."

Archie, Liz, and I always ate together, and I wasn't sure how Corliss could fit so comfortably at the table like she'd known us our entire lives. She leaned back in her chair with her feet kicked casually onto an empty seat, laughing freely whenever she wanted. I envied the life of a travelling baker. Corliss seemed to enjoy everything with an ease I hadn't felt... ever.

"What do you mean Osty's not part of the troupe anymore?" Archie asked. "He *founded* the original Travelling Baking Show."

"Obviously I'm aware of that," Corliss replied, wrapping one arm over the back of her chair then pretending to smack him on the side of the head with the other, hitting his shield. "But he went and met some lovely, silver haired woman up in Teredor, *accidentally* dropped an anvil on his toe, and can't travel for six months." Corliss gave a huge, unamused eye-roll at the inconvenience. "But then we picked up Shadar a few months back — you remember him, the storyteller from Tabriel Vale — and we've been bringing news and spreading stories across the continent ever since. They even let us onto the sky stage in Glaria, which I'm sure you'll remember, has been a lifelong dream of mine."

"They *willingly* let you up there?" Archie asked, looking impressed despite his best efforts. "You're sure you didn't have to break in?"

"Yes, I'm sure. We were the first ones to bring them word about the Dincaran survivors, so they let us use the stage to announce it. Shadar's voice can carry for miles, so he narrated how the Escalis dumped every survivor from the battle on the shores of Tekada, and the rest of us acted out the heart attack King Kelian probably had at the sight of so many mages on his precious continent." She snickered to herself. "We did a whole scene where he panicked and gave the order to quickly build a hundred ships so he could send them back. We had every citizen in Glaria hunched over laughing. We'll act it out again for everyone here when we get the chance."

"I'd love to see it," Liz said, looking more excited than I'd seen her since West's disappearance.

Corliss grinned and I wanted to add something, but couldn't think of anything that seemed appropriate. And since I was still stupidly dwelling on the thought of Archie and Corliss hugging, I found myself twirling my fork around against the tabletop, feeling strangely out of place with my closest friends. Even Corliss's harmless fidgeting began to bother me as she scratched her fingers mindlessly across the top of the table. *Down down down over. Fidget fidget fidget fidget.*

"So Archie, you used to travel with the Baking Show?" Liz asked.

Archie shrugged. "For a short while —"

"We kicked him out," Corliss said. "He couldn't get anything right."

Archie jabbed her in the side. "That's not at all what happened."

"He broke half our cooking utensils, poisoned the customers, and almost burned the operation down."

"I didn't," he insisted. "Allie, you saw me in action with the Baking Show. Help me clear my name here."

"Hmmm?" I looked up from my fork at Archie's expectant smile. He was trying to include me in the conversation, which warmed the bitterness in my chest enough to reply, "Yeah, you weren't half bad."

"Allie's worked with us once or twice too," Corliss told Liz, which was a disgusting lie. I had only worked with them once. "The girl can't cook, but she's an excellent washer of dishes."

"She broke less than I did, from what I hear," Archie said.

Archie was trying to make me look at him. I knew he was trying to get me to like Corliss, but some weird part of me didn't want to, and didn't want to explain herself, so I left my gaze on my twirling fork and bowl, already emptied of today's venison stew.

"In other news, Archie," Corliss said with a grin, "Karissa found her power a couple weeks ago. She can turn invisible."

Archie laughed and said, "I bet Emery couldn't be happier."

He kicked me under the table, and I flicked my eyes up to him. "What?"

Archie only frowned and said, "Nothing. Corliss and I were just talking about some of our friends outside the Dragona."

The two of them glanced at each other, like I was the butt of a private joke between them, but Corliss' finger scratching distracted me again.

Down down down down across – ooohhhhh holy life. She was drawing tally marks. And she knew Emery and Karissa?

Archie met my widened eyes with a tiny nod of his head as their long-time friendship suddenly took on a new meaning. She was probably an old friend of mine too!

"I'm still hungry," Liz said to her empty plate on the table, entirely oblivious.

"Me too," I told her. "Would you be the best sister in the world and get me something while you're up?"

"Fine. But you owe me. Anyone else?"

Archie and Corliss both shook their heads, and Liz had no idea how eager the three of us were to see her go. As soon as Liz reached the food area, I threw my forearms onto the table top and leaned forward to whisper, "You're a Tally?" Then I turned on the one person who was supposed to be explaining my past. "Archie? Couldn't you have mentioned that?"

Corliss also frowned at him. "Thanks for that, Archie, after I went to all that trouble to get you into the Dragona and introduce the two of you."

Archie replied, "You may have gotten me in, but you did *not* introduce us. Don't you remember? Allie jumped me."

I looked up at my eyebrows as Corliss chuckled at the memory, and I didn't admit that I found it mildly funny in hindsight.

Corliss said, "I was the one who found out about your amnesia stunt. If it weren't for me, nobody would have even known you needed help."

"Thank you then," I said, finally allowing myself to warm back up to her, at least a little. If not for Corliss, Archie wouldn't have come to the Dragona to help me. "I don't know what would have happened if I'd been left alone to figure out who I was. It would have been a disaster. Who else is a Tally that I don't know about?"

Corliss looked to Archie, and I could feel the good natured humor drain from the air before he said, "I don't think there's anyone else left."

Corliss tightened one corner of her mouth and dropped her eyes to the table, giving me the feeling that there had once been more of us.

"Here you go," Liz said, handing me a bread roll as she swung a leg over her chair.

I held up the piece of bread smaller than my fist and asked, "Is this supposed to hold me over?"

"What are you? A hibernating bear?" she shot back, making me smile. "You can get up and get more. Hey Corliss, do you have a power?"

"I can move things without touching them," Corliss said, and the roll in my hand lifted into the air with only a slight twitch of her fingers.

"Hey, I still want it," I exclaimed, snatching it and taking a massive bite to claim it as my own. I added through a full mouth, "No wonder you're so good with Travelling Baking Show tricks."

"No no no." Corliss held both pointer fingers up to correct me. "*That* is all skill. You learn a thing or two when you travel with the Baking Show. Which reminds me..." Corliss reached down to her travel sack, which looked more like a conglomeration of pockets than an actual bag, and she pulled out a tight roll of leather. Corliss unwound it until she reached a pouch in the center, revealing a handful of dried green *something*.

"Are we supposed to smoke that?" Liz asked, drawing snorts of laughter from me and Corliss.

"*Nooooo*," Archie said in disbelief. His entire face lit up like a child's as Corliss set the bundle in his hands. "They're tea leaves. I mean, the real, grown and dried in the north, tea leaves." I could smell them from across the table, a mix of autumn wood smoke and spicy warmth. They smelled like comfort.

"You!" he turned on Corliss, "are the best. I owe you my life."

Archie put an arm around her shoulder in a one armed hug, and Corliss shrugged with an unsurprised smile. "I do what I can."

The biting sting of loneliness crept through my veins and toward my heart as I heard him whisper something faint and unintelligible to Corliss before they broke apart.

Liz set her warm hand lightly on mine and pulled, making me realize I had stabbed the prongs of my fork into the wooden table.

"I think I'm ready for bed," Liz said, mostly to me. "Allie, do you want to come over to my room for a little while?"

I looked at Archie who smiled and said, "We can talk tomorrow. I think I'm ready for bed too."

"Sure, tomorrow morning," I said, forcing a smile in return. "And you can make us all tea."

Archie laughed and asked, "What makes you think I'm sharing?" He pressed the leaves tightly back into their pouch as he stood, as though afraid they might escape, and exchanged a brief but meaningful glance with Corliss before he left. And the sting spiderwebbed deeper.

It was almost funny to me, that something as small as the direction Archie turned his eyes could invoke such a strong response, but it was also anything but funny. I felt my cheeks turn red, angry with myself for pushing him toward somebody else. Was there really nothing between us? Was I really so unlovable?

My blood grew warmer the longer I sat, so I stood and pretended I needed more food, although the thought of eating suddenly made me sick. Liz and Corliss struck up another conversation as I strode away.

Come *on*, Allie.

It was just a glance between friends, and I reminded myself that Archie was allowed to have other friends. I had spent many nights wondering why overreacting was such a hobby of mine, why I always let strong emotions smother all my rational thoughts. When I was upset, my instincts just handled situations for me.

A hand fell lightly on my shoulder, and I whipped around to see Liz leaning back, like she knew she would startle me. "Are you alright?" she asked, searching my eyes.

"Yes," I replied, "I just..." my words fled from me as Corliss slipped quietly into the side tunnel.

She was following Archie.

My breath froze in my lungs and my chest hurt, like my blood had carried a shard of ice into my heart.

Liz frowned at my response. "Allie... You might as well write your feelings across your forehead and have a bard sing them beside you. You're transparent."

"I know," I replied, trying to keep myself grounded in calm, rational thoughts so Liz wouldn't think I'd lost my mind over nothing. "I just need time to think. That's all. I'm going to bed."

"Well if you're taking the long route to your room, you know, the one that takes you past Archie's room first, then I'll come with you."

I sighed and found myself strangely grateful that she knew me so well. "Thanks, Liz."

Liz took strides almost the same length as mine as we stepped into a side tunnel, the air around us cooling a few degrees while the noise from the Wreck faded.

"Do you really think there's something between them?" Liz asked.

I felt my stomach squirm as I stopped in the middle of the hallway, feeling the need to defend myself. "Look, I know it's stupid—"

"It's not stupid, Allie. What's stupid, is that you and Archie are closer than foxes in a den and not doing anything about it. You two obviously have fun when you're together. There are times when I think Archie cares about you more than I do, and the guy is not exactly ugly." I found myself smiling. "*And,* if he thinks there's anyone in the world better than my sister, I am going to hit him."

I laughed and some of the tension escaped into the air. "I like how similar our thoughts are," I said, and we both slowed as Archie's door came into view.

I didn't like that the door was closed, I didn't like that their muffled voices sounded so comfortable with each other, but most of all, I did *not* like the words I heard from Corliss.

"You know you're always welcome to come with us if you want to leave the Dragona."

I held my breath, waiting for Archie to laugh and tell her the Dragona was his home. That his friends were here, that we were his *family.*

Instead, he replied, "I think I'll take you up on that. A change of scenery might be nice." ·

Shock welled up so quickly that I thought I might choke on it. He couldn't go. Archie was the constant in my life, the *only* person in the Dragona I could talk to, one of the few who could put a smile on my face when I didn't want one.

"But you can't just leave without telling Allie why," Corliss said. "She needs to know. Honestly, Archie, she already should."

"I know, and I've been trying to tell her, but… it's so hard. There's never been a good time."

Liz's eyes had doubled in size. "Allie, we should go."

I nodded quickly, but my feet remained planted as I heard Archie ask, "When are you guys leaving?"

"Probably a couple days—"

"A couple days?" he repeated. "But you just got here."

"I'm sorry, Archie, did you get us confused with the Stationary Baking Show again?"

They shared a chuckle, and my blood turned into a fiery, liquid anger in my veins. He was leaving. He was leaving me, laughing about it, and had not *once* thought to tell me there was someone else.

My hands shook as I thought of bursting in to hit and kick and bite and yell at him, and Liz stepped quickly between me and the door. "Allie, let's go. Don't do something you're going to regret."

I could see her preparing to lunge at me, ready to wrap her arms around my shoulders and make me drag her into Archie's room if I really wanted to go after him, and I appreciated it. Her willingness to get in my way grounded me just enough to know my rational self wouldn't want this either. Rational Allie just felt so far away right now.

So I turned around and sprinted. If it wasn't a problem I could bare my teeth at, then I could at least run away from it. Rational or not, it was my solution. I just… couldn't get far enough. Every time I felt tears seep into my vision, I would take a longer stride and push my legs to run faster until I escaped the confining tunnel walls. I finally reached the fresh air where cedars towered over a dimming forest, and I slowed to take deep breaths from the wooded breeze as pink clouds surrendered their vibrancy in preparation for night.

What was I going to do without Archie? *How* could he actually be planning to leave me?

I ground my palms against my forehead and held my breath, making a furious attempt to pull myself together. I was a whole person without him, wasn't I?

Yes. I was. And it was stupid to feel like an earthquake had just ripped a gaping fissure through me.

So what if he left? I could find a new sparring partner, and a new friend to hunt with, and a maybe there was somebody else in the world willing to chase me down every time I got myself into danger. Surely I could find somebody who knew my past and had the patience to stay up all night answering my questions with stories that left us both in stitches.

I leaned against a massive cedar, trying to convince myself that my need for Archie was strictly practical as the sky grew nearly dark enough for the stars to emerge. Night life in the forest began to stir as the crickets struck up a chorus and a nearby duskflyer began whistling its evening melody. The local birds only knew one song... One mourning, haunting song with low notes that brought an unnecessary level of feeling into my thorn-wrapped heart.

I looked all around for a distraction and spotted a tendril of smoke rising in the distance, grey against the blackening sky. I pushed myself away from the peeling tree to trot toward it because anything was better than where I was now, and I was curious to know who in their right mind was outside at night. It was no secret these woods were dangerous.

A muffled shriek cut through the trees and I slowed my approach as dread stiffened my limbs. Were there Escalis out here, or possibly the Zhauri brotherhood who'd just arrived? Had they grabbed somebody from the Dragona?

Logically, I knew I should turn around and distance myself from the situation, but then I'd have to wonder all night if that scream had belonged to a friend. Whereas if I crept a little closer, I might be able to figure out who was here. In fact... It would be irresponsible *not* to move in and listen. I might be the only person who could.

Seeing without being seen is an art, and while most people try to escape notice by moving slowly and crouching often, neither of those things are the key to stealth. The real secret is to get a good look at your surroundings and step casually about them, the way you'd navigate furniture in a room you've known all your life.

I've never been particularly patient, but I do know how to move with discipline and grace. By the faint starlight glowing through the canopy, I could see the outlines of every leaf and twig around which I had to maneuver, and I slipped silently toward the commotion until flickers of firelight began to dapple the foliage.

Being a Tally meant I could hear conversations from a great distance, and the drifting voices sounded distinctly Escali. I caught the words *can't, never,* and *Epic* before I could hear a full sentence, and I leaned silently against the base of a mossy tree to hold my breath and listen.

"Prince Avalask hasn't even revealed his son to us yet." The feminine voice sounded desperate. "Nobody knows where he is."

A deeper voice answered rather politely, "I have no interest in the location of his son." He spoke Escalira, but his words were wrought with the vowels of a Human accent. "I asked where he would hide something of great value."

A second shriek rang through the night, and I clapped a hand over my mouth to keep from gasping. I couldn't let this happen. Not at the Dragona. This wasn't how we did things.

I wasn't stupid enough to think I could run in and stop them, but I could get back inside and alert Tarace — alert everybody.

"Pity. I thought a servant to the royal family would know more." The deep voice had switched back to Human. "Kill her. We've got another one back in the trees."

My heart stopped as icy dread trickled down my neck. I shrank back against the moss because it was *impossible* they'd heard me, and I wasn't about to give my position away by panicking.

The man laughed softly and said, "Not Escali, either. She understands Human."

63

He had to mean me. If he could sense me and knew I understood him, he had to be a shanking mind mage. I hissed silent profanities for getting myself into this position and heard a different taunting voice say, "Don't you dare, Kit. You know how Iquis gets when you take his kills."

A new, horrific scream was stifled into silence, and I froze as indignant rage pounded into my ears. One of the hunters began to approach me, taking no care to muffle his long strides, and I was too shocked and furious to bolt away.

The laughing voices of the group had switched to yet *another* language, and one said *"Zhev nol' silnat dierevismos,"* which was answered with a few chuckles and, *"Silnat? Falrieg on nekrie."*

I recognized the Icilic language spoken up north because I knew two of the words. *Silnat* meant five, and *nekrie* meant ten. I should absolutely be making a run for my life right now, but I stepped out from behind the tree in livid defiance instead. A man approaching forty came to a stop, his blue eyes cold and piercing beneath thick, steep eyebrows.

"You southerners don't fear the Zhauri name yet," he said, the same chilling voice that had just ordered a woman's death. He had a lean, clean-shaven jawline and stood much taller than me with a cloak of white fur draped over his massive shoulders. "But you will."

My entire body shook, but more with anger than fear as I spat, "They're taking bets back there. I hear them." I took a step closer and added, "What's the wager?"

"How long you'll last."

"Against who? You?"

"No," he said with an interested smile. "All good hunters have their dogs. You're about to meet mine."

I sneered and was about to ask how he'd like his dog cooked and served to him when I heard the eerie squeak of a door swinging on

64

rusty hinges. The hunter whistled sharply, and as much as my pride demanded I stand tall, instinct finally reared its head and I bolted away.

There wasn't a dog alive who could match my short swords, but killing the thing with its mind mage master nearly at arm's length didn't appeal to me. I dodged trees as I ran and skidded down a hill of loose dirt that stuck between my feet and the sole of my sandals, but I couldn't hear anything pursuing me.

I was nearly back to the Wreck entrance when an unnatural sound rumbled through the entire forest — like a growl, a hiss, and a long scrape of metal on metal.

I whirled around and just about screamed when I saw the thing — a massive red-eyed wolf with a barbed tail and metal plating growing around his chest like a mane. I didn't usually freeze with fear, but his blood-washed eyes bored through my defenses and nearly paralyzed me as he crouched.

Chapter Six

The beast sprang on powerful hind legs, and I jammed both blades between the metal plates on the dog's chest as he bowled me over, his paws larger than my hands. One sword stuck into the ground, keeping the snapping teeth away from my face as I landed on my back, craning my head away as hot drool peppered my face. With the blade rammed between his neck-plates and the hilt stuck into the ground, his ferocious teeth fell just short of ripping me apart.

White magic leapt into my hands and eyes, and I brightened the entire forest with a crackling stream of destruction. It crashed into the wolf with the same force that had once blown a hole in the back of a ship, and he barely shuddered.

"DON'T LET IT BITE YOU," I heard Archie shout as he scrambled over the Wreck's entrance boulders to dash toward us.

I took a horrible risk and rolled to my feet as the wolf turned to see Archie and I made a mad leap for the safety of the tree limbs above.

The wolf twisted back and lunged, but the blade in his neck caught against a gnarled root in the ground and jerked him to a stop, sparing me half a second to pull myself up as more drool spattered onto my legs. He thrashed sharply to dislodge my sword, then leapt with snapping jaws as I got my first knee up to safety. And by the thinnest hair of fate, the beast's teeth missed my dangling foot and sank into the leather sole of my sandal. I wrapped my arms tightly around the rough limb as he shook his head rabidly and tugged, hind legs dragging the ground beneath us. My sandals were too durable to tear and laced all the way to my knees, so I couldn't just shake one off.

"ARCHIE!" I shrieked as the tree bark ripped against my forearms and I struggled to tighten my grip on my only lifeline.

Archie had at least thought to bring a bow, and an arrow pierced into the wolf's neck, right above the metal plated mane. A second and third arrow joined the first before the monster even squealed, and I had nothing but fingertips holding me up as a fourth arrow slammed into his jaw, forcing him to let go with a yelp.

I regained my grip and pulled my feet quickly up as the unnatural beast changed targets and bolted toward Archie. I yanked my hunting knife from the laces of my sandal to hurl it, and the dog stumbled as the blade stuck between his shoulders, but he didn't slow.

Archie was already sprinting up a steep incline, toward one of our dragon caves further up, and I leapt quickly back to the ground to grab my closest sword and pursue as the vicious wolf gained on him. I wanted to scream. He was going to reach Archie in four, three, two—

Archie disappeared into the black cavern, and the predator darted in after him.

Everything fell completely silent as I raced up the moonlit slope in terror, but a sudden cacophony of roaring and squealing echoed over the mountainside as the wolf met the dragons inside. I thought my lungs might explode as I forced my legs to push through long strides, and I grabbed every shrub in my path to pull myself up faster.

I reached the mouth of the cave just as the monstrosity dragged himself out on powerful front paws, his hind legs bloodied and mangled while half a quiver's worth of arrows protruded from his neck. The injured beast snarled at me as I ran forward to drive my sword through his ribs. I knocked him down and pushed all the way through his chest until my blade sank into the ground, pinning him in place, and *still* he twitched and snarled at me.

Archie emerged from the cave and shot two more determined arrows into the massive wolf before looking up to meet my eyes, and just as I took a breath to say, *I am so sorry,* Archie ran at me. I jumped skittishly back, not sure if he was going to maul me with a relieved hug or *what.*

When he collided with me, he wrapped both hands around my neck and shoved me back against a tree, rattling my nerves. I had never seen him so frantic, and I froze as a different kind of terror shot through me.

"Tell me it didn't bite you!" His voice was hoarse with fear. The moon cast shadows across his face as his blue eyes pierced mine with desperation. He had a tight grip on my jaw, like he was ready for me to lunge and bite him.

I shook my head as much as I could with his hands crushing my wind pipe. "No," I gasped. "It didn't. Look."

I stood on one leg and pulled my foot up to show him — dirty but unbloodied.

Archie looked down and took a full three seconds to make sure, then collapsed against me, pressing his face to my shoulder. He took a steadying breath, then stepped back. "It did bite one of the dragons. We've got to go kill it."

Archie turned, but I put a hand on his shoulder to ask, "What happens if it bites you?"

Vicious snarls erupted from the cave again, as though the dragons inside had turned on each other, and I guessed the answer.

Archie glanced at me and said, "I'll go take care of the dragons. Can you make sure that thing is dead?" The wolf struggled and I nodded quickly. Archie dashed back into the cave and I stooped to wrench my hunting knife from between the monster's shoulder blades. The brute reeked like a wet dog who'd died three weeks prior, and he bared yellow teeth at me with a snarl until I drove my knife in just beneath his jaw. I held my breath as the life haunting his red eyes finally faded to an aimless, dead stare, and I removed my blade to take a step back and breathe again.

Another roar echoed from the cave, startling me back into action. I darted inside and ducked under the rocky overhang to see a black dragon lying dead and a furious green dragon stomping two clawed feet onto Archie on the ground. Archie had thrown his hands defensively over himself, and the golden shimmer of his shield power stopped the dragon from crushing him into the floor as he gritted his teeth and hissed at the strain.

The dragon turned to greet me with an angry wave of flames just as Archie's shield shattered beneath the weight. I dove to the side and landed on my elbows behind a short boulder, but not before I saw blood welling up from Archie's chest where two taloned feet held him down. I clambered back to my feet as the beast snapped at Archie's face and he flung his right hand up in desperation, forcing the rows of sharp teeth to sink into his forearm rather than his eyes. Archie released a tortured scream as the dragon pulled his arm back with a sharp jerk, trying to rip it off.

Every blade I owned was outside, so I panicked and leapt onto the boulder I'd hidden behind, launching to land on the dragon's back. I sank my own teeth into the scales on its neck as the most natural response in the world — anything to make it stop tearing into Archie.

Releasing Archie, the dragon snaked its head back to snap at me, forcing me to jump off the other side and dart away. The thing jerked its feet off Archie in an attempt to maul me with a shriek of rage, but heavy chains prevented it from reaching me, giving Archie just enough time to scramble away. We were both out of its reach, but Archie had barely stumbled to his feet when I saw the dragon take a massive breath, and—

"NOOOO!" I screamed as the scorching flames washed over my best friend. The fire roared and crackled against him with a blazing heat that curled even the ends of my hair. When the dragon ran out of breath, Archie stood alive and wincing with his hands held in front of him, the golden shimmer of his shield just barely present.

I ran straight to him and dragged him behind a sharply angled boulder before more fire blazed out to roast us, and we crouched from sight. Archie groaned and coughed as he sat back against the rock, blood dripping from his arm and smoky sweat from his face.

"What's wrong with it?" I asked quickly. "What happens when that Zhauri dog-thing bites you?"

Archie gritted his teeth with a pained grimace and touched his mouth several times, looking for an explanation. "It's... the spit," he said, squeezing his eyes closed. "The Zhauri call it a death hound, and its teeth are coated in a poison that makes you lose your mind before you die."

"Is the dragon going to die on its own then? I can still—"

Archie threw his good arm out to grab mine in a crushing grip. "Leave it. I already killed the one that was bitten. This one's just panicking."

"Oh shanking life," I whispered in relief, glancing to where twenty teeth had torn into Archie's arm and raked across his very bones, a sight so awful that my own skin stung and cried out in sympathy. His chest, thankfully, wasn't nearly as bloodied. "Here, let me help—"

"Don't touch it," he growled as I reached for him, and it finally hit me that Archie's expression of agony was laced with an angry glare. "I'm a Tally. I'll be fine in five minutes." He held the wound tightly to himself as he began to shake.

"I'm so sorry," I said as drops of blood pattered rhythmically onto the floor. "But we have to do something, Archie. The Zhauri will be here any minute—"

"The Zhauri? You mean the hunters who have never been evaded in Human history?" Archie wasn't just angry — a livid ferocity had darkened his face. "The ones I *just* warned you about?" His jaw twitched several times, and I nearly expected steam to pour from his nose as he demanded, *"What. Were. You. Thinking?"*

"I'm..." I nearly choked on my words. "I... saw the smoke from their fire, and I didn't think they would hear me—"

"And I'm sure you went running straight toward it! Didn't you?" Archie looked to the cave ceiling in disgust and snarled, "You're shanking lucky sometimes that your insanity is at least predictable! Liz came in and admitted why you'd stormed off, because she was worried you were about to do something stupid. And you know what, Allie? I *knew* to come straight outside, because this is literally the dumbest place you could have possibly come! The *Zhauri?*" Archie growled sharply in frustration, looking ready to murder.

Justified or not, killing their death hound *wouldn't* go unpunished. The Zhauri would be here any minute, and Archie's injury put us in a terrible position. The skin was so mangled that his good hand couldn't cover the whole wound, and when I reached again to help, Archie twisted away, his glare warning me back.

"Does it ever cross your mind that your actions might affect other people?" he demanded. "I watched that death hound grab hold of your foot, and I thought I was going to have to kill you, Allie. To say you gave me heart attack doesn't come close to what

71

you just did to me. And for *what*?" he shouted. "Because you misunderstood something you heard eavesdropping?"

A sick new sense of guilt twisted into my stomach, and I tried to respond, but only ended up speaking empty air and closing my mouth again. "Yeah, you heard me. Corliss and I are just friends. The same way you and I are *just friends*."

"I get it, alright? I'm sorry," I said. The message that we were to remain as friends couldn't possibly be clearer, and it wasn't exactly a surprise. "I'm sorry for getting us in this situation, but we need to pull ourselves together and figure a way out of it."

"And what do you suggest we —"

"If we can't run from the Zhauri, then I'll walk out with my head held high and try to talk our way out of this. I just need to know what to expect from them."

Archie glanced at the ground, and I seized the opportunity to lunge and wrap my hands around his mutilated arm, putting immense pressure on the skin to hold it together while his Tally blood healed it. Archie winced and let the smallest groan escape, leaning his head back against the jagged boulder as he released his arm to me.

"It's the only thing we can do at this point," Archie growled reluctantly. His entire body shook and he wiped a shiny layer of sweat from his forehead with his good hand. "But you're not going out there alone. I'll —"

"I'm not offering for altruistic reasons," I cut him off, not knowing how much time we had. "I don't want them to know you have anything to do with me. If things go sideways with the Zhauri, which they very well could, I'd rather have you in a position to help me than sinking in my boat. Do you think your shield can keep that mind mage from sensing you?"

"They have two mind mages," Archie said. "Maverick's a reader, Iquis is a writer."

72

"A writer?"

"I mean Iquis can cause pain, bend ideas, and take control of your mind — but he can't sense anything. Maverick's the one who can read your thoughts, and he's the leader of the group."

"Alright, but can he sense *you*? Since you've got your shield?"

"I don't think so. But you have to be so careful, Allie. Aside from their mind mages, they have two telekinetics and a shade who gives them their brutal reputation. I know I already warned you—"

"You don't have to warn me again," I said. "I know you're serious. That was why I approached them. I heard them..." I froze because breathing became harder at the thought of the word *torture*. "I heard... screams."

Archie's eyes widened as I bit hard at my inner lip, trying to detach myself. "They... had an Escali, somebody who would have known Prince Avalask. They were asking her where the Epic would hide something of importance."

Archie held his breath for a moment, then asked, "What did she say?"

I took another moment to gather a false sense of calm. "Nothing. Their leader, Maverick I guess, said she didn't know anything... And they killed her when they realized I was close."

All of Archie's anger vanished with his next exhale as his shoulders sank and his eyes softened. "I'm sorry," he said as I gritted my teeth and stared at the ground, "but... it's nothing you could have prevented." I nodded quickly, but a bitter ache had crept into every crevice of my chest. Archie gripped his uninjured hand into his hair for the duration of a stressed thought and said, "They must be after Prince Avalask's son."

"Maverick said that wasn't it. And the only other thing nearly as valuable would be Sir Avery's daughter."

Archie groaned and took a stuttered breath. "The Zhauri are Human, but if they get ahold of Ebby, they're not going to hand her

73

back to her father. They're held accountable to *no one*, and she's more powerful than anything else they could attain. But if we get away from them unscathed tonight, we might be able to reach her first and get her back to Sir Avery."

I readjusted my hands around Archie's arm, causing him to screw his face into a pained grimace. "Have you considered that it might be better to leave her with Prince Avalask?" I asked. "He... could protect her."

Archie hissed a chuckle of mockery through his teeth. "I thought Sir Avery was joking with me. Prince Avalask *actually* tried to convince you to leave Ebby with the Escalis?"

I squinted back at him, unamused, and replied, "*Yes.* He made some very good points about the future of the world and such small things."

Archie watched me like I might be delusional, and said slowly, "She's been *kidnapped.*"

"Yes, and that's not *necessarily* a bad thing."

Archie's frown turned into disbelieving disgust. "Look... Let's deal with the Zhauri right now," he said, "and afterward, we'll sit down and come to an agreement. Because if I'm trying to help Sir Avery and you're trying to help Prince Avalask, we're worth nothing. We have to take the same side."

"You know, it's sort of funny," I mused. "That is *literally*, exactly the reason Prince Avalask is keeping Ebby, so she and Vack can grow to be more than enemies. Those kids could change the world, Archie."

"Oh good," Archie said scathingly, "a better world brought about by child abduction. I can hardly wait."

I felt my jaw drop in exasperation and asked, "*What* did Sir Avery offer you? And how did it make you blind to everything else that matters?"

74

A dog yipped loudly outside the cave, startling us both. I leapt to my feet as Archie quickly said, "We'll talk about this later." I flicked my gaze to the cave entrance, wary of the still angry dragon eyeing me. "But listen to me, Allie. Fighting the Zhauri isn't an option. Running isn't an option. Use your brain, and don't provoke them. Just get through this, and we'll leave the Dragona tonight."

"Alright," I said, feeling my exhausted heart begin to accelerate again. "Stay hidden, and I'll say I came out here alone."

"Don't say it, just imply it. Maverick will know if you're lying."

I turned away and Archie hissed, "Allie!" right before I stepped out into the moonlight. I peered back, and he brushed his fingers against his mouth, raising his eyebrows.

I touched my fingertips to my lips, and they came away with crimson dragon's blood, reminding me I'd bitten the thing. Archie broke a smile, and I wiped the blood onto the cave wall as he whispered, "Go get 'em, Tally."

An evening breeze drifted through the late summer leaves, making the entire hillside whisper like running water. The cool air felt good in my lungs as I padded toward the dead, armored wolf, the white light of two moons reflecting off his metal plated chest.

I stopped and peered into the dark to watch for the Zhauri, spotting a furry snow-dog staring at me from a safe distance. Grey with a black raccoon-mask of fur around his eyes, he sat with the patience of a statue who'd been sent to keep an eye on me, and I held perfectly still to listen for his owners.

Flickering torchlight bounced out from the trees before I heard any sound from them — a frightening thought, because even *Escalis* weren't that quiet. I would have been entirely oblivious to their arrival if they hadn't brought light to announce themselves.

Even though the Zhauri were Human, they carried a foreign feel. Their clothes were grey and silver with white fur cloaks draping from their shoulders, each boasting a skinned wolf head near the top. They had well-groomed and meticulously shaped beards, thick enough to suggest they had seen many rough winters, and with the exception of the one in the back who had lopsided eyes, matching in neither size nor shape, the rest were striking.

Tall, broad shouldered Maverick looked the oldest of the five and was the only one clean-shaven among them. To either side of him stood the strongest looking thugs, one with hair so blond it was nearly white and the other midnight black, both in their early twenties. The last two Zhauri looked to be mid-thirties, one of them entirely unremarkable and the last pure ugly.

My heartbeat picked up the longer we stood still and I finally said, "I don't believe I've welcomed you to the Dragona."

Only the thug with the thick blond beard broke a smile.

"I've had that dog twelve years now," Maverick said, tipping his nose toward the monster on the ground. "I was holding a bottle in his mouth the first time he ever opened his eyes. I *liked* that dog."

And, idiot that I was, I snorted a laugh and replied, "Maybe you should be more careful with what you feed the next one."

My insolence brought a look of disbelief to every face except Maverick's, who replied, "Believe it or not, there's a difference between a whistle to kill and a whistle to hold, and now that I realize who you are, I'm glad I didn't order your death too hastily."

My smile lost its luster. "I'm sorry," I said, my politeness an utter mockery. "Have we met?"

The man with the darkest facial features asked in a thick, northern accent, "Do you know where Sir Avery's daughter is?" His black beard blended into his dense hair, and then into the night.

"No," I replied flatly, determined not to sound pleading or desperate, like the woman they'd just killed.

76

Maverick smiled with interest and said, "Sir Avery told us you would be a good source for finding her, you and a friend of yours named Archie."

"He doesn't know anything either," I said as a sick sense of unease seeped in. They thought we were a means to their end, a resource to be exploited.

"I understand you lack such information at this very moment," Maverick said, "and that's why I'm giving you a week to find her."

"A *week?*" I repeated.

"Sir Avery has offered us a rather enticing reward if we bring her home, so I expect you to be both cooperative and effective. I'm not asking you to rescue the girl, just retrieve her location."

I opened my mouth to ask *or what,* then instinct demanded I close it again, proof that I have inhibitions in me *somewhere.*

"Now listen, we have a busy day planned tomorrow, so I'll speak with you again in a week's time." Maverick looked back to the disfigured man and said, "Iquis, get those arrows out of Beast and see if you can't wake him."

Iquis moved with a slight limp before kneeling to tug arrows out of the dead dog's hide, and I watched in horror as the death hound blearily opened his eyes to the man's touch.

"Perhaps you'd like us to escort you back to the Dragona?" asked the thug with the blond beard. His eyes were warm and friendly, completely the opposite of his serious, black haired counterpart — two very different embodiments of the word dangerous. "A young lady like yourself shouldn't be alone in the dark."

The hairs on my neck prickled angrily, and I had to consciously decide not to fire an insult back at him before I nodded my loathing thanks. "Sounds like I've got a busy week to prepare for."

And it *would* be busy, because Archie and I now had to decide whether to help Sir Avery or Prince Avalask, and I had to figure out how to handle the Zhauri's wrath — since there was no way in shanking life I was going to disclose Ebby's location to them. Maverick flashed me a sharp grin as soon as the thought crossed my mind. It was a knowing, taunting smile, daring me to enter next week without providing him information and see what happened.

We were going to find out.

Chapter Seven

Prince Avalask had said that princesses once lived in this tower made entirely of black glass, where pale amber light filtered through the very walls and made the room around Ebby glow with every sunset. Ebby would have felt like a princess if the city beneath her window wasn't Escali, or if she wasn't a prisoner, or if her clothes weren't in tatters because she couldn't control her powers.

Ebby flexed her fingers beneath her seventh pair of white leather gloves in the last month and rubbed the tight straps around her wrists as the sun sank behind distant mountains.

She had accidentally burned holes through pairs one and two, reduced pair three into flaky white dust, exploded pair four at Vack when he called her weak and obnoxious, and pair five had vanished in the middle of the night, the result of another nightmare. Pair six had gotten stuck in the side of the glass building when Vack tried to push her *literally* through the wall to get her out of his life. Her current pair of gloves, pair seven, had teeth marks on the right glove where Vack had tried to bite her, and she would certainly never be insulting his mother again.

Life was a nightmare, to be sure. Vack was getting stronger every day while Ebby tried to stay isolated and not harm herself.

She was no closer to finding Ratuan or her father, but she had at least discovered enough powers on her own that she could try.

"So you wasted another day looking for Ratuan?" Vack asked, pushing her door open, though he usually knocked.

"It's not a waste," Ebby muttered. "Now, let's get this over with. What's the conversation for today going to be?"

Vack closed the door behind him and Ebby got immediately to her feet, startled. He always left the door open. She pulled her gloves quickly from her hands and asked, "What are you doing?"

Vack scowled back at her, but to her relief, left his on. "I want to make a deal," he said, approaching the middle of the room to simply sit, waiting for her to join him. Ebby wanted to feel suspicious, but couldn't. Vack was mean and intolerable, but brutal honesty was his one redeeming quality.

"And what's the deal?"

"I want to see my friends again," he said. "And I want you to just stay in your room while they're here so they don't see you."

Ebby almost laughed with relief. "You don't need a deal for *that*. I would rather clean an outhouse than meet your friends."

"And I won't be telling my father that they're here, so I need you to make sure you don't tell him either. That's the deal, Tear-salt."

Lying to Prince Avalask? Ebby narrowed her eyes and fidgeted with the gloves in her hands, afraid to even address the scariness of that idea. Prince Avalask had accommodated her request for white gloves, simply because she'd asked. He'd often invited her to train with them — she refused every time — and always gave her things she needed. He even seemed to genuinely worry about her at times, but Ebby wasn't deluding herself. The Epic could easily bring an end to her if she became a hassle to keep around, and she had no desire to see that day come.

"I can make it worth your while," Vack said, looking up at her from the floor. "I found Ratuan. I can tell you where he is."

"You... *You found him?*" Ebby nearly shrieked, dropping to her knees across from Vack. He could have set the bargaining table in the Breathing Sea and she would have joined him. "Where is he? Tell me he's alright."

"He's fine," Vack replied, as though Ratuan's wellbeing wasn't of monumental importance. "So what do you say?"

"I'll do it. I'll do anything. Where is he?"

Vack leaned away from her and sneered. "You're awful at bartering."

"Please, tell me where he is." Ebby's hands shook, with fear or excitement, she didn't care.

"If I can get my friends over here tonight, I'll tell you where he is in the morning."

"You tell me now!" Ebby nearly screamed as green flames leapt into her hands. Vack had his gloves off in half a second and was back on his feet, hands glowing purplish-black and teeth bared. Ebby leapt up as well, and for once, didn't back off a step.

"Tell me now," she hissed again, and Vack raised his eyebrows in the direction of her flaming hands, taking her seriously for the first time *ever*.

Prince Avalask appeared very suddenly in what little space remained between them. "Gloves on. Now." His serious command rattled Ebby's nerve, but she held her ground and peered around the Epic's sweeping black robe to glare venom at Vack, who already had his black gloves on again. "Ebby," Prince Avalask repeated, his deep voice scaring her but not enough to put her gloves back on. "You don't know what you're doing."

For the first time since being kidnapped, Ebby glared up at Prince Avalask. Her defiance was just cut a little short as the green flames escaped her hands and raced up her right arm. Prince Avalask's hand shot to her arm in a flash, before the fire danced into her hair, and the flames quickly vanished leaving a wicked burn across her skin.

Ebby cried out in startled panic, and Prince Avalask repeated, "Gloves on." She pulled her gloves on, but the sting sank into her bones and she didn't think she could survive another moment without his help. "This is skinfire," he said, crouching to her level as numbness spread down her arm to keep the excruciating burn from killing her. "And it's why you have to start learning what you're doing. I know you don't want my help, but it's probably going to save your life."

Ebby sniffled as water filled her eyes and snot clogged her nose. Prince Avalask removed his hand from her arm and stood again to tell Vack, "You don't know what destruction was in your hands either. Ebby will join us for training tomorrow morning, and I expect *this*," he waved a hand around the area of dispute, "not to happen again."

Vack glared dangerously at Ebby as he said, "It won't."

Ebby only vaguely heard the older Epic's instructions on how to heal her arm, and something about how it would be good practice to learn how to heal others, but she had her full attention on Vack's green eyes, ever so faintly tinted with fog. His thoughts and emotions were dead silent. He was going to kill her. The moment Prince Avalask left the room, left them alone again, he was going to kill her.

And that moment came before she was ready. Prince Avalask said he'd see them the next morning, then disappeared. But instead of murdering Ebby, Vack watched her silently. He had learned to block his thoughts in the past months, but she knew him well. He was waiting for her to retreat in a sobbing mess.

She stood her ground for a full minute before Vack folded his arms. "Tonight. I'll tell you tonight after I see my friends." Then he turned and left.

Ebby let her tears begin to flow freely and crawled beneath her bed to cradle her injured arm. The pain was the only reason she was crying though. She had just won. She had stood up to Vack, and he had compromised. A greater accomplishment may never have existed.

And when she was honest with herself, it was a relief that Prince Avalask would start teaching her the things he was teaching Vack. Watching Vack's powers get stronger over the past months had put her in a bad position. She needed to be able to stand up to him so she could get back to the families who loved her, and so she could face Vack as an equal when the time came. Training with him would be better than allowing him to train alone.

No amount of training will make you my equal, Vack's thoughts reached her from across the hall.

I will be, Ebby shot back in sudden determination. *And then I will be better.*

Who knew that mere *thoughts* of laughter could sound so scathing or condescending? Ebby fumed and tried to withdraw her mind as far from him as possible, focusing on the pain in her arm as she attempted to lessen it.

She'd learned over the past months that healing wasn't as simple as Vack made it look. *There's nothing simpler,* Vack jeered, and so instead of putting her full effort into healing, she focused her thoughts where Vack would be disinclined to listen.

She envisioned the moment she would be reunited with Ratuan, hoping Vack would gag on it. She would escape from here, find him, hug him—

Gross, Vack thought, indeed gagging before he withdrew from her.

Ebby had dedicated every hour over the past months to scouring the area around Tabriel Vale in her mind's eye. How could Vack have found Ratuan first? And where could he possibly be if not in Tabriel Vale?

Warmth filled her and made the pain in her arm disappear as she thought of the homes she used to have, the pictures she used to paint, the books she used to read, and the dreams that used to fill her sleep with Ratuan's bed nearly close enough to touch.

She vaguely sensed Vack leave his room before he came back with two young Escalis. One boy and one girl, all overjoyed to see each other. She tried to pretend they didn't exist and found herself miserably unsuccessful. Joy. From Vack.

It just served to remind her how pathetic life had become, allowing a crippling sense of loneliness to seep in where any triumph may have lived. Nothing could ever be as unfair as her situation. Vack had his friends, his family, and the knowledge that he was safe, so safe that he could feel *joy.* Ebby's envy was unfathomable — the kind that few people in the world could possibly live to experience, the kind that might drive her to do something incredibly stupid. She was so broken… she wanted to join them.

"You know we've heard the rumors," the newest Escali boy said in excitement as Ebby abandoned her attempt to ignore the group. "They say that you found the Humans' Epic, and you've already started battling him. You can get him, Vack. If you kill him this early, all you'll have left is Sir Avery."

"I haven't been fighting the Human's Epic," Vack said through a grin. "But go on, continue your foolish guesses."

"I've heard he's here," the girl said, watching Vack carefully for a reaction. "Right here in the Obsidian Tower. I hear you've already caught him."

"Where did you hear that?" Vack asked, his cheerfulness taking a hit.

"It doesn't matter. But is it true? Is Sir Avery's son here?"

84

Vack stared at the girl in an unresponsive standoff. *Just tell her no,* Ebby hurled her thoughts at him. *Sir Avery's son isn't here! It's not even a lie.*

Yes it is. You're just giving me the excuse of a liar.

It's a half-truth! Who cares?

The three Escalis took Vack's silence as a yes, and the boy asked, "Can we see him?"

"No."

"Why not?" the boy asked. "Let's fight for it. If I win, we get to see him."

"No deal. We never needed an excuse to fight before. Are you suddenly afraid to challenge me?"

"I challenge you, Vack, to a decent fight since nobody else seems able to give me one."

Ebby withdrew as far as she could from their conversation, baffled by the absurdity of it all. Vack had never been happier than with his friends, and all because he got to fight with them?

Ebby didn't want to witness the brawl about to occur, so she focused on searching for Ratuan one last time.

While scanning eagerly through the inhabitants of Tabriel Vale from afar, Ebby sensed something else only a second before it was too late. The boys were tumbling and struggling for the upper hand, and the girl was opening the door to Ebby's room. One second was enough to turn invisible, and Ebby froze, huddled beneath the bed, not breathing.

A loose braid of wavy brown hair hung over the girl's shoulder, and she cautiously scanned about the empty room, her head tilted inquisitively. Her eyes were dark and her nose pointy. She was terrified to enter where she knew a Human Epic lay in wait, but she was driven by a thirst for knowledge that overpowered her fear. She wouldn't have been able to sleep at night if she hadn't investigated Ebby's room.

85

"Jalia!" Vack shouted, running across the hall. The other boy came after him, and Ebby was struck by how similar he looked to Vack, his hair messy and his eyes frighteningly cloudy.

"You can hear her heartbeat," the girl whispered, peering straight at Ebby.

"Her?" the other boy asked.

"Come on, Mir. You'd have to be Human not to smell her."

"You need to leave," Vack said. "You can't be in here."

"Have you misplaced your good sense?" Mir demanded. "You're protecting a *Human*?"

"Listen, you know I don't want to, but I said nothing would happen to her. I'm not about to become a liar for your sake."

Mir looked at Vack in disbelief, then turned to leave the doorway in disgust.

Jalia took another moment before following, analyzing everything in Ebby's room with too much intuition for Ebby's comfort. Jalia quickly theorized that Ebby was hiding either because she was very young or not competent in defending herself. Jalia took Ebby's frantically beating heart to mean these were the first Escalis she had seen outside of Vack, which was nearly the truth. The emptiness of the room also gave away that she wasn't there by any choice of her own, otherwise it would have been personalized.

"Jalia. Let's go," Vack said to her. Jalia took one last squinted gaze through Ebby before she stepped on Vack's foot and retreated. Vack showed absolutely no visible reaction, and as soon as he shut the door, Ebby began breathing again and sat back in relief.

She expected some sort of an apology from Vack, but he wasn't about to supply it. He was with his friends, already enjoying himself again and not caring how much danger Ebby had just been in. He was only relieved that he hadn't suffered the embarrassment of them seeing her.

Ebby chewed on her inner lip, positively fuming. Lately she had fooled herself into thinking that Vack might not be the worst creature in the world to be stuck with, but he *was!*

She reached angrily toward the black glass floor beneath her and scorched words into the obsidian with intense, concentrated heat. It was a song with no tune, composed with hatred instead of harmonics.

Vack is a monster. Vack is a snake. It won't bother me if he drowns in a lake.

There are no lakes around, and you can't even conjure a leaf of water, Vack responded from across the hall. *Although, there is always the chance you might cry one into existence.*

Ebby clenched her fists together and exhaled slowly, wondering if anybody had ever hated anyone the way she hated Vack. She melted a new line into the glass walls.

He can fall off a cliff or be crushed by a tree. If he's eaten by wolves, it won't bother me.

I could fight a wolf with my hands tied behind my back, Vack taunted her.

And so it went. Every once in a while Vack would detach himself from his friends just long enough to shoot mockery across the hall toward the terrible limericks Ebby was using to personalize her room.

She finally ran out of poetic ways for Vack to die right around the same time she ran out of steam, and also right about the time Vack left to walk his friends home. Feeling so livid was physically exhausting, and she would have just gone to sleep if not for the thought of Ratuan.

Vack jumped into her room a while later without opening the door, and although Ebby wanted to scold him for his uncaring callousness, she hated the thought of another confrontation.

87

"Here's your precious friend." Vack threw her a directional thought that couldn't possibly be right. Ratuan wasn't in Tabriel Vale. In fact, he wasn't in a Human city at all, and he wasn't very far. According to Vack, Ratuan was *beneath* them.

"Is this your sick idea of a joke?" Ebby asked, her insides writhing as she tried to hold on to some hopeless hope. "He's not beneath your stupid city."

"Why don't you act like an Epic and *look*." Vack's condescension had Ebby ready to throw a lightning bolt at him before humoring him. "There are over a thousand Human kids down there."

"That's not possible."

"Yes it is. There was a battle in a city called Dincara, and we leveled your whole fortress before finding all the kids who were fleeing to the next city. It's no wonder you all grow up to be such spineless—"

"D-Dincara?" Ebby stuttered, her heart stopping and her breath catching at the entrance to her throat. Reso and Sembla lived in Dincara. Her friend Penny lived in Dincara. She knew the names of the vendors on the pavilion and had a favorite old dog who wandered across the bridge from time to time. "B-but, I would have known."

Vack laughed. "I guess not. It happened not long after you arrived here. And since your kind lost all their mages in the battle, we've been able to start reclaiming whole territories."

Panic made breathing harder. "My... friends," Ebby gasped, flinging a hand to the wall to keep from collapsing. They had been dead for months?

Vack stopped laughing. "I'm sure they're fine," he said, trying for once to disarm the situation. "My uncles found the kids and brought them here—"

"The same uncles who brought ME HERE?"

Ebby had never gotten the memory of Margaret's vicious murderers to leave her head, and thoughts of them with their hands on Ratuan again made her violently ill. She sank to the floor as sobs overtook her control, and she felt no shame crawling back beneath her bed as Vack watched.

But he wasn't wearing a sadistic grin. He had frozen, as though he felt guilt or sympathy or something else impossible.

"You win, alright? You win," Ebby whispered, leaning against the wall, pulling her knees to her face as her entire body shook. "Please go away." Vack stayed put, and it didn't even matter.

How could more of her friends be dead? And Dincara... gone...

There was no reason left to fight. Escaping here would just be an escape to the miserable existence where nothing was permanent. Where everyone died or was already dead. Why even continue?

"Look, I made it sound worse than it was." Vack crouched and set his hands and knees on the floor. Ebby refused to look up through her breathless sobs. "It's just the city that was leveled. Most of the people are fine. There was a last minute decision to spare everyone, and we just put them on boats and took them to another continent. Tekada. The one you're all from to begin with."

Ebby left her face pressed to her knees and said nothing. This freak niceness would vanish any second.

"Tear-salt?" When she remained silent, Vack crawled beneath her bed and sat against the wall beside her. "Look, I'm sorry."

"What?" Ebby snapped her head up to see Vack looking at his knees.

"Oh come on, you heard me. I said I'm sorry. I've seen that Margaret-woman in your head so many times that I want to hate my own uncles. I still don't like you, but I'm sorry that happened."

And that was, hands down, the nicest thing Vack had ever said to her.

89

Stop that. You know I can't be nice to you, Vack thought. *If we treat each other like friends, that's eventually what we'll become. Neither of us want that.*

Yeah... I know. But Ebby would honestly prefer this weird, kind version of Vack any day.

"I just... feel bad," he said, biting at his fingernails as he wrapped an arm around his knees. "I've never seen anyone killed, but I know what it's like to have somebody and then suddenly not have them anymore. And you went from having lots of somebodies to nobody. And who even knows where your parents are. I at least have one..."

"You're not very good at being nice," Ebby said, though she knew this was the closest he was capable.

A knock on the door startled them both, and Ebby used magic to peer into the hallway as she went invisible, feeling her heart freeze with dread as Vack whispered, "*No...* They must have followed me back."

Two Escalis stood outside her door. Vack's uncles, Savaul and Gataan.

CHAPTER EIGHT

Vack leapt up from beneath the bed as Savaul pushed the door open. "Vack!" he exclaimed, delight masking the evil in his eyes. "We haven't seen you in months! Get over here."

Savaul stooped with his arms outstretched, and for having just admitted that he didn't like his uncles, Vack didn't hesitate to hug Savaul. *I'll get them out of here*, he thought quickly to Ebby as she masked the sound of her heartbeat.

Where in life was Prince Avalask when she *actually* needed him?

"You've gotten so big," Savaul said with a genuine grin, still made scary by his cloudy eyes and the spikes of bone protruding from his elbows. Gataan, the brother whose teeth had torn into Margaret, stood as a quiet looming force, smelling the air with interest. "Seems like your father's been keeping you busy, hasn't he?" Savaul asked, glancing around the room. "Teaching you the ways of the Epic?"

"Yes. You should see what I can do now. I can light things on fire, shoot lightning, turn rocks into dust, and shield myself."

"I'll bet he's taught you a lot about shading too, so the Human mages can't find you? Or anyone you're trying to keep hidden?"

Everybody knew Savaul was trying to bait him into bringing up Ebby. Vack replied, "That was the first thing he ever taught me. Years ago."

Savaul studied his nephew for a moment, then asked bluntly, "Do you know where she is?"

"Yes."

Ebby wasn't going to wait for her fate, invisible beneath her bed. She crawled to her feet as silently as a rabbit on glass and edged toward the doorway where the larger brother stood.

"What would it take for you to tell me?" Savaul asked.

"My father's permission," Vack said, making his uncle chuckle.

Gataan, the larger brother of so few words, said, "She's here."

Savaul squeezed Vack's shoulder in reassurance. "We'll take care of her for you. You don't even have to do anything."

Vack froze and Ebby could feel his mind spinning, trying to find a way to stop exactly that from happening. He didn't want her dead, but Ebby couldn't see him standing up to his uncles either.

She became visible for two seconds and ghosted through the back glass wall, emerging in the hallway to sprint away as she heard calmly behind her, "There she goes."

Ebby was faster than her pursuers and her footfalls surprisingly quiet. At this speed, her biggest problem was actually that every corner of the glass tower was like a sharpened knife waiting to cut into her.

She reached an intersection with another hallway and grabbed the corner to push off in a new direction, shrieking as the black glass sliced her palm wide open. She sprinted on, past at least twenty doors in the glass. At the next intersection, she tried to stop her momentum to turn, and only barely touched the corner of the wall, but received another slash across her fingertips like the bite of a hundred hornets.

Ebby clenched her teeth and pushed herself to keep running as she heard heart-stopping laughter behind her. "*She's bleeding,*" said one of her pursuers, and Ebby tried to keep her despair from coming out in a sob as she descended three steep staircases in a row.

She *could* outrun them for a while, but she couldn't hide. Escalis were built for tracking, for hunting — and she was leaving a blood trail.

She wasn't about to turn and face them either, so she took a deep breath, got a running start down the next narrow glass hallway, and leapt into the air to vanish.

But instead of landing outside this time, she reappeared at the end of the same hall where the glass floor dropped abruptly to another black set of stairs. She skidded right off the uppermost step and tumbled immediately down, throwing her arms in front of herself in a plea for survival. A shimmering golden barrier prevented the steps from shredding her into a bloody mess, but she still crashed down the whole flight of stairs and landed at the bottom, bruises everywhere and her spirit broken.

Ebby curled into a ball as pain enveloped her the way it had nearly every day of the past month, and she whispered to the uncaring world, "Just let them end this." She let out a long, resigned sigh and closed her eyes, ready.

Gataan's deep voice rumbled from the hallway above, "Her scent ends here."

"*What?*" Savaul exclaimed before swearing loudly. "She can't know how to jump yet. She wouldn't still be here." He paused and said, "She must have turned invisible and backtracked past us."

And right before the twins reached the staircase, they turned around to hastily retrace their steps, giving up an easy view of helpless prey. Ebby took a deep breath and lay still, certain this stroke of luck had to be imagined. She rubbed her arms and focused on healing them, silent and unmoving for several minutes of disbelief, until an ornately carved door at the end of the hall began calling to her.

She'd lost track of how far she'd just run, and delirious hope suggested that Ratuan might be on the other side. Ebby set her hands on the cold floor, where a thousand lines of grey rock spider-webbed through the glass, and she pushed herself to her feet. She could have stopped to read the multitude of Escali symbols carved into the door, or even used magic to look past them to the other side, but she ghosted herself straight through instead, stepping into a several degree colder space as the only living being.

She'd joined twelve looming statues of black glass that were larger than life — all of them Escali women — and after a calming breath, she slumped back against the door to marvel.

They looked like queens, each of them draped in glass imitations of thick furs and leathers. Each stood with the confidence of a woman who had an army behind her and a few held knives while others had falcons landing on a shoulder or an arm. Ebby stepped forward so she could lay a hand on one of the cloaks. Somebody had been talented enough make obsidian look and feel like frozen fur, which meant there *were* Escalis who cared about creating instead of destroying. And for whatever reason, they had created just one of the Escali women from solid gold rather than black glass.

Ebby saw the splitting lines of a family tree carved into the back wall and crept closer to see a name she recognized, spelled in tiny gem stones at the bottom.

Vack.

It was clear that only the Epics' names glittered, as Avalask's shone the same above him. A thin line connected Prince Avalask to a woman named Dreya, obviously Vack's mother, and then a thicker line led to his siblings, Savaul, Gataan, and Glidria. The father of the four also had a name of gemstones, *Gramsaf,* and a thick line connecting him to Izfazara, a name gilded in gold, probably to show he was the king. Ebby's eyes roamed all the way to the top, to the first Escali Epic, Juhdect, whose brother was also a king. In fact, every Epic on the tree had a king for a brother.

A latch rattled lightly behind her and Ebby released an exhausted breath, too tired to keep running, hiding, and wiping tears from her eyes.

The massive door swung very slowly inward, stirring dust into the still air, and Vack's friend Jalia stepped cautiously into the room. Her slightly cloudy eyes were piercing, and her intense observance led her to a hundred theories about Ebby within seconds, all of them scarily accurate. The ratted clothes, the dark circles beneath her eyes, the way Ebby stood so loosely and resigned, they all gave her away. This incredibly perceptive girl actually understood her brokenness, and that thought made tears well in Ebby's eyes.

Jalia tilted her head and said, "Vack told me you were a crier." Ebby laughed to herself. These Escalis were all the same. "Why are you crying?"

Ebby gave her a tearful shrug. "I don't even know anymore."

"Then *stop*." Jalia clearly didn't have patience for something so irrational. "What do you need?"

Ebby bit her cheek with uncertainty. In the silence that followed, Jalia repeated, "What is going to make you stop crying?"

The question made her want to dissolve into further tears, but the supportive nature of Jalia's thoughts made her realize this was some weird version of a friendly gesture. It wasn't kind or gentle, but at its heart, it was an offer of assistance.

Asking Jalia to help her escape Prince Avalask would be a waste of a wish. There had to be some way Ebby could actually use this kindness. "I have friends beneath this city, and I don't know how to get to them."

"The kids from Dincara?" Jalia asked. "You're an Epic. Just jump down to them."

"I don't know how," Ebby replied, painfully aware that Vack was already practicing jumping. The way Jalia frowned, as though Ebby was wasting her precious abilities, made her feel further sick. Here Ebby was, the hope for the Human race, and she was as close to useless as could be.

"Can you at least turn invisible again?" Jalia asked.

Ebby vanished on the spot, but not to impress. It was because Vack's other friend, Mir, slipped through the open doorway and peered quickly into every corner.

"She could understand you?" he asked Jalia warily, worried about the threat of invisible ambush, unaware that Ebby was actually crouching behind the gold statue now.

"She understands," Jalia said. "And she's learning. You can't hear her heartbeat this time. She found a way to hide it." The boy froze and Ebby felt a sense of cautious trust from him that Jalia had the situation under control.

"Why did she come here?" he asked.

"She's here by accident. She doesn't know what this room is," Jalia replied. Even mind-reading Ebby didn't know how Jalia had figured that out. "And I'm going to take her down to see those captured kids beneath the city."

Panic and excitement flooded Ebby at the thought of seeing Ratuan, but Mir turned on Jalia and demanded, "Did you eat stupid-meal for breakfast?"

"No I didn't, Mir," she snapped back. "But you're stupid if you haven't realized what Prince Avalask is doing. Obviously he doesn't want her to grow up and murder us. Only an idiot wants to make an enemy of the deadliest weapon in the world."

"I would rather be an idiot than a groveling coward. You can do her all the favors you like, but she's not going to spare you in the end. Not you, not any of us."

Jalia shook her head and said, "I'm done with this conversation. Go let Vack know we found her, and I'll meet you both in his room when I'm back. It's a long walk down there."

"This is a bad idea," Mir told her as both kids turned and promptly exited the room.

Ebby's jaw had fallen open and landed on the cloak of the statue in front of her. Neither of the friends saw that conversation as anything more than a pleasant exchange of thoughts and ideas. This was *normal*. And since Jalia had declared the conversation ended, they had both immediately taken off toward their next intended goal. Jalia had already covered a long hallway and turned the corner by the time Ebby got her invisible feet moving to pursue.

The grey veins of rock beneath Ebby's feet grew thicker and more wildly abundant as Jalia led her deeper. Then they began passing Escalis. There was a room full of them on the right, gathered around a large table and laughing scary, throaty laughs.

"Are you following?" Jalia asked as she walked, keeping her eyes fixed straight ahead.

Yes, Ebby projected her thoughts, too frightened to speak. Jalia gave her the slightest head nod that meant she had heard. *You were right, about that room,* Ebby added. *I didn't know what it was.*

"It's a room of remembrance," Jalia said. "For all the women in the royal family who have been killed by the curse."

Ebby frowned to herself since nobody else could see her. *Curses aren't real.*

"This one is. It was your Epic grandfather who put it on them, and now every woman in the royal family is dead. Murdered, drowned, killed by freak illnesses — the royal family has had to watch them drop, one after another, and couldn't do a thing to prevent it. I'm fairly surprised that Vack can stand the sight of you, actually."

Ebby distinctly remembered Vack saying they'd been killed by Humankind, so he must believe curses were real. *Well... If there are no women left in his family, then there's no reason left to hate me. It wouldn't matter anymore.*

Jalia shot a reproachful glance back at the thin air where Ebby walked. "*Yes,* it matters. Because assuming that Vack survives to be a grown up, he'll have to do the same thing his father did and marry somebody he knows will die. That curse is real. Vack's mother barely made it long enough to have him after marrying into the family."

Was Vack's mother the gold one? Ebby asked.

"No. Prince Avalask, Savaul, and Gataan used to have a sister. The whole royal family is known for their black hair, but for some reason Glidria was born with hair like spun gold, and the world called her the Golden Princess. Prince Avalask tells stories about her sometimes, how every Escali alive loved her for more than just her beauty." Jalia sounded entirely detached as she said, "She was captured and killed long before any of us were born though. I mean, her brothers rescued her first, but she was so sick that all they could do was watch her die. That's their curse for you."

Ebby felt sick, and Jalia stopped at the sight of two Escali adults blocking the tunnel ahead.

The Dincaran kids are straight down from here. Jalia thought to her. *Just keep walking. You would have to be worthless to miss them.*

"Are you lost?" one of the men asked Jalia.

"Of course not," Jalia replied, and Ebby watched her take a step toward them with fearless curiosity. "I want you to let me in to see the Human kids."

Neither of them looked particularly irritated, and the first who'd spoken said, "Not right now. We leave them alone for the night hours. Come back tomorrow if you want to meet one."

Jalia's eyes widened like she'd been offered an entire devil cake and didn't have to share. "You'd let me do that?"

The second Escali glanced behind himself and said, "Somebody needs to remind those insolent little monsters where they are. You could probably get away with more than we could, being young yourself."

Jalia frowned inwardly, but said nothing because she didn't want to endanger her chance.

"Appreciated," Jalia said, tipping her head to them both before spinning to walk away.

Ebby stood frozen, like the glass-freckled ground had swallowed her feet and filled her lungs. She just had to walk past those two guards on either side of the tunnel. But what if they heard her? What if they sensed her presence, or smelled her?

Her heart began to beat furiously because there were other kids like her at the bottom of those stairs, and she needed them more than she needed to breathe. She *would* get down there.

Ratuan was worth the risk.

CHAPTER NINE

"The Zhauri are at the Dragona," Archie explained to the three Tallies we'd found in their usual cavern, still awake despite the late hour. We'd left the Dragona as fast as it took me to throw two sets of clothing into my hunting bag.

Robbiel, the one who could run faster than anyone alive, closed a book as soon as he heard the word *Zhauri*. Nessava, probably the kindest and most energetic of the group, stood from a deep stretch she'd been holding, while Emery, the Tally with the power of fire and cruel sense of humor, glanced at the door behind us as though we might have been followed. "They're on the hunt for Sir Avery's daughter, and they've told me and Allie that we can either help or suffer the consequences," Archie said.

The three hadn't seen us in months, and we'd just thrown their door open to announce it was doomsday, so it was only fair to expect the ensuing stares of shock.

"Sir Avery…" Robbiel said slowly, "had a daughter?"

"Well, he *had one*," I said with a hint of a chuckle, an entirely inappropriate attempt at humor, judging by Archie's distasteful glower, "but Prince Avalask whisked her away at the beginning of summer. It sounds like nobody's heard from her since."

100

Nessava's brown eyes grew even larger than usual while Emery cocked his head to the side. "But why are the Zhauri after you?" he demanded. "Sir Avery should be the one threatening your lives. It's *his* offspring that's caused this mess."

I gathered by the sour look that Emery wasn't fond of children, or maybe just Sir Avery.

"Sir Avery came to us too," Archie said. "He asked for our help and hired the Zhauri, and the Zhauri gave us a week to find her."

Robbiel, who was usually one of the calmer Tallies, set his book aside and got to his feet. "You can't help them," he said, joining us. "A young Epic has more raw potential than anything else in the world. She *can't* fall into their hands."

"What are you most worried about?" I asked.

Robbiel glanced at Emery, but Nessava was the one who softly said, "Maverick..."

Robbiel nodded slowly. "Maverick is a power-hungry-"

"Monster," Emery finished for him. "He's a power-hungry monster, and we need to stay clear of him until he takes his crowd back north where they belong. And they should probably take Sir Shanking Avery with them. Get him out of our lives."

I could see a few easy alliances to be made, and said, "Sir Avery's not the only one who approached us." I shot Archie a sideways look, daring him to interrupt me. "Prince Avalask could keep Ebby safe, and he's training her with his son right now so the two don't grow up to be enemies. I say we leave her where she is, and then Prince Avalask can help keep *us* safe from the Zhauri."

Archie shot back an irritated scowl and said, "No, we'll find a way to bring her home that doesn't involve the Zhauri. Sir Avery happens to be her actual father, and she belongs with him."

"Yeah, not to mention he's bribing you," I said, returning his scowl with a heated one of my own, "With something you won't speak of."

101

Archie sighed at the ceiling as Emery told him, "I would tell you to come live here and get away from her, but Karissa nags the rest of us even worse."

"I'm not nagging," I growled. "Prince Avalask is holding onto Ebby with everybody's wellbeing in mind, *not just his own*."

Archie ignored my jab and said, "Either way, we have no idea how to find her. We asked a few people about the captured kids from Dincara on our way in, and it sounds like they're down in the old dungeons below —"

"Everybody knows they're down there," Robbiel said. "But the entrance is guarded... unless..."

Emery huffed a mocking laugh. "You're *not* trying to use the old back passages, are you?" he asked, folding his arms as he glanced back to the fireplace. "They were too tight to move in when *we* were kids."

"The back way to the kids is through here?" I asked, realizing that Archie probably hadn't mentioned it because we'd spent our entire trip here passionately discussing the Ebby situation.

Emery rolled his eyes and said, "There are a thousand cracks in the rocks between caves. That doesn't mean you can fit through them."

"Shanking life, Emery. Neither of us doubled in weight since the last time we saw you," Archie said, drawing another jeer from Emery. "It'll be tight, but we'll make it work."

Nessava smiled with her bright, large teeth and said, "Celesta has a hammer and chisel we can borrow if you get stuck. I'm sure she won't mind us wrecking the second half of the fireplace to prevent you becoming fossils."

Half of the stones around the fireplace had been ornately carved and then smashed in a game of *try-to-kill-your-fellow-Tallies* last time we'd been here. We apparently played it often.

102

Emery leaned back against the wall with a smirk and said, "I will eat my left foot if the two of you fit through there."

"Deal. You ready?" Archie asked me.

"Yep."

Every cave-dweller's fireplace has to vent to the surface, but the dark gap in the rock that led upward also extended to the side in ours. Archie went first with some difficulty, and I followed into the cramped crevice. The fissure was so tight that a large meal could mean the difference between getting through and getting stuck, and then it narrowed even further.

I was forced to stand straight while attempting to slip between the jagged stones, and then I had to slouch at strategic angles to accommodate their curvature. Rocks scraped across my front and back as I sidestepped after Archie, wedging myself in further as everything grew impossibly tighter. I didn't like the lack of breathable air around us, and further disliked each time I gouged my ankles because I couldn't look down to see the uneven floor.

Archie slowed and finally stopped, laughing softly to himself.

"Emery's going to be keeping his left foot, isn't he?" I asked, nearly knocking my teeth against the rocks in front of me.

"No, I'll make it," he said. "It opens into a little air pocket after this." I could hear him wriggling, but couldn't turn my head to see him. My knees began to protest their position, pressed against the sharp stones while my ankles grew upset with the angle on which my feet were perched.

"Archie... what did Sir Avery offer you?"

I heard him release a deep breath and say, "It's a long story... and... tough to talk about."

"Well, we're *stuck*," I said, drawing a chuckle from him. "And Corliss knows, doesn't she? So why's it hard to tell me?"

Archie took a moment to gather an answer. "Because for you to truly understand, I would have to tell you everything. Who I am, the things I've done… And once you know, it's going to be the end of us."

I exhaled a laugh so forcefully that my spit hit the wall in front of me. "Archie. There's nothing in your past bad enough to end us." I heard him work himself free of the jam and scrape into a section of easy moving. "You're a good person. You prove it all the time in the way you help me, and sacrifice for me, and come running straight into danger any time I need you." It wasn't news to anyone that he did more for me than I could ever deserve.

"And I appreciate that you think all that of me, more than you know," he said, "but I've really messed up, Allie, and I didn't exactly learn from my mistakes." The crevice opened into Archie's promised air pocket where I could almost extend my arm straight in front of me, and Archie pressed himself into the next narrow section. "I'm not saying Sir Avery can undo what's been done," Archie said, "but there are things he can fix, going forward… Things that Prince Avalask can't fix."

He looked back and I waited in silence, hoping he would feel obligated to explain further. Archie hesitated and tugged at his hair in deliberation before he finally said, "Allie, please help me bring Ebby home. I promise, I'll never ask you for anything again."

I took a second to respond, because I sort of owed him my life several times over. How could I possibly say no?

"Listen," I said slowly. "Let's just find her first, alright? Then we can decide what to do, because I *want* to take your side on this, Archie… I just don't know if I can."

"Yeah… It's a pointless conversation if we never find her, isn't it?" Archie's somber demeanor disappeared like he controlled it with a switch, and he said, "We're here anyway. I think this is the tunnel that leads to the Dincaran kids."

I widened my eyes. "What do you mean *you think—*"

104

Archie stepped through a hole in the floor and lowered himself into an empty cave, so wide that either of us could have laid across it and not been able to touch the sides. I slid down after him and landed on an ancient staircase, covered in small flecks of black glass. Our entryway was just an unnoticeable fracture in the ceiling. I could pass a hundred just like it without a second thought.

Dead silence extended eerily in either direction, and the air grew colder and smelled faintly more like bad breath as we descended the stairs. Sympathy couldn't describe the shock and sadness I felt when we finally reached the bottom, the entrance to what could only be called a dungeon. A long hall stretched ahead of us with at least twenty small cells on each side and at least five kids nestled together in each one.

"How…" I stuttered as discomfort and guilt attacked. "How are we going to explain how we got here?"

Archie stared down the long hallway and released a deep breath. "It's not as though they've got anyone to tell. Let's go find Leaf."

We silenced our footfalls with rolling steps, and the kids slept quietly as we reached the end of the hall without seeing Leaf's shock of orange hair. The dungeon took a dip and a turn, then led to an even longer corridor of cells. At the end of this hall was another dip in elevation before another stretch of darkness.

"How many kids did they get a hold of?" I whispered, climbing down a fourth turn. I finally saw the orange hair I was looking for.

Leaf was in with three other boys and a girl, and was by far the smallest of them. I knelt to get a closer look and clenched my fingers over my mouth when I saw his arms. Dark, swollen gashes marred his forearms where the unmistakable imprints of teeth had torn in. Two of the other boys had similarly bloody injuries, but Leaf's were inflamed and fiery red beneath the darkened crust.

105

I looked up at Archie and mouthed, "We are getting him out of here."

Archie nodded back with a disbelieving frown, as though offended I might doubt him.

I reached in and lightly held Leaf's hand, hoping that whatever he was dreaming about, it was far away from the Escali tunnels and a lot better of a world.

Archie nudged my shoulder and breathed, "We'll get him help." I let go and pulled my hand reluctantly back through to my side.

"Allie?" Leaf whispered, opening his eyes a fraction.

"Shhhhhh, go back to sleep."

Leaf rubbed his eyes sleepily to get a better look, cringing just from lifting his hands to meet his face. Archie pulled me to my feet then off to the side, out of his sight. I felt awful as we slipped away, but I was pretty sure Leaf had gone back to sleep because we didn't hear anything else from him.

I scraped myself through the final stretch of the tight crevice as Archie said, "We will blow our cover trying to get these kids out."

"Sure, but nobody's going to be able to charge us with treason after we bring them home," I said. "I've spoken to Prince Avalask about helping us, but we can't wait around for him. Did you see Leaf's arms? We have to do something now."

"We'll do what we can to help, and then get back to the Dragona and tell Tarace where the kids are," Archie said. "They're too important not to rescue."

He had almost dislodged himself from the fireplace, myself right behind him, and asked our friends, "Where's Karissa?"

Nessava and Robbiel raised their eyes to Emery, who froze in place looking both guilty and amused. I twisted my left foot to get it unstuck as Archie hardened his gaze and said, "Some of the kids down there are in rough shape. Where is she?"

"Look," Emery said, raising his arms defensively, "I didn't know there was going to be a sudden emergency where we'd need her."

Nessava rolled her eyes and said, "Emery stole her bag and climbed to the top of a tree —"

"She left it unattended!" Emery said. "I had to steal it. I didn't light the tree on fire though, which I think we can all agree, means I've grown as a good, moral person."

Archie huffed an irritated sigh and told me, "Karissa knows more about medicine than all the Dragona's healers combined. You could saw yourself in half and light yourself on fire, and Karissa would be able to stitch you back together."

I looked at Emery and asked, "Where is she? I'll go —"

"I could help," Robbiel cut me off. "I'm not Karissa, but I mean, people and animals are essentially the same. How bad is it?"

I found myself fidgeting with the ends of my hair as I shrugged, knowing next to nothing about what made an injury serious. "We were hoping somebody else could tell us."

Robbiel said, "Let me grab my bag — I'll be right back."

"You… help animals?" I asked as he pushed the marble doors open.

Robbiel shrugged. "Just the ones I can catch. It's more or less of a hobby."

"For when he's not out stealing books," Archie said.

Robbiel was already gone, but called over his shoulder, "It's not stealing if you put them back."

He disappeared and I found myself twisting my hands together. Waiting is something I've never learned to do properly.

"Hear that?" Emery asked. "Robbiel says it's not stealing if you put it back. The three of you are my witnesses when Karissa gets here."

Nessava glanced at my nervous hand-wringing and said, "She's is going to throw a fit when she finds out she missed this." I glanced up at her, not sure I understood. "Seriously. Karissa's started chanting *stitches, stitches* every time somebody does something dangerous. She lives for this stuff."

I flashed her a small smile, not even sure if it was fake or genuine.

Robbiel returned in less than a minute and handed Archie a large bag to hold while pulling a billowy white shirt over his head.

Archie chuckled quietly and said, "I don't miss wearing those."

"They do look ridiculous." Robbiel grinned, pushing the poofy sleeves up to his elbows. He looked almost perfectly Human without any arm spikes to give him away. "Gets the job done though."

Robbiel was smaller than either of us, so he went first through the fissure and dragged his bag along behind him as we struggled through it once more. When we reached the kids this time, several were awake in the upper tunnels. I stupidly thought to myself that we might be able to walk past them unnoticed, but that wasn't about to happen. A small girl was the first to leap to her feet and silently grab the bars on her cell before we could pass. She said nothing, but her eyes asked a million large questions.

"Shhh, it's alright," I whispered, hovering a finger over my lips as I bent my knees to speak on her level. "We're here to help." She nodded and took a step back to let us continue unhindered. I heard her wake her friends as we disappeared from sight, and a boy in the next tunnel leapt up to gape at us as well.

I was glad that those who saw us had enough sense not to shout and give our presence away to the world, but the hope that lit their eyes nearly tore a hole through me.

108

The five kids in Leaf's cell were still asleep when we reached them and Robbiel pulled a set of long black pins from his bag to pick the lock.

The door creaked on its hinges as it swung open and woke all five in a frightened startle. Leaf was the first to rub his eyes and realize the Escalis weren't dragging them out of the cell.

"Allie?" he whispered, glancing at the others as though worried he might be dreaming.

The inefficiencies of the Human language became suddenly apparent. There weren't any appropriate words for this situation. *I'm sorry? I've missed you? I'm so glad to see you're just injured and not dead?*

I sank to set my knees and palms on the rock floor, and Leaf took a careful step toward me, then abandoned all caution. He wrapped frail arms around my neck, so loose I could barely feel the embrace, but with more love and trust than the tightest hug of a family member.

"I told them I had friends," Leaf said as I tried to steady him with my own arms, pressing my cheek to the side of his red hair. "I said you'd find us. But how are you going to rescue everyone with just three people?"

"We're going to tell everyone on the outside where to find you," I told him. The idea of not escaping tonight paused Leaf's breath, and I leaned back to see his eyes again, now full of fear. "But for tonight, I brought a friend who can help you."

Robbiel knelt on cue and whispered, "Hi there."

Leaf blinked at him several times, looked to me for reassurance, and still hesitated before he softly replied, "Hey."

"This is my friend," I assured Leaf, and Robbiel gave him a smile both friendly and harmless.

"I'm Robbiel. Do you think I could see your arms? They look like they hurt."

109

Leaf gave a shy nod and reluctantly lifted his hands, palms up, to reveal the hideous gashes. Robbiel gently grabbed both of his arms and said, "You must be pretty tough," as he turned them over to reveal multiple blood-crusted bites. "These bites would have me crying for days."

I saw a proud smile at the edge of Leaf's mouth before the kid with shaggy blond hair and bloodied arms said, "He didn't deserve those bites. We're the ones breaking the dishes."

"And spitting in the Escalis' food," said the last of the three bearing injuries, swiping his overgrown black hair from his eyes. "We didn't stop until they went after Leaf."

"Well, the good news is, you can keep the arms," Robbiel said. "We do have to clean and wrap them though. It might hurt a little."

Leaf nodded as Robbiel dug through his pack for a grey glass bottle and a roll of white cloth.

The last boy hadn't taken his gaze off me to so much as blink, and a sense of unease shook me as I returned his stare. His eyes were a cross between green and brown and not particularly striking, but something about them froze the breath in my chest and made me feel anxious to the point of dizziness.

"Who *are* you?" he asked in a flat whisper that made the hairs on my neck prickle. I didn't know him, but I recognized him.

"Ratuan?" The name rolled off my tongue, and I pressed my knuckles to my mouth in confusion.

Everybody in the room sensed the tension with this unknown kid, and Robbiel took the opportunity to pour something onto Leaf's arms, causing him to shriek and lurch back against me. Leaf kept his arms out to endure the worst of the torture and I looked back to Archie, pretending I couldn't handle the sight of gore.

Archie's slight squint and head tilt asked me what was going on, and I returned his frown with a tiny shake of my head to say, *I have no idea who he is.* I knew that didn't make sense when I knew the boy's name, but Archie's tiny nod meant we'd talk about it later.

The kids down the hallway began shouting, and I picked out the words, "You've got one coming!"

"There's an Escali coming," Leaf said, choking on his words. "Where are you going to hide?"

Archie, Robbiel, and I exchanged worried glances, knowing nothing good could come from an Escali encounter in front of a whole hall of Human kids.

"Are you kidding me?" exclaimed Karissa as she rounded the corner and saw the three of us with the door to the cell open. Archie was the quickest of us to respond, and pulled a knife from his side as though ready for her to jump us. "I've spent the last three months complaining that I missed fixing people up, and you come down here *without me?!*"

I opened my arms, palms up, to silently exclaim, *we can't answer you.* She hadn't thought ahead to cover the spikes on her elbows, and wasn't speaking Human either.

I also stood and pulled one of my short swords from my side. "*Are you both shanking psychotic?*" Karissa demanded.

Archie had the quickest idea and said to me, "It's fine. Robbiel is a mind mage. He can keep her from attacking us."

I never would have guessed it was a lie if I didn't belong to the group.

Robbiel continued wrapping Leaf's arms, and said, "We'll be fine. She won't even remember seeing us."

Karissa flung her gaze up to the ceiling in irritated disgust, then said, "I will kill every," she glared at Archie, "single," she glared at me, "One of you." She glared at Robbiel last and with the most venom, as though he had committed the worst betrayal imaginable. Robbiel frowned back, as if to ask what he was supposed to do, and

111

Karissa demanded, "Was it infected? Did you sanitize your tools? Did he need stitches? Has he lost much blood? Is he in shock?"

Leaf looked like he might go into shock when Karissa took another step toward him, and that seemed to be the only thing that convinced her to rethink her strategy.

"Fine," she said, resigned to let her anger out in one large breath. "When the three of you get out of here, I want *every* detail."

She looked longingly at the injury one more time, then turned to go.

One of the other boys with bites down his arm looked at Robbiel and said, "You're really good. At the mind stuff and the medicine."

"It still doesn't explain who any of you are," Ratuan said. The question was mostly aimed at me.

"We're friends," I said. "And we're here to help make a plan." This seemed to intrigue them. "We also need to ask your help," I said, making eye contact with all five kids. "Do any of you know where our Epic is?"

Ratuan widened his eyes. "The Escalis got our Epic?"

I wasn't sure how to answer that without making everything seem even more hopeless, but they understood that the following silence meant *yes.*

Ratuan said, "He's not down here."

"Are you positive?" I asked.

"Yes, because our group is the one planning the escape," Leaf said. "Eme's been keeping track of how many mages we have." Leaf turned to the one girl. "Nobody's shown a sign of more than one power, have they?" The girl silently shook her head.

"We need help from the outside too," Ratuan said. "But we don't have any reason to trust you."

"We're the only ones down here offering help," I said with a sad smile. "Your options are pretty limited, buddy."

"That's not a reason to trust you," Ratuan replied. I had to admit, I admired his style. "What we need is information. How to get out of here, how many Escalis will be in our way, where to go. We need a map. Can you get us that?"

"We'll see what we can do," Archie said as Robbiel let go of Leaf's arms and took a step back.

"I want to see yours too," Robbiel said to the other boys with bite marks. "Is anybody else down here hurt?"

Each of the kids closed their mouths and turned to Ratuan, who hesitated. "We've got a few injuries. They're in the cells at the very bottom where we take care of the babies and toddlers. We were trying to keep them as far from the Escalis as we could."

I studied Ratuan before asking, "You've organized who's staying where down here?"

Several kids, including the quiet girl and the boys listening intently from across the hall, giggled at my question.

"Yes," Ratuan said, barely trying to fake humility when he was clearly very proud. "We've put a little thought into who's staying where."

CHAPTER TEN

Ebby wrapped her small hands around two thick iron bars and gaped past them to see four boys and one girl, huddled in a tight circle and completely absorbed in a whispered conversation. White strips of cloth circled three of the boys' forearms, one of whom had the strangest reddish-orange hair she had ever seen.

"Ratuan?" The word escaped Ebby's mouth as a puff of air.

Ratuan whipped around and froze as the other four fell silent. She could feel his confusion and a flood of hope welling up, which he tried to suppress because this was too absurd to believe.

Ratuan glanced all around before meeting her eyes, nearly on the brink of a panic attack. "Ebby?"

Ebby forgot how to speak and screamed with delight instead, ghosting herself through the bars to throw her arms around Ratuan. "It's me!" she exclaimed. "It's me, it's me, it's me."

Ratuan took two sharp breaths as uncontained hope and relief threatened to spill out his ears. "You can't be here," he said, his voice cracking as his trembling worsened. "I looked. I looked a hundred times. I learned the name of every kid in these caves, and you weren't here!" But he suddenly hugged her back in that lung crushing way she had missed so sorely.

"They've been keeping me separate," Ebby said, tightening her grip as joyful tears streamed from her eyes. "I have so much to t-tell you. So much has ha-happened."

Crying overrode her ability to speak, and Ratuan had even less to say since he was surrendering to certain delusion.

Can you hear me? she asked in his head.

Ratuan jerked his head back. "What the —"

I'm the new Epic. I'm Sir Avery's daughter. That's why the Escalis took me. That's why they've been keeping me separate.

Now Ratuan took a step back. "Girls... can't be Epics," he said, and the other four kids gaped at Ebby in sudden disbelief.

"It's not that girls can't, it's just n-never happened before," Ebby said, wiping her cheeks as she gathered her courage. "But you just saw me walk through those bars. You just heard me in your head. Look at this," she held both hands out and conjured a flame in one while the other palm spat a fountain of green sparks. "I can freeze things, shoot lightning bolts... I can levitate your shoe! I can do all of it."

Ebby was struck with a sudden fear that hadn't occurred to her. What if Ratuan wouldn't like her anymore? What if he didn't want to be best friends with an Epic?

Ratuan just stood flabbergasted. It was the smaller boy with the orange hair who asked, "What are you doing *here?*"

"He's right, you shouldn't be here," said the boy with black hair falling into his eyes. His name was Eric, and the other boy with shaggy blond hair was Steph. Every young girl in Dincara with a set of eyes knew these two boys, though they usually had tans from helping their fathers out on the boats. "If you're an Epic, can't you just escape?"

"I can't," Ebby shook her head tearfully, afraid because Ratuan still hadn't spoken. "Prince Avalask is the one keeping me here, and he's got this horrible son named Vack —"

115

Ratuan interrupted, "His son? You've met the Escalis' new Epic?"

"Yes, and he's horrible!" Ebby said, stamping a foot on the ground at the injustice of it all. "He's mean and vile, he *bites...*"

And so began the very long story of all that had happened since she'd been torn away from Ratuan. The others asked questions and clung to her every answer. They introduced themselves as they laughed, cried, and planned. At the end of it all, Ebby found herself in the middle of a kid-pile for the night. Judging by the other cells around them, that was their normal way to sleep and keep warm with no blankets in sight.

She faced Ratuan in the middle of the huddle, and he'd entwined his fingers with hers, filling her with a sense of warmth and hope she hadn't felt since the last time she'd held his hand. "I looked for you too," Ebby whispered as everybody else fell asleep. "I searched Tabriel Vale every day and never found you."

"Nobody in Tabriel Vale would help me," Ratuan said. "I told them you were alive, and they just tried to put me in the orphanage. So I left for Dincara to find Reso and Sembla. I thought they might know something."

"What did they say?" Ebby asked.

"I never found them," Ratuan replied, squeezing her hand. "The Escalis attacked before I could, and Dincara sent every kid in the city to take refuge in Kellington. But the Escalis caught us before we ever got close."

Ebby clenched her jaw tightly because it was her fault Ratuan was here. He could have easily stayed in Tabriel Vale, but she'd needed him and he'd come to find her. And even if it was wrong and selfish, she was incredibly grateful to have him, a friend in the nightmare.

"You remember the girl we found before the Escalis got you?" Ratuan whispered, even more softly. "That Allie girl you've talked

116

about before?" Ebby nodded. "She was here just a few hours ago. She's looking for you."

Ebby scrunched her eyebrows and breathed, *"What?"* That was one unsolved mystery she hadn't thought about in a while. "Do you think she's trying to rescue me?"

"She seems like she is," Ratuan said. "She said she wanted to get us all out of here. She brought two others with her, and they bandaged everyone up before they left."

"Really?"

"Yeah, but there's something strange about her, Ebby. I don't trust her."

"I don't know if we have a choice," Ebby said as a brilliant idea came to mind. "But I can listen to her thoughts if she comes back. I can figure out who she is."

Can you hear how much I've missed you? Ratuan thought very loudly.

Ebby laughed. "No need to break my ears over it," she said. "But yes. And I can still say I've missed you more."

Ebby slept well for the first time since her old life had been ripped away. There was something wonderfully comfortable about being warm, feeling wanted, and the anonymity that came with a city's-worth of other kids around her. Small comforts like these made the cruel world livable.

Several peaceful hours sank in before Ebby woke to a voice that caused her heart to sink into the floor. "What are you doing?" Vack demanded from outside the cell, startling everybody around them.

Ebby blinked a few times before Ratuan whispered, "Don't worry about him," and he moved slightly closer to Vack, protecting her. "They know we can't understand them."

Ebby nodded and thought back to Vack, *I'm not doing anything.*

It's nearly morning! My father is going to be back soon to teach us. You don't want him to find you down here.

I belong down here, Vack. The only thing in my life that matters is down here.

Vack rolled his eyes up at the ceiling. *Well don't be an idiot about it. We'll both be in trouble if you don't show up to practice, and you won't be able to come back here at all. Stand up so I can jump us out.*

Ebby crossed her arms and huffed out a sigh. She didn't want Prince Avalask to prevent her coming back. *Can you at least make it look like we're still enemies? I don't want my friends to see me get up and leave with you.*

"Oh, gladly, Tear-salt," Vack said, stepping through the thick iron bars.

"Hey, whoa, what is he doing?" Leaf exclaimed, waking everyone in the cells around them.

Vack grabbed Ebby by the arm, hauling her to her feet, and the other four kids immediately latched onto her clothes to yank her back.

Ratuan was the one who leapt straight onto Vack, trying to claw at his face and strangle him. "Get away from her! Get OFF!"

The boys across the hall began shouting, "Leave them alone!" along with "Get out of there," and "You're dead!" Vack's grip on her arm become searing hot, enough to melt a handprint into her flesh if she wasn't able to freeze her arm into a block of ice, but Ratuan still tried to tear Vack apart, screaming like a demented animal as red blisters boiled up beneath his skin.

"VACK! STOP IT!" Ebby screamed, lunging forward to slam Vack into the iron bars. Vack flung Ratuan away with one hand, brutally reminding Ebby of the day Sav had thrown Ratuan into the dirt and nearly killed him. Ratuan hit the wall this time and immediately rebounded to charge again.

But Vack had already yanked Ebby out of everyone's grasp, straight through the bars, and into the tunnel where shouting came from every side. New words were coming through the clamor now as chaos erupted.

"He just used magic!"

"He's the Epic! He's the new royal Epic!"

"Get a good look at him!"

Ebby's ragged screams were the loudest of them all. "You don't hurt my friends! Don't you ever touch my friends!"

Ebby threw herself into Vack with raging, loathing fury, intent on tearing into him, but Vack caught her and used the momentum to jump them both into the air. Seconds later, they hurtled into Ebby's black glass room and landed in a heap.

Ebby immediately scrambled to her feet, lowered her shoulder, and crashed her whole body into him as he regained his footing, pulling her gloves off in frenzied haste.

"What is wrong with you?" Vack shouted as she screamed again and tried to get her fingers around his throat. Vack crushed her shoulders and hurled her sideways into the obsidian wall. The haunting squeak of splintering glass filled the entire room as Ebby ghosted herself straight through Vack and turned to shoot a pillar of fire at him. Vack caught the entirety of the flames before they reached him, and he reshaped them into a gigantic fireball between his hands.

"You really want to play this game with me?" Vack asked as Ebby eyed the swirling ball of death he could easily retarget.

Ebby flung her hands out, and a wave of conjured water broke over Vack, quenching the ball of flame. Ebby shot a lightning bolt with no accuracy whatsoever, and it struck the ceiling, splintering the glass further.

Vack dove to the ground anyway, anticipating *something* being shot at him, and he swung an arm forward, causing Ebby's feet to fly out from beneath her. The second she hit the floor, Vack pounced on her. He grabbed both her white gloves and pinned her beneath him, snarling as he tried to get them back on her hands.

"Stop it!" Ebby screamed, struggling to shake him off as he grabbed both her wrists. He was doing something to keep her from ghosting through him a second time, and she'd be defenseless as soon as he got those gloves on her. "I hate you! I hate you! I hate you!"

"WHAT IS THIS?" A deeper voice roared. A soft black boot landed on Ebby's chest, pinning her where she had already been pinned, and a cloaked hand grabbed Vack's clothes and yanked him high into the air. "What do you two think you're doing?" Prince Avalask demanded.

"Her friends attacked me!" Vack shouted, dangling from his father's hand.

"They were trying to protect me!" Ebby shouted back, trying to sit up despite Prince Avalask's foot holding her down, smelling strongly of smoke. "You can't keep me away from Ratuan! Neither one of you. And if anybody hurts him again, I'll kill them. I'll kill them, I'll kill them, I'll—"

"I barely did anything to him!" Vack shouted from above her. She squirmed harder, but couldn't get up.

"I DON'T HAVE TIME FOR THIS!" Prince Avalask bellowed, which was a first. Ebby had never heard him raise his voice.

"You don't have time for anything," she replied, wanting to cry now. She knew she wasn't supposed to like Prince Avalask, but he had never been unkind to her, other than keeping her trapped, of course. Hearing him yell hurt deep in her chest, and she whispered, "You don't even have time to notice when I'm being murdered."

Prince Avalask looked to the ceiling and let his shoulders slouch, as though he couldn't believe this was happening. He took his foot off Ebby and said, "Alright, stand up," as he set Vack on the floor.

120

Vack eyed Ebby hatefully and she finally noticed shining red welts running from his eyebrows to his chin where Ratuan had scratched him.

"Both of you listen," Prince Avalask said. "Vack, you are going to go back to your room, and Ebby, you are going to stay right here. I will be back in exactly one hour, and then the three of us are going to sit down for a good, long chat. Any questions?"

Ebby shook her head no, and Vack spat on her feet. He actually spat a gross wad of slobber onto her feet, making Ebby leap back and yelp in disgust.

Prince Avalask didn't miss a beat. He snatched Vack's arm and *bit him* as Ebby gasped and Vack silenced a cry. She could tell this was normal for them, but that didn't make it any less barbaric. She might as well be living with wolves!

"Get back to your room, and don't you *ever* do that again," Prince Avalask said, his deep voice dangerous. Vack turned to go, and his father repeated, "I'll be back in an hour," before he leapt and disappeared.

Vack paused at Ebby's door just long enough to shoot her a vicious glare, then he retreated back to his room. Ebby normally would have withdrawn to her bed to have a good cry, but pure adrenaline coupled with strength from seeing Ratuan gave her the will to do something incredibly bold.

She pursued Vack and shoved open the door to his room, which she had never before even had the courage to approach. She opened her mouth to give him the scolding of his life but had to close it again as her eyes widened in shock. Vack lived in *filth!*

Every piece of clothing he owned lay scattered across the floor, mixed in with dishes, old food, crumpled papers, and the remains of old possessions he had apparently burned to ashes. A few wind instruments, balls, and strange looking tools were mixed in among the wreckage.

Vack was utterly unashamed, and whipped around to bare his teeth at her.

"You *live* here?" Ebby nearly shrieked, all other accusations seeming suddenly less important.

"Are you insane?" Vack asked, retracing his trail through the clutter to approach her. "You just found out my father is going to be incredibly busy for the next hour, which means *you could be escaping right now*, and instead you are here nagging me? You are a new breed of stupid, Tear-salt. Get out of my room, and get out of my life."

Ebby lost a bit of her nerve and took a step back. "I... We don't know that he's actually busy. This could be some sort of test, to see if I'll try to get away."

She knew it wasn't a test — the thought of escaping was just suddenly more terrifying than before. How could she just leave, now that she'd finally found Ratuan? And where could she go where Prince Avalask couldn't follow? And what did she even have to return to?

"Look," Vack said flatly. "You know how to spy on other areas with your mind. It's all you've been doing for the past month. Just find my father, see if he's truly busy, and then make your escape."

"I don't know if you've been paying attention, *Vack*," she spat his name, "but finding people hasn't exactly been a strength of mine."

"I will show you where he is," Vack growled. "And if he is busy, then you will get out of here."

"Fine," Ebby said, folding her arms uncomfortably. She wasn't about to admit she was having second thoughts about escaping. Not to Vack.

Vack grabbed one of the gloved hands she held tightly to herself and peered into her eyes. It was teeth-grittingly uncomfortable, but it had to happen to see what he could see.

122

Vack's thoughts had a unique feel to them, a strange mix of aggression and caution that she could probably pick out of a crowd by now, as he showed her a location hundreds of miles away.

He'd brought them to a moonlit Escali town where screams echoed across the icy hills and a fire tore across the rooftops. The sun was still an hour from rising and the panic in the air was thick enough to make breathing hard for Ebby, even from miles away. People dashed between buildings, making sure their neighbors were safely away from the flames and shouting where to meet.

The source of the disturbance was a group of five Human men wearing white cloaks, striding between the buildings as though touring the place.

A bolt of lightning struck from the sky and clashed with a blue shimmer of a shield that protected the group like a dome, sending a loud clap of thunder roaring through the valley. Prince Avalask appeared high in the sky and fired bright red bolts down at the intruders, but those also crashed into the magical barrier around them.

The tallest of the five released a fearsome dog with eyes the color of blood and metal plates shielding its chest and neck. She'd heard stories of the Zhauri death hound before, but her imagination was nowhere near as terrifying as the real thing, and she couldn't deny who the group was any longer. The Zhauri had come south.

The dog tore away from them, bolting toward a trio of armed and ready defenders. He slammed straight into them and wriggled fiercely past their defensive weapons, grabbing one of the thinner women by the arm as though he couldn't feel the others' blades slashing into his hide. He shook his head wildly, but her Escali skin held together despite his effort, and Prince Avalask leapt into the air and grabbed the hound by the scruff of the neck, slamming it into a wall. He carved a deep, flaming line into the earth around the demon, effectively trapping it against the building, then looked back to the group of invaders.

Prince Avalask leapt again, but something invisible knocked him straight back out of the air, crashing him into the frozen grass to the screams of everyone watching. A new man, tall with thick hair and a regal stance, had appeared twenty cubits away. He lifted glowing hands to call another lightning bolt from the sky to strike Prince Avalask.

Still on the ground, Prince Avalask threw his arms up to shield himself as the bolt hit him. The following crack of earsplitting thunder struck Ebby with a panicked realization. This was Sir Avery — the father who'd never wanted her, and the only person alive who could end her nightmare.

Chapter Eleven

The death hound paced wildly in its makeshift trap as a kid no older than Vack emerged from one of the nearest buildings, arms wrapped around a furry animal he meant to protect.

"Run to the others!" Prince Avalask shouted, getting just enough footing to dash away from Sir Avery's next lightning strike. The group of defenders yelled for the boy as he took off and the hound crouched, ready to spring and pursue as soon as a gap opened in the flames.

"Funny seeing you here," Sir Avery laughed, leaping back toward the buildings to set fire to one more thatched rooftop as Prince Avalask flung his hands out, causing the hound to yelp and stumble.

Sir Avery reappeared to blast Prince Avalask off his feet, but Prince Avalask threw up a shield between them, staggered back, and managed to jump and disappear before he fell. He landed among the buildings where Sir Avery quickly joined him.

The two Epics fired all hues of flames and destructive bolts at each other, along with obscene threats and curses as they dodged in and out behind broken pieces of the town. And while Prince Avalask tried to subdue the death hound and battle Sir Avery, the Zhauri with the black beard and thick arms had reached his hands toward the ground and everything from his fingertips to halfway up his forearms had turned purplish black.

The ground before him shook and cracked apart as massive stones the size of buildings rose to the surface of the world from below. Ebby couldn't fathom *what* they might possibly be after, so deep in the ground.

Their excavation pulled the ceiling off a room far beneath the ground, and Ebby's heart stopped as she realized it was the first chamber she and Vack had occupied together, with no doors or windows, shattered black glass still littering the ground.

Nobody occupied it anymore, and Sir Avery shouted, "Where is she?"

"Clearly not here!" Prince Avalask retorted, firing a white stream of destruction.

Sir Avery snarled, "You better hope I find her before I find your shanking son—"

Prince Avalask swung his arms in a huge sweeping gesture, and an entire building collapsed sideways onto Sir Avery. The charred remnants of wood and stone only buried Ebby's father for a second before he blasted the debris away and charged back toward his opponent with fire in his hands.

The death hound finally found a break in the flames trapping him and sprang free as a young Escali woman with long, tied hair pulled herself from beneath the pile of rubble created by the Epics. The closest defending Escalis spotted her as the death hound tore toward her, but the only person with a hope of reaching her was the young boy who had time to turn around and race back.

The death hound sprang and landed his massive paws on her, sinking his teeth into her shoulder. She screamed as the metal-plated beast dragged her out of the wreckage, and her scream continued to echo in Ebby's mind as the death hound clamped its jaws around her throat and crushed it. The boy who'd dropped his

126

furry friend jumped onto the back of the hound to sink his teeth into the dog's neck with a snarl of his own.

Desperate panic overwhelmed Ebby as the beast jerked its head around and grabbed the boy's leg, shaking its head violently as he screamed and bit back on its neck. The wolf threw the young boy off and was about to grab his throat too when a sharp whistle jerked him to attention. The broad shouldered leader of the Zhauri whistled again and the beast took off toward its master as the five hunters retreated casually between the burning buildings and screams.

Prince Avalask was desperately hitting Sir Avery with massive, invisible blows which struck an invisible shield but reverberated around the hills until Sir Avery finally leapt into the air and disappeared along with the Zhauri. Prince Avalask also leapt into the air, but reappeared next to the dead woman just as the other defending Escalis reached her.

More began to gather as angry and mourning shouts of denial echoed for all to hear, and several armed guards circled to make sure none of their attackers dare return in their moment of grief.

The boy who'd been bitten was convulsing on the ground with a grey bearded man who was probably his father kneeling beside him.

Prince Avalask knelt down too and spoke hurriedly as the boy's mouth began to foam and he arched his back, coughing in the direction of the rising sun.

"No, please!" his father was begging. "There has to be a way you can help him."

Ebby felt ill as two tears fell from Prince Avalask's cloudy eyes.

"I've tried before," he said, placing a hand on the boy's neck as he began to thrash harder, lunging suddenly to bite anyone within reach. "This is truly the kindest thing I can do."

127

Ebby knew what was coming, but Vack was the one who whimpered and stumbled back from her, forcing the scene to vanish as he threw a hand to his own neck.

Ebby immediately retreated into the numbness that was beginning to feel like a familiar friend. Death was a constant in her life, and for the first time, the person being killed wasn't somebody she knew or loved. This didn't feel too much worse than reliving Margaret's murder every day.

Vack, on the other hand, was gasping for air with his eyes wider than she had ever seen them, glancing all about himself as his lips turned blue. Ebby felt waves of revulsion and despair pouring off him. He had never seen death, and it was a shock that seemed to hit newcomers pretty hard.

"Vack?" Ebby asked, her entire body tense because numbness could only go so far to dull the stirring of old memories.

Vack took a sharp breath, and that was the only response she got from him.

"Do you want me to leave?" she whispered.

Vack nodded and set a hand on the back of a chair for balance, even though the chair itself was lopsided, one leg perched on an overturned basket.

Ebby padded back to her room on silent feet, closing Vack's door, and then her own door softly behind her. She sat back against it and reached her hands out so the blanket from her bed floated gently into her lap.

She tried to recreate the time Prince Avalask had taken all her suffering away in forced calm, because an Ebby without emotion was an Ebby who could think with clarity. Numbness just seemed to be the closest she could get.

And she knew what she should be doing right now. Escaping. She still had time. Prince Avalask was definitely preoccupied and Vack wouldn't stop her. But when Ebby looked this problem in the face with complete honesty, she knew she was afraid to go home. That stranger who was supposedly her father was just as ruthless as any Escali.

Her fear of escape was wasting precious time. She needed to go.

Alright, I'll count down from three, she thought to herself. *Then I'll get up and jump out of here.*

One.

She thought of Sir Avery and Prince Avalask snarling at each other as they clashed.

Two.

And Ratuan was so close. She might never see him again if she left him here.

Three.

She trembled and stayed on the glass floor, bowing her forehead to her knees as the tears came. It just wasn't fair that the world depended on her bravery and then gave her *nobody*. She was the wrong girl for all this power. High stakes couldn't change the fact she was weak and afraid, and she hated herself for it.

Ebby tried several more times to count down from three, but held less hope for herself with every digit. Her indecision ended up becoming her decision when Prince Avalask appeared in the late afternoon and she still hadn't moved. She wasn't sure she ever wanted to move again.

Prince Avalask went straight to Vack's room, and Ebby kept her thoughts to herself to give them privacy as the Epic spent the next hours with his son. Loneliness stung her as she tried to imagine a big warm hug enveloping her, assuring her everything would be alright. But she knew it never could be, not while there was magic in the world.

The Everarcs had cursed them all. First the Escalis, then the Breathing Sea, then the mages and Epics. Ebby didn't want to be an Epic, she didn't want to be at war with the Escalis, and more than anything, she just wished her stupid ancestors would have left the Everarcs untouched. Why was that so much to ask?

Most of the day passed before Prince Avalask appeared in her room without making use of the door, and Ebby failed to even startle.

He nodded to the glass floor beside her and asked, "Is anybody sitting here?" Ebby shook her head, feeling guilty because she was relieved he'd come.

Prince Avalask swept his black fur cloak off to the side and settled in next to her, lacing his fingers around his knees.

"Ebby…" He sighed a deep, sincere sigh that bore the weight of everything wrong. "I am so sorry."

"It's ok," she muttered, rubbing the destroyed fabric of her tunic between her fingers. Of course, nothing was ok, but she didn't know how else to acknowledge his apology.

"I'm sorry that Savaul and Gataan were able to get up here without me noticing. And I'm sorry for what you just saw."

"I've seen it before." Ebby shrugged, feeling as little as possible. "Is Vack ok?"

"He's… Well, no. The first death you see is always the hardest. He'll be alright though."

Ebby nodded slowly, then whispered, "Does it ever stop hurting?" The question made her feel vulnerable. One mean comment would be enough to break her right now, but Prince Avalask looked at her with sympathy. "To see a life lost? No. I don't think that's ever supposed to not hurt. Not even after a thousand times." In a way, Ebby was glad to hear so. She never wanted death to feel normal. "Do you see now why I've done all this?" He lifted his hands to the black glass walls. "I would go to any length to prevent you and Vack living this nightmare. You don't deserve it."

Ebby sniffled, grateful for the effort. She didn't want this either. "Is every day like this?"

"Not all of them, but far too many."

"And my... my father..." Ebby's eyes teared up at the mere mention of him. "He's not evil, is he?"

Prince Avalask's eyes hardened for a moment before he covered his thoughts. "I don't know how to answer that, Ebby."

Ebby never would have believed it before, but now, after seeing Sir Avery setting fire to the rooftops and allowing a death hound to kill a child... Prince Avalask would never have done that.

"Look," Prince Avalask said, shifting uncomfortably, "I'm not trying to convince you I'm better than your father. I've done terrible things too, and he's not usually this violent. He's just ripping the world apart looking for you, which we both know is my fault."

"Sir Avery doesn't want me," she said, taking a sharp breath. "He's never wanted me."

Prince Avalask chuckled in exhaustion. "Oh no, I can guarantee he does. I've gotten an earful about it over the past months."

Ebby bit her lip to keep it from quivering. She'd lived her entire life with a hole in her heart where her parents were supposed to reside. She'd always tried to hide how much that hurt, because the families she stayed with always took good care of her and she didn't want them to think her ungrateful. But Ratuan knew. It would be ok if Prince Avalask knew.

"When I was little," Ebby said softly, "I dreamed every single night that my mother and father were on their way to come get me. They were such happy dreams that I'd get out of bed before everybody else and stare out the window, looking for people who looked like me. I spent every morning imagining what I would say the first time we ever hugged as a family, wondering what they would say and think of me." Ebby shrugged quickly and said, "It was so stupid, but I just thought that... maybe they loved me."

Ebby wiped her eyes quickly and said, "Sir Avery has never once said hello to me in eleven years. I'm not a little girl anymore.

131

I know he's going to say he loves me now, but it's only because he doesn't want you to have me."

Prince Avalask released a long sigh of understanding, then caught her eyes and said, "I've known Sir Avery for a long time, Ebby. I don't have a lot of pleasant things to say about him, but abandoning you was probably the most loving thing he's ever done." Ebby scoffed in disagreement. "He didn't want this life for you either, and even though he needed you, he let you have a childhood instead. I've been a little less generous with Vack."

"Having a father is better than being lonely," Ebby said bitterly. "Vack is lucky."

That drew a sad laugh from Prince Avalask. "I don't know that I would call him lucky."

His distant eyes reminded her of a dozen statues in a room far below them. "Is there really a curse on your family?" she asked.

Prince Avalask studied her for a moment before asking, "Where did you hear that?"

"Jalia told me. Is that how Vack's mother died?"

Prince Avalask released his knees unthinkingly and bit at his thumb nail, something Vack also did in moments of discomfort. "Yes. She fell ill before Vack was born."

"But couldn't you save her? Since you're an Epic?"

"I tried everything, but… fate had decided her time was up. There was nothing I could do."

Ebby bit her lip, knowing she should be quiet, but finding herself boldly curious. "Jalia told me the same thing happened to your sister, the one they called the Golden Princess. Jalia said she got sick. You couldn't save her either?"

"Well, there was a little more to it than that." Prince Avalask looked uncomfortable. "But yes, it was awful. She was supposed to be queen too. The second sibling to the Epic always takes the throne, and she was going to be wonderful."

Ebby couldn't help wondering if Savaul had something to do with her death, because that would make him king after Izfazara.

"It's nothing like that," Prince Avalask said to her thought. "There was an age gap, but Savaul and Glidria were close — very close. We all were, but losing her hit Savaul the hardest. A curse is a truly terrible thing."

"I've always been told curses aren't real," Ebby said.

"They're..." Prince Avalask hesitated before he glanced at her, as though deliberating if she was old enough. "People have thrown the term *curse* around lightly for so long that we've lost sight of their severity, I'm afraid. A genuine curse can only be cast in death, and only by somebody hateful enough to stick around *past* death to fulfill its intent."

Ebby had never heard of such a thing. "So... Somebody sort of leaves their soul behind when they die?"

"If they have a purpose large enough to remain for, then yes," Prince Avalask said. "But to do so requires imprisoning yourself somewhere between life and death, and it's not meant to be that way."

It certainly sounded horrible to Ebby. "Who would do that?"

"Your grandfather," Prince Avalask said. "It was in the battle where my father lost all his power, and your grandfather lost his life. He was angry enough to commit his entire soul to ensure every man in the Escali royal family would suffer the grief he'd endured losing his own wife. It was shortly after that fight, about twenty years ago, that we began losing every woman in the family. Now none are left."

Ebby looked up at him, giving him a moment's peace before curiosity bested her. "So... when Vack's mother married you, did she know?"

"She knew. We both knew," he said with a sullen nod. "But Dreya chose to be my wife despite the death sentence — well, she

133

competed for it actually." Prince Avalask bit several nails off in deep thought before he smiled faintly at his legs. "This will sound weird to you, but we had a competition to find the strongest woman in the world. Everybody had a shot, and I agreed to marry the winner because we needed somebody who could survive long enough to give me Vack. She would be our best chance."

Prince Avalask grinned at an old memory and said, "I didn't get to meet her until the day of our wedding vows, for her safety of course, and Savaul teased me for weeks that I was marrying an ox. You have no idea how relieved I was to see she was beautiful, inside and out — her hair so dark and her eyes delighting in life. I didn't realize when I met her that she would share in all my pain, or handle half my problems... And against all my better judgments, I fell in love."

"You... didn't want to?"

"I thought that maybe if I didn't love her, she wouldn't die. But there was no stopping it. Everybody loved her."

"Even Vack?" Ebby asked. "Was there enough time for him to love her?"

"He loves her memory, but no. We lost her less than a week after he was born."

Ebby just felt sorry to hear so. Sorry for herself, for Vack, for Prince Avalask. The world hadn't been fair to any of them.

"She wrote him letters though, knowing she wouldn't be here to watch him grow up. Letters for every birthday until he's twenty, for when he makes his first big mistake, one for the day he gets married, one for if he ever falls in love..." Prince Avalask leaned his head back against the wall and groaned. "I miss her so much."

Tears gathered in the bottoms of Ebby's eyes. How could this be happening, that the most powerful fiend in the world was giving her the heartbreaking story of his life?

She asked softly, "How did you make it stop hurting?"

"I... cheated. I forced myself to forget her." Prince Avalask ran a hand over his eyes and said. "Sir Avery gave me ten days to grieve, and it wasn't enough. I couldn't pull myself together." He pulled his hand away and a bittersweet thought darkened his face. "I can still remember meeting her for the first time, when she laughed at me for being nervous about the *continent-wide* wedding my family had assembled. I remember the very last week with her too, and all the last things she told me to hold onto. And I remember a couple times in between... But I forgot the rest of that beautiful year." Prince Avalask gazed sadly up to the ceiling. "I had to."

Ebby wrapped her arms around his middle and hugged him tightly, though her hands barely reached far enough to clasp on the other side. Prince Avalask smelled like smoke and destruction, a smell that had become familiar over the past months, and one that didn't bother her.

"The world is cruel," she said.

"It can be," Prince Avalask said, hugging her with one arm and tucking the other behind her legs to pick her up. Ebby hadn't been carried to bed in years, but it didn't bother her now. It just made her sleepy and strangely comfortable as she pressed her face into his shoulder and closed her eyes.

She knew she wasn't supposed to feel safe in his arms, but the second he set her down, her heart began to race. She didn't want him to leave. She couldn't go to sleep while Savaul and Gataan knew her location. She might never sleep again.

Almost on cue with her thoughts, a light knock resonated through Ebby's room, and she bolted back to her feet to tug her gloves off. It was only Vack though. He pushed her door gently open, lacking all his usual fire.

"I can sleep in here," Vack said, looking at their feet as though reluctant to be present. "It's my fault Uncle Savaul knows where she is."

Did you listen to our entire conversation? Ebby asked in her mind.

Vack frowned and said, *You let your thoughts drift like flood waters. That's not my fault.*

We'll work on it tomorrow in practice, Prince Avalask's powerful voice broke in. *I'll show you how to block them and how to keep your conversations a little more private.* "Now what do we want to do?" Prince Avalask asked aloud. "Is everybody going to sleep better with Vack in here?"

Ebby hesitated because she and Vack had nearly bargained their lives away to get separate rooms. It seemed like a huge step backwards, but she would feel safer with Vack in front of the door, and even if Vack didn't want to admit it, Ebby knew he didn't want to be alone.

She shrugged as though it made no difference to her, then said, "It's better than sleeping in Vack's room. Have you seen that place? I mean, honestly."

Prince Avalask's booming laugh filled the room, startling them both. "She does have a point," he said to Vack, who simply rolled his eyes. "Alright then. Tomorrow we'll train, and we also need to get you both new clothes. Start thinking about how you want people to see you, because you can't show up to save peoples' lives dressed like ragamuffins. Vack, come help me grab your bed and we'll get it moved over here."

Ebby lay awake in her Escali bed, staring at the vaulted glass ceiling, still sporting carved limericks about all the ways she wished Vack would die. They had shoved Vack's bed in front of her door so nobody could get through it without bowling him over, and Vack's deep breaths finally sounded like he had fallen asleep.

They hadn't spoken since Prince Avalask left, but something else happened in the silence. Ebby had the constant, tiny feeling that

136

Vack was grateful for her presence, and she had the tiniest urge to be thankful for him too, because the dark was much less scary when shared.

She waited until Vack had been asleep for a little while, then ghosted herself past him, became invisible, and trotted down hallways and stairways until veins of grey rock crept through the black glass walls.

"Ratuan?"

Ratuan snapped awake at the sound of his name, and Ebby could feel heaps of anxiety evaporate as he saw her outside the cell.

"Oh thank life you're back," he said, leaping up to grab the bars as the other kids woke. "You had me so worried. Did he hurt you? Are you alright?"

Ebby nearly shrieked as Ratuan gripped the bars. His hands were burned and blistered, and his pain rang through her like the skin of her own palms being ripped off.

"Your hands," she said, grabbing Ratuan's in her own. He took a sharp, stuttered breath as she pulled them off the bars. Ebby winced just as hard and said, "I can fix them."

Ratuan smiled gratefully as she narrowed her focus. She had never healed another person, but this was Ratuan, and she could do anything for Ratuan. He leaned his forehead against the bars and asked again, "Did he hurt you?"

His entire life seemed to rest on the fear that she might say yes. "No," Ebby said. "It was really more of me trying to hurt him."

"Any luck?" Ratuan asked.

"No," Ebby said, suppressing a smile. "I've never been a match for Vack. I'm not sure I ever will be."

Ratuan flipped his hands around so he suddenly had a grip on hers, despite how they pained him.

"You have to be safe, Ebby. Don't ever take a risk like that again. Don't fight him unless you know you can win."

137

"I'm... We fight, Ratuan, but he's not going to kill me."

"You don't know that," Ratuan said, desperate to make her understand. "It's like when you hear about people taming wild animals, and the animals turn on them without warning. He's going to turn on you without warning, Ebby, and I don't know what any of us are going to do. Nothing matters more than getting you out of here."

Ebby slouched forward and pressed her forehead between the bars so it just barely touched Ratuan's. She still felt incredibly shaken from all she'd seen in the day, and she was going to collapse if she couldn't admit her guilt. "Ratuan... I had a chance to escape today, and I didn't take it. I was too afraid," she said, eyes on the floor where the metal beams buried themselves in rock.

"Afraid? What were you afraid of?"

"Of leaving you here," she said as a few tears fell onto her cheeks. "Of meeting Sir Avery, and someday having to fight Vack. Of everything."

"Hey, it's alright," Ratuan said as another large tear hit the ground and she slid her hands down the bars. "Come in here so we can sit and talk."

Hysteria crept in, and Ebby screamed, "I can't just leave while you're still here!"

Ratuan barely startled, and didn't distance himself a single step. "Ok, that's alright," he said gently. "I just need to know you're safe, Ebby." She looked up to meet his eyes, embarrassed by her outburst. "It's not a bad thing for you to stay here. If you play along with the Escalis, you might eventually gain their trust and get a free shot at killing Vack. We'll never get an opportunity better than that."

Ebby fell unnaturally still because that was the last thing she ever wanted to attempt, and a small voice of caution warned her *not* to mention that Vack was currently asleep in her room. "I don't know—"

"You know how important it is to kill him, don't you?" Ratuan asked, and Ebby nodded quickly. "Because he's going to grow up to hunt you, Ebby. He's going be a danger to all of us, and if you don't stop him now, while he's weak, you'll have to stand up to him later when he's powerful. You understand that, right?"

"Yes," she whispered, although trying to kill Vack sounded like the surest way to kill herself. She quailed, however, at the thought of Ratuan's disappointment if she didn't try.

"But what if we weren't enemies, and I didn't have to fight him?" Ebby asked, feeling her face redden as dread swept through Ratuan. She couldn't believe she'd just said those words.

"I know they're trying to convince you that's an option," Ratuan said slowly, carefully. "But Ebby, Vack was born to kill and do harm. Think of everything he's already put you through. Look what he's already done to me." Ratuan turned his palms up to show the angry welts and boils from the ten seconds he had been exposed to Vack.

Ebby could feel Ratuan looking into her eyes, but she couldn't tear her stare away from his hands. She felt so guilty, so ashamed, that she had fallen this far into Prince Avalask's trap when she had seen through it every step of the way. Her throat constricted into a painful knot.

"Ebby?" The smallest boy with the orange hair, Leaf, approached with slow caution to set his hands on the bars. "Have you ever heard the story of the scorpion and the frog?"

"Yes," Ebby said with a miserable nod.

Ratuan frowned and asked, "How does it go?"

Ebby glanced at Leaf, then said, "Reso could always tell stories better than me." She longed to have that life back more than anything. "But there once lived a scorpion who needed to cross a river, and of course, he couldn't swim. So he asked a frog to carry him across, and three times the frog told him no, for surely the scorpion would sting him and he would die." Ebby hesitated, because she suddenly couldn't remember how in the world the scorpion had convinced the frog to do something so stupid.

Leaf said, "The scorpion promised not to sting the frog, and the frog believed him, because if the scorpion stung him in the water, they'd both drown. So he decided to carry the scorpion across."

"They both drowned," Ebby said, feeling the weight of the story in her stomach. "The scorpion stung him and they both drowned, because it was in the scorpion's nature. The circumstances didn't matter."

Ratuan set his hands on hers again, and waited until Ebby raised her eyes to his. "No matter what anyone says, Ebby, a scorpion will sting you, and Vack *will* hurt you."

Ebby looked at the ground again because she knew Ratuan was right. Vack was an Escali, and he had a predator's instincts in his blood. There were times when he didn't seem so bad, when he panicked at the sight of death or helped her when she hurt, but there were also times when he was vicious and fearsome.

"Do you remember when we used to play chess?" Ratuan asked. Ebby could feel him running through things he could say, knowing her well enough to pick exactly the right words. Always the strategic one, he was.

"Of course," Ebby smiled, glad to be off the subject of Vack. "You could beat anybody. You even beat your father when he finally agreed to play."

Ratuan smiled too and said, "That's all this is now. We're playing chess, and I just need you to trust me to control the board." He squeezed her hands and said, "I will get everybody out of here, and I will keep you safe, but I *have* to know I can count on you. I can't win without a full set on my side."

140

"You can count on me," Ebby whispered, feeling the warmth that came with his care.

"You are my best piece, and I will keep you safe at any cost," he said again, rubbing a thumb across the backs of her hands. "And I know it sounds scary, but all you have to do right now is gain their trust. You have time to get ready, and I'll be right here if you need anything. You were made to kill Vack, Ebby. I know you can."

Ebby nodded and pushed the fear of the deed into the future where it belonged. "I know I can too," she said, because for Ratuan, she could do anything.

CHAPTER TWELVE

I was back in the cedar forest, outside Tabriel Vale, in the wildflower patch with fire searing through my mind. Sav and Gat had just tricked me into leading them to Ebby, and now she was right shanking next to me.

"Ratuan, no, come back!" echoed through the trees. The woman shouting it was about to have her throat ripped out. Ratuan was about to be crushed into the ground. Ebby was about to be torn away and probably killed.

"You've got to run," I sobbed, curling in on myself in unbearable pain. My shame was almost as excruciating, and I wished I could just die, right here in a disgraced heap. I'd given away the location of our *Epic*, and I couldn't fight for her, or scream, or even pull myself up to my knees.

"Allie!"

I thrashed as somebody got a tight grip on each of my arms. "Allie! It's a dream!"

I fell instantly still, breathing hard, looking through a tangle of hair to see Archie holding me. We were back at the Dragona, in his pristinely kept room where dust didn't dare invade, where never a single article of clothing was left on the floor. I must have drifted off. We'd been out all night, and the last thing I remembered was

142

sitting on Archie's perfectly made bed, planning out how we would explain the Dincaran kids' location to Tarace without revealing who we were.

"Still a violent sleeper?" His smile calmed me as I took a sharp breath. My racing heart finally slowed and Archie let go of my arms.

"I know who that boy is," I said, shoving my hair out of my eyes, lingering to toy with the ends. "Ratuan. He's the friend from when all of this started, with Sav and Gat..."

Archie watched me for a confused moment. "What are you talking about? I thought you didn't know who he was."

"I just dreamed about him, about the day I woke up without my memory. Archie, I'm the reason Sav and Gat found Ebby. I somehow led them to her, and Ratuan was there too. That's why he recognized me."

I pressed my palm to my forehead and took short breaths.

"He probably has no idea that Ebby's the new Epic," Archie said.

"Probably not," I agreed, closing my itching eyes. I needed to return to my room and get some sleep, but I just couldn't convince my limbs to move.

I sat still for moments longer to gather myself, and Archie startled me as he stood, grabbed my feet, and set them up where he'd just been sitting.

I pried my eyes back open as he grabbed two blankets from the foot of his bed and laid them on the floor.

"What are you doing?"

"Well, you're clearly not moving," he said, crawling between the two and making himself comfortable, which was tough when the ground was solid rock. "And neither of us will be able to speak a full sentence to Tarace if we don't get an hour of sleep first."

I smiled, grateful for the generosity. "You don't have to do that. I'll leave."

143

"Do what you want. I'm comfortable here."

I rubbed my stinging eyes. "Honestly, you can have your bed back."

Archie put a finger to his lips and said, "Shhhh. I'm sleeping," burying his face beneath an arm to end the conversation.

I rolled my eyes and turned over, crawling beneath the welcoming blankets that smelled like spiced tea, and like Archie. Of course, I had to practically rip the sheets up first, as they were all tucked in tightly with the corners folded and creased, but every muscle in my body thanked me for the warmth and comfort as I finally sank down beneath them.

Exhaustion was upon me like wolves on a steak dinner, but I knew nightmares loomed close for me. The best way to combat them was confronting my most pressing dilemmas, and life had handed me some big ones.

Murders, kidnappings, the torments of war — they could all end if the two new Epic kids became friends. And while I wanted to do everything in the world for Archie, pulling Ebby away from the Escalis might just be the worst thing we could do.

If I didn't fight to help Prince Avalask, then I wasn't standing up for everyone's greater good. And we're *supposed* to stand for what we believe is right, no matter the consequences, aren't we?

I slept dreamlessly for hours until I heard somebody whisper, "Not worth it."

I pried my bleary eyes open to find Archie still on the ground, staring straight at the ceiling.

"Hmmmm?" My question went unanswered. "Archie?"

"We're all just pretenders," he replied, and I smiled faintly to myself as I realized he was sleep talking. At least he wasn't violent.

144

"What are we pretending?" I rose to one sleepy elbow to watch him, hoping he would respond.

"Everything." He continued to gaze straight up. "But mostly that we're happy. We're always pretending life is worth living."

My smile vanished. I slowly rose and set my feet on the cold floor as Archie turned away and muttered, "Some of us are just really good at it."

I padded toward him as his breathing hastened and his inhales became sharp gasps. I knelt quietly. "Archie?"

I tried to set a hand on his shoulder, stopped by his shield until he rolled back toward me and curled into a ball. And since he'd moved to touch me, I was able to grasp him tightly as he whispered, "I'm sorry." A pang of sadness and maybe even fear hit me in the chest. I had never seen him shed so much as a tear before, but here he was, dissolving in his sleep. "I'm sorry. I'm so sorry. I didn't mean to."

I rubbed his shoulders and tried to comfort him, if comforting the sleeping was even possible. "Hey, you're alright," I whispered, lying face-to-face beside him. "You have nothing to apologize for."

He released a deep, shuddering breath before settling, and I continued rubbing his strong shoulders as he drifted back into peaceful stillness. Behind his good looks and beneath his positive outlook, lay an Archie who was afraid and ashamed and hiding… but *why*? What could he have possibly done to feel so guilty? The loss of his sister was the only trauma I knew of in his life, but even if that was *somehow* his fault, it wouldn't be a friendship-ending revelation for me. I couldn't imagine anything that would be.

The dissonance I'd fallen asleep with worsened, because I knew that bringing Ebby home could somehow fix the horrors tormenting him, and I had a sense now for how important that was… But as much as I truly cared about Archie, I couldn't bring myself to change my mind for him. The world was better off with Ebby in Prince Avalask's care.

I didn't remember moving back to Archie's bed, but I woke the next morning lying atop a mess of blankets, and Archie was gone.

I sat up uncertainly, not sure if I should be worried, or embarrassed, or... *Why in shanking life wasn't he here?*

Archie pushed his door open with guilty eyes, and I narrowed mine, trying to understand his clenched jaw and hands thrown restlessly in his pockets.

"Sorry," he said, "I needed to get out and think for a bit."

He sat beside me on the bed, searching for words.

"What's going on?" I asked, making my suspicion sound playful.

Archie shrugged and looked at the ceiling, taking a deep breath.

"I've been thinking a lot, and I've decided to take Corliss up on her offer to travel."

I froze.

"What?" I tried to turn my breathless question into a laugh, but my heart had stopped.

"I'm serious. I've stayed here longer than I ever meant to."

I pushed myself back from him as angry heat crept into my face. "Enough of this stupid nonsense about your past. What is the real shanking reason you want to leave?"

Archie restlessly started to tuck his blankets down into the bed, and I tried *hard* to fake patience while I simmered inside. "I can't get close to others, Allie, and you and I are getting too close. Being with me puts you in danger."

I stood in a flash and said, "That is the biggest load of bullscat I have ever heard." He must be a new breed of idiot to think himself the source of my peril. "We have exactly the same enemies, and

146

most of the danger we encounter is *my* fault. I'd already be dead three times over if not for you. How can you just leave me after all that?"

I wished I sounded kinder, like somebody worth staying with, but I couldn't keep scathing anger from my voice. I knew, deep down, this was part of the reason he wanted to go.

"Look, there are things you don't know —"

"Oh what?" I sneered. "Something to do with your *big secret* is putting us in danger?"

"I'm not making up stories so I can run away," he said, finally taking offense. "But I didn't want to leave my sister either, and she was killed because I didn't."

A better person would have softened their words at the mention of his dead sister, but I didn't flinch. "You told me she was killed by Sav and Gat. And you think they're going to leave me alone just because you're gone?" Archie looked almost entirely composed, except he dug his nails deep into his palms as I said, "You're not playing the hero by leaving me to them, and to the Zhauri, and Sir Avery, and whoever else I manage to infuriate."

We both stared hard at each other until Archie said decisively, "I have to leave."

"Well, good riddance then." My voice became suddenly, irrationally flippant. "I'll go talk to Tarace myself and hope the Zhauri don't murder me by the end of the week."

I turned to skip toward the door, and Archie grabbed my arm to stop me. "Look, I'm sorry," he said, looking truly disheartened. "I'll help you get through this mess with the Zhauri, but that's as long as I can stay."

"Alright, sounds great," I said with a bright smile. I felt like a lunatic, like it was the only way I could cope with the idea of being alone so soon. "Let's go see Tarace like we planned then, shall we?"

I put an anger-inspired spring in my step and tried not to think about how much it was going to hurt to lose him. I tried not to scold myself for being such an idiot and relying so heavily on another person. People will always let you down — it's a fact of life — yet I'd willingly given away a piece of my independence since meeting Archie. What a *fool*.

We reached the long hall to Anna's old study, where Tarace now resided over stacks of paperwork, and were still five steps from the door when it creaked open of its own accord. My heart sank as I saw Tarace sitting behind Anna's old oak desk, Sir Avery leaning against it, and Maverick standing with his hands folded casually behind his back. The whole room reeked of fearsome authority, some left over from memories of Anna, but mostly from the power trio facing us now. I wondered for a moment if I could crawl under Anna's large desk and just die. It would be a kinder fate than this.

"I'm amazed to see you back so soon," Maverick said, eyes fixed on Archie instead of me. "You must have even better methods for obtaining information than I do."

Archie said nothing, so I stepped up to say, "We came back to speak with Tarace. We didn't expect to run into you."

"Anything you have to say to Tarace can be said in front of us," Sir Avery said impatiently, spinning one of his thumbs around the other. Tarace stared silently over folded hands, the perfect image of a man who was picking his battles.

"We found where the Escalis are keeping the Dincaran kids," Archie launched in. "They haven't seen sunlight in months, and some of them are hurt—"

"Did you happen to find Ebby among them?" Sir Avery asked. Archie fell silent, gritting his teeth in distaste. "Because the kids' location isn't news to us. You're wasting our time."

I stared hard at Sir Avery, because if he knew their location, something should have already been done for them.

"Are we just... leaving them there?" I asked, specifically to Tarace.

Tarace, without any particular inflection or emotion, replied, "The Dragona doesn't have the resources right now to retrieve them. We have allies among the other cities who will help us, but until last night, the matter hasn't been a priority."

"Not a priority?" I repeated.

"The children from Dincara are none of your concern anyway," Maverick said, rather politely. "Your task is to find our Epic so Sir Avery can keep Prince Avalask at bay and my team can extract her."

Archie turned to Sir Avery and asked, "You honestly want us to give your daughter's location to the Zhauri? You know their history. They shouldn't be anywhere near her."

Sir Avery chuckled and said, "Their history is the reason I brought them down here. Prince Avalask is shading Ebby from being tracked; he can move her to a new hideout at a moment's notice, and even if I *do* find her, he can fight me long enough for his son to relocate her. The Zhauri are our best shot at getting her back. Maybe our only shot."

"But you're *trusting* them?" Archie demanded as though Maverick weren't in the room.

"No, I'm *paying* them," Sir Avery replied. "We've discussed the reward you'll receive if you contribute to her rescue, and if the Zhauri can bring her home, I've told Maverick that one of his boys can marry her."

Archie's jaw fell open, and I felt a protective beast rear its head in my chest as I growled, "She's *ten.*"

"She's almost twelve," Maverick corrected me, "and next year she'll be thirteen, and three years after that, she'll be sixteen. We all understand the nature of aging. What's important right now, is that you two locate her."

149

"Oh, I'll find her," I said, my lip curled back in disgust, "but you are going to be the very last person to find out when I do."

Archie stood on my foot, telling me to shut up as Maverick replied, "I've given you your deadline. I can give you motivation not to miss it, if that would be helpful."

Archie grabbed my hand tightly enough to suggest he might break it as I spat, "I don't take orders from you," and Archie groaned as though I'd just signed for our deaths.

Maverick broke into a frightful smile and said, "Such brave words for one in such a vulnerable position."

I was just about to spit a string of insults regarding his character and his mother, but hesitated as he exchanged a conspiring glance with Sir Avery.

"I can point Allie's sister out to you if they're not cooperative," Sir Avery said, his tone suggesting that this entire conversation was beneath him and he had other places he'd rather be. Maverick shot me a patronizing smirk as Sir Avery continued, "Archie's got a group of friends they'd both hate to lose, and neither of them would be particularly keen to see the other maimed or given Time, if you really need to get persuasive."

My jaw fell open and I breathed, "What are you *doing?*"

"I don't think you understand the severity of this situation," Sir Avery replied, leaning toward me with his eyes narrowed dangerously. "That's my little girl the Escalis have. They haven't killed her yet, which means they're trying to turn her against us, and I can only imagine the methods they're using. What's it to me if you have to lose a couple fingers in order to rescue her?"

Tarace finally stood up and said flatly, "The threats are unnecessary. None of those things will happen as long as I lead at the Dragona." He turned his sharp gaze to me and Archie, ignoring the other two men in the room, but I couldn't help but wonder if Tarace's protection meant anything against the threats of Maverick

150

and Sir Avery. "But you both need to understand how important it is to get Ebby home," he told us, "especially after what we learned last night. Humanity might not survive if we don't retrieve our Epic. Rescuing her and the Dincaran kids just became urgent."

I glanced at Archie, whose frown looked nearly serious enough to be permanent. "What did we learn last night?" he asked.

"That's right, they wouldn't have been here," Sir Avery said dismissively. "I'll leave you two to explain the situation. And I'll see your boys later tonight," he said, giving Maverick a curt nod before leaping to disappear.

Tarace fell thoughtfully quiet, and Maverick was the one who cordially explained, "The situation, as Sir Avery calls it, has grown quite dire."

"It sounds like you already know Sir Avery didn't have a son like he was supposed to," Tarace said, irritation finally creeping onto his face. "Messed that right up with some tavern girl who gave him a daughter?"

"We've heard of Ebby," I said defensively.

"So that's where our Epic is, being brain-washed to side with the Escalis," Tarace said, his composure slowly leaking away. "Meanwhile, those children the Escalis captured consisted of our young mages from the Dragona, and every child who had just been exiled from Tekada to Dincara for the ability to use magic — which means the Escalis have all our future magic-users."

"Do *you* have any news for us that isn't a waste of time?" I asked, wishing Sir Avery was still in the room for the jibe.

"You asked why we haven't done anything about those children yet," Tarace said. "And the answer is because we were waiting for our adult mages from the Dincaran surrender to come home so we could mount a real rescue. But they're not coming home."

Fearful dread crept into my chest as I said, "What are you talking about? The Escalis took the survivors in Dincara across the ocean

151

and dumped them on the shores of Tekada. Everybody knows that."

"Yeah, that's what everybody heard," Tarace said, choking on a sudden surge of emotion that made my breath catch. What could be wrong? Corliss had said the survivors were already released. Izfazara had promised they would be.

"The Escalis did drop them on the shores of Tekada," Tarace said, struggling to keep his voice steady. "We all thought King Kelian would send them right back to us, since magic is banned there."

Several large veins emerged on Tarace's temples as he clenched and unclenched his jaw several times, and I glanced at Archie to see fear on his face too as Tarace set a closed fist on the desk.

Maverick, his voice maddeningly calm, explained, "Instead of sending them back, King Kelian declared the mages criminals for returning to his sacred lands, and one at a time, he executed them." Maverick spoke like he was discussing the weather. "Every mage involved in the Dincaran battle is now dead."

CHAPTER THIRTEEN

My spit grew hot and bitter in my mouth, and my limbs fell numb. Our mages, my friends, Humanity's only hope against the Escalis, had all been murdered?

Murdered. And it was my fault.

Archie was saying something, maybe to me, maybe to Tarace, but I was seconds away from vomiting on the floor of Anna's old study, and the words sounded like a jumble.

All our mages?

I fled the room in a confused mess, flew through the caves without a care as to who I passed, and stumbled over the boulders that separated the Wreck from the forest. My feet took me into the fresh air and crunched through fallen pine cones and tree needles, trying to escape the horrible word…

Executed.

I leapt over a tiny creek and crashed straight through two huckleberry bushes before nearly tumbling over the edge of a massive cliff cut into the mountainside. A beautiful green expanse stretched below me, dotted with trees and open fields beneath a deep blue sky, and I released an angry, hideous shriek to echo over it all.

It wasn't their fault they'd been sent back! How could anybody be so disgustingly cruel?

I braced one hand against a crumbling stump and used the other to grab my hair as I hunched over in violent illness.

Once my watery venison stew from yesterday lay on the bed of moss in front of me, I grabbed a massive fallen limb, wrenched it from the wild vines holding it down, and slammed it into the nearest tree with an angry snarl. It broke, so I smashed my hands onto either side of the trunk and tried to crush it, sinking my teeth into the bark in an attempt to make it feel some fraction of my own pain.

Something crashed through the huckleberry bushes and I whipped around with bared teeth, ready to bite and claw through whatever had decided to pursue me now, but it was Archie, and ripping one of his arms off wouldn't necessarily make me feel any better.

Archie skidded to a stop and froze, watching my face as though he *also* harbored concern that I might try to dismember him.

Of all the things I needed to scream, the one that mattered most came through first. "Archie, you can't..." I gasped a frantic gulp of air. "You can't leave. Don't leave me to do this alone."

I stared hard at him, ready to defend myself and shout that it wasn't *him* I needed, I just needed his ability to hunt, and his memories of my past, and his sense of humor, and his nearly-unending patience. I was still entirely self-sufficient, but having him around... well, it helped.

Archie curled his fingers into his hair and tugged at it, watching me warily. "I was... trying to make things better by leaving," he finally said, dropping his hand back to his side. "But I'm not about to abandon you. I'll always be here when you need me."

Archie took a step toward me, using a caution I would usually reserve for approaching rabid wolves, and I turned my gaze to the

154

rolling hills of green below, wishing he'd given me reason to shout at him. On any other day, the bright sunlight and cloudless sky would have been beautiful. Today, they were just bright, a strain on the eyes.

"This is my fault," I finally said as hollowness rotted me away, sluffing off every bit of my soul that had ever existed. "I made the wrong decision."

And Archie *laughed*.

"You've got to be kidding," he said as my throat tightened around a large lump. "For making the deal that spared their lives?"

I rubbed at my eyes, which were thankfully not leaking. "They never would have been sent to Tekada if not for me."

Two hands grabbed my shoulders, and when I pulled my hand off my face, Archie pressed his forehead to mine. I felt one degree calmer with him so close and closed my eyes to appreciate how steady he felt. "Allie, every survivor from Dincara belongs on the *Saved* side of your list. What Kelian did wasn't our fault. We never could have guessed this would happen."

"It was *our job* to guess," I said, opening my eyes to glare at the grass beneath my feet as the blades shuffled in the breeze. "We know King Kelian is a dirty bastard. We know he hates magic. We should have given the Humans information before the battle instead of the Escalis."

"Look, you can't do this to yourself," Archie said rather unkindly, stepping back from me. "We didn't have any good tips to give to our side, and we barely gave the Escalis any information at all. That battle was going to be lost, and if not for us, it would have just ended in slaughter."

I leaned against the mossy, needly stump beside me and dug my nails in, hoping for a second to *not* talk about slaughter. "How are you just... holding yourself together right now?" I asked weakly.

"This is just how I cope," Archie said. "I just... push the situation into the back of my mind and pretend it isn't happening. I laugh and tell everyone I'm fine, and then I can go about my life. It's how I've always done it."

Even now, his only emotion was a caring smile. "That can't be healthy," I said, wiping my nose on the back of my hand.

Archie just shrugged. "Yeah, well, neither was crying in a corner for two years of my life. Sometimes you've got to pick your unhealthy."

I closed my stinging eyes for a moment. If I was capable of burying this hurt under a mountain of distraction, it would be tempting... But guilt, anger, and pain don't just disappear because they're ignored. If I put them out of mind, they'd be left to fester and eat at me in the space between thoughts, returning as dreams and haunting the quiet moments when all I had was myself.

"You created a saying once," Archie said, wrapping his fingers around my hand. "Well, actually, you carved it in big letters across my wall. You told everyone, *all darkness is only shadow.*"

"*All darkness is only shadow...*" I repeated, the next words surfacing from a place of deep familiarity, "*for unless light has ceased to exist, it is merely an obstacle away.*"

Archie didn't hide his surprise and studied my face in uncertainty. "You remember that?"

"I... don't know. It feels engrained, I guess. Like I've been saying it all my life."

"Well, you're not wrong," Archie said, chuckling airily. "We've all said it so many times over the years, it's become a long standing joke among the Tallies, and a way to identify each other. But... all too often, we're brought back to its real meaning, which is that there's always good in the world, and a happier tomorrow if you can get through today."

I sighed heavily because the saying was hopeful and personal —
a reminder than no matter how low we fall, no shade of darkness is
permanent. *Light is merely an obstacle away.* At least in theory.
Practically though, some places just never see light. Like the inside
of a cave, or the bottom of a dungeon.

I shrugged and said, "Some obstacles are just too big to be
moved."

Archie squeezed my hand and said, "I once told you the exact
same thing, and you replied that sometimes you have to move
yourself."

I rubbed my palms down my face, startled as wings stirred the
air above my head. Flak landed on my shoulder, and I gritted my
teeth as she dug her sharp talons in to stay up. My grey-flecked bird
butted her head against mine, making me smile.

"What... are we going to do?" I finally whispered, taking a
steadying breath. "We *can't* give Ebby's location to the Zhauri, but
Humanity needs her back. The Escalis are too strong to withstand
without mages."

"There are still the Dincaran kids," Archie said. "Tarace and the
other city leaders are going to find a way to rescue them — they
have no choice now. As for Ebby..." Archie let go of my hand at a
clear loss for words, and we both jerked in surprise as Prince
Avalask appeared beside us.

"Hey, you two," he said softly. "I've heard the news. I'm so
sorry."

Flak leapt off my shoulder and flapped twice before Prince
Avalask held an arm out and she landed gracefully, bowing her
head to the Epic.

"Our friend Michael was one of the mages on those ships," I said
heavily.

"And Sir Bruscan, our sword trainer, could use magic," Archie
added.

157

"And I'd hoped maybe Anna survived the battle and would be coming back," I said, blinking several times to avoid the shame of tears. "I just don't understand. They were mages. Even with an *army*, King Kelian shouldn't have been able to kill them."

"It was…" Prince Avalask cleared his throat, settling his eyes on Flak as he went on, "Kelian used the one-at-a-time technique. Took them individually for questioning, starting with anybody who could communicate by thought. And by the time they realized nobody was coming back, it was too late."

Half of me wanted to vomit and the other half wanted to sail to Tekada to set the place ablaze. "*Why* are we still calling Kelian our king?" I demanded of Archie. "We should be rebelling against him, not sending supplies across the ocean to appease him. We should be… renaming our continent, and sending him ships of horse scat."

"Believe me, you're not the only person who wants to," Archie said, eyes narrowed bitterly like he wished he could conspire with me. "But we have a standing deal with Tekada. As soon as we stop sending supplies, Kelian's made it clear he'll kill every child who can use magic rather than banish them, and we *need* those mages."

I clenched my fists and said, "Why can't we go conquer Tekada?"

"Because if our forces are all on Tekada, who's going to defend against the Escalis?"

"It's possible the Human-Escali war won't be lasting much longer," Prince Avalask said rather casually. "So perhaps Kelian could be your next focus after all."

Archie and I fell silent, waiting for him to mock our shocked faces and say he was joking. I finally cleared my throat to speak, then stopped again to avoid sounding foolish.

Prince Avalask smirked like a mischievous child who'd pulled off the heist of his life, and said, "I spoke with a couple people, made a couple promises, and threatened to turn every hair on

Savaul's head stark white if he sabotaged me. And in the end, I persuaded my uncle to release the kids from the Dincaran battle."

My jaw fell open. There was no way. There was just no way.

Archie asked, "*Why* would he give them up like that?"

"As part of a bargain," Prince Avalask said. He stroked Flak's feathers thoughtfully, but she hopped sideways to avoid him, drawing an amused smile from the Epic. "War has grown tiresome, and we could easily kill those kids from Dincara, dooming Humanity to certain defeat, but it would be a tedious victory. We'd still have to stomp on Humankind until they're all dead — stubborn mules that they are. Whereas if we offer to return those kids unharmed, that puts us in a strong position to negotiate for laws and lands. And I have one rather large demand of my own that's not negotiable." Prince Avalask looked abruptly from me to Archie, the jerky movement reminding me he wasn't Human, or a Tally. "We'll return the Dincaran kids, but I'm keeping Ebby."

Archie's entire body slouched as he ran a hand down his face. "That's the *one thing you can't do*," he groaned.

"Listen," Prince Avalask said, "I know how much you need to bring her home, but you don't know her. Ebby is a malleable, pliable little girl. She will become whatever you tell her to become." Prince Avalask narrowed his eyes and said, "Neither of you know Sir Avery as I do. If he gets her back, this war will recommence in five years, tops. He wants her because she's powerful, not because he loves her."

"You have no idea how much he loves her," Archie said sharply. "You can't just run around kidnapping kids because you think you'd make a better parent."

"I can, and I have," Prince Avalask replied. "And I will continue to do so for as long I like."

"Archie." I tried to grab his arm, but his shield blocked me. "Think about it, this is perfect," I said, taking my hand back.

"Ebby's safe from the Zhauri, *we're* safe from the Zhauri if the war is over, and the Dincaran kids will be home — no bloodshed required."

Prince Avalask glanced gratefully to me and said, "Thank you. Now, I need a hand meeting the right people, starting with Tarace—"

"Hang on," Archie said, taking a step between us. "There's another side of this to consider, and we're not rushing to help you before we address it."

Prince Avalask raised his eyebrows and asked, "Have you explained to Allie *why* bringing Ebby home is important to you?"

"She's. been. *kidnapped*," Archie growled.

"She and Vack could change the world if they became friends. We'll bring an end to the war now, and then they can prevent it from ever rekindling," Prince Avalask replied in scathing annoyance. "*Your* need to bring her home is entirely selfish."

"Allie and I aren't helping you until we've come to an informed decision," Archie said, standing stiffly. "And if Ebby's not part of the deal, we won't be helping at all."

"*Archie,*" I hissed.

Prince Avalask's gaze sharpened as he asked, "Do you know how hard it's going to be, contacting Human leaders without somebody to get me past their interaction spells?"

Flak leapt off to soar over the fields rather than endure the jostle of his angry hands.

"Not my problem," Archie retorted. "I'm willing to help you, but we're not negotiating over Ebby. You can keep pretending life with you is the best thing for her and the rest of the world, but it's *delusional.* She'll have influences in her life other than Sir Avery once she's home. She and Vack could have play dates and become friends in other ways, without you holding her hostage."

Prince Avalask scoffed like Archie's suggestion was stupid enough to be offensive, but a piercing falcon cry echoed across the hills, and we all fell silent to look over the green expanse. Flak's warning had come just in time.

Four men clad in white cloaks strolled below, carelessly letting their voices drift on the breeze. The two strongest Zhauri dragged the lifeless body of an Escali between them, each holding one arm. The other two walked behind, one with a pack on his shoulders, and Iquis with a hobble to his step. Four massive, furry snow-dogs trotted dutifully in their wake — black, white, brown, and grey with a few variations on their faces and paws.

Prince Avalask turned to Archie, jaw gaping. "The Zhauri are staying at the Dragona?"

"Yes," Archie replied, eliciting a look of outrage from Prince Avalask. "I was going to tell you," he said in exasperation. "They got here yesterday and insisted that Allie and I help find Ebby."

"They're already wreaking havoc looking for her, and I couldn't track them because of that shade," Prince Avalask said, clasping his hands together with a sudden hunger in his eyes. "Zeen, the one with the pack. This is very good to know."

I glanced down to the Zhauri brother with the chestnut hair and thick beard like the rest of them, getting the feeling that Prince Avalask had a score to settle. And I already hated the Zhauri enough to add, "They've been told they can marry Ebby if they bring her home."

Prince Avalask snorted in revulsion. "They will *never* get anywhere near her or Vack. Not them, and not Sir Avery."

Archie was about to argue the point further, but I quickly cut in, "It's good you're here. This isn't the first Escali they've grabbed to question, and they killed the last one. We couldn't do anything to stop them."

161

Prince Avalask took a pensive second to adjust his wind-ruffled black cloak, staring at the rolling field. "Neither can I."

He held up a finger to cut me off before I began to protest. "Listen. The Zhauri are unmatched, Allie. On the rare occasion they participate in matters of war, they're Humanity's most dangerous weapon. See the one with the black hair, looks like he's half werewolf?" Prince Avalask pointed at the brother with the thick, dark facial features, dragging the Escali. "His name is Kit, and I've seen him singlehandedly demolish an entire stone fort up north. Exploded it from the inside, killed everyone in a fifty cubit radius. The one with the ugly face and the hobble is a mind mage of the worst sorts, called Iquis. Can't read minds, but he can rip them apart. Zeen is a shade, but he's also their lead interrogator. Don't you two get mixed up with them. *Ever.*"

"But you're an Epic!" I exclaimed as quietly as possible.

"Ebby's an Epic too, but the girl would die if a sloth attacked her," Prince Avalask exclaimed. "The Zhauri only have five gifts between them, but they're the strongest mages in the world. That is *far* more dangerous than having access to all the powers."

I turned my gaze back to the field, not wanting to imagine the horrors in store for the Escali below.

"What about Blond-beard down there, with the muscles?" Archie asked. The only one I'd seen smile. "He's the second telekinetic?"

Prince Avalask shook his head slowly. "No, he's new. I managed to kill the brother who could stop motion a few years ago, and this is his replacement." A triumphant smile crept onto Prince Avalask's face as he studied the newest member. "Hakkrui could stop flying arrows or catapulted stones — he could freeze rioting crowds if he wanted to. He gave the Zhauri control over any situation. I can't read the new one with Zeen so close, but I'm pretty sure he's got your power, Archie."

Archie's bitterness lightened as he tilted his head in interest.

"I mean he's what you could be if you actually trained and put some discipline into getting better," Prince Avalask said, drawing another scowl from Archie. "And I *think* he might also be Maverick's son. Tall, wide shoulders, same jaw, and just about the right age... It would certainly explain why he's powerful enough to protect the whole group."

Zeen, the shade carrying the pack, made a mocking sound like a squeal of pain, and the other three laughed as more joking words were exchanged in Icilic.

"None of them are more powerful than you," I insisted.

"No, but the group is. That new brother is their defense, Kit can wreck anything they come across, and Iquis can cripple anyone who tries to stand against them, myself included."

They set the Escali down for a moment to rest, and I flung an arm out to grip Archie's shoulder, tight as my fingers could squeeze.

"What?"

"Archie, we know him." My heart had stopped entirely.

Archie got down beside me to look. "Oh no... It's Tral," he said, recognizing the Escali.

"You know his name?"

"They mentioned it several times while you were sleeping," he replied.

Months ago, two Escalis had been ordered to drag me and Archie down a mountain, but everything had gone wrong and I hadn't been able to walk. Tral was the one who had ended up carrying me the entire way, out of pure compassion even though he thought I was his enemy.

The Zhauri had captured *him*.

163

"Allie, come on, you have to stop," Archie said, grabbing my sleeve as I dashed into the tunnels on my way to Anna's old study.

His grip was tight enough to pull me to a halt, and I whirled on him furiously.

"We can't let this happen," I said, my voice hoarse with fear. "They're going to hurt him. Tarace won't stand for it if he knows — we have to tell him."

"Allie, Tarace has no authority over the Zhauri," Archie said.

"Then we can find out where they're taking him, and we can stop them—"

"Allie!"

When I fell silent, I realized that he just looked hopeless. I was toe to toe with him with my shirtsleeve still clutched tightly in his hand, and he whispered, "We're just two people."

"*So?*"

"So… we can't fix everything," he said. I glared angrily, feeling more and more helpless as he gave me a sad, half-hearted shrug. "I wish we could."

I hissed my heated breath through my teeth and demanded, "What are we supposed to do then? Leave him to the Zhauri?"

"Yes, but not for long. Listen, Sir Avery will do literally anything for us if we can get Ebby home. We can get him out of here that way."

I fidgeted with my fingers, nearly rubbing the skin off. "And then what about Ebby?"

"I know you want to leave her with Prince Avalask. I really, truly get it. But we can bring Ebby home *without* the Zhauri and then ask Sir Avery to release Tral. The Zhauri would have no claim to Ebby and no reason left to stay here, so they'd return to the north and we'd *all* be safer for it."

"And what about the Dincaran kids?" I asked. "Prince Avalask won't negotiate to send them home unless he gets to keep Ebby."

"Either he'll come around, or we'll find another way to rescue the kids." Archie stared hard at me in sincerity. "This is the better way."

I took a deep breath and tried to remember why I wanted to leave her with Prince Avalask. My reasons felt suddenly distant in light of so many looming threats. "Alright, let's go find her," I said.

Archie nodded and said, "Grab everything you might need. We're not coming back until she's with us."

CHAPTER FOURTEEN

Time has a habit of passing fastest when we need it to slow down, which is always horribly inconvenient.

My quick steps resonated around the empty cave walls, making it sound like ten people were dashing up the glass-flecked steps with me, away from the Dincaran kids. I reached the narrow fissure in the ceiling in record time, leaping up to grab two familiar hand holds, straining to pull myself into the tight gap that would lead back to our Tally caves. The rocks cut into my hands, but this jump was a normal part of visiting the Dincaran kids when they returned from their daily labors in the Escali kitchens.

Karissa had donned a disguise last week so she could join Robbiel in the dreamland of bandaging and disinfecting. Archie had come with me twice to see the kids, but I'd been down here mostly by myself as he inquired about Ebby around the city.

Without a faint scent trail, or a lock of hair left in a tree, or a madman claiming to have seen her, we'd made no progress at all in the two weeks we'd been here. A chronic sense of panic had settled into my stomach because the Zhauri's deadline had been six days ago, and a discouraging voice in my head began suggesting I might want to hide out and avoid going back to the Dragona altogether. Archie seemed to be losing hope as well.

166

I squeezed myself through the crevice which hadn't widened one bit since we'd first used it, and I cursed as the sharp rocks dragged me to a stop. I finally had information worthwhile, and getting stuck was absolutely the last thing I needed.

I sighed and tried to slow down despite my excitement. We'd been asking the Dincaran kids for two weeks if they knew anything about our new Epic, but they kept insisting they hadn't seen her. I would have given up and left to look elsewhere, except for one glaring red flag. Any time we asked about Ebby near Ratuan, the kids would glance at him before answering.

Something about him set me on edge, so I'd taken special care to ask about Ebby when Ratuan was far from us, but the answers had still been the same.

"We haven't seen her."

"We don't know anything."

"We would tell you if we did."

I dislodged myself from one of the tighter squeezes in the rocks and pushed into the last stretch toward our fireplace as I heard the scrape of the large marble door opening.

I heard Robbiel ask, "Who won?"

He was answered by a mocking laugh that I recognized as Emery's. "Go on, tell him the score."

A sigh that sounded like Archie's was followed by the admission, "Fourteen to three."

I dragged myself out of the fireplace to see Archie and Emery both covered in a shiny layer of sweat, wooden practice swords in hand, while Celesta worked on a tedious piece of stitch work and Nessava assaulted her hair with all manner of braids. Robbiel sat against a wall with a book open in his lap and let out a low whistle. "Somebody's out of practice," he said, returning his gaze to his reading.

167

"Yeah, well it's been months since I've been able to spar," Archie replied as I hopped twice on my left foot to twist out of the cave's clutches. "Sorry Allie, I spent the rest of the afternoon looking, I swear."

"Actually, I would hate to see how bad Allie's gotten lately," Emery mused, tossing his practice sword to catch it mid spin.

I made a note to scold Emery later, and exclaimed, "Ebby's been down with the Dincaran kids."

All attention turned to me as Emery asked, "Is this also based on your weird *they-keep-looking-at-Ratuan* theory?"

I faked an ugly laugh that clearly told him to knock it off. "It's more than that," I said. "The Dincaran kids keep telling us they haven't seen her. Has anybody thought twice about that?"

I threw my arms wide in epiphany, but my friends just stared at me with varying degrees *are you crazy?*

"They shouldn't know to be calling the new Epic *her*," I explained with determination. "There hasn't been any information in or out of those caves in months, but every kid we've spoken to knows she's a girl. *We* didn't tell them that. They must have seen her."

Archie knocked a palm against his forehead as Robbiel glanced sideways at him and muttered, "How did we not notice that..."

"You know who we need to confront about this?" I asked.

"Ratuan," Archie said immediately. "He's the first one she'd see. Let me drop my gear off in my room, and we'll pay him a visit."

Karissa pulled the door open just in time to pass Archie on his way out, and entered our cavern with a book in hand.

"Robbiel, I stole this from your room," she said as Archie disappeared down the hall.

"That's fine, I stole it from the Dragona," Robbiel replied. He glanced up at her, then closed the book in his hands and held it out to her. "You'll like this one better though. It's got blood, gore, drama —"

Karissa quickly traded, then sat beside him and opened to page one.

"You should grab your stuff," Emery told her. He stooped to snatch the book from her hands, but she jerked it back on reflex. "Allie thinks she's got a lead on Ebby, and they're planning another trek down to the Dincaran kids."

Karissa glanced at me and said, "I could do with another trip down there."

"They're going *now,*" Emery insisted. "Put your hair in that weird style that looks like a butt —"

"It's *a bow,*" Karissa said, staring at the book to ignore him.

"Yeah, whatever. Do your hair, grab your poofy sleeved shirt, and go with them."

Karissa snapped the book closed and looked up at him in greatest dislike. "Why are you trying to get rid of me? *What* do you have planned that you need me to leave for?"

I'd lost interest in their bickering my first day here, and decided to see what was taking Archie so long. I pushed past the marble door and started down the hallway, passing my own room. I'd barely set foot in my sleeping space since taking on the quest to find Ebby, and under the pressure and stress of the Zhauri's threats, I'd completely forgotten to pull up the false bottom I'd found in my wooden chest a while back.

But at the same time, a low whistle was drifting from beneath Archie's closed door, pulling me closer, and whispering that I could check the bottom of my chest later. It was the deepest and saddest movement of the duskflyer song, a song I hadn't heard him whistle in a while. Archie drew each note so their meaning would echo and last, and a strange stir in my chest startled me, because music... well, music had never caused a feeling like this in me before — a feeling like love, and longing, so deep in the heart that it couldn't possibly be pried away.

Archie's melody had a soul, mourning something long lost even though the notes were full and warm. Duskflyers themselves couldn't sing like this, and the hairs up and down my arm prickled in response.

Archie startled me by pulling his door open, looking a little surprised himself as the whistle came to an abrupt stop.

We locked eyes for a brief moment before Emery *destroyed* the moment, bolting down the hall toward us, hissing, "Get inside!" He pushed us both into Archie's room, closing the door with only a crack left open.

"What are you —"

"Hang on," he whispered, holding both his hands out with a gleeful smile. He motioned frantically for us to come watch the hallway with him, and I exchanged an uncertain glance with Archie before noticing the massive words *All Darkness is Only Shadow* carved into the wall behind him — Human words spelled with Escali letters. Maybe they had inspired his sad whistling — a reminder of the past.

"I found a snaptree out in the woods," Emery said, throwing a hand over his mouth to muffle his laughter.

I glanced at the ceiling and said, "You are *such* a child."

Emery whispered, "Shut up, old woman. You used to be more fun."

Karissa strode to her room, and I threw my hands over my ears before she reached her door. As soon as she touched it, a loud cacophony of cracks and snaps rattled the tunnel like pitchy branches in a roaring fire.

"EMERY!" Karissa's scream echoed over top of them as she jerked her hand back. "Snapping sap?" she exclaimed to the empty tunnel.

170

Emery barely stifled a laugh as she tried to wipe some of the sticky substance off on the wall, but the friction caused a hundred more deafening snaps to shake three miles of tunnel rock. Even covering my ears couldn't block it, and Emery's laughter was the next loudest thing as he hunched forward and lost the ability to breath.

"I'll kill you for this!"

Karissa lifted one powerful leg to kick open the door across from hers, and Emery suddenly took the situation more seriously as she darted into his room. He fled Archie's room to bolt after her, and a crash of scattered belongings echoed through the tunnel as the two collided and Karissa shouted, "I GET NESSAVA!"

Nessava and Robbiel had just poked their heads out from behind the marble doors.

"Get out of here before they drag you into it," Robbiel warned.

And right before she took off to join the fray, Nessava turned to me and Archie with a grin. "It's good to be home, isn't it?"

Another crackling chorus of snapping sap made it impossible to reply as we heard multiple items clanging to the ground and Emery shouting, "Robbiel! You're on my team! HELP!"

I couldn't help laughing, feeling a little of the toxic worry in my stomach subside. "Actually yeah," I said. "More than you know."

The buzz of activity among the Dincaran kids didn't cease when we reached them. They'd seen me here less than an hour ago, but I hadn't visited Ratuan's cell, and we reached it this time to find the door swung open and Ratuan missing.

"You're back!" Leaf said, his freckled face lighting up. "Your friend Robbiel was here yesterday with his friend Karissa." He held his freshly bandaged arms wide to show us. "Come in! I swiped some extra food from the kitchens tonight. We'll share."

His excitement warmed me so I couldn't help smiling. "I've told you, Leaf, you don't have to share with us. I'm the one who should be bringing you food."

He scrunched his face like my response was silly. "You're my friends. I don't mind."

Eric with the angular face said, "Ratuan's not here. We can tell him you stopped by."

I crouched to give Leaf a hug as Archie asked, "How about Ebby then? Is she off with Ratuan too?"

Leaf stiffened in my arms and glanced back at the older boys, who also froze in hesitation. The girl in the cell pushed herself silently into the corner and stared at her nails.

Leaf tried to smile up at me through a guilt-ridden face. "Who's… Ebby?" he asked.

I gave him my best disappointed smile and said, "You know who she is. What's going on, Leaf?"

Steph, the one who looked the oldest of the group, came to Leaf's defense with a supportive hand on his shoulder, and said, "There are things we can't talk about here."

I narrowed my eyes and asked, "Why? Because Ratuan told you not to?"

Leaf's hesitation turned into something closer to fear, sending a tingle of unease down my spine.

"Where's Ratuan?" Archie asked.

Leaf bit his lip before saying, "Ratuan and Ebby —"

"Leaf!" Steph cut him off, but Leaf had grown bold.

"What? They already know she's here, and they want to help. I could take them to —"

"Leaf, you've got to stop," Eric warned.

"I'll take them," Leaf said. "I don't think Ratuan will be mad." The older boys gave him looks of pity and disbelief as Leaf said,

"Really, I don't think he will be. Come on." He glanced at me with a smile and a slight quiver. "I'll show you where they are."

Five hallways deeper, the tunnel forked and I began to hear a soft voice speaking ahead. "I think they realized we don't heal like they do." The relaxed voice was almost certainly Ratuan's. "They've started pulling us from the kitchens to make sure we're healthy and figure out which powers we've got." Ratuan fell silent for a moment before saying, "There are two we know of who can speak Human, and I've told everyone to keep their powers hidden, but-"

Ratuan fell silent, and excitement sped my pace. Ebby must be with him — he was certainly speaking to somebody, somebody who'd warned him of our arrival.

An angled fissure in the wall led to a small dome-cavern, seemingly empty except for a peculiar work of stone art descending from the ceiling like a tangled chandelier. A thousand stone snakes of varying widths twisted around each other with bubbles attached to the entwined spirals and tubes, reaching nearly to the floor.

"Is it a map, Ratuan?" I asked, recognizing a tunnel system with bubbles everywhere the caves opened into caverns.

Ratuan stepped from behind it with his eyes narrowed in distaste, glaring first at Leaf, then at me and Archie.

"I hope the three of you have a very good reason to be here," he said.

"Well, we know Ebby's with you," I said. "Good enough?"

His expression soured even further as I broke a smile and changed to a more gentle tone. "If you care about her, Ratuan, you'll let us take her home."

Ratuan fell still, eerily thoughtful for an awkward moment, and then ten moments more. The perturbed look on his face gave away

173

that he was arguing silently with an invisible somebody. He must not want her to show herself.

But a small girl appeared behind him, wearing vomit colored clothes that looked like they'd been torn and mended at least once a day since she'd gone missing. I vaguely remembered seeing her wispy hair and thin frame, although I mostly remembered her screaming and crying as she was ripped away from Ratuan. She gripped his arm now, as though to make up for the separation.

"I can't go," Ebby said, her voice even smaller than her gloved hands.

I closed my mouth, and Archie asked in pure shock, "You'd rather stay *here*?"

I crouched to her level. "Ebby, I know you don't know us—"

"I've been watching you since you got here." She twisted and stretched her tunic nervously as she added, "I also remember you from before."

"We're just here to help," I said, changing direction. "Your father sent us to find you."

Fear flashed across her face as she said, "I can't go. It's all part of the plan that I..." Ebby stopped mid-sentence and glanced at Ratuan before swallowing and restarting. "What I mean to say is, everybody here needs me. I can't leave without my friends."

I glanced between the kids, trying to figure out why everybody was so afraid to speak. I squinted at Ratuan, hoping he got the message that *yes, I did pick up on that.*

"You'll help your friends the most by coming to the Dragona, where you'll be safe," Archie said. "Because we could all end up dead in the next few years if anything happens to you. We can't have the next Escali Epic unopposed."

Ebby bit her lip and shook her head. "I can't go." Ratuan set a comforting hand on hers, and Ebby pulled it together enough to look right at me and say, "You have your answer now. Is there anything else you'd like to contribute, or will you be leaving?"

Bitter anger flared in my chest, because I knew without doubt those words had not come from the shy girl in front of us. Ratuan was in her head, and making his way into everybody else's too.

Leaf stepped up beside me and said, "I was thinking..." He stopped as Ratuan turned him a piercing glare. Leaf took a moment to gather his courage and say, "We can trust them, Ratuan. I wouldn't have brought them down here if I didn't believe it. They can get us the mages we need. They could even create a distraction above ground while we're—"

"Leaf, I get it," Ratuan interrupted him, but Leaf was infected with a great idea that couldn't be silenced.

"And we could give them the spider marks! It can be like they're part of us—"

"Leaf!" Ratuan barked at him, and Leaf shrank back in a fearful way that made me bristle.

Ratuan and Ebby looked at each other again, clearly exchanging thoughts before Ratuan glanced back at us. "Giving them the spider marks *would* give us the time we need to talk," he said.

"Let me guess," Archie said, tapping the back of his own shoulder. "You're all getting tattoos of a spider on your shoulders, like they did in Dincara when you proved your worth."

Ratuan said, "Everybody down here is more than deserving, so yes. Ebby and I found a sort of ink while we were making this room." Ebby winced and glanced at Ratuan's hands, which were stained black like he'd spilled ink over his palms and accidentally smeared it across his fingers. I couldn't see Ebby's beneath the white gloves. "It's permanent, as far as we can tell."

"I can show each of you around while the other gets their spider," Ebby said, smiling hesitantly at us both.

175

Ratuan watched her for a short second, and something happened so quickly that I almost missed it. His face lit up like Ebby's smile was the most beautiful in the world, like she was his warmth in the cold. He hid his admiration by the time the second ended, but I realized Ebby meant more to him than power, and that was a thought I liked.

Ratuan looked at us, his serious self once more. "It turns out I'm the only one around here who can draw a halfway decent spider," he said. "If you want one, I can do it for you."

"I'm interested," I said, because while one of us was occupied with Ratuan, the other would get to speak with Ebby, free from his tight grip. And what did I care if I had a spider tattooed onto my shoulder?

Ratuan disappeared behind the three dimensional map and came back with a tiny utensil like a thin paint brush and a flat spoon with a sticky black gel coating the end.

"Do you want to go first?" he asked.

I felt suddenly more uncomfortable than I cared to admit, and I glanced down at my leather jerkin and pale undershirt. "I don't think I can roll my sleeves up to the shoulder—"

Ratuan laughed, not like I was funny but like I was stupid, and I felt my face turn red. "Well obviously you have to take it off, just like everyone else did," he said. "That isn't a problem, is it?"

I yanked on my jerkin's front lacing to loosen it and ripped it over my head and shoulders, because *no, it was not a problem.*

I dropped the warm leather on my feet and had my undershirt halfway off too when I realized how incredibly stupid and impulsive this was. It had taken one condescending comment, one implication that I was a coward, and here I was, literally taking my clothes off to prove I wasn't intimidated. Ratuan must be absolutely dying with laughter. And yet, I was too far in to change my mind now. I dropped my undershirt on the leather jerkin and folded my

176

arms where one last undergarment covered my chest and straps laced over each shoulder.

I sat and crossed my legs, refusing to look vulnerable while cold air drafted across my back and stomach. "This spider had better look good," I said, staring straight ahead at the wall. I didn't want to see Archie or what he thought of me right now.

"It will," Ratuan said as he moved behind me and I got the sinking feeling in my stomach that usually accompanies a mistake. "Leaf, why don't you head to Production, *where you're supposed to be,* and Ebby can show Archie each of our tunnels so the Dragona knows what we're up to here."

I could feel Archie's eyes burning a hole in the side of my head. He was waiting for me to make eye contact and let him know I was fine with him leaving me here. But I couldn't take my eyes off the wall and he eventually turned his attention to Ebby instead.

Everybody left, and I interlaced my fingers tightly before setting them between my crossed legs. I'd rather be eaten alive than let Ratuan see me fidgeting, or showing any other signs of nerves.

"I can grab a blanket if you're cold," Ratuan said.

"I'm fine."

I pulled my hair off to the left and Ratuan grabbed my right arm, squinting at my shoulder. Chills shot down my back even though Ratuan's hands were perfectly warm.

"I'm actually glad we can finally talk without everyone else here," Ratuan said. From the corner of my eye, I saw him coating his brush in ink.

"I didn't think you were interested in talking to us," I said.

"I am now. Ebby says she can't read your mind, which is perfect. I need you to get a message to Sir Avery." I stared straight ahead until Ratuan said, "This is going to sting."

All I felt was a cold dot of liquid on my shoulder, and I found myself bored with it until it really did begin to sting. And then it started to burn. And as Ratuan touched the brush to my skin again, I began to fear a hole was burning through my flesh. My breaths grew sharper as water pooled at the bottom of my eyes and my nose began to run. Ok, I was pretty sure he was stabbing the superheated brush through my skin.

"You've got me curious," I said, struggling to keep my words even. I hadn't felt pain like this since I'd been shot.

"I need you to tell Sir Avery who I am, where I am, and that I can do more for him than he might expect," Ratuan said. "He'll find a way to speak with me if he knows what's good for him."

"I dare you to talk to him that way," I said with a snort of laughter, which was really just meant to cover a sniffle I couldn't keep contained. Ratuan laughed lightly behind me as I used my knuckles to wipe the tears from my eyes. The sharp sting wasn't dissipating, and I was seconds away from clawing at it to make it stop.

Ratuan said, "I have big plans and I need his help."

"You could tell me what they are," I said. "I'd like to know how you plan to get out of here."

Ratuan blew on my shoulder, which sent a hundred more unpleasant chills down my back, and then he pressed the heel of his palm against the mark with all his strength. The burn subsided under pressure and became more bearable.

"Every time these tunnels take a turn, we've split them into a different section," Ratuan explained. "The one above us is Language. Any time we figure out a new Escali word, we get it back to that corridor. If you're sleeping in that hall, then you're doing everything you can to learn Escalira before you fall asleep. Above Language is Strength. That's where you pretty much do pushups until you're dead. Eric and Steph are in charge up there, trying to get everybody strong enough to fight the Escalis when we escape."

"You're going to try to fight your way out of here?" I asked. For a moment, the pain in my shoulder didn't seem so bad considering these kids were all about to commit suicide.

"I know it doesn't sound smart. But below us is Production, where we're making weapons. Real weapons. And everybody down here is finding their powers left and right. I'm telling you, we're getting at least one more mage per day. We are going to be able to fight."

"And what's the name of the corridor we're in right now?" I asked.

"This is Planning. Ebby's been making this map of the tunnels for weeks now, and anyone with information knows to bring it to me here. I've been to the Dragona once," Ratuan said, grabbing the front of my shoulder so he could push harder, which to my relief made the pain subside almost entirely. "I remember the whole layout, and I remember seeing a giant chore chart on the wall in the Wreck. We've made something similar down here in Planning, where we assign everyone to a different corridor each night. Turns out this ink can blacken solid stone."

"So, you've got everyone rotating through the different sections?"

"Yes. I'll even go up and work Guard sometimes, and I think it's important that everybody spend time in Language. I'll be honest though, I hate Strength. Eric and Steph think it's hilarious how much I hate sore arms, but I'll do anything to avoid that tunnel."

I didn't want to say I was warming up to Ratuan, but a small smirk did grace the corner of my mouth at the irony that he was afraid of a few pushups. I also appreciated the pressure on my shoulder, even though I was pretty sure the ink was burning his blackened palms too.

"But at the end of every night, I do like my team to come back here to Planning with me."

179

"Eric and Steph look like little hellions. I get why you want them, but I don't understand why you're keeping Leaf so close, or that other girl you've got."

"Eme is a shade," Ratuan said, taking his hand off my shoulder to examine his work. "She can keep my plans and thoughts hidden from Vack and Prince Avalask. And I just like Leaf. He's... different. I'm still trying to figure him out."

"You mean you're still figuring out how he might be of use to you?"

"Don't tell me you wouldn't do the same," Ratuan replied.

"And what about Ebby?" I asked, not able to argue that I wouldn't do *exactly* the same. "If you really cared for her, you'd ask her to get out of here."

Ratuan stepped back from me, and I turned around to face him, barely aware anymore that I wasn't wearing a shirt. "I tried," he said. "Honestly, I asked her to go, but she's too afraid to leave, and it's better for me if she's here."

Ebby and Archie returned, seeming at ease with each other, and Archie asked, "How's it look?"

"You tell me," I said, getting to my feet and turning my back to him, pulling my hair off to the side. I craned my own neck to look, but it was difficult to make out any details on the back of my own shoulder.

Archie came closer to peer at it. "It... looks like a spider," he said casually, brushing his fingers over the mark to feel it. His touch sent a fiery tingle racing across my skin. Warmth filled every bit of my core with ticklish joy, and I knew that sounded incredibly stupid, but it was real enough to chase away the cold, clammy discomfort from Ratuan.

Archie picked up my undershirt and handed it to me. "My turn then."

180

I pulled the pale shirt over my head as Archie began to take his off, and Ebby asked, "Allie, do you want me to show you the caves too?"

"Yes, just let me get this back on," I said, grabbing my leather jerkin to pull over my head. Archie settled down with his legs crossed, and it dawned on me rather harshly that I had never seen Archie without a shirt, at least not in this life. His entire back was more muscular than I'd imagined, and his shoulder blades more sharply defined, even when he barely moved them. It hit me with sudden remorse that I had never set my hands on that powerful strength and I had never run my fingertips down the indent on his spine that was so masculine and so *him*.

I was clearly losing my mind, and so I escaped the situation in a hurry.

Ebby came with me, having to trot to keep up with my long strides, and when we were far from Ratuan, I stopped and crouched to her level, meeting her eyes to figure out what she was thinking. She looked fearfully away, then back to me, then nervously down to her feet as she bit at her lip. "Ebby, I really am here to help you—"

She threw her arms around my neck as she began to cry, and I nearly panicked before deciding it was best to put my arms around her as well.

"Are you alright?" I asked, nearly choking as she trembled and cut off the circulation to my brain. "Has anybody hurt you?"

She shook her head and cried into my shoulder, "I just don't know what to do. I can't leave Ratuan here, but I can't stay with Vack and Prince Avalask. I'm afraid something horrible is going to happen when they try to escape, but I can't ask him not to try."

"It's alright, you're ok," I said soothingly, prying her incredibly strong arms off my neck. I held onto her gloved little hands and said, "I might be able to get them out before the escape attempt."

181

"What?" she whispered. I could see desperation in her eyes, and didn't know how to explain that my rescue plan wouldn't include her. I wasn't even sure it was the plan we would go with. "That would fix everything!" She snatched my shoulders in a bruising grip. "Please, get them out of here. You only have three days before they do it themselves."

I studied her face closely and asked, "Why are you so afraid? You just don't think they stand a chance?"

I saw hesitation in her pretty eyes before she tucked her chin down to cry more torn sobs.

"It's alright, you can tell me," I said, settling down onto my knees. "Oh, you poor girl. Come here." I pulled her in close to hold her again.

"I d-don't know what to do," she repeated.

"We'll get you through this, alright?" I said. "Just tell me what you're afraid of, and we'll fix it."

"It's m-more than an escape," Ebby said. "Ratuan is going to try to kill Izfazara on the way out, and I just know something's going to happen to him."

"Ok. Ebby, think through that for a second. There's no way —"

"You're underestimating him," Ebby's voice dropped into hoarse desperation, and she pushed away from me. "I've told him everything. He knows exactly what he's up against, and he's making plans. I just, I know things about him. He's more than anyone expects."

"What sorts of things?" She froze, and I asked, "Can you show me?"

"I... think I can," she said, sniffling loudly as she scrunched her eyebrows and I felt her presence reaching into my mind. "Look at me?" she asked.

Her eyes were muted blue and kind, but I struggled to keep my gaze on hers and relax my sense of control. Letting somebody inside, letting them see everything that makes you *you*, is incredibly difficult on multiple levels, requiring trust that Ebby hadn't really earned.

I felt like my mind was made of butterfly wings, and when I finally convinced myself to let Ebby in, she stepped inside wearing boots three sizes too big for her feet. I immediately regretted it, but couldn't open my mouth to say the word *stop*, and braced myself for the inevitable damage.

Ebby removed one of her white gloves and set a hand on the side of my face, placing her own trust in me as the armor around her mind vanished. She then moved timidly, gracefully even, among my thoughts, reaching tender points where her feelings seemed suddenly indistinguishable from my own.

I expected flashes of images like when Prince Avalask had been in my mind, but Ebby's thoughts were unrefined, raw, and confusing. Her memories were a scatterscape of feeling, seeing, smelling, hearing, and emotions. But through it all, I could see a hundred different chess games she'd played with Ratuan while they laughed, and talked, and sipped at the tea his mother had brewed.

Ratuan played to win. He always stared at the board much longer than seemed necessary, and his strategy never varied. He sacrificed almost every piece in his color, but he won every game. Ebby had never beaten him, but he'd never finished a game with more than three or four players standing.

And I understood why she was so afraid.

Ebby's thoughts began to wander, not in paths that made perfect sense, but in directions that vaguely connected and intersected. An image of Ratuan telling her that Epics were the queens of the chessboard. Then Prince Avalask telling her the story of the royal curse, which would one day impact Vack. Then Ebby falling asleep in the same room as Vack, feeling sympathy for him and feeling

183

safe with him. Then the conflicting feelings of joy when Ratuan looked at her and told her how important she was to him. Knowing Ratuan hated Vack, but that Vack wasn't the sort of evil Ratuan thought.

Ebby jerked back from me, startled. "I didn't mean to show you all that," she said, looking frightened once more. "I'm sorry."

"You don't need to be sorry," I said. "Please, believe me Ebby, I understand what it's like to be torn in two directions."

She blinked a few times to hold back the tears pooling between her eyelashes.

"Can you tell me what to do?" she asked.

I sighed, reminded of Prince Avalask calling her pliable, and it dawned on me exactly what we were doing to her. We were turning her into a mindless tool, a *thing* to be controlled by whoever had her instead of a strong young girl with a mind of her own. And all of my arguments for the situation suddenly fled my mind because I needed to be more than another voice in the conflict, another set of hands tugging at her.

"Honestly, Ebby, bringing you home would solve a lot of problems for me. But... People are going to try to control you your whole life, and you *can't* become a plaything to be fought over." I looked straight into her eyes and said, "You are so much more than a pawn in everyone else's hands."

She stared at me like I'd suggested she go fight the Zhauri death hound. "You want me to decide?" she whispered.

I couldn't help laughing at her shock, and her cheeks flushed red as I squeezed her hand. "Yes. The secret is, you listen to what's in here," I said, setting a hand over my own heart. I knew it sounded dumb, but it was advice that I held dear enough to share. "You'll never in your life regret a decision you believed was right."

Ebby continued to stare at me like I'd asked the impossible.

184

"So ignore everybody else, and tell me what you want," I said. "Do you want to stay, or do you want to leave with us?"

She bit her lip and stared for another full minute before saying, "I want to stay. Please though, get my friends out. You only have three days."

I gave her an encouraging nod and felt a sense of warmth toward her as she broke into a grateful smile.

"I'll do the very best I can," I said.

CHAPTER FIFTEEN

Allie and Archie had gone, and Ratuan's team of five was back in their cell for the night as everybody around them settled down to sleep. Ebby's hand was warm in Ratuan's, but her chest ached with longing, wishing she could be their sixth member instead of leaving every morning.

"It's official. Everybody older than eight can swing a stone club fifty times without resting," Eric told Ratuan with a gleam of pride, giving Steph a triumphant high-five.

"Production has also finished sculpting a club for every kid," Steph said, "and enough keys to get every door open in thirty seconds — just like you ordered."

"And you thought they couldn't do it," Eric sniggered.

Ratuan wore a proud grin as Eme said softly, "Two new girls came down to Magic with powers today too. One of them is just water, but you need to see what Arctica can do. I don't know what it is, Ratuan, but you're going to like it."

Ratuan raised surprised eyebrows and asked, "The same Arctica we put in charge of the babies and toddlers?" Eme nodded and Ratuan tilted his head thoughtfully. "Alright, I'll pay her a visit as soon as we're done here. I also learned a couple things from Leaf's friends." Ratuan settled his gaze on Leaf and said, "Giving them

186

the Dincaran spiders was a good idea. I was glad to speak with them alone."

A proud smile crept onto Leaf's face. "It was nothing," he said, scuffing one foot against the other. "I like to help." Ebby decided she liked this red haired boy who was just about her size. She would like to get to know him.

Ratuan's hand grew icy on hers, even though his face showed no signs of change. It felt like jealousy, like he'd heard her warm thoughts toward Leaf and didn't like them.

"But you *knew* I didn't want outsiders knowing about Ebby," Ratuan said, letting go of her hand to step closer to Leaf. "Now because of you, they know she's here." Leaf's cheeks reddened as he opened his mouth, and Ratuan struck him across the face with the full strength of his right arm. "You made a decision that was not yours to make!"

Leaf fell back against the stone wall with a startled yelp as Eric and Steph stumbled to their feet uncertainly and Ebby threw a hand over her mouth. Ratuan put two calming hands out to the boys on either side and said, "I am more than proud of the two of you and all you've done up in Strength. But listen, we each have a role to play down here, and we can't operate as a team if everybody thinks they can call the shots. I am the leader here for a reason, and you all know better than to undermine me."

Leaf set a small hand on the side of his face and cringed back against the stones as Ratuan grabbed him by both shoulders and said, "Listen, I'm not mad at you." Leaf grabbed Ratuan's wrists helplessly while tears threatened to spill onto his cheeks. "I'm not mad. But there are a thousand kids down here, Leaf, and we would be nothing if not for discipline. You'll sleep alone in the corner tonight, alright? I hope that doesn't seem too harsh, considering how serious this is."

Leaf glared up at Ratuan, and for a moment Ebby thought Leaf might try to stand up to him. But he shook his head to say it didn't sound too harsh, and Ratuan gave him a smile both encouraging and strangely caring. "I'm sorry it has to be like this, but it's just for one night. I know you don't make the same mistakes twice."

Leaf shook his head again and Ratuan let go of his shoulders. "Good. Now, Ebby and I are off to congratulate Arctica. Nobody talk to Leaf until tomorrow morning. We're a group, and if you want to act alone, then you sleep alone."

Ratuan startled Ebby as he grabbed her hand again and gestured to the cold metal bars to ask, "Shall we?"

Ebby's heart hurt as Leaf sank down in the corner and pressed his forehead to his knees, but she quickly squeezed Ratuan's hand and focused on ghosting them both through the barred doorway. Ratuan led her off down the tunnel, and she focused on not letting her thoughts stray while his hand was in hers.

What would he do if he knew how much she'd just told Allie?

You can hear me if I think like this? Ratuan asked in her head as they walked.

Ebby glanced at Ratuan and nodded to him.

You're not upset with me, are you?

She could never be angry with Ratuan. It would be too devastating. But at the same time, she couldn't really say she was happy with him.

I know you didn't like that, but I didn't hurt him. His pride is just wounded, that's all.

Ebby shrugged and hesitated, replying, *I just think there might have been a better way to handle it.*

Ratuan stopped her and looked straight into her eyes with an intensity that made her blush and feel guilty for questioning him.

Listen, I like Leaf as much as anybody else. But remember when we talked about me controlling the board?

Ratuan waited until Ebby whispered, "Yes," then he thought, *Please, just keep trusting me with it. This is what everybody down here needs — a real leader who can strike fear and respect. Anything less than that, and we'll all fall apart.*

Ebby nodded that she understood, but she found her eyes on the ground as Ratuan squeezed her hand. "You ready to meet some more Dincarans?" Ratuan asked aloud. She let herself smile at his excitement to show her off and then nodded as Ratuan pulled her over to a cell of kids she hadn't seen yet. "Ebby, this is Carder, Tess, and Nathan. Back there is Jules and Codiea..."

CHAPTER SIXTEEN

"What did Ratuan say when you were with him?" Archie asked as we wedged ourselves back through the tight fissure that led to our friends. I'd already recapped to him my conversation with Ebby.

"He wants me to get Sir Avery here to talk to him. Needs his help."

"He's all sorts of clever, Allie." Archie stopped moving and I didn't know if he was stuck or just thinking. "I talked to several of those kids, and Ratuan's figured out the secret to... undying loyalty, I think. Part of it is painting all those spiders on everyone and getting to know them individually, but... I don't know. He's just got something figured out. Those kids would die for him if he asked them to."

I stopped moving too, wedged uncomfortably between jagged walls as my breath left my chest in dread. "Ebby thinks that's what he's going to do."

"What?"

"Ratuan is a chess mastermind, but he wins by sacrificing all his pieces. She thinks it's about to come true in real life."

Archie fell silent and I pushed myself into the opening that marked the midpoint of our struggle. "I don't know what to do,

190

Allie," he said quietly. "I tried to convince Ebby to come back with us, but she's too afraid to leave Ratuan. We could fix all our problems by telling the Zhauri where she is, but we would also be two of the worst people in the world for it."

I stared hard as Archie dragged himself through the tight crevice. "Not to mention," I said casually, "she doesn't want to leave just yet, and if she stays with Prince Avalask, he's willing to negotiate over the Dincaran kids. If the war ends, you and I will have no value left to Sir Avery or the Zhauri. That's a good thing, Archie. Leaving her here is our best-case-scenario."

Archie pulled himself free and stood face to face with me in the close-quartered air pocket.

"If we don't get Ebby back, we don't have any bargaining power to get Tral away from the Zhauri," he said.

"Yes, but there will be other ways to rescue him. I mean, what if Ebby's already friends with Prince Avalask's son?" I avoided his eyes so close to mine. "A friendship between those kids will save thousands of lives if they play it right."

Archie finally took a deep breath and said, "I know."

"Then what could Sir Avery have possibly promised you, Archie?" I asked. "What is worth more than all of that?"

"You are," he said softly.

I had just opened my mouth to respond and literally choked on my own breath. I threw an arm over my mouth as the horrible spit-in-windpipe tickle brought on a bout of hacking coughs.

"Don't act like that's a shock," Archie said with a laugh. I could barely move back half a step in the cramped space. "You know how much you mean to me."

I closed my mouth to stifle three smaller coughs as my face reddened from embarrassment and the duress of choking. It took me a moment to draw a full breath and say, "Does *'you and I are just friends'* sound familiar?" I coughed one final time, taking the extra second to collect my flustered thoughts.

"That's not what I *want*," Archie replied. "I've told you before though, it's too dangerous to be —"

"You don't have to humor me," I said, sounding more scathing than I intended. "I understand why you only want to be friends, and I honestly don't blame you. It's my hot temper. It's the way I live and fight like a man. I've never been... quiet... Nobody wants a girl like me."

Archie narrowed his eyes like I'd lost my mind. "*That's* what you think the problem is?"

I scowled furiously as he just looked bewildered.

"Look. I've never cared that you're loud. And maybe you do fight like a man, but I'm not..." he hesitated, looking for the right word, "I'm not intimidated by that. I would never want you to be weaker, or less of a match. Sparring would never be fun again. And, I mean, you've had a temper since we were kids fishing in the creek. I know that about you. I always have. None of that bothers me."

He was so close I could feel his breath, and when I glanced up to meet his eyes, jitters attacked me inside and out.

But nothing this good could ever happen to me, and I knew it. So instead of closing the remaining distance between us, I froze exactly where I was. *"But?..."*

"But..." Archie paused and his smile hardened. "Just being my friend is like tanning on the banks of the Breathing Sea. Being *more* than friends is like diving in. And I want you to know I'd do anything to change that."

I think my heart might have melted on the spot.

"So that's what Sir Avery's promised you?" I asked, wondering suddenly if this might be an elaborate dream. "Some sort of safety, where you and I can be together?"

I could see hesitation in his eyes as he nodded. He wanted me. He wanted to be with me and had an adorable sheepish look in his eyes like he was nervous to say it aloud.

I blew air through my lips in disbelief. "Archie, we don't need Sir Avery's blessing to be together," I said, nearly giddy with relief. "So what? We live dangerous lives. There's no reason we shouldn't just live them together."

Archie shook his head sadly and I reached to grab his hand, stopped again by his shield. "I'm more dangerous than anything else in your life," he said.

"Right, you've got a dark past, blah blah blah," I said, drawing a surprised chuckle from him. "I don't want you to explain yourself right now," I said, "but after we get these Dincaran kids home, we should spend some time with just the two of us and figure this out. If you want to," I added, still not sure I believed that he wanted to.

"I would love nothing more than to try," Archie replied.

"So..." I said slowly, "you're agreeing with me, that we need to get the Dincaran kids out more than we need Ebby? We're taking Prince Avalask's side?"

Archie sighed. "Yeah, I guess we have to."

"Then we need to let Prince Avalask know the kids are making their escape in three days. We'll avoid a lot of bloodshed if we're quick."

Archie nodded at the fissure behind me and said, "You're the one blocking the way."

I strained to pull myself out through the fireplace, but my face immediately reddened in horror at what I saw.

Emery, Nessava, Celesta, Corliss, and Robbiel were seated with their legs crossed, like kids at story time around the cold fireplace.

193

As I dragged my last arm into the open space, they all began to applaud.

"A truly heartfelt performance!" Corliss cheered, making everybody laugh as she clapped loudest of them all. She'd arrived to visit her fellow Tallies yesterday. "I had a tear in my eye, you two. Bravo!"

"Oh shanking life," Archie muttered from the crevice behind me as he tugged himself free.

Karissa was the only one still on her feet, not looking the least amused. She glared straight at Archie, and said with her voice dangerously low, "You haven't told her?"

I expected Archie to brush the comment off with a humorous one of his own, but he froze beside me, and even more strangely than that, nobody else piped in to tell Karissa to cool it.

"*Thank you* all for listening," I said, "but now that the laugh is over, why don't you go back to your own business?"

Karissa's gaze turned sharp. "You need to know what Archie's hiding and how much it affects you."

"Archie's dangerous, I get it," I said, "but I live a plenty dangerous life already. I don't understand what you're all worried about." I threw my hands out to stop everyone who looked more than happy to explain. "And he and I will talk about it in our own time."

Karissa scowled and turned suddenly invisible.

"We also have another problem to worry about," Archie said, glancing at me to say *thank you*. "We have three days before the Dincaran kids try to make their escape, and it's going to be violent."

"Well, we can't exactly subdue them," Robbiel said. "They've got more than enough mages to fight their way out, and Ratuan set up leaders to replace him if he goes suddenly missing."

194

I gave a discouraged nod and added, "Ratuan is trying to arrange for Sir Avery to show up too, which would stop Prince Avalask from doing anything at all. But if we talk… to…"

I trailed off as something brushed the wall beside me. Karissa must have moved to our side of the room, and my shoulders tightened in warning.

A high pitched squeal startled us, and everybody sitting leapt to their feet. Karissa became suddenly visible, peering all around herself like she was on the hunt.

"One of those kids followed you back," she said. "I caught hold of her, but she… vanished in my hands."

"Well that sounds like two powers to me," I said.

I could have heard a drop of water fall three rooms away, such was the silence that fell around us.

"Ebby?" I said to thin air. Nothing changed and nobody moved until Archie jumped beside me at the sight of Ebby, appearing behind my legs like she trusted me enough to hide behind.

"I'm sorry," she said immediately as everybody's eyes widened. "I didn't mean to eavesdrop. I was just…" she clasped her hands together and held them tightly to her chest in fear. "I'm sorry."

"We can't have her here," Emery said, looking angrier than anybody else with his palms full of fire. "I know half of you enjoy running around trying to change the world, but she is in the middle of a tug-of-war between *Sir Avery and Prince Avalask*. We *can't* have her here."

"Being in the same room with her doesn't hurt anything," Karissa said flatly, standing up straight and pushing her large dark curls back from her face as she turned to Ebby. "Are you alright?"

Ebby nodded but stayed as far behind me as she could. "I'm sorry," she said, glancing up at me. "I just, I wanted t-to know more about you."

195

"What exactly were you trying to learn?" Emery demanded. "And who did you plan to tell?"

Ebby shook her head quickly. "Nobody. I just wondered..."

"She needs to go," Emery said to me. "There are not many of us left, and I don't want us ripped apart by feuding Epics."

Ebby's eyes caught on the table next to Robbiel and grew wide in shock. She finally stepped out from behind me in astonishment. "Is th-that... Is that a book?" she asked, moving toward it like she'd never seen one.

Robbiel looked startled to realize his hand was resting on it as she took hesitant steps toward him and asked, "Written in Human?"

Ebby pressed two fists over her mouth before whispering, "Can I hold it?"

Robbiel handed her the book with hesitation, and watched as Ebby cradled it in her arms like a precious baby. Corliss superficially coughed into her arm, "We've lost Robbiel," as Robbiel broke into a smile.

Emery rolled his eyes to the ceiling and said, "We can't keep her."

Robbiel ignored Emery and said, "I have other books I could give you. This one is Karissa's."

"She can borrow it," Karissa said. "But bring it back. It's my favorite."

Ebby gripped it tightly to herself and said, "I will. I've read books before. I know how to treat them."

"Great," Emery said. "Could you leave now?"

Ebby nodded quickly, but a young Escali with ragged clothes and a mess of royally black hair appeared next to her. He had to be Prince Avalask's son.

Emery stabbed a knife into the wooden table beside him and muttered, *"Oh shanking life."*

"I'll leave," Ebby said, glancing at me one last time before turning to the new Epic. "Come on, Vack. We can go." She held her hand to him, but Vack didn't take it.

"Tallies?" Vack asked to no one in particular. He flicked his gaze between each face, then turned his unnerving attention to Archie in the intrigued, wolf-like way I expected from an Escali.

Archie, in return, lowered his shoulders very deliberately, not the least bit welcoming.

"I've wanted to meet you," Vack said, taking a bold step forward.

"*You* are going to leave me alone," Archie replied, sinking into a dangerous crouch.

Vack smirked *exactly* like his uncle Sav, and asked, "Who's going to make me?"

I was ready for Ebby to step up, as she was Vack's only equal in the room, but it was Emery who lunged, grabbed Vack by the shoulders, and shoved him to the ground.

Vack snarled from the stone floor and shot a wave of green flames at Emery, which never made contact because Archie dashed to his side and threw his shield out to block the magic.

Emery stood with his arms crossed, utterly calm as Vack's green flames collided harmlessly against Archie's shield. As Vack let up his assault and got to his feet, Emery unfolded his arms and lit both of his hands with angry red flames.

He raised his eyebrows and said, "Get. Out."

Vack vanished on the spot and we all looked to Ebby, whose eyes were wide in shock.

"Where'd he go?" I asked.

She shook her head quickly. "I don't know. He's shading himself. I can't track him."

"Thanks," Archie said, giving Emery a rough clap on the shoulder.

Emery shrugged with an air of triumph and said, "I knew you'd have my back."

Archie sighed and glanced around the room before saying, "I should probably go fix this."

Emery's gloating turned into a scowl of disbelief. "*Why?* You don't have to explain yourself to him."

"I know. But we'll be better off in the long run if we smooth things over. I'll be back."

As Archie pushed through the doors to venture out alone, Karissa moved next to me and muttered, "Just so you're aware, everybody else in the room understands what that exchange was about... Except maybe Ebby."

"I'm ready to hear about it," I said, turning to look straight at her. "*If* Archie doesn't find out that I know."

Karissa blew air through her lips like my words were a stale joke told for the hundredth time. "Not a problem. We never tell Archie what's really going on."

"What? Why?"

"Because he can't handle things like the fact Jonnath died with the rest of our mages on Tekada. You know how they tear him apart."

"What?" I exclaimed.

"Sh! I'm telling *you.* Jonnath was from Dincara, so he was feeding them information about the Escalis and ended up getting involved in the battle and sent to Tekada. We've all agreed to keep that little fact on the down low from Archie though. He falls apart at stuff like this."

"And you're... sure? You know for sure?"

Karissa nodded bitterly and I gaped at her, expecting to feel dreadful hurt in my chest, but the news barely registered. I'd hardly met him, and knew nothing about him for which to miss. Just one more thing the world had stolen from me.

Robbiel had opened the book in Ebby's hands to show her something within the pages while Emery and Corliss both had suspicious eyes on our whispered conversation.

Karissa shot a glare at Emery and said, "I'm about to tell Allie Archie's big secret. You going to try to stop me too?"

"Nope," Emery said flatly. "I'd rather not see her die because Archie's being a little girl about the matter."

Karissa lost her focus, distracted by the hands touching her book.

"Did you show her the section about always cleaning your tools?" she asked Robbiel as he flipped the pages.

"No," he replied, *"But it's in chapter one."*

Karissa moved closer to point in the margins. "I've written all sorts of notes in here," she said, "about things I've tried that have and haven't worked. There are some especially important ones you should look at in the section on open wounds—"

"Karissa?"

"I just need two half-seconds," she said with a dismissive wave, pulling the book from Ebby's hands to flip toward a few of the more riveting sections.

I gave Corliss an impatient look and said, "Can you make Karissa understand we're short on time? I'm going to run and grab my short swords, and then we need to find Prince Avalask to tell him about the kids."

"Sure, but it'll probably be several half-minutes before she even hears me talking to her," Corliss said with a smirk. Karissa missed the joke, as she was too absorbed telling wide-eyed Ebby the order in which her book really should have been written.

I headed out the doors and straight for my room, trying to conjure feelings of loss and sadness about another death among the people I cared about. But they weren't coming. It was cruel, the way the world had turned all my friends into strangers.

I reached the hall of doors, and fury leapt into my throat when I realized my short swords were no longer propped against the wall where I'd left them. Whoever thought this was a funny prank was about to meet their end. There are some things you just don't touch.

I almost stormed back to the group in outrage, but thought twice and realized one of them may have just moved my possessions inside for me. I pushed my door open and shrieked in surprise at the sight of my short swords in the hands of Sav, sitting on my trunk, casually sharpening them.

CHAPTER SEVENTEEN

I flung the door back shut like I'd just stuck my hand in a nest of spiders, and I shriveled back against the wall, glancing both ways down the corridor, ready to make my escape.

I heard a dark chuckle resonate through the tunnel, but absolutely couldn't tell from which direction it'd come. It had to be Gat. He must be waiting to give chase when I ran, and I would rather take my chances with Sav.

I threw the door back open and demanded, "What do you think you're doing?"

Sav tilted his head sharply and said, "You must have a death wish, talking to me like that."

I was tempted to throw a hand over my eyes and admit that yes, I must.

"Why are you here?"

Sav looked me up and down in a way that made me shudder, like he was taking measurements for my coffin. "Please, have a seat," he said, motioning toward my hammock, dangerously close to him. "I think you've forgotten who owns these caves."

"You're not king yet, Sav."

"You speak the truth, but since my father was killed in the Dincaran spire explosion, there's no longer any doubt that I'm next in line. It's about time you showed some respect."

Several lethal looking etching tools lay next to Sav while he carved a design into the face of a short sword. *My* short sword.

"Believe it or not, I'm here to offer you assistance," he said.

I peered skeptically. "No. You're not."

Sav shrugged and then dug the sharp engraving tool into the steel face of my blade, as though content to not tell me if I didn't want to hear it.

"What's the offer?" I asked.

"I'd like to help return Ebby to Sir Avery."

I snorted with disbelief and asked, "Her wellbeing is suddenly of importance to you?"

"Let's not kid ourselves," he said, his full focus on carving the next swirl in my blade. "We both know I'd like to put her in the ground, but I can't with my brother protecting her, and she's turning our new Epic into a sympathetic fool. I can't let this continue."

"No... something's missing," I said. "You should be plotting to kill her, not to help her escape."

Sav glanced up at me with his wicked grin. "You are one of the more intelligent Tallies," he said, adding a casual shrug as he switched tools and began to deepen his lines. "The simple truth is that I'm patient. We have an old family tradition where kings make the decisions, and the Epics execute them." He lingered on the word *execute,* and I hardened my gaze to hide how his words chilled me. "When power passes to me, I can send Vack after her. But it's important to me that Vack not become a soft little flower in the meantime. His father is trying to ruin him."

"And how are you going to help me return her to Sir Avery?" I asked.

"I'm sure you've heard of interaction spells. Every member of our family has one to keep us safe, but give Sir Avery this. I need to speak to him." Sav lifted an envelope wrapped in what looked like silver spider webs. "It includes a time and a place for him to meet me so I can introduce myself. And if you open it, lose it somewhere, or let it fall into the wrong hands, I will see to it that every Tally in these caves is violently tortured and killed for it. You understand me?"

I reached and took the message from him, nearly laughing at the fact I was becoming Sir Avery's personal secretary. Sav's threat rolled off my back. I believed him, but I believed he would try to do exactly that, whether this letter reached Sir Avery or not.

"Out of curiosity, Sav... If you ever do become king, does peace even interest you? At all?"

To his credit, Sav did pause to consider before he said, "Mankind doesn't deserve to exist after all they've done. Some acts can never be forgiven." I frowned, and he added, "You can go now. I'll be finished with this shortly."

"What happened?" I asked as he returned to his engraving, the eerie squeak of metal on metal sending a shiver across my shoulders. "The entire Human race can't have done you wrong, Sav."

Sav jerked his head up to look at me with sudden realization. "Your Tally friend hasn't told you, has he?" I froze and tried keep my expression hard as disbelief lit Sav's eyes. "He's letting you run around and take care of him, and he hasn't told you who he is?"

I heaved a heavy sigh through my nostrils because I was truly the last person alive to know Archie's secret.

"You probably just think I was born hating Humans, don't you? You have no idea how hard they worked to earn this," Sav said, pointing my blade at me as I scoured the room for a weapon not already in his hands. I had a knife in the laces of my sandal, but

203

nothing else. "I might have been able to move on after seeing my mother murdered. I like to think of myself as an understanding man. I may have been able to forgive Humans for killing her in front of my five-year-old self, given enough time. I was almost killed as a kid too — would have been, if Gataan hadn't saved me from the three men drowning me in a pond. I like to think I could have gotten over that too. But my sister..."

Sav narrowed his eyes, thinking of something outside this room and outside this time, where anger tore at him with claws I knew too well.

"I've heard of her," I said, keeping my voice as flat as possible, afraid he might lash out like any wounded animal. I'd actually *just* heard of her, when Ebby's thoughts had wandered to the royal family's curse. "People called her the Golden Princess."

"Whatever you've heard of Glidria was *wrong*." Sav slammed the etching tool onto the trunk beside him, nearly causing me to scramble back. "You've probably heard she was beautiful, but you have *never* known the meaning of the word. You've probably heard that her hair gleamed brighter than gold, or that she fought with unmatched grace, but nobody knows how she took care of us. They can never know how many hours she spent teaching Gataan to fight, teaching me to read, cooking dinner every night and demanding that we all sit together to eat it. She and Avalask were much older than us, but even after she married, she still ate dinner with us every night. The four of us were powerfully close."

"I know what happened to her," I whispered, my calm becoming more and more forced.

Sav repeated, "Whatever you've heard about her capture was wrong." He moved to the edge of the trunk, perched to spring. "Avalask, Gataan, and I were frantic when she was taken, and our world erupted with the kind of outrage that turns into an army overnight. Every Escali alive came together to help rescue her, yet it *still* took us an entire month to get her out of Human hands."

"And she had gotten sick during her capture," I said, wanting to end his story quickly so I could put distance between us. "I still don't see what this has to do with Arch—"

Sav stood very suddenly, which sent me nearly into the hallway in my startle. "To say she was *sick*," Sav's words caught in his throat, as he took a step toward me, "is the most disgusting perversion of truth in history. That *disease* she picked up killed her when it crawled out of her nine months later."

And those words struck me like a bolt of my own destruction. She must have had a Tally, one with her beautiful golden hair.

Sav took another step toward me, teeth bared. "And past that, her only living daughter grabbed the creature before it could be dealt with, *named it,* and then disappeared with monster in hand, never to be seen again." Another step closer. "But you know which part was truly the most hideous insult to the Escali race? We could have eradicated mankind that afternoon. Every Escali alive would have joined together to do it if they'd known what killed her. And instead, Izfazara ordered her abuse and murder a secret. Our own uncle ruined our chance to avenge her, and still to this day, that truth remains buried."

Sav was within two steps of me, and his eyes bored straight through me, making it almost impossible to draw a breath.

"Sav..." I whispered, gathering my wit. "How... How can you possibly blame Archie for this? None of us chose our parents. It's not his fault—"

"I think you're missing everything important in this story," he breathed as I stepped back into the tunnel, only stopping when my back pressed against the opposite wall. "I've continued existing for one purpose, Tally, and that is to bring justice to the most

205

disgusting crime of our age and avenge my beautiful sister's death."

"But what will that take? Is watching Archie die going to fix anything?"

Sav regarded me for a moment of disbelief before he threw his head back in vicious laughter.

"You think I've spent all these years plotting his *death*? No, when I become king, everybody will discover what happened to their beloved princess." Sav closed the remaining distance between us and towered over me. "Killing your friend would be easy. I would rather account for the grief that crippled every Escali on the day he was born. An entire race cried for the loss of my sister, and your friend can only make up for that by grieving over the loss of the entire Human race. I will not let him die until he watches every building burn and every child rot unburied in the fields. And lastly, Tally, after you've served your purpose, your time will come."

Sav pinched a strand of my hair between his fingers and tucked it behind my ear, making me want to throw up, cry, collapse, and run, a chaos that kept me rooted to the spot in horror as he leaned forward to whisper, "So grow closer to him. Because there will come a day when you are the only hope he has left, and I want him to have to hold you the way I held Glidria in her last minutes, watching your chest rise and fall without knowing which will be the last."

Sav and I were both startled by a snarling commotion, further down the hallway.

"Sounds like Gataan found your friends," Sav said as a shriek echoed off the stone.

I glanced at Sav before dashing from reach, straight toward the raucous snarls and swearing. I got there just in time to see Gat throw Emery into Karissa with a sharp yelp before she vanished.

Robbiel darted around Gat to keep him from pursuing Emery and Karissa, landing punches and kicks to the knees, ribs, and every exposed part of the larger Escali, infuriating him.

Emery got back to his feet with a snarl as Gat managed to grab a piece of Robbiel's clothing, taking the opportunity to tackle and flatten him. Emery had blood all over his back, but that didn't prevent him from jumping onto Gat to bite him and try to pull him off by his snarl of a pony tail.

The second I realized Gat was trying to get his teeth around Robbiel's throat, I ran at him too, lightning in my hands. "Get off, get off, get off!" I warned, mostly to Emery, even though I knew he wasn't going anywhere. I threw my hands around Gat's neck and released a crackling, explosive current of destruction. Emery, Gat, and Robbiel screamed as I shocked the fighting spirit out of all three and immediately shoved my shoulder into Gat to roll him off. His jerkin bunched up near the shoulders where Karissa had also grabbed to help drag him.

Everybody who'd been hit groaned in pain, but Gat was nearly back to his feet when Sav came in behind me and said, "We were just leaving."

Emery rolled into a ball on his side in agony, but still managed to say through gritted teeth, "You were never welcome."

Gat got strenuously to his feet and growled, "Let me finish this."

"Another day," Sav replied, looking pointedly at each of us. "This won't be forgotten."

I didn't think Gat was going to be able to walk away from the fight, but he surprised me with each step. His grumbled argument with Sav echoed faintly as they retreated into the distance.

"I'm so sorry," I said as Emery curled in tighter and wrapped his arms around his head.

"Thank you," Robbiel said, also on the ground, clutching at his throat, double checking it was present.

207

Karissa reappeared, looking positively giddy. "There's blood everywhere!" she exclaimed. "Do you know what this means?"

Emery scrambled to get his bloody back to the wall. "Absolutely not. I'm fine!"

Robbiel pulled himself to his knees, took a moment to collect himself, and leaned in to see the back of Emery's bloody shoulder. "You may actually want to let us take a look at it," Robbiel said. "He got his teeth in pretty deep."

Emery stumbled to his feet to get away from them, but Karissa got right in his way as Robbiel slowly stood. "I'm not one of your rescued animals," Emery growled at Robbiel. He turned to Karissa. "And you are a demon. The two of you need to stay away from me."

Emery brought a bright flash of flames into his hands as they closed in, and he said, "Oh, I will shanking murder you both."

"I need to go," I said, and my friends turned like they'd forgotten I was there.

"Why are neither of you accosting Allie?" Emery demanded, the flames in each hand growing brighter. "Nobody's even asked if she's alright."

"I'm... fine," I told them with a tired smile. I tapped my temple and said, "It's just psychological damage. Nothing a needle and thread can fix."

"You need to be careful," Emery said. "She'll still try!"

Karissa shot me a joking look of manic glee, and Robbiel asked, "Seriously, are you alright? Why were they here?"

I looked up at the ceiling, preparing for their scoffing disbelief as I said, "Sav wants to help get Ebby back to Sir Avery."

"What?" the three of them demanded.

"I don't know any more than you do," I said, hands up in exasperation. "We need to talk to Prince Avalask. He might be able to explain Sav's sudden interest in her. And he *needs* to know the kids are escaping in three days."

"We'll get down to his hall, and if he's not already there, we'll get his attention," Karissa said. "Archie still hasn't come back though. Somebody should wait here for him."

"I will," I said. Naturally.

"I'll wait with you," Emery said. "You shouldn't be by yourself, considering what just happened. And the less of Karissa's face I have to see, the better."

"Alright," Karissa said, ignoring Emery entirely. "Come down to Prince Avalask's hall as soon as Archie's back. I have an idea to get us in."

CHAPTER EIGHTEEN

I crouched in front of my wooden chest to examine my short sword while Emery stood attentively at the door, watching for the return of trouble. As angry as I was to see my blade tainted, I had to admit the swirls, dots, and twisting shapes were... beautiful. Sav must have been in my room half the day etching them.

"Sav left you a message?" Emery asked.

"Ohhh, they *are* words," I realized.

In Escalira, words are made by thick shapes to represent vowels, surrounded by smaller dots, loops, and slanted lines to represent consonants. A name like Allie only contained three marks. Two side by side shapes, for the A and the E, and a tilted loop that meant L, positioned above the E to lead.

Savaul's thick vowels had a style of their own, nearly running together, and hardly looking like letters at all.

"What's it say?" he asked.

The vowels were disorienting, so I read slowly, "*I am the one from whom you cannot hide.*"

"Shanking scat-brained lunatic," Emery muttered as irritation crept into my chest as well. These blades had been with me longer than I could remember. The simple sun on each pommel was usually a glimpse of familiarity and comfort, and every scratch and dent in the metal had been my own doing, until now. *Now* they'd been violated.

My irritation began bubbling into anger, so I set my etched blade off to the side and opened the lid to my chest, digging down to the bottom to occupy myself with something else. "Hate to ask, but... Did Karissa get a chance to tell you about Archie?"

"No," I said, "but Sav did. I know where he comes from, and I know Sav will use me to get to him, in all the worst ways."

Emery just folded his arms and leaned against the doorway. "What joyful lives we lead," he muttered.

I tugged at the knot hole in the bottom of my chest, pulling up the false bottom with a woody creak as it scraped the edges.

I gasped as my eyes fell on something even more precious and valuable than I'd imagined.

I would have been happy to find a bar of gold or silver.

I would have been thrilled to find some sentimental family heirloom from my past.

But I was absolutely ecstatic, as I reached down and ran my fingers over an aged leather cover in disbelief.

"Hey," Emery said, glancing over my shoulder. "It's your old diary."

I brandished the book of worn, uneven pages, and would have thrown it at him if it wasn't so valuable. *"You knew this was in here?"*

He scowled back and said, *"No.* If I'd known where you hid it, I would have torn all the pages out and slid them under everyone's doors." He shook his head and grumbled, "It's like you don't even know me."

I ignored him and flipped carefully through the pages, past rough sketches and scrawled passages in both Human and Escalira. I saw the little nuances that made my handwriting mine, like the extra curl I always added to my L-loops, and the way my Escali vowels were always taller and thinner than necessary.

I ran my fingers over the beautiful ink strokes, the light indents all over the page sending a thrill of sentiment into my heart.

"Archie's back," Emery said.

I gently closed the diary and wound the attached leather cord around three times to secure it as Emery took off and something else occurred to me.

It was no wonder Vack knew of Archie. The Golden Princess would have been Prince Avalask's sister too, which made Archie and Vack... cousins?

I heard a quick, "You alright?"

And a short, "Yep," before Archie reached my room. I expected him to look distraught, but he carried himself with casual ease, like the unwelcome family reunion hadn't ruffled him.

"You spoke to Vack?" I asked, not sure how he could look so unaffected.

"Yeah. Turns out he would *also* like for Ebby to leave with us." He grinned like I couldn't begin to guess the understatement, and then he drew his eyebrows together in uncertainty. "Why are you looking at me like that?"

"Like what?" I replied. "I'm not even... looking at you. Where did Emery disappear to?"

I couldn't hide emotions to save my life, so I stepped past him to the hall where he wouldn't have a clear look at my face.

Emery had left the furthest door ajar, a door which certainly did not belong to him, and Archie noticed too. "Why in life is he in Robbiel's room?"

Emery emerged with what looked like a puppy in his hands.

Curiosity drove me to approach him until I recognized black fur with one white stripe running down the middle, and I hissed, "Are

212

you insane?" I would have shouted the question, but we'd all smell for days if the monster in his hands startled.

Emery used one hand to open the door to Karissa's room, and he shut the creature safely in without incident before shooting me a look of wide-eyed innocence.

"What?" Emery asked. "Stripes is an upstanding member of society. Robbiel rescued him a few weeks ago and he's been nothing but a beloved companion."

Archie broke into laughter as I gaped in disgust.

"Why," I demanded, "has Karissa not put a lock on her door?"

Archie tried to compose himself enough to ask Emery, "What was it, five years ago we had the great doorknob war?" He turned to me to explain, "There's a whole graveyard of disassembled doorknobs and hinges out in the woods from when people started trying to lock their doors."

Emery said with a gloating smile, "Let's get down to Prince Avalask's hall. I'm sure Karissa will love to tell you all about it."

We encountered one small problem outside Prince Avalask's hall where two guards refused to let us in, saying the Epic was out on business. But when the massive glass doors opened of their own accord, the guards stood at attention and allowed us to pass.

Once they'd swung shut, Karissa became visible with a proud smirk. "They think Prince Avalask is the one opening the doors. That's their cue to let people through."

I should have commended her for the idea, but I found myself gaping at a large fire built in the middle of the beautiful glass hall, on the stone walkway that ran down the middle.

"This is how we're getting Prince Avalask's attention?" I asked, gesturing toward it. Firelight flickered off every glass pillar lining the hall, dancing brilliantly into every corner, and Corliss and

213

Nessava had pulled up fancy chairs which looked incredibly out of place beside the bonfire. Celesta must still be up in the Tally caves, because I didn't see her.

"Well, now he can't possibly ignore us," Karissa said, walking to sit on an upholstered bench beside Nessava. "Now be quiet. We're playing funniest moments, and the three of you just interrupted Corliss' story."

Corliss directed a grin at me and said, "I was just telling everybody about last year when you introduced yourself to Archie."

"You've got to be kidding," I said as I felt my cheeks redden. "That isn't fair. I can't remember any stories to tarnish your good name."

Emery leapt into a chair and said, "Sh! We can tarnish her good name later. I want to hear."

"So, you'd both just made it into the Dragona?" Karissa prompted her.

I cringed inwardly and moved closer to the fire as Corliss touched a hand to her laughing lips and went on. "Yes, so Archie and I have made it in, and we've planned this thing out meticulously," she narrated with her hands. "We've got our entire fake backstory memorized, I've got Allie right next to me, we've even rehearsed how the conversation will go—"

"You're the one who made us rehearse the whole thing," Archie said, sinking comfortably into the nearest armchair.

"—and I'm about to introduce the two of them, when BAM! Allie falls off the roof and smashes him." Corliss swung her arms into a dramatic clap and could hardly continue the story through her laughter. "The *irony of it!* She just knocks him over, knocks everything he's holding to the ground — I laughed so hard I cried. My stomach hurt for the next three days, worse than the time I bet Karissa I could eat three pounds of prunes—"

214

"Ugh, can we not relive *that* night please," Karissa said, which inspired a round of light laughter, myself reluctantly included.

"Here I was, just about to introduce him, like *hi Allie, this is my super attractive friend, Archie, and I want you guys to be friends* – "

"Come on, Corliss, can you give somebody else a turn already?" Archie said as I tried to look unaffected. Having flaws is the worst.

"Allie could go next," Emery suggested, dancing away and holding up the diary that had *just* been in the pack on my side.

"You thief!" I said, getting to my feet, glancing at my opened bag in shock. He brought fire into his hands to keep me from lunging at him, which by some miracle wasn't leaping onto the paper — but that diary was my lifeline!

I shot Archie a look that said, *fix this!* and he threw up his arms, saying, "I have no control over what he does."

Karissa was the one who gave me a look that could form alliances, right before she turned invisible.

Emery jumped onto a fabric chair, flipping through the pages. "Alright, lots about Archie, blah blah blah, pretty blue eyes and a pretty-boy smile. Ugh, Allie, you're making me nauseous."

Archie leapt to his feet, suddenly taking the matter more seriously. "Alright, give it back." I was about to be sick.

"I'm kidding, just kidding," Emery said, glancing at a few more pages as Archie took a threatening step toward him. "Haven't even seen your name yet, friend."

"Wait! Find a part with all of us!" Karissa became visible between the two of them, the turncoat. She threw her arms wide and crouched to keep anyone from pushing past her, exchanging a grin with Corliss. "I want to know what she's said about us."

"Close it." Archie deepened his voice to a growl. "Or I will rat both of you out for all you're worth." Emery just raised his eyebrows and Karissa folded her arms. "I will tell Robbiel exactly what happened to his first pet rabbit. I will tell Corliss who broke her entire set of ceramic cooking bowls—"

"I already know it was Emery." Corliss grinned as though she couldn't be bothered.

Archie didn't pause for breath. "Karissa, I swear on stitches themselves, I will take care of all my own wounds for the rest of my life—"

Karissa interrupted, "Good, I'd love to see you die of dysentery. Start reading!"

Emery cleared his throat loudly, and I moved closer so I could tackle Karissa, giving Archie a clear shot to the diary, but Archie held up one finger to say *wait.*

Robbiel had suddenly clenched his jaw and glanced between every face in the room. "You guys told me Sparky escaped."

Everybody froze like his words were the rattle of a desert snake.

Karissa was the only one who didn't sense imminent danger and rolled her eyes. "Ok, so he escaped into a bowl of stew," she said without remorse. "We were all starving. Do you even remember that winter?" She got the hint when he lowered his shoulders and got to his feet as well. "Emery's the one who did it!" she exclaimed, vanishing on the spot as Emery's eyes grew wide and he leapt down to grab a large stick from the fire. "He and Jonnath snuck into your room, back before the great doorknob war!"

"Where *is* Jonnath?" Archie asked. "I thought he'd be back by now."

The mood in the room shifted noticeably.

"He's up north visiting family," Nessava said quickly.

I wanted to grimace as Archie tilted his head in clear suspicion. "What are you talking about? Jonnath doesn't have family in the north."

Nessava's eyes grew suddenly and unforgivably large. "Friends! Did I say family? I meant to say friends."

The prior game of keep-away was suddenly forgotten as Archie looked straight at Emery. "Where's Jonnath?"

Emery let his breath out before shutting the diary and tossing it back to me. "Come on," he said, throwing his burning stick back into the fire. "Let's go outside."

"Why don't you just tell me in here?" Archie asked, anger creeping into his features. "It looks like I'm the only one who doesn't know."

"Because," Emery said, grabbing Archie by the shoulder to push him toward the door, "neither of us are about to get emotional in front of Karissa. She'll diagnose us with something and try to feed us witch-craft stew."

Archie shot me a look that asked *did you know about this,* and I mouthed the words *I'm sorry.* Archie shook Emery's hand furiously off his shoulder before leaving the hall with him, silence following their departure.

Karissa was the first to sigh and explain, "I tried being nice to him *one time.* I made him soup when he was sick, and this is what I get for it."

I gave her half a smile, but I found myself dwelling again on the loss of Jonnath and the fact it barely troubled me. Maybe I should count myself lucky that I didn't have to endure one extra bit of misery… but looking around at the faces of Corliss, Nessava, and Karissa as they fell solemn and thoughtful, I felt like I'd lost something important.

Without any fond memories on which to ponder, I was forced to remember why we were here, waiting patiently, hoping Prince Avalask would show up. We were cutting this way too close…

The kids were escaping in three days.

Assuming we talked to Prince Avalask by morning, we'd have all day to introduce him to Tarace and start negotiations, then one more day to hopefully get the kids home, or at least convince them to sit tight. The next day was the escape. How could we possibly pull this off?

I fell asleep with flames dancing through my eyelids and woke much later to a loud, exhausted sigh of frustration.

"All I want to do is go to bed," Prince Avalask said, leaning heavily against one of the obsidian pillars. "There was a flood, and I've been up for thirty-six straight hours, and..." he gestured to the smoldering embers, looking like he might just cry. "Then you Tallies build a fire *in my hall*. Why do you hate me?"

I was the first to gather my wits and say, "We needed to talk to you. The Dincaran kids are planning to make their escape—"

"In three days. I know," he said. "I *do* glance down there every once in a while. So while your concern is touching, unless you've decided to help negotiate their return, I've pretty well got the situation handled."

Emery and Archie were back, and I glanced at Archie to see a look of pure disinterest on his face before I said, "We'll help."

"You're aware I'm keeping Ebby, and that's final?" Prince Avalask rubbed at his eyes, causing a shift in his black fur cloak which shimmered in the firelight.

"We know," I replied, "but we'll still help you. Also... I'm not sure if you know this, but Sav has suddenly taken an interest in getting her back to Sir Avery."

Prince Avalask frowned before taking a deep breath and closing his eyes. "I'm not surprised. He and I argued pretty hard about this attempt at a truce, and our compromise in the end was that we wouldn't give back the mages *and* the Human Epic. It's just one or the other."

He watched us like he was ready for outrage, and when none of us reacted in alarm, he said, "We're either giving back the mages and keeping Ebby, or we're giving back Ebby and keeping the mages. Sav strongly prefers to send Ebby home and hold onto the rest of them. If he can get Ebby back to Sir Avery, then the decision's been made."

Karissa stared at him and asked, "What would you even *do* with a thousand Human mages?"

Prince Avalask looked ready to collapse on the spot, incredibly tired, but also sad and hopeless.

"Another source of debate. I think we could train them to our own benefit, but it's wishful thinking. Savaul will likely convince Izfazara to kill them."

A chilled silence swept through the room, and I tried to catch Archie's eye, but he had his teeth gritted like a bad taste soured his mouth.

"We can still fix this," I said slowly. "We just have to get the Human leaders to agree to peace in exchange for the kids. They'd be idiots to pass it up. We could introduce Prince Avalask to Tarace tonight, and then we'd have two days—"

Archie jerked his head up, revealing the fury that had been festering behind his indifferent stare. "That's the *dumbest* thing you've ever said," he snarled. "You want us to walk in and introduce Prince Avalask to Tarace? Why don't we just…hand them a map of our family trees while we're at it! Why don't we just give ourselves ten thousand years of Time for being traitors and save them the trouble?"

"I am sick to death of bickering," Prince Avalask snarled, his dangerous voice inviting no argument. "I'm going to bed, and we'll approach Tarace in the morning. If you don't want to help, then *go home.*"

219

Prince Avalask waved a hand, and Archie disappeared from the room, causing a startled stir among the rest of us.

"Where did you send him?" I asked, getting quickly to my feet.

"Were you not listening?" Prince Avalask snapped back, all his usual patience gone. "I sent him *home.*"

"Send me too," I said. "I'll talk sense into him."

"You're not going to change his mind about how dangerous this is," Prince Avalask said. "And the last thing I need is for him to change yours."

"I'm as bullheaded as they come!" I exclaimed, drawing a few amused snorts from around the room, quickly stifled. "You just sent him to the *Dragona* where the Zhauri are living, where Sir Avery visits. He shouldn't be there alone. Send me too."

"Fine," Prince Avalask grumbled, rubbing at his eyes one last time. "The Zhauri are in the Dragona's east wing, near the cave where the third Everarc was found, but they're living in the northeastern caves. Talk to Archie and avoid the Zhauri until morning, and I'll come find you both after I get a few hours of sleep. Remember why we're doing this."

CHAPTER NINETEEN

	Shields	
Spying	Intentions	Speed
Tracking	Jumping	Strength
Mind Reading	White Destruction	Earthquakes
Thought Blocking	Black Destruction	Motion Stops
Mental Manipulation	Fire	Telekinesis
Voice Throwing	Ice	Invisibility
Illusions	Lightning	Shading
Levitation	Cancelling Magic	Healing

he last two weeks had been eventful to say the least. Jalia had decided to visit Ebby every afternoon to learn more about her, and strangely enough, Ebby didn't mind talking to Vack's most curious friend. Every night was spent with Ratuan, making maps, providing morale in the dank caves, and sharing knowledge with every new mage in the deepest, most hidden corridor they called Magic. Ebby had lots to learn and contribute among the gifted, and they'd all grown together as the weeks passed.

Then Ebby left every morning for training with Vack and Prince Avalask in a beautiful, far away field surrounded by pear trees. Prince Avalask showed up later and later every day, looking more and more exhausted, but he never explained himself and Ebby and Vack knew better than to ask.

On their first day of training, Prince Avalask had handed Ebby and Vack a list called *The Twenty-five Powers of Conflict,* and he'd taught them a new game every day to help master each gift. They'd raced to track wild game through the woods, run obstacle courses at incredible speeds, and learned they were both entirely inept when it came to hovering above the ground, to the point that they couldn't make a remotely safe game of it.

Ebby's skillset was incredibly different from Vack's. When they learned to use fire, her flames were small and concentrated whereas Vack accidentally set the surrounding woods ablaze. Ebby could not, for the life of her, control a bolt of lightning like Vack, but when they learned to cast illusions, Vack could barely make his own shadow. Ebby could actually make *things* — gnarled trees with flawed leaves and intricate caterpillar nests, flowers, the illusion of flickering flames... She was a creator. Vack was a destroyer.

They'd spent three days of the past week learning to hide, playing a game called *try-to-stay-invisible-while-somebody-throws-rocks-at-you.* Vack thought the game was brilliant until he realized Ebby could throw a rock nearly as hard as he could, and staying invisible while dodging wasn't easy.

Ebby sat on her glass floor and rubbed at a welt near her shoulder, smiling because she'd given Vack one that would turn an equally deep shade of purple, and then she went back to meticulously rechecking her stitches. She'd heal it later.

She even found herself humming *Stitch Me a Thistle* as she scrutinized the white fabric draped over her hands, feeling almost entirely at ease amid so many comforting things — a needle held between her teeth, a spool of white thread on the floor to her right, a blanket across her lap to keep her warm, and Karissa's book about Human anatomy lying open to her left.

Stitch me a thistle, a thistle or two, sew me a song and I'll whistle for you.

222

This dress... this sparkling white dress was the greatest masterpiece she'd ever embellished, and after countless hours of love and labor, it was done. She'd never in her life seen anything like it.

"You left this in Vack's room," Jalia said, pushing Ebby's door open with a scrap of parchment in hand.

Ebby glanced up from her fortress of comfort and spotted several lines of her own handwriting. "Oh. Thank you."

Jalia handed her the list with a piercing, expectant stare, and then sighed. "Well? Tell me what it says."

"It's just a list," Ebby said. "They're the *Twenty-five Powers of Conflict* that Prince Avalask had us memorize."

Even with her focus returned to her beautiful dress, Ebby couldn't miss Jalia's displeased scowl. "It is not. There are too many words."

Ebby set her hands in her lap with a sigh. "It *is* the list, it's just... Prince Avalask said Vack and I had to memorize all twenty-five, or he'd knock down the walls between our rooms. And, I mean, you've seen Vack's room...." Ebby caught Jalia's stern glance of agreement. "So I made a song of them to remember better."

Jalia's eyes widened and she said blatantly, "I'm impressed." Ebby couldn't help smiling at the things that impressed Jalia, and she glanced at her own neat, perfectly spaced handwriting. The lyrics were an embarrassment to music — simple, childish rhymes she wouldn't show to her closest friend. Thankfully, Jalia couldn't read the first word of them.

> First you use your power that can scout the battleground,
> Don't lose sight of who's around you, track your rivals down.
> Read the minds about you, don't forget to guard your own,
> Manipulate them if you can, try not to let them know.
> Distract them when you throw your voice, illusions catch their eye,

But if a battle must take place, fight them from the sky.
Keep your shield around you strong, and sense their next attack,
Jump often so you can't be hit, then throw destruction back.
Fire, ice, and lightning bolts keep enemies at bay,
Drain the mages' magic, and remember speed and strength.
Surprise them with a shaking ground, or freeze them on their feet,
The plants can grab, the rocks can stab, but don't forget retreat.
Make yourself invisible if ever you must flee,
Be sure to shade your whereabouts and heal your injuries.

The list didn't include every power Ebby could use, and she was pretty sure things like *mind reading* and *sensing intentions* should have probably been combined into one power — but on the whole, the list was useful.

"Are you done with the dress?" Jalia asked. "I can bring more thread if you need."

"No, I think I'm done," Ebby replied, holding it for Jalia to see. Over the course of several weeks, Ebby had embroidered white flames across the entire hem, white lightning bolts striking across the chest, leafy white vines twisting around the middle, water droplets raining down between the leaves, icicles draping off the neckline, and a spider on the left shoulder, like the tattoos her Dincaran friends now proudly sported.

"I'm more impressed with the outfit you made for Vack," Ebby replied. "Well, with the fact you got him to wear it, actually." Because while Ebby stitched Epic powers around her dress, Jalia had made an equally intensive black outfit for Vack. "Is he still being a baby in his room?"

Shut up, Vack thought from across the hall, and Jalia smirked. "Yes. It took us fifteen minutes to get it on him, and now he's looking at himself from every angle, trying to make sure he doesn't look stupid. Will you hurry up and take that filthy old tunic off so we can see yours?"

Ebby glanced down at the torn, tattered, and indeed filthy shirt that had once reached to her knees and been painted to look like the sunset. It had *once* been her proudest masterpiece, and parting with it was like... parting with a huge piece of herself. This fabric had been through all her terrors and had taken even more damage than she had over the past months.

Jalia noticed her quiet contemplation and asked, "Is it *rude* to call your tunic filthy?" Ebby smiled at Jalia's harsh pronunciation of the Human word. It turned out the Escalis didn't have an equivalent for it. Also not in their language was *manners,* or the idea of *polite society.* But Jalia was at least attempting to learn Ebby's backwards ways and values.

"Yes, I think that was the definition of rude," Ebby said, wanting to giggle at Jalia's perplexed stare.

"Well... I'm *sorry.* But move faster, will you? I want to see the dress," Jalia said, gesturing for Ebby to get to her feet.

Ebby pushed the blanket from her lap and stood slowly, hesitating until Jalia grabbed the shoulders of her tunic and helped her remove it. Ebby slid the new dress over her head and poked her arms through the open holes at the top, pulling the fabric into place around her middle. When she looked down at herself, at the crisp, white dress that fit her so perfectly, she didn't even feel like Ebby anymore. It was like the dirty, hopeless girl she'd come to know had disappeared and been replaced by somebody beautiful and new.

Her insides twisted, and she felt the sudden urge to tear her hard work apart and put the rags at her feet back on. This was wrong. This pretty girl wasn't her.

Vack finally pushed through the door to Ebby's room and she blushed because if he had been ten seconds earlier, he would have seen her changing.

Vack stopped abruptly and gaped. His black outfit had a multitude of crossing straps along the legs and around the middle to keep it cinched comfortably against him. Jalia had forgone sleeves and given him black leather bracers instead, lacing from his wrists to the spikes on his elbows. His black Epic's gloves covered his hands. If Jalia was shooting for an intimidating look, Vack's messy midnight hair and foggy eyes completed it perfectly.

"Wow," Vack said. Ebby blushed harder, embarrassed to know he had even noticed what she was wearing. The burning desire to get it off turned into a desperate need.

"And wow to you too," Jalia said, nearly skipping around behind him. "What do you think of the shoulders?" she asked, grabbing them playfully. "I made them broad. I think they make you look tough."

Vack was trying to stifle a grin as he twisted and adjusted his black bracers. "I think I like the whole thing."

"What do you mean *you think?* Of course you like it — it's grand and spectacular. Ebby, is that considered *rude*, that he can't just admit it's wonderful?"

Ebby had no breath in her lungs with which to respond. She felt disgusting, like she was trying to cover her life in lies, masking her true self in beauty she didn't deserve.

Prince Avalask knocked soundlessly on her obsidian door-frame. He looked exhausted, but awake enough to notice their drastic change in appearance. "Would you look at that..." He glanced between the nearly unrecognizable Epics before turning to Jalia to ask, "Would you mind having my headstone engraved with the words, *'Prince Avalask did not approve of Ebby's dress?'* Because her father is going to kill me, and it's going to be your fault for bringing it to her."

Ebby looked down at herself in horror as Jalia crossed her arms and glowered. "You *knew* she was making it," Jalia said. "Why did you wait until now to say something?"

"I didn't realize she was planning to live and fight in it-"

"Well where did you think she was going to wear it?" Jalia interrupted, holding her arms wide in exasperation. *"To a ball?"*

Ebby almost couldn't believe Jalia's audacity, and even Prince Avalask looked a bit taken aback before he chuckled at her wildness.

"I like it," Jalia said, a flat, inarguable statement. "It's the opposite of Vack in every way. It's white, it's beautiful, and Ebby's the first Epic girl. Why shouldn't she wear a dress?"

"For obvious reasons, I thought," Prince Avalask said, raising his eyebrows in amusement. "Like how frequently Epics fight up in the air."

"She'll just move so fast that nobody can see her," Jalia reasoned with a clever grin. "You have to let her wear it. Look how long she spent on the embroidery."

Prince Avalask took one last look at the sparkling white designs. "I'm not saying it isn't beautiful — I'm just asking that you put the same level of effort into my headstone. You both look distinguished." He set a hand on his chin and considered his son again. "You and I will make quite the pair in front of the crowds next week, Vack."

Ebby glanced between them and asked, "Crowds?"

Jalia shook Vack by the shoulder and said, "You didn't tell Ebby it's almost your birthday?" Jalia looked at Ebby. "Vack is turning six next week."

"Six?" Ebby repeated.

227

Jalia narrowed her eyes and said, "You can't be more than six yourself."

Ebby gaped indignantly. "I'm almost twelve!"

Jalia shot her a scowl. "No you're not. Who do you think you're kidding?"

Prince Avalask seemed amused by the exchange and said, "She really is. Humans have a childhood two or three times longer than ours. It's funny to watch. In two years, you'll both look older than she does. In ten years she'll look older than you again."

Jalia gaped like Ebby had offended her by keeping this information to herself.

"I only have half an hour for training today," Prince Avalask said, seeming distracted. "And then, Vack... I need to speak with you before you get your day started."

Ebby saw a happy grin flash across Vack's face before he could hide his excitement. He rarely saw Prince Avalask without her.

"You both ready to practice in your new clothes?" Prince Avalask asked.

Vack nodded as Ebby grabbed two handfuls of the fabric around her and gritted her teeth, her chin beginning to quiver. Ok, she would wear it to practice in. She would give it a chance, and then she would take it off.

When Ebby reached Ratuan this time, he was waiting at the bars of his cell as though he knew she was coming. Her legs grew wobbly and her hands began to shake like she was approaching her own death.

"Where did this come from?" Ratuan asked, trying to keep his voice even as he figured out how to react.

"I... made it," Ebby said, her nerves nearly on fire and tears very close to the surface. "I wanted to take it off, but I don't have anything else, and…" Her voice cracked. "I'm sorry. I shouldn't pretend to be something I'm not."

"You look amazing."

Ebby glanced into his eyes. "Really?"

"You look like an Epic," he said, and Ebby's heart lightened. "But why white on white? Nobody's going to be able to see what you made."

"I thought it would make a good story," Ebby said, feeling her eyes drift to the ground with how childish her idea sounded. "Someday, people might tell their friends *I got so close to the new Epic, I could see the flames on her dress.*"

"You are so beautiful," Ratuan said, and Ebby blushed once more, feeling her insides tighten with something that felt like love. "The thoughts you have, the things you make — you are just so beautiful."

Ebby twisted her hands together and smiled, *finally* feeling like she could continue to wear it.

"Thank you," she whispered, feeling more confident when she looked back up at him. If Ratuan liked it, what else mattered? "It… makes me feel like I'm dancing, even when I'm running and fighting."

Ratuan reached through the bars and set a hand on her upper arm, making her wince as his fingers brushed the beginnings of the dark bruise. Ratuan cringed too, like her pain hurt him even more. "Ebby… you don't have to stay here."

"No, it's alright," she said, setting a hand on his. "It was an accident. And you should see the bruise I gave Vack yesterday." She smiled, because she'd done so well in the game they'd played. "Prince Avalask took us out in the woods, and we were tracking each other out in the trees. And Ratuan, I tricked Vack by hiding under this log and knocking a limb down behind him—"

Ratuan's thoughts grew cold with jealousy.

229

"I mean, it was perfectly horrible, of course," she quickly added, realizing her mistake too late. Training with Vack wasn't supposed to sound fun. "But I'm still figuring out his weaknesses, and I'm... gaining their trust."

"I see," Ratuan said.

"Ratuan, please don't look at me like that," Ebby said, her limbs feeling weak. "I'm still on your side. I'd do anything for you. You know that."

Ratuan dropped his tense shoulders and said, "I know. I'm sorry. I just worry about you. They're trying to change you, and I don't want you to change."

"I'm ok," she said with an encouraging smile, feeling relieved when Ratuan smiled back, even if it felt a little forced. "I'm not changing, just getting stronger."

"How do you feel about bending these bars apart so you and I can take a walk?" he asked.

Ebby laughed and said, "Maybe not that strong. Can we go up to Language tonight? I love the way everyone looks at me when I can tell them what the Escali words mean."

"Actually, I was thinking we might spend some time in our map room, just you and me."

"Oh. Yeah, that sounds fine too," Ebby said, grabbing Ratuan's ink-stained hand to pull him straight through the bars.

Ebby! Ebby!

She heard thoughts being shouted at her as Ratuan kept hold of her hand and they took off.

Ebby glanced back at the cell to see Leaf standing at the bars, looking straight at her.

Please be careful, he thought to her. Ebby frowned back, upset that anybody might suggest she wasn't perfectly safe with Ratuan.

I'll be fine, thank you, she thought back, promptly turning back around to walk with Ratuan's hand comfortably in hers.

"Where is Vack right now?" Ratuan asked as they approached the hidden crevice that opened into their map room.

"I'm not sure. Probably with Jalia or Mir."

"Who are Jalia and Mir?"

"His best friends," Ebby replied. She pointedly hadn't mentioned them because she'd grown a little fond of Jalia while they'd shared stories and poked their fingers full of holes, creating the Epic outfits. And Mir had made her laugh at least twice now. He spent hours every morning, running along cliffs between falcon nests to check on their eggs and acquaint himself with their tiny hatchlings. He'd recently gotten permission to take Ebby, Vack, and Jalia out to see them too. "They're both almost as bad as Vack. No manners at all. They fight all the time."

Ebby and Ratuan slipped into their cove they'd worked so hard to create, and Ebby was immensely proud of the system of caves coming down from the ceiling.

"So you've said Izfazara spends a lot of time in this cave?" Ratuan said, setting his hand on one of the bubbles of rock. "And Prince Avalask's hall is over here." He let go of her hand to walk around the map. "And where is Vack right now?"

Ebby focused her thoughts, but already knew where she'd find him. "He's exploring abandoned caves with Jalia. He usually spends his free time with her."

"With *her*?" Ratuan repeated, looking the map up and down the same way he looked at a chess board. "So, where at, exactly?"

Ebby felt suddenly, unexpectedly uncomfortable.

"Why... does it matter?" she asked, folding her arms with an uncertain tickle in her stomach.

Ratuan looked up and gave her the slightest frown. "I just want to know. Is something wrong?"

231

"No. Of course not," she said. "Have I ever told you about this room over here?" She smiled her best, most loving smile to ease the tension. "There are all these statues inside, made of black glass. You would never believe how real they look, Ratuan. They represent all the women in the royal family who've been killed by their curse."

"Sorry Ebbs, I still haven't been out of the kitchens or the dungeons. I can't say I can quite imagine it."

A bitter chill crept into Ebby's chest, like Ratuan was angry with her. "So where exactly is Vack right now?" he asked.

Ebby glanced back at the map, knowing she could point straight to the caves Vack and Jalia liked to explore, and knowing Ratuan would smile with relief as soon as she showed him. But a small voice in her head cautioned her.

You're more than a pawn in everyone else's hands.

"Ebbs?" Ratuan moved around the map to grab her hand, but it wasn't warm. It felt jealous again, and she couldn't figure out what she'd done wrong this time. "Are you afraid they'll do something to you if you tell me?"

She could easily get out of this by saying *yes*, but it wasn't the truth. "No," she said softly.

"Then what's wrong?"

Ebby glanced up at him and said, "I don't want you to hurt Jalia. Or Vack."

"Because you want to be the one to do it?" he asked.

Ebby took a quick breath and nodded. "Well, of course," she said, trying to take a step back from Ratuan.

"Hey, Ebby, look at me," he said, stepping with her and setting his hands gently on her shoulders as a tear escaped each of her eyes. "I know what's going on, and I'm not mad at you, alright? You're under more stress and pressure than any of us, and I never thought you'd be able to keep them completely out of your head. I was ready for this."

232

"It's just not what you think," Ebby said, wiping at her cheeks, wishing she could just make him understand. "They're not what you think."

"Do you remember the day we were separated? The day the Escalis ripped my mother's throat out and took you from me?" Ebby nodded, feeling perfectly awful. "And do you remember when you first realized the Escalis were trying to make you join their side, you promised yourself you wouldn't let them take away your Humanity, no matter what happened?"

Ebby nodded and was about to explain how things had changed, but Ratuan said, "All I need you to acknowledge is that they've already changed you, compromised you. Because you don't hate them the way you did that day. You're barely opposed to them at all anymore. You can at least see that, right?"

Ebby nodded, knowing a secret part of her enjoyed Jalia's reactions to the strangest little things, and would trust Vack with her life. Neither of them were evil.

"We both know they're in your head. The proof is there, and I'm not mad at you, Ebby. It's just that I'm watching them take you from me, one little piece of you at a time until you're gone."

Ebby shrugged miserably. "What do you want me to do?"

"Just tell me one thing. Do you still trust me, and I mean absolutely trust me with no reservations, when I say I want what's best for you?"

Ebby nodded, and not because she felt obligated. She did truly trust him, with everything.

"Please Ebby. I need to know you're still on my side."

"I am," she whispered, looking into his familiar eyes, brown with hazel around the edges, so caring and concerned.

"Can you tell me where Vack is?"

Ebby nodded and reached to the map, where a section of the caves glowed blue at her command. Ratuan smiled with the relief

233

she'd expected, but for the first time in all memorable history, his smile didn't warm her.

"I want you to know how much I trust you too," he said, squeezing her hand. "Can you keep a secret?"

"I don't know if I can," Ebby said. "Minds are so... tricky sometimes."

"You'll be fine," Ratuan said. "I know you will. I've told everybody down here we're escaping in two days, because I wanted Prince Avalask to read our minds and think he could stop us. But we're doing it tomorrow morning."

Even though it was just one day's difference, Ebby felt a stab of fear through her heart. "T-tomorrow?" she repeated.

Ratuan quietly shushed her as he nodded. "You're the only one who knows so far, but I had to tell you so you weren't left behind. The rest of the plan is the same — I still need you to distract Prince Avalask so he doesn't notice us, and if anything goes wrong, just find me. I'll keep you safe."

"Ok," Ebby said, nearly choking on the fear of her friends putting themselves in incredible danger.

Ratuan sounded perfectly confident and reassuring as he said, "I'll be fine, and so will you. Just get through today, then one more night, and we'll be free of this."

CHAPTER TWENTY

I sat pensively on a hill outside the Dragona where ice from last winter still whitened the highest peaks and crunchy orange leaves skittered past me on their way down to the sparring field.

My earlier argument with Archie had gotten heated. I'd yelled a little louder than I intended. He'd told me to go outside and cool off, saying he'd come talk to me when I was *a shanking sensible person again.*

He must think himself quite clever, telling me to come out here when that was obviously my intention anyway. I wasn't about to calm myself in the caves of the Dragona, sandwiched between the dark, oppressive walls like an earthworm. Thinking is easier in the presence of happy bird chatter, surrounded by the smell of the forest, with open spaces allowing escape in any direction...

And I understood Archie's concern. Yes, introducing Prince Avalask to Tarace would expose us as the Escali-sympathizers we were. But today was a new day, which meant we only had two more before those kids made their escape. Even if it went according to Ratuan's plans, there would be blood on the way out. Whereas if Prince Avalask's proposal worked, the whole war would be over.

Archie stepped onto the sparring field and spotted me in the bright sunshine as a warm breeze picked up, rustling more leaves down from their branches.

The knotted tendons in my neck began to unravel as he climbed the hill to reach me, and I risked a hopeful smile. "Did you decide to help me after all?"

Archie shook his head, and said, "This is a bad idea, and I'm asking you *not* to get us both the ten thousand year sentence." I withheld an angry retort as Archie crossed his arms, readying himself for it. I think I surprised us both with my restraint, and once it was clear I wasn't about to bite him, he relaxed his defensive front enough to say, "I'm sorry I shouted at you."

"I'm sorry too," I replied. I was still seated, but the hill put us nearly at eye level. "Your concerns are more than valid. I shouldn't have called you an imbecile." I met his eyes in sincerity, and he returned a brief smile to say all was forgiven. He made these things so easy.

"But... we have to do this, Archie," I said softly. "*I* have to do this. The ends justify the risk."

"Yes, but we should be looking for other ways to get Prince Avalask past that interaction spell, ways that don't endanger us."

"There are no other ways with only two days to go. And nothing's going to happen," I tried to reason kindly. "What's Tarace going to do to me when I have an Epic at my side?"

Archie sighed and said, "I'm not worried about Tarace giving you Time right on the spot. But as soon as you show up with Prince Avalask, all of this is over." He glanced at the edge of the forest and then down to the sparring field, speckled with fallen orange leaves whose edges fluttered in the breeze.

"If things don't go well with Tarace, you'll lose Liz, your home, and the chance to influence any sort of future here," he said. "Have you really thought all that through?"

My heart hurt because I *had* thought through those consequences, and fear gripped me at the reality this could be my last time standing outside the Dragona. "Archie, how can we claim we're here to influence the future if we pass up a chance like this?" I asked. "I really do get it. This is probably the biggest risk we could ever take, but if it works, I won't have to lie to Liz anymore. And can you even imagine, being able to sleep at night knowing everybody you care about is safe?"

Archie softly replied, "There's only a slight chance that will happen, against a very strong possibility Tarace will react poorly and will grant you ten thousand years of Time."

"Come on, Archie," I said, trying to keep myself from smiling. "Since when have I feared consequences?"

"Never!" Archie threw his hands up. "I have to fear them for you, and I have no way to undo the damage you're about to do."

I watched him, letting silence fall between us, knowing neither of us would give. I couldn't. Sometimes we have to take risks.

In a low whisper of apology, I said, "I wouldn't be me if I didn't go for this."

And with his eyes on the ground, Archie nodded sharply to say he understood.

I waited alone for Prince Avalask, lying with my diary over my face to block the sun while the day grew hotter and windier. My first entries were pure rage on the paper, right after Prince Avalask had rescued me from certain death on Tekada, right after my father had been killed and my pregnant mother taken into custody. I read through meeting three people like me, named Robbiel, Archie, and Emery, all of whom were funny and good friends through my many struggles. I even reached a section about meeting Archie's sister, and it became abundantly clear through the next several pages that I'd idolized her outlook on the world and her belief in right and wrong.

Several years passed with no entries before I found a much improved version of my penmanship, saying I'd gotten word my mother was dead and Liz was being exiled to Kelianland because she was a mage. I knew she'd be landing in Dincara and wanted more than anything to meet her, but I was also terrified of stepping into a Human city and trying to pass as normal. I deliberated about it for pages.

"You're alone?" Prince Avalask landed on the hillside, glancing around as though his Epic senses may have missed Archie among the crunchy leaves.

"Yep."

He peered at me as I closed my diary. "Care to talk about it?"

"Nope." I swatted a stray leaf out of my eyes as a rattling gust knocked several more from the trees.

Prince Avalask looked out over the sparring field and said, "The Zhauri are hours away from here, chasing shadows, and I've ensured Sir Avery is quite occupied outside Teredor so we won't be bothered."

"Good," I replied. "Let's get this done."

My heart began to race as we approached Tarace's study. I'd faced worse dangers than this, I tried to remind myself, but I felt like I was being hunted and couldn't run. Like I was sticking my foot in a steel trap, even though I could see its shiny metal teeth glinting in the sun.

"This is worth it, right?" I demanded from Prince Avalask as the door came into view. "I mean, you better make Ebby's life the best in existence. And, these kids had better come back to us in better condition than we left them."

238

Prince Avalask cast me a sideways glance and said, "I would have second thoughts too, if I were you."

His casual reply made me feel somehow more frantic, and I stopped. Even though this was the right thing to do, I suddenly wasn't sure I could.

"But if I were you," Prince Avalask said, glancing back at me as he slowed his pace, "it would calm me to think about the consequences of not acting. Think about what's going to happen if those thousand kids from Dincara are left to Savaul. You could also think about Ebby. Because she'll eventually escape back to Sir Avery and be made into a weapon if this doesn't work out. And if you don't help me now, you'll regret for the rest of your life that you had the chance to change the world, and didn't."

I sighed as Prince Avalask vanished, and I pushed Tarace's door open to find him alone, startled by my barging in.

"Could have sworn I locked that," he said, getting to his feet with more haste than I'd think him capable, judging by his tired eyes. He shut the door and asked, "I assume you have news about Ebby. Here, have a seat. Where's Archie?"

I sat in the chair across from his desk, the smell of papers and leather-bound books nearly overwhelming.

"Archie couldn't come," I said, "and I know this isn't what you want to hear, but I'm not here about Ebby."

Irritation tainted his usually controlled expression. "We talked about this," he said flatly. "The children from Dincara have been *my* priority since we last spoke, and Ebby was supposed to be yours. Did you even try to find her?"

"I actually was able to speak to her," I said, glad to catch him off guard. "She still knows who she is, she hasn't been hurt, and she doesn't want to come home."

Tarace threw his hands open in outrage. "Of course she doesn't! She's being manipulated by Prince Avalask!" He set his palms on

239

the edge of the desk and leaned against them, thinking quickly. "I'll send somebody out to let the Zhauri know you've got her location—"

"I had the chance to speak with Prince Avalask too," I cut him off. "That's why I came to you, and not Sir Avery or the Zhauri. The Escalis want peace, Tarace. You're the only leader I know who's sensible enough to entertain that idea."

Tarace gaped at me in disbelief and revulsion, like I'd suddenly sprouted arm spikes and turned rabid. He touched his fingertips to his forehead for a moment, then said, *"Excuse me?"*

I slowly went on, "If we leave Ebby with the Escalis, they'll give us every one of the Dincaran kids back, along with a truce. Those thousand kids are more powerful than our one Epic, by far. We can't afford to pass this up."

Tarace ground his teeth together before asking in a low voice, "Have you misplaced your common sense, Allie? Escalis don't want *peace* or a *truce*. They'll never let those children return freely."

Prince Avalask became suddenly visible beside me and said, "You're not entirely wrong. It's more a surrender than a truce, considering your position."

Tarace froze in alarm, glancing at the closed door behind us, edging back from Prince Avalask, and looking to me in appalled horror. "This was why you came?" he whispered in betrayal. "To introduce him?"

I completely understood Tarace's fear for his life, and tried to explain, "We were too short on time to do this any other way. The Dincaran kids are days away from a devastating escape attempt. And honestly Tarace, if we don't make this deal now while Izfazara's in power, we won't get another chance. The heirs lined up to replace him wish us worse than dead."

"Izfazara's no different," Tarace spat. "Am I supposed to forget the Escalis razing Dincara? My family's lived there since my great grandfather built the city walls, and now it's *gone*."

Prince Avalask sighed. "No harm came to those who surrendered," he said patiently, "and we took no part in Kelian's decision to kill your mages." Prince Avalask swept his black fur cloak off to one side and sat comfortably in the chair Sir Avery had occupied last time I'd been here. "You can sulk about the loss of your father, but mine was also killed when that spire exploded, and I'm still here. There's a greater cause at stake."

Prince Avalask kicked his feet onto Tarace's desk, and Tarace threw me a furious glance, full of so much hate that I knew everything was ruined. Archie was right. I'd just given up my life at the Dragona.

"You and I never have to get along, Tarace," Prince Avalask said, folding his hands in his lap. "But we do need to talk about the children we found after the battle in Dincara."

Fearful hesitation mixed into Tarace's loathing, and he slowly lowered his shoulders. "What do you want?" he asked.

Prince Avalask held an open palm toward me and said, "Allie did a pretty good job of explaining. We're tired of this war, and we'll give them back as a gesture of good faith in exchange for a truce — a surrender, my uncle wishes to call it."

Tarace tried to conceal it, but I could see interest in his eyes, a hunger almost. "How specifically do you plan to go about this?"

Prince Avalask stood, and the stacks of paper on Tarace's desk moved politely to the floor without fuss. Prince Avalask said, "Even among Escalis, it's well known that Humanity hates their king, and lacking a ruler makes our task difficult. We have to somehow convince every Human city to agree to this truce if it's to be made." He focused on Tarace's desk where scattered points of yellow light gleamed to life.

241

"But the Dragona's been the head of continent-wide decisions in the past, and you're well known because of your father. The other cities may yet listen to you." A tint of blue crept around the sides of the desk, and I began to recognize the shape of both the main ocean to Tekada and the Breathing Sea. "These points of light are the major cities you'll need to convince. Tabriel Vale will follow whatever you decide here at the Dragona, obviously, but you'll need Nella up in Glaria and Jack from Terrintel on your side before you approach the northern cities. Lakama is giving us more problems than you would believe. I'd be surprised if Jory even wants this war to end."

Prince Avalask had an impressive, but not surprising knowledge of Human cities and their leaders. He'd even lit points of light far into the west, past where I'd ever travelled.

Tarace stared at the desk in silence and Prince Avalask sighed, drumming his fingers impatiently on the blue of the Breathing Sea. "I've been trying to put this in a positive light," he said, "but Tarace, my brothers will kill the children from Dincara if we don't find something to do with them. If you thought it was painful to lose your city, you're going to crumble when you see the rest fall because Humanity is too disadvantaged to defend itself."

Prince Avalask leaned toward him and said, "You don't even have your second Epic right now, Tarace, while my son is just a few years away from being able to wreak havoc. I hold all the cards to destroy you, and I am here offering you life instead. Don't. Be. An idiot."

Two painstaking hours passed as Tarace and Prince Avalask argued over details. Four different people rapped their knuckles against the door during their conversation, and Tarace patiently told each of them to come back in the evening.

Prince Avalask struck me as quite the accomplished negotiator as they spoke, except he refused to even entertain a discussion about Ebby. She was staying with him, and Sir Avery would stop tearing apart Escali cities looking for her, or there was no deal. Tarace was hardly in any place to make demands, so he let that one go and focused more on territories.

I learned more about Human and Escali history in that hour than I'd ever known, regarding which cities had changed hands over the years, which areas had been the most contested, and where the most people had died. Tarace seemed to know every detail of every event that had ever happened, and he wielded his knowledge well, arguing aggressively for every territory, reciting details and reasons it should belong to Humans and not Escalis.

"I think I can reach Terrintel, Glaria, and Lakama by the end of the night, and maybe head west of the river in the morning," Tarace said. "Give me... until tomorrow afternoon, and I'll at least bring them to the bargaining table."

"I'll come back tomorrow afternoon then," Prince Avalask said, rising to his feet.

"Wait," I said, speaking for the first time since the introduction. They both looked at me like I'd been napping. "What about the Escali the Zhauri brought back?"

Tarace glanced between us, and for a moment, I questioned if Tral still lived. "He's inconsequential," Tarace said.

"Then we could let him go," I said. "As a token of our own good will."

Tarace's face fell absolutely blank as Prince Avalask said, "I think that would be the perfect beginning to a successful peace. I can take him with me."

"Certainly," Tarace said, but his voice sounded so... void, it gave me a strange feeling in the pit of my stomach. "Let's go get him."

I leapt to the bottom of an eerily dark staircase and gasped like I'd been submerged in icy water, hunching immediately forward to catch my breath.

"I don't know why he's not answering," Tarace said from above. "He's down there."

"And likely dead," Prince Avalask bit back. "What could have possessed you to turn the third Everarc Cave into a dungeon? I would expect this cruelty from the Zhauri. Not from you."

I gripped my upper arms tightly and tried to convince my lungs to expand when all my insides seemed to have shriveled.

"It's not that bad," Tarace said. "Step inside. See for yourself."

"Magic is the thread that weaves Escali blood and bone together," Prince Avalask said in disgust. "I would be no stronger than a child in there. A single Human would be able to subdue me."

There were three caves like this in the world, where the Everarc Crystals had been excavated, leaving behind caves entirely void of magic. I'd never been inside one, and it was decidedly awful.

"Doenn khahhgna?" Prince Avalask asked.

"Yeah, I'm fine," I replied, glancing back to them as Prince Avalask nodded his understanding.

It made me sick to think how much worse this would be for an Escali, and how many hours Tral had been stuck here.

"You'll need this," Tarace said, tossing a key down to me. I normally would have been able to catch it in my sleep, but my reflexes were sluggish and I barely had my fingers unclenched by the time it clattered to the floor. I coerced them open and closed several times before massaging a little feeling into them, bending carefully to pick up the key.

Four doors dotted the cave walls, three of which gaped open. I felt uncomfortable, knowing we'd turned something so rare into a place of despair, but also relieved only one cell had an occupant.

I twisted the key and stepped quietly inside to see Tral sitting against the opposite wall of the tiny cell, and he was… *bleeding.*

His arm spikes had been tied tightly to his upper arms so he couldn't bend his elbows, and then they'd been tied behind his back. Deep gashes marred his arms with some slashed across his neck and face, and I had the feeling I wasn't even able to see the extent of dried blood and open wounds.

He snarled when he saw me, then muttered, "Isn't this just fitting." I distinctly remembered his friend telling him, *If the roles were reversed right now, I can guarantee that it would be dragging you.*

I held my hands apart, far from the short swords on my belt, and switched immediately to Escalira.

"Gifted favors never go forgotten," I said, and his face darkened.

He looked at the ceiling and said, "You speak well. Much better than the Human *glorsch* before you."

"I'm so sorry," I said, scratching my fingernails into the pads of my thumbs, wishing I could find a more sincere way to express my remorse. "It's over now. I'm here to let you out."

He shook his head and said, "You toy with me." I didn't see even a glimmer of hope in his eyes.

I pulled my hunting knife slowly off my side and said, "I'm cutting you free."

He bolted upright in one startling movement, glaring dangerously, daring me to approach him.

I had three ropes to cut through, and I knelt hesitantly to saw at the tie around his left arm spike, freeing his arm to bend once more. I started on the other arm, careful to avoid a deep gash that hadn't begun healing, and asked, "You remember me?"

He said nothing, breathing deeply, his cloudy eyes boring frightfully through me. I shifted slightly to get around him and cut the ties off his wrists, incredibly uncomfortable with his teeth so close.

245

Tral wriggled to get the cut ties off and then looked at his hands as though he'd never expected to see them again. I couldn't help noticing bloody scabs where his fingernails had once been, and my stomach rolled.

He met my eyes, and I heard a rumble of a growl in his throat before he lunged at me.

I scrambled back with a yelp, but was nowhere near fast enough to get away before he landed on me. I threw a hand over my face to block his teeth, snarling furiously back as I dug my other nails into the gash along his shoulder. He cried out and leapt off, dashing for the open door as I got my feet beneath me.

"What is this?" Tral asked from the dark hall. He must have stopped abruptly.

"It's real," I heard Prince Avalask reply. "Come out of the dark."

I stepped through the door in time to see Tral sink into a pained bow before the Epic, and then he vanished into thin air. Prince Avalask raised his eyebrows, asking if I was alright.

"I'm fine. You can go," I said, and then Prince Avalask jumped away as well, leaving me with Tarace, whose face was emotionless as a cliff's.

I climbed from the Everarc Cave and warmth flooded back through me like love and a familiar hearth combined. The feeling was punctured by a stab of guilt as I met Tarace's empty gaze.

"I assume this has been going on for a while?" he asked.

"Yes," I replied. "I've known Prince Avalask a long time. He's not the monster we've made him out to be."

Tarace watched me before simply turning to walk away.

"Tarace?" My fingers tingled nervously as he turned back around with no discernible expression. "Can we acknowledge I just put my life in your hands?" I wanted a tip of his head or an understanding sigh, and he gave me nothing. "I guess... I'll ask you to remember that as you decide what to do about me. I came to *you*."

I could see I would be getting nothing from him, so I turned to head back toward the Wreck.

"I have a lot of thinking to do. And quite the list of cities to visit," Tarace finally said, and when I looked back, he simply looked tired. "If you have any goodbyes you'd like to say, now would probably be a good time," he added.

I gave him a sad smile in return. "Alright."

CHAPTER TWENTY ONE

Since Tarace had us filling out the large chore chart in the Wreck a month in advance, I knew Liz was supposed to be out digging up potatoes this week, accompanied by a string of hilarious complaints, I'm sure. But as I neared the Wreck, a catchy song echoed out to me, and I found Liz still inside.

She was *dancing on a tabletop* with Corliss, and I felt the heaviness in my chest loosen as I caught a glimpse of my sister's gleeful eyes, finally looking alive again as she spun sharply. Three other members of the Travelling Baking Show were hashing out drumbeats as Corliss recanted some funny, rhythmic tale, and Liz shouted specific parts with the rest of the crew when necessary. The Wreck only held ten people at this time of day, but all had smiles on their faces as they adjusted their chairs to watch.

"Your sister's a natural," Corliss called to me, laughing as they both turned left in a step-skip-turn and jump. They landed next to each other, arms thrown wide, inviting applause, and I clapped with the rest of the sparse audience. Prince Avalask must have sent Corliss back here as well. She certainly didn't look like she'd run the whole way.

"Come join us," Liz said, offering a hand to help me onto the table top. She was out of breath, cheeks red, and her infectious smile hit me hard enough that I felt a pull at the corners of my own lips.

"Actually, I was just on my way out to pull potatoes with you, if you'd like the company."

Liz looked quickly around herself and said, "I lost track of time." She leapt lightly from the table and landed beside me. "You disappeared on me for a while there... Now you reappear and want to help me dig for potatoes?"

"No place I'd rather be," I said, trying to fake a smile as we took off toward the sunny day. "Also, when did you learn to dance?"

Liz shot me a sly, sideways grin. "I sort of became an honorary member of the Travelling Baking Show."

I snorted a laugh and asked, "When did that happen?"

"A day or two after you disappeared."

My face fell. Finding out she'd joined the circus was a pretty clear sign that I hadn't been paying her enough attention.

"I don't want you to be angry," she said, "but you and Archie left. Corliss was here, and she's a lot of fun. I used to be fun too, don't you remember?"

"I do. And I'm not angry," I said sincerely. "I'm glad you found something you enjoy. Just... be careful. Cooking's not exactly in our genes."

Liz elbowed me in the side and said, "Not in yours, maybe, but I can make ice cream on hot days. I'm a commodity!"

I laughed as she began to tell me all about her ice power, and I found myself clinging to the sound of her voice. This might be the last time I would ever hear it, and that terrified me beyond all other fears.

We neared the dried up field of potatoes, and I jumped as she squeezed my shoulder.

"Where did you go?" she asked, her eyes speaking a language of kindness I didn't deserve.

I just shook my head as words were hard to find. "Sorry. Just... a lot to think about."

"Yeah, I figured," she said. "Which is why I don't understand why you're out here pulling potatoes."

I let out a deep breath, feeling like I'd been holding it in for five minutes. "I... just want to be close to you." My shoulders sagged beneath the weight of too many secrets, and fear flashed through Liz's eyes.

"What's wrong?" she asked. "Are you alright?"

I nodded and tried to force a small smile. "I'm fi —"

"You are not fine. It's written all across your face. You know you can tell me anything, don't you?" She grabbed my other shoulder and gave me a rough shake. "I could help you, Allie. Why won't you ever let me?"

I wanted so badly to tell her everything. I couldn't keep it in. "I think I'm in trouble, Liz," I said, glad to feel her fingers tighten.

"What happened?"

"I'm... I had a choice to make," I said, gripping my left hand tightly in my right, watching my knuckles turn white. "I had the chance to fix everything, or watch it all stay the same. And... I tried to fix it."

"What does that mean, to fix everything?" she asked.

I looked up at her and whispered, "I mean, I had the chance to fix *everything*."

She was searching my eyes for answers but stumbled across the worst question instead. "What was the cost?"

I looked straight back into her dark gaze, reminded of my own reflection, and raised my shoulders in a halfhearted shrug. "I don't know yet."

I was about to drop my eyes to the ground when they caught on a deep red scratch right below Liz's throat. "Liz, what happened?" I grabbed the collar of her jerkin as she lurched from my reach. I caught a glimpse of swollen red scrapes all over her chest before she tugged the jerkin up to her chin

"What happened?" I demanded.

She just looked ready to cry. "Liz," I softened my voice. "I'm sorry. I'm sorry, just tell me who did this."

She shook her head quickly.

"Liz—"

"You did, alright?" she said, rubbing at her neck. "West is gone. And you've got me so worried, it hurts... The days have gotten better, but I wake up at night, scratching myself like this." She curled her nails in around her throat. "I don't mean to, but I never know where you are. I never know if I've just seen you for the last time, and I have these dreams..."

She nearly choked on her words and I closed the distance between us. "I'm sorry," I said, setting a gentle hand on her arm. "I didn't realize—"

"Well? Is this it then?" she growled. "This could really be the last time I'll have you in my life, and we're out here digging for stupid *potatoes?*" She kicked at the ground.

"I don't know," I said softly. "And... I'm afraid." She glared at me, demanding I explain. "I don't want to involve you, in case everything goes wrong. But if it goes the way I've planned, then there won't be any more reason to keep secrets."

"When?" she asked. "When will all of this be over?"

"By the end of the week," I said. Because by then, we would either have a truce or the Dincaran kids would attempt their escape. Tarace would either keep my secret or expose me.

"And what am I supposed to do if I lose you?" she asked.

251

"You won't," I said, resolved that this would be a promise I could keep. "I don't know what's going to happen, but you won't lose me."

"Alright," she said, folding her arms as though warding off cold despite the hot day. "I guess that's as good as I'll ever get."

We really did spend the next hours loading potatoes into buckets under the bright sun. The first hour passed in silence, the second in forced conversation about topics that didn't matter, and the third was spent sweating and catching up about everything we hadn't had time to discuss lately. Liz told me legends about the most powerful ice mages over the centuries, and said she aspired to one day use her gift for combat like them. She asked if anything had progressed with Archie, and I reluctantly explained nothing had. We talked about Corliss and her funniest moments, and finally, we talked about the massacre on Tekada.

Liz said the non-mage survivors were scheduled to land in two days, and I had to wonder if Ratuan was somehow aware of that. What a coincidence it was the same day as the escape…

She also said they were bringing back some sort of weapon, but she knew nothing of its nature. I couldn't even guess why Tekada would send us a weapon to combat the Escalis, after they'd *just* murdered Humanity's best defense.

Liz wanted to return to the Wreck, and Prince Avalask had said the Zhauri were hours from the Dragona, so I agreed to come too.

I approached the entrance boulders cautiously, comforted by the sounds of the Travelling Baking Show livening the mountain. But we climbed inside and my heart plummeted at the sight of five men in white cloaks, seated around a table with four furry dogs lying at their feet, death hound not included. They spoke in melodic Icilic as Kit's voice grew louder, telling a story while the other four laughed with him.

Maverick had already spotted me, and he finished chuckling at Kit's tale before mouthing across the room *somebody's in trouble.*

I yelped as a hand fell on my shoulder and Corliss met me with a grin. "Hey, Archie's looking for you." I froze for a moment, knowing the Zhauri would follow me if I left the Wreck. Maverick could probably already tell I had Ebby's location.

She squinted at me and said. "Now. He needs you right now."

I nodded quickly and glanced at the cave that would take me to Archie's room.

"And Liz, we need you back to help with dishes," Corliss said as Liz squinted at me. Corliss clapped loudly and said, "Alright team, break!" She shoved me toward the tunnel and Liz toward the Baking Show. I strode with purpose, but felt a new sense of dread as I glanced back to see Corliss walk boldly to the Zhauri table and pull up a chair as they began rising to their feet.

"It's dawned on me that I haven't introduced myself," she told them with a grin, always one for shock. "My name is Corliss, and I'm embarrassed to realize I haven't yet invited you to experience the joys of tabletop dancing."

I reached the tunnel and ducked from sight before peering back into the Wreck. I wanted to dash away, but I couldn't tear my gaze off Corliss in all her insanity.

I strained my ears to listen, even as the Zhauri stared at her in surprised silence. Maverick spoke in Icilic, and Iquis fixed his intense, lopsided stare onto Corliss. Her confident smile faded in a hurry.

Kit set a hand on her arm, and each of his words came iced with his thick accent as he threatened, "If I see your teeth again, funny girl, I will see to it you swallow every one of them."

Corliss, never one to miss a joke, pulled her lips over her teeth and said, "Alright, I can take a hint."

The new, blond one laughed openly and Kit narrowed his dark eyes. "Leave," Kit said, "and be grateful you are funny."

Their pitch black dog with white paws perked his ears in my direction as a voice behind me demanded, "What are you doing?"

I flipped around to see Jesse, and scoffed loudly. "What I always do, Jesse. None of your business."

"What's wrong with your face?" he asked.

That had to be the pettiest insult in history, and I rolled my eyes before striding past him in calm ignorance, urging myself not to run from the real danger. If the Zhauri wanted to pursue me, running would just make me look guilty.

I glanced anxiously back to make sure they weren't following, but just saw Jesse turn straight around and head for Tarace's study, the snitch. And from the corner of my eye, I caught a glimpse of something stuck to my left elbow, a stray hair or piece of lint. I brushed at it, then tried to pick it off and felt a gentle tearing sensation creep up my arm.

I had just pulled off a long, translucent strip of my own skin.

I pounded on Archie's door then shoved it open as he grabbed the handle to pull. I charged inside as his surprise became worry.

"Archie, I just saw the Zhauri in the Wreck and now I'm... *molting!* I look like a snake! Like I'm half Human, half Escali, and half snake!" I gestured to the foggy edges of skin peeling away from my arms and face. "What did they do? Have you ever seen anything like it?"

I peeled a strip of skin from the top of my shoulder to the bottom of my elbow and watched it drift softly through the air, my stomach a bind of panic.

"Alright, I see it. Would you mind *not* doing it on my floor?" Archie grabbed his waste basket to plunk down between us as my jaw fell open in disgust.

"And don't look at me like that," he said, his eyes amused. "You're not dying. This is the Tally version of a sunburn. Your skin has already repaired itself and is getting rid of the dead layers. It's not pretty, but you're going to be alright."

I could hear the laughter in his reassurance, and I felt a flush of embarrassment flood into my face at how incredibly *ignorant* I was. I could have puzzled this out if I'd just put a little thought to where I'd been all day.

"Oh," I muttered, knowing this might become the next campfire song if word of it ever reached Corliss. "Well... Sorry for molting on your floor then."

Archie laughed a full, deep laugh from the pit of his stomach. I was ready for a lifetime of mockery to begin on the spot, but he brushed my idiocy off and asked, "You ran into the Zhauri?"

"I more... ran past them," I said. "Maverick mouthed across the room that I was in trouble, but they haven't followed me here. At least not yet." I glanced at Archie's door and said, "We should leave before they get the chance."

Archie shook his head and said, "They're like Escalis, Allie. Running from them is the surest way to make them chase you." He also glanced nervously at the door before asking, "How was talking to Tarace?"

"He's speaking with the other city leaders right now, convincing them to take the deal."

Archie gave me a low whistle of amazement, and started to say something else before his door was thrown open with a frightening thud against the wall.

"Oh, how hot the fire in which you play," Sir Avery snarled, his jaw trembling with terrible anger. The veins in his neck bulged like

255

he was ready to tear someone apart. "I just spoke with Tarace," he spat. *Oh shanking life.* "Did you think for one second I wouldn't find out about this?"

"I... hoped maybe you would understand," I said, jittery with fear as the Epic huffed like an enraged ox. "Listen, I know you want your daughter back—"

"And I know what you think, that I only want her because she's powerful. You are wrong, you stupid Tally. She's *my* daughter, and Avalask cannot keep her from me."

I scrambled to find words that might placate him. "It's not about that," I said slowly. "We'll make a deal so you can see her, but we have to think about the thousand other kids—"

"I don't care about those other kids! Where did you find her?"

"Hang on," Archie said, coming to my defense. "We *happened* to run into her. We still don't know where Prince Avalask keeps her hidden."

"You shut up," Sir Avery fumed, "and *you* show me where you found her."

He held a hand out to me and I tried to skip back, already at the edge of Archie's bed.

"You are awfully bold," I said, growing sicker. "Nobody gets a free pass into my mind."

"I'm Sir Avery. I get what I want," he replied. I felt thoughts prodding at my own thoughts, and I responded with an angry flash of lightning in my hands and eyes. Anywhere I could feel an intruding influence, I shocked it senseless, feeling sizzles in my head everywhere I decimated a tendril of thought. I threw my palms to my skull as Archie grabbed my shoulder, erecting a sudden wall of safety between my mind and Sir Avery's. The Epic's invading presence vanished in a flash.

Archie had never shielded me before, and I could tell he was angry by the tight grip of his fingers, but he remained calm and reasonable on the outside. "Listen, we went to Dekaron with every intention of bringing Ebby home, but things—"

Archie jerked me back to throw both hands in front of us as Sir Avery flicked his glowing fingers, but the Epic's burst of red light hit the wall, and it crumbled away to reveal a long, open tunnel.

The tunnel was wrong. We should have just been looking into the room of Archie's closest neighbor, but my jaw dropped as two people ran past the opening. One was Tral, the Escali we'd just released. The second was a girl with her blonde hair tied back, dashing by on long, strong legs with sandals laced to her knees.

"What are you doing?" I whispered as the long tunnel disappeared, replaced by a clear view of the Wreck.

"Nothing to harm your health," Sir Avery replied, his furious glare replaced by one more sadistic. "Just throwing a few illusions around for the Dragona's entertainment." People crowded around the tables in the Wreck, eating food and laughing with their friends, and my heart stopped as I saw myself seated at a table with all my Tally friends who had taken no care to cover their arm spikes.

"These are real? People can see them?"

"They'll see juuuust as soon as they look," Sir Avery said in lingering amusement. "And I wish you luck, convincing eye-witnesses you *haven't* been collaborating with Escalis. I'll be among the first to recommend a ten thousand year sentence for your crimes."

The Wreck disappeared and I saw one more vision of myself strolling casually across the sparring field with Prince Avalask.

"Ok, stop," I said, swallowing my angry pride. I was better off giving Ebby's location to Sir Avery than waiting for the Zhauri anyway. "We found her down with the Dincaran kids, alright?"

"There are three *yous* milling about the Dragona right now," Sir Avery said, lazily holding up three fingers. "So I'm going to need three more things worth my while."

I took a quick breath and glanced at Archie to make sure he wasn't telling me to shut up, but I only saw loathing and bitter resignation in his eyes. "The Dincaran kids have been working on an escape plan—"

"An obvious conclusion, and not helpful to me," Sir Avery cut me off. The Wreck came back into view on the wall and a few people began to glance sideways at my group of Tally friends.

"No, you don't understand. It's a good plan," I persisted. "Ratuan's got the cave split into sections where they've been training, and they're breaking for freedom in two days—"

"Boring," Sir Avery said, yawning cruelly.

"—and he wants you to come talk to him because they're trying to kill Izfazara on the way out."

Malicious interest lit Sir Avery's eyes, and he put a finger down. The group of Tallies in the Wreck disappeared before I was watching myself outside, walking casually and chatting with Prince Avalask.

"Savaul wants to speak with you too," I said, panicked even though I couldn't see anybody else near the sparring field.

Sir Avery sneered and asked, "Why would Avalask's brother want to see me?"

"He says he wants to help bring Ebby home. He's even willing to introduce himself to you."

"See? This isn't so hard," Sir Avery said, putting a second finger down. The Allie and Prince Avalask on the sparring field turned to smoke and disappeared, but one more me was running through the tunnels with Tral on their way out of the Dragona.

"What else do you want to know?" I demanded.

"What else is worth knowing?" Sir Avery asked, sickly playful.

Jesse, none other than shanking Jesse, caught a glimpse of myself and Tral running by his connecting tunnel. He tilted his head uncertainly, then trotted after them to investigate.

258

"Better find something," Sir Avery said as Allie and Tral rounded a corner and stopped running so Jesse could catch up.

What else was relevant?

"Ratuan has Ebby in the palm of his hand," Archie said as Jesse made it to the end of the hall, nearly to the corner behind which I was standing with Tral. "She says what he wants her to say and does what he tells her to do."

Allie and Tral evaporated into nothingness *right* as Jesse came around the corner, one second from being face to face with the two, and Sir Avery cocked his head as the wall returned to its normal rocky self.

"What makes you say so?" he asked.

"We've seen it," I said flatly.

"I'd like to see it too," Sir Avery said, holding a hand out to me. I had the overwhelming urge to dance back again and spit at him, but it would be an idiotic mistake I couldn't afford.

Archie held me back by the shoulder, and I set a hand on his to mutter, "I'm alright," before I stepped away from his protection and grabbed Sir Avery.

I thought back to seeing Ebby down with Ratuan, but Sir Avery didn't merely share the memory with me like in the past — he reached into my mind, grabbed a thick handful of my thoughts, and brutally ripped them out.

I screamed as my knees buckled beneath me and Sir Avery grabbed my shoulders with crushing strength to keep me standing. If thoughts could bleed, my blood would have been spattered around the walls of Archie's room.

I could hear Archie's snarled words, but more than that, I could feel my memories being directed to everything I knew of Ratuan's planning. Sir Avery stripped away copies of all I knew, and I gritted my teeth to suppress a cry as my heart lurched in fear of what this could do to my mind. I couldn't start over. Not again.

"I still put up with you, Tally, because you once looked out for my daughter when I couldn't. But she is *not*," he hissed, "staying with Avalask." His breath was hot on my face as he growled, "Learn your place. My heart will not ache if I need to be done with you entirely."

Sir Avery reached into my front pocket and snatched Sav's spider-webbed envelope.

He let go of me to rip the letter open, and I barely got my hands out to soften the impact of crumpling to the floor. Sir Avery's eyebrows rose further with each line he read, and he shot me one last look of disgust before muttering, "Teach the two of you to betray *me*..."

He leapt into the air, and vanished as I threaded my fingers into my hair and pressed my hands to my skull. I closed my eyes and tried to isolate the pain, but my brain felt like it had been grated, sanded, and left to scab over, resulting in the sharpest headache I'd ever endured.

"Allie?" Archie whispered beside me on the floor, his voice choked.

"We have to get Jesse," I groaned as my head throbbed. "He saw me."

"It's alright. We just have to prove Tral is in the Everarc Cave. Jesse will have nothing."

"Tral's already gone," I said. "If Jesse accuses me of letting him out and Tarace isn't here to vouch for me..."

I heard Archie sit up and imagined he was tugging at his own hair too.

"I can go take care of Jesse," he said. I nodded and felt two of Archie's hands grab one of mine. "Don't move. I'll be back."

I nodded again, smaller this time, because every movement hurt.

I just lay still after he left, feeling ashamed Sir Avery had pulled information from me that wasn't his to take. That made me weak, and not the secret keeping vessel I wanted to be. Logically, I knew shame was the wrong response, but I felt it all the same.

I also couldn't help but wonder... How was Archie planning to take care of Jesse? He could try to talk him down or... kill him... But Archie wasn't a killer. Maybe he would tie Jesse up and hide him somewhere until all of this was over.

The morality of that option didn't concern me as much as... well, where would he put him?

I pressed my palms to the rock floor, pushed myself to my feet, and despite the lingering headache, I pulled myself together. He was going to need help.

I stumbled into the hall and glanced either way down the abandoned tunnel. If Jesse went to Tarace, he would find him gone, and the next best thing...

The Zhauri. He probably hated me enough to take this to the Zhauri.

Prince Avalask had mentioned that the five hunters lived in the northeastern caves, which made sense because they were the nicest the Dragona had to offer. I headed northeast in the familiar tunnels, hoping Jesse didn't know the Zhauri were in the Wreck. I was almost to the Zhauri's quarters when I heard Archie's voice ahead, low and urgent.

"She's a traitor, and she deserves ten thousand years for it," Jesse hissed back. "And you're probably going down with her, unless you can convince everyone you're an idiot and she played you. Now get out of my way."

"You have no idea what you're talking about," Archie said. "You saw an illusion, Jesse. That's all it was."

"I just ran to the Everarc Cave, and all four doors were open. The Escali is *gone*, Archie, and it's because she let him out."

I rounded a corner and saw loathing light Jesse's eyes at the sight of me. "Listen," I said, the perfect image of calm, "Tarace gave the

261

order to let the Escali go. Take this to him, Jesse, not the Zhauri. He'll explain."

Jesse just sneered. "So one of you tells me I saw an illusion, and the other says the Escali was released on Tarace's order?" I could see by the way he was glancing between us, he was about to try something.

"Just *ask* Tarace," I said. "If you take this to the Zhauri, you'll start a chain reaction that'll get me hurt or killed."

"Isn't it great?" Jesse asked, pure triumph on his face. "All I have to do is scream, and the Zhauri will hear me. You can't escape them, and who knows what they'll do to you before they hand you over for Time. We all know what they're famous for." Archie's fingers twitched as Jesse jeered, "And who ever thought *I* would be the one to catch you?"

Archie looked like a contained storm, and he shot me a stone-cold look that asked if I was ready to witness a murder.

I said flatly, "The Zhauri aren't here. They're in the Wreck."

"Good," Archie replied.

Jesse's eyes widened, and he grabbed a knife off his side as Archie whipped around to punch him in the gut. Archie grabbed his arm in two places and twisted it behind his back, catching Jesse's knife from the air before it could clatter to the floor.

Archie shoved him into the wall with the blade at his throat and snarled, "Don't test me, Jesse. Nobody's about to wander through this section to save you. Get it?" Jesse just stared at me in shock, making no move to get away and no sound above his ragged breathing. "Now listen for a second, will you? We need her to stay here," Archie pointed his free hand at me but kept his eyes on Jesse, "for reasons I am not about to explain to you. All that matters to me, is finding a way to shut you up."

Jesse looked good and terrified, but managed to say, "Just do it then."

Archie frowned and said, "That's it? You want me to kill you without hearing the other options?"

Jesse screwed his face into a hateful glare and said, "What then? You'll let me live if I stay quiet?"

Archie patted him roughly on the side of the head, and said, "Allie and I aren't going to kill you, Jesse, but we have very powerful friends who are more than happy to do our dirty work. You breathe a word about this to *anyone*, and I will personally send them straight to Keldrosa to make you regret it. Don't look shocked — yes, I know where you're from."

Jesse swallowed loudly and his glare lost its bite. "And what do you think you'll find there? It's a big city."

Archie snorted a laugh and said, "It's the *north*, Jesse. If our friends get up there and ask ten people where to find your house, all ten will kindly point to it and give them a bite to eat on the way. And we all know about big northern families, so think twice about how many brothers and sisters you're endangering with your antics, because you will find nothing left of them but ashes." Archie cocked his head dangerously and asked, "Still feel like taking this to the Zhauri?"

Jesse looked to me again, begging me to tell him this was an elaborate joke. When I kept my face callous, Jesse finally breathed, "I won't tell anybody."

Archie grinned and said, "*Good.* Because if you mess this up for us, it'll be the worst mistake of your life." Archie looked to me and asked, "Anything to add?"

I shook my head, knowing that shock was seeping through my cold expression.

Archie resheathed the knife onto Jesse's side and took a second to smooth the wrinkles he'd left on Jesse's shoulders.

"Good talk, friend," Archie said.

Archie walked back to me with a spring in his step, put an arm around my shoulders, and we left without looking back. I felt sick. Beyond sick. Guilty, disgusting, and dizzy to name a few. And a little worried, because the care-free person next to me *looked* like Archie, but everything else about him was wrong.

We were two turns away from Jesse before I looked up and asked, "Are you ok?"

Archie nodded a calm, lighthearted nod as he lowered his arm and said, "I'm fine. This is my hidden talent. I can play any part that suits me. I can fool anyone."

I would have believed him too, except the color in his face wasn't quite right. I also found myself looking at his hands, where the slightest of tremors rattled his fingers. I reached to set my palm in his, and the strangest thing happened. His shield didn't stop me.

"Are the two of you lost?"

We both startled at Kit's deep voice. He had two other Zhauri with him — the new blond one, and Iquis.

"Sorry," I said, quickly dropping Archie's hand as I clenched mine into fists. "Just tried a new shortcut and it didn't play out. Didn't mean to bother you."

I ducked my head to pass them, and none of the three stepped aside to let us by, but they also didn't stop us.

Archie glanced back as they began conversing in Icilic. "We're *beyond* lucky Maverick wasn't with them."

"Could you understand them?" I asked.

Archie laughed softly and a little color returned to his cheeks. "Emery taught me some of the northern language years ago, so I can say *yes, no,* and all the swear words."

A faint smile crossed my face too, but I still felt sick.

We reached his room in silence and ended up sitting on his bed with a hand of space between us, both leaning back against the wall

264

with our own thoughts. I wished I had my old box of sand to spill in front of the door and secure it, but I hadn't seen it since Dincara.

"I... just threatened an innocent family," Archie finally said, looking straight ahead, his gaze falling hollow.

I sighed, because I couldn't exactly deny it. "I'm sorry I put you in a position where you had to."

"Don't be sorry," Archie replied. "Sir Avery's the one who's going to be sorry. Worst shanking Epic of the century..."

"Yeah... but you didn't want to talk to Tarace because of the danger, and I dragged you into it anyway." I played anxiously with my fingers. "Now if I go down, I'm taking you with me."

Archie let a laugh escape. "Well, you sure as life aren't going down without me."

My stomach twisted with something that felt like guilt. "Maybe you should let me suffer my own consequences sometimes," I suggested softly. "I don't listen to you, I'm not always very nice to you, I haven't really done a lot for you... I don't know why you feel so obligated to take care of me."

Archie shot me a smirk like I was being ridiculous, and said "We've been friends a long time. And I mean the laugh together, cry together, face the best and worst times together kind of friends. You were there for me when my life was a wreck, and I'm here for you now." He shrugged and said, "You're worth taking care of."

He stopped like he'd said too much and wouldn't look at me.

"I know your secret," I said, surprising even myself with the sudden confession. "Sav told me who your mother was. I understand why you're worried about getting close."

Archie clamped his jaw shut and nodded sharply.

"And I hear you don't do well losing people you're close to."

Archie closed his eyes and let his shoulders sink back against the wall. "It's easier to live with everyone at a distance," he said, releasing a deep breath. "I never meant to let you slip through the cracks."

We fell into a sleepy quiet once more, and I leaned my head back against his wall to let my eyelids fall closed, listening to my breathing, to his breathing, and the silence of the deep underground.

"No, I told you," Archie's frantic voice woke me.

I didn't even hesitate this time, setting my feet on the cold floor, dragging my blankets to where he lay curled in a tight, unmoving ball beside the door like the last time I'd stayed over.

I laid one of the thicker blankets on the floor beside him as he twitched sharply. He shook his head, getting even more worked up. "I tried to tell you," his voice broke halfway through the plea, and he tucked his head down to cough a deep sob from his throat.

I intertwined my fingers with his, noticing again that his shield wasn't stopping me, and he squeezed them tightly. "I'm sorry," he cried to his own chest as his entire body trembled. I used my free hand to toss the extra blankets I'd brought over us both, and Archie gasped, looking straight at me. I wasn't sure if he'd woken, or if this was part of the dream.

"I have to leave," he told me, breathing loudly through his nose to clear it. "I can't keep doing this."

"We'll talk about it tomorrow," I whispered. "Get some sleep."

He shook his head again and said, "You're in danger when you're with me. I dreamed..." he tried to gesture toward all of me, but I refused to release his hand. "The blood was everywhere. I tried to stop it, but—"

"That's all it was," I said gently. "Just a dream."

He pulled his free arm over his face and continued to shudder and take sharp, irregular breaths as I wriggled closer and draped an arm over his shoulder.

I pressed my chin to his forehead and whispered, "Hey, I'm right here. We're both safe."

Archie laughed to himself and said, "No we're not. I don't know how we ever could be."

I couldn't help but sigh, because he was right. We'd left too many loose ends too close to the fire.

Tarace was probably in another city right now, gathering opinions from our other leaders. Sir Avery was likely out talking to Ratuan and Sav, which couldn't bode well for anyone. Jesse could turn us in at any moment, or the Zhauri could come to collect on our information.

"But I'm glad you're here," Archie murmured, almost too softly to hear.

I smiled into his hair and said, "Me too. Go back to sleep."

I woke up on the floor this time, bolting upright as I realized nobody was next to me.

"Hey! I'm still here," Archie said, standing next to flickering orange flames in the fireplace. "I was just about to wake you."

I gazed at the fire to let my eyes adjust, smelling deep spices in the air. "What's that smell?"

"This is the tea I've been telling you about," he said, carefully handing a cup down to me on the floor. I wrapped my hands around the heated porcelain and made sure it was steady before bringing it beneath my nose, letting it cool.

"I can't believe you decided to share," I said, the sharp scent of autumn filling me with warmth.

"Yeah, well..." he smiled hesitantly. "Nothing says *sorry about last night* like a good cup of your favorite tea."

I smiled at him and took a sip, finding the tea spicy and lightly sweet. Archie sat on his already-made bed and sipped at his own, and I could see why he lived for this stuff.

"Archie?" I asked, drawing his attention as I set a hand on his knee. "Is something wrong with your shield?"

He settled his eyes on my touch before placing his warm palm on mine. "I think... I've come to consider you a part of me," he said slowly, giving me a sad smile as he pulled my hand up and returned it to me. "I've heard of things like this happening with mages, but... I think we can both agree we shouldn't-"

A sharp rapping on his door cut him short. I leapt to my feet as Archie pulled it open and Corliss hunched forward, breathing heavily like she'd sprinted to reach us. "You need to get out of here," she said between quick breaths, eyes on me. "Sir Avery just came into the Wreck and told the Zhauri to detain you. The Dincaran kids are making their break this morning."

"What?" I exclaimed, already grabbing my belt of short swords to fasten around my hips. "The Dincaran kids aren't escaping until tomorrow!"

Archie handed over my knife to put in my sandal-laces as Corliss said, "Sir Avery is about to start sending teams to help the kids escape, and I just watched Kit and the new blond Zhauri leave the Wreck on their way to your room. Archie's is probably next on their list."

I glanced fearfully at Archie, but I didn't even need to ask the question. He already had his own sword sheathed at his side and was pulling on a light pair of boots.

"Has the escape already started?" Archie asked. "Or do we have time to warn the Escalis that Izfazara's in danger?"

"I have no idea," Corliss said, "but I'll come with you to find out."

Archie fixed a determined stare on both of us as I stuffed my bag beneath his bed, opting to leave it behind for the sake of speed.

"We're not letting the Zhauri take us," he said. "If we run into them on the way out, do everything in your power to fight back. Especially if they've split the group in two."

CHAPTER TWENTY TWO

Ratuan-day came but twice this year, and this time Ebby clamped her hands together, holding them to her chest on the edge of her bed as she waited. This was what she wanted. She would be going home with everyone she cared about.

A knock on her door violently startled her and she tightened her mind as Vack pushed it open.

"Aren't you coming?" he asked, stepping in with a frown. "We're supposed to meet down at Jalia's house. Let's go." He held a hand out to her, since Ebby was still struggling to jump properly, and she froze. "What's wrong with you? I thought you were excited for Mir to show us the baby falcons."

"I was..." she faltered, pulling her feet onto her bed and folding her legs with her dress draped over her knees. "I just don't feel like going anymore."

Vack walked all the way over to her with a scrutinizing squint, trying to read her face as she clamped her mind shut. "What's wrong?" he demanded.

"Nothing," Ebby replied. "I'm just not feeling well."

Vack stepped back with a hint of worry in his eyes. "You're an Epic. You can't be sick. We should tell my father—"

"No! No, I'm not that sick," Ebby said, trying to maintain an illusion of calm while keeping her thoughts locked in silence. "I'm really just thinking, that's all."

Vack frowned and held his palms up like a scathing question. "*About?*"

"Just... thinking," Ebby said. It was incredibly hard to think up a lie while keeping her thoughts on lockdown.

"You're leaving today, aren't you?" Vack said.

Ebby felt her cheeks flush red at the thought she might singlehandedly destroy all Ratuan's hard work and planning. "What makes you ask?"

"I just wanted to see how you'd react," Vack said, grinning at his own cleverness. "You look guiltier than a chicken thief, Tearsalt. It's alright, I'm not going to tell anyone." He looked behind himself, then swept his hand to the side, shutting her door. "I guess... It wouldn't hurt for us to talk before you go."

His grin faded quickly as he glanced around the room, like an animal suddenly realizing he'd trapped himself.

Ebby gestured to the empty space on the bed beside her and found herself smirking at Vack's hesitation. "Vack, you look like you're in pain."

"I just don't like..." he gestured back and forth between them, at a loss for words. "These conversations."

"We can keep it short," Ebby said, and Vack finally leapt onto her bed with both feet, settling to face her with his legs crossed.

They fell silent and Vack bit at the side of his thumb nail.

"What are we going to do?" she whispered. Vack just shifted his eyes up to her, waiting for the rest of the question. "About each other. What are we going to do when everybody wants us to kill each other?"

"We could agree not to," he said. Ebby liked the sound of that. "It would haunt me my entire life if I killed you," he said.

Ebby raised her eyebrows and asked, "Would it really?" Vack nodded and then shot a meaningful glare her way. "And I hope you feel the same?"

His defensiveness made her smile. "I don't want you dead," she said. "I don't want anybody to die."

Vack shifted uncomfortably and then folded his hands in his lap, arm spikes protruding to either side as he chewed on his next words. He *never* thought about what he was saying before he said it, so maybe this goodbye meant something to him after all. Finally, he asked, "Are you sure you want to go?"

She'd also *never* expected to hear those words from him. Was he serious? Before she could even think what to say, Vack pressed on, "I just think it's stupid for us to be fighting when we could actually do something that matters. And... I'm sorry if I haven't always been exactly nice to you."

Ebby launched her eyebrows into the sky at *that* understatement and let out a laugh of disbelief. "No. You haven't been." And yet, the poorly worded apology took a giant weight off her shoulders.

"I just... I was mean because I didn't want to like you," Vack said, immediately adding, "I still don't like you very much, but I don't want to be your enemy. And we've seen Sir Avery. He doesn't want you back because he loves you. He wants to use you as a weapon."

Ebby didn't argue that point. She knew it was hopeless.

"And... Jalia likes you," Vack said, running out of persuasion rather quickly. This wasn't a strength of his.

"That's why you think I should stay? Because Jalia likes me?"

Vack looked at his hands and said, "I'm worried what will happen to you if you go back."

Ebby just watched him for a minute, knowing his insides were squirming more with every second of silence. "Vack... That's the nicest thing you've ever said to me."

Vack just shrugged like he had given up all hope of being a respectable man one day. "Yeah, well... I think you should stay."

Ebby found herself considering it, then thought how badly Ratuan would be hurt if he could hear this conversation. She'd just die if he ever found out.

"He's using you, you know," Vack said casually, as though merely pointing out Ratuan's hair color.

Ebby realized she'd let her guard slip, and she frowned heavily. "Ratuan loves me," she said, emboldened by the words, even if Ratuan had never said them.

"I know he does. But he also knows everything about you, and he knows how to manipulate you. You give him power."

Ebby squinted at him, because she wouldn't back down when it came to Ratuan. "I only give him power to do things that are good. That's all he asks of me."

Vack shrugged as though it didn't matter to him, but Ebby caught a brief taste of care and concern in the air before Vack realized he'd let his thoughts slip too. "I'm going to leave before Mir and Jalia come looking for me," he said. They'd officially breached his acceptable level of discomfort.

"Alright," Ebby said to her bedframe, reluctant to let Vack walk away so quickly. She just wanted to argue a little longer, or spend an extra minute sharing complaints about the *Twenty-five Powers of Conflict.*

Vack was on his feet but hadn't moved, as though torn between the desire for a swift getaway and something still needing to be said.

Ebby turned her eyes up to him and waited, knowing he couldn't survive the silence for more than a minute.

Vack folded his arms and said, "I just want to tell you... You can always come back. If you want to." He shrugged, still unable to

273

look at her. "Even after we've fought a hundred times and claimed we were never friends, there will always be a place for you here."

Ebby's throat began to constrict, and she tried to hide it with a scoff. "We never *were* friends, Vack."

"I know," he replied. "But we could have been."

Ebby's throat grew painfully tight as she realized Vack had his hand out to shake hers. And he was finally looking at her. Ebby grabbed his thickly gloved hand in hers and shook on what was probably goodbye for a very long time.

Vack caught her thoughts and replied, *yes, but not forever.*

Ebby curled her knees up to her chest as a cold sense of loneliness crept through her. She didn't know why it was there. She'd never liked Vack. Jalia, yes, maybe a little, but never Vack.

The escape began quietly below as the kids opened every cell door in the whole dungeon with their keys from Production. Ebby prepared to jump down to Prince Avalask's hall, and realized with sudden fear that he wasn't there. He had been! Less than an hour ago!

She checked the quarters where he sometimes slept, realizing in a panic that she had no idea where he'd gone, and she still couldn't locate people.

Ebby wanted to cry in frustration, but since so much was at stake, she invented a way to find someone right on the spot. Being the artist she was, she tried to recreate Prince Avalask's distinct presence in her mind. She used *everything* from the smell of smoke and ashes embedded in his clothes to the sense of authority and humor he carried with him. Then Ebby cast a wide and receptive net of open thoughts through the city, simultaneously feeling the joys, worries, and purpose of every soul in a three mile radius.

Ebby had to dim the overwhelming sea of thoughts as she looked for just one set. It was like looking for a red wildflower among rolling fields of orange. Except, this was much more beautiful. Every life below her was a brilliant spark, and when she looked at the city like this, it positively glittered.

Ebby was lucky Prince Avalask was even in the city, and she found him in the crypts where majestic, feminine beauty had been captured in glass and frozen in time. Prince Avalask was sitting on the glass base of a woman holding a fist and a falcon to the sky. Savaul leaned against the one statue wrought from gold while Gataan picked at his teeth with the tip of a knife. They had no idea what was happening beneath them.

Savaul rolled his eyes up to the vaulted ceiling as Prince Avalask argued, "Their idiot king crippled them by killing all their mages. If we don't count the kids below us, they've probably got less than fifty left."

"And that's why we should kill those kids — so they only have fifty," Savaul said.

"We're not killing children. How many times do I have—"

"How many family members do we have to lose before you wage this war seriously? Don't you miss our mother? Don't you remember what they did to our sister?" Savaul turned his gaze up to the golden face of his sister, the one with whom he'd never speak again. Loneliness stung him the same way it ached in Ebby's heart, and Ebby pulled her thoughts away to avoid empathizing.

"We don't have to wage a war that's over," Prince Avalask said.

Savaul lowered his chin and said, "This is the greatest mistake we could ever make." Now Prince Avalask flicked his eyes toward the ceiling in irritation, a gesture that caused Savaul to snarl at him. "And what, Avalask? You think they're going to keep to themselves for the rest of time? You give them ten years, and those Dincaran and Dragonan kids will all be mages. They will decide this entire continent is rightfully theirs, *again*, and then we will be exactly back where we started. Give them time to train those kids unhindered, and they'll destroy us."

Prince Avalask just stared at his nails, waiting for the rant to end, and his disinterest rubbed a nerve with Savaul. "You know, I'm sure we'd all be docile if we could forget the past as quickly as you forgot Dreya."

"Don't drag my wife into this." Prince Avalask brought no magic to his hands, but his angry words would be enough to terrify the wits out of anyone. "Don't you *ever* talk about her."

"We all cared about her, Avalask. I don't relish the thought of killing children, but sometimes hard decisions have to be made so we don't have to live like this anymore. What about *our* kids?"

"I'm tired of death," Prince Avalask said, brushing his dark hair behind his shoulder. "You have no idea what it feels like, experiencing the fear of the victim you're laying hands on. Even if we can only get ten years of peace, I'll take it."

"I can't feel it like you can," Savaul said, "but I can see fear in their eyes. And I know you like to think the worst of me, but I don't enjoy that."

Gataan got a particularly stubborn piece of food out of his teeth and chuckled as he held the knife point up to look. "The fear is my favorite part."

Prince Avalask didn't even acknowledge Gataan, but shot Savaul a glare of revulsion severe enough to declare a silent end to their argument. Then his mind began to wander, checking on cities and family members out of habit to make sure all was well.

Ice flooded into Ebby's heart because she knew she needed to keep him distracted for five more minutes, and she was seconds away from failing. She would have been too frightened to move if not for Ratuan relying on her. But by the end of the day, she would

276

be back with him, protected by Sir Avery while the Dragona celebrated her return. She *would* be brave.

Ebby knew she was the worst jumper on the face of the continent, but she focused on Prince Avalask, got a running start, and leapt into the air. The glass room disappeared and the entire world spun around her, spitting her out in the crypt with disorienting momentum.

Ebby didn't have a hope of landing on her feet, but even worse, she slammed straight into Savaul as he leapt back with a startled yelp. He immediately grabbed her, and Ebby panicked at the feel of his hands. She thrashed and punched him twice in the ribs and once in the mouth before kicking his shins and jerking away, by which time Prince Avalask had grabbed her upper arms to yank her back anyway.

"What's gotten into you?" Prince Avalask demanded as Savaul hunched forward breathlessly to grab the leg she'd kicked.

"I heard what you're trying to do!" Ebby shouted at Savaul as he spit a mouthful of blood to the ground. "Those are my friends, and you don't touch them!"

She could hear the shock in Prince Avalask's voice as he asked his brother, "Did she break it?"

Savaul winced and nodded before shooting a livid glance at Ebby, startling her because she hadn't realized she *could* break somebody's leg. She squinted back as though she'd intended to hurt him, and she felt a sense of power she never had with Prince Avalask and Vack. She was stronger than Savaul.

"Nobody is touching your friends," Prince Avalask said from behind her. "We're sending them home."

Ebby froze and turned around with wide eyes. *"What?"*

"They're going home. We're ending this war today, on a good note."

Prince Avalask let go of her, and Ebby stood where she was, wary of Gataan watching her hungrily, and realizing why Savaul thought they were making the worst mistake of their lives.

"Today?" Ebby repeated, overwhelmed by sudden panic and indecision. She needed to tell Ratuan, but it was already too late. The escape was already in full effect.

"What's wrong?" Prince Avalask asked. "I thought you'd be happy."

"I am," Ebby said a little too quickly. The lines of his brow deepened as he tried to analyze the situation, and Ebby clamped her mind shut until Prince Avalask glanced back at Savaul again.

"Let me see it," he said, crouching as Savaul rolled up his dark pant leg. A deep purpling welt had developed where internal blood surrounded the wound. Prince Avalask set a hand against it and Ebby could feel he was letting his mind wander once more.

"I don't..." Ebby stuttered, hating herself for not being able to think of a better distraction. "I don't know if I want to go back."

Ebby cringed as nobody said anything in response. It was a lie. She wasn't actually considering staying. No. Never. Not her.

Prince Avalask shot Savaul an *I-told-you-so* glance, while Savaul's expression looked more like *dear shanking life, you have to be kidding me.*

Gataan just looked like he was barely refraining from leaping at her, and as Ebby took a step away from him, his gaze followed her like hunter on prey.

Prince Avalask cleared his throat and asked, "What's changed your mind?"

Ebby shrugged and folded her arms tightly across her chest, wishing Ratuan could be here to help her lie convincingly. "Jalia's always been nice to me, and I've learned so much here. And I don't want to hurt Vack, and I don't want Vack to hurt me, and..." her breaths became sharper as the real fear came to the tip of her tongue. Sir Avery. She'd seen him, and he was terrifying. She didn't want to hug him or call him *father*.

"Ebby?" Prince Avalask stayed crouched at eye level, even though Savaul's leg seemed all better. "Nothing would make me happier than for you to call this your home. If that's what you want." He looked pointedly at both Savaul and Gataan. "Could you leave us for a couple minutes?"

His brothers looked irritated beyond all measure, and before either of them could move, a sharp jab of panic stabbed through Ebby. Prince Avalask leapt to his feet as the same desperation tore into him, and Ebby threw her sight and senses out to a massive glass staircase where a high pitched wail echoed piercingly.

"HEEEEEEEELLLLP!"

Jalia was sprinting up the black glass steps in sheer terror, and Prince Avalask leapt quickly from the crypts to investigate.

Ebby was suddenly alone with Savaul and Gataan, looking peeved and hungry, respectively.

Without hesitating to wonder about her abilities, Ebby jumped after the Epic and landed next to Jalia in a clumsy stumble, lucky to have her feet beneath her as she fell against the glass steps and sliced both her palms open with a shriek.

"He took Vack!" Jalia sobbed, grabbing Prince Avalask's hands to stay up. In one expulsion of distress, she cried, "We were down exploring caves while we waited for Mir, and Sir Avery found us, grabbed him—"

"Where did they go?" Prince Avalask asked, his voice a cold stone.

Jalia shook her head frantically and gulped in air. "I don't know."

Prince Avalask turned to Ebby for only a second, but the fury in his eyes stopped time for her. He knew this was her fault.

She stood frozen as Prince Avalask jumped into the air.

Jalia sobbed and shuddered, holding a hand over her mouth. She took a steadying breath and asked Ebby, "Where'd they go?"

Ebby's throat constricted and her hands began shaking as she swept the area in her mind, looking for any of the three Epics.

She should have known this would happen. No, she *had* known it was coming, and she'd told Ratuan exactly where to find him.

One of the kids who could communicate by thought shouted across the city to her, *We're meeting at the western surface entrance. Sir Avery's there with the Dragona's mages, and Ratuan's almost there too.*

Ebby's knees partially collapsed, forcing her to lean against the wall. That was probably where Prince Avalask had gone too, if Sir Avery had Vack.

"Where did Sir Avery take him?" Jalia asked again, wiping her eyes to read Ebby even though she could barely speak. "You have to tell me he's alright!"

"I… I didn't mean for him to get hurt." She tried to breathe, to shake the guilt from her soul.

"Are you saying you helped plan this?" Jalia demanded.

"No! I helped, but I didn't know the plan. I didn't know… they would…" She couldn't bring herself to say *kill Vack.* And she couldn't let it happen.

Ebby found Prince Avalask in a split second, then told Jalia, "I'll fix this," and leapt into the air.

CHAPTER TWENTY THREE

Archie grabbed our shoulders and jerked the three of us to a skidding stop in the autumn leaves, *right* before we reached the entrance to the Escali world and an entire ring of Human mages gathered around it.

"*What?*" I whispered frantically, seeing my sister among the tense, waiting group, along with Tarace, Jesse, Terry, Sir Avery, and two of the most dangerous Zhauri brothers — Kit and Iquis.

"They must be planning to meet the kids out here," Archie said. "Come on, there's another way in about half a mile north."

I took two sharp, panting breaths to reacquaint my lungs with something other than pain, and then we took off again.

The three of us leapt quickly down between boulders and gnarled tree roots to enter the Escali caves further north, and bolted down toward the dungeons.

It was nowhere close to a straight shot. The tunnels twisted and corkscrewed into the earth, forking several times in directions that made me thankful I had Archie and Corliss.

"Whoa, stop," I hissed as we came out on level ground and sped past a split in the cave. I screeched to a halt and turned around.

Three Escalis lay unmoving on the ground in a connecting room, two covered in purpled bruises and welts like they'd been beaten to death, and the third scorched and charred.

Corliss took a tentative step toward the closest and crouched to look for signs of life before turning back to gape in astonishment.

"They're just *kids*," Archie whispered. "How could they do this?"

I heard a whisper from further down the flat tunnel, sounding suspiciously like, "Shoot them."

Archie whirled as I did, grabbing me as an arrow screamed through the air and stopped dead in front of my face, falling to the floor at his golden shimmer of a shield.

Lightning leapt into my hands, and Archie let me go as I threw my arms out to unleash on our attackers. My destruction crackled harmlessly into the wall as they dodged back from view, and I kept my hands out, antsy and ready for them to reappear.

"How could you?" The Escali's distress echoed harshly around the cave walls. "Izfazara was always good to your kind!"

My heart plummeted. Izfazara couldn't be dead.

But the other muttered, "Savaul will be king, and we'll never have to deal with them again."

Corliss was still in the room beside us and mouthed the words, *Run on three.*

She counted down on her fingers, one, two, then three, and bolted toward us as we spun to sprint back the way we'd come.

"We need to get back to the Tally caves," Corliss said quickly. "Turn here!"

"What?" Archie exclaimed, eyes wide. "The Tally caves are back this way."

"This is a shortcut," Corliss said in haste, her eyes begging us to trust her. "I *promise*. Let's go."

Archie shot me a hesitant glance before taking off after her, as though I might have any clue where we were.

We tore through the tunnels, spotted only once more before we reached the Tally caves, but those who saw us decided we were worth pursuing as well.

"Oh shanking life," I breathed as we ran past large, blackened scorch marks along the walls, probably from Emery.

"Whoa!" Corliss shouted, flinging her hand to the side, her power sweeping an arrow off its course at the last moment as those in pursuit caught up.

"Both of you go," Archie said, shoving us ahead. "I'll follow in the back."

He threw an arm up to stop one more arrow, and Corliss and I took off toward the large marble doors, hopefully harboring our friends. There was one word written across the door, *literally in blood,* a Human word, but written with the Escali vowel for *UH*, with a curl above it that represented the sound *R*, and a slashed arc below for the sound *N*.

Corliss yanked the doors open, and slammed them closed once the three of us were inside.

"They're already gone," I said in a panic as Archie threw a metal bar through the door handles and somebody rammed a shoulder against them.

Archie and I had identical thoughts and dashed back to the fireplace, our only escape without trying to fight our way out.

"No," Corliss said, glancing between us in desperation. "Come on. You know how I get with tight spaces."

I nearly let out a bark of laughter, because given the circumstances, a close squeeze was the very least of our worries.

"We don't have a choice," I said as another loud crash startled us. "Closed doors are only temporary."

283

"Come on, we'll both be with you," Archie said. "I'll go first. If I can make it through, you know you can too."

I could not, for the life of me, understand why Corliss was eyeing the fireplace with greater fear than the banging doors behind us, but she seemed truly mortified.

"This won't kill you. *They* will," Archie said, pointing to the doors, then extending his palm to her.

Corliss reached hesitantly toward him before Archie grabbed her hand and just about dragged her back to the fireplace. He wedged himself into the crevice, and I heard him muttering encouragement before she finally pressed herself in after him.

A vicious smash against the doors shook my nerves before I followed.

"I shanking hate this," Corliss said, taking a rattled breath in the dark space. "This is shanking stupid, and when we get out of here, we are all going on shanking diets."

I snorted a laugh and followed it with a quick, "Sorry. I'm sorry. You're doing great."

Archie leapt down to the massive staircase below, and Corliss eagerly jumped after him.

I got my feet into position to drop through the floor, but stopped when I heard words below that weren't from Corliss or Archie.

Archie asked, "Why does everybody think we killed him?"

I maneuvered low enough to see Archie and Corliss holding their hands up, away from their weapons. Three Escalis ascended the stairs from below, two with swords, and one with a double bladed staff.

Archie and Corliss slowly backed up the stairs as a long-faced Escali replied, "Savaul says Tallies betrayed Izfazara. Your kind introduced him to the kids, breaking the spell that protected him, and the kids used about twenty different powers to kill him. Have you *any* idea what fate awaits you now?"

"Why would we want to kill Izfazara?" Corliss asked, just as the Escalis walked beneath me. "He gave us a place to call home. Savaul is going to have us hunted to the corners of the continent."

I rained lightning down on the three Escalis, watching them jerk in surprise to see me before they crumpled to the ground. I kept the stream up for a good five seconds longer than necessary because I didn't want them getting back up for a long while.

"Thanks," Archie called up to me. "You can come dow — wait! Stay up, STAY UP!" he shouted.

Corliss shrieked, "Go go go!" She and Archie took off up the stairs in a frantic dash, and I felt my stomach drop.

The Zhauri death hound, the lightning fast shanking *death hound*, bolted up the stairs after them, and I heard them collaborating in a panic to keep the thing at bay as it nearly caught up. Maverick, Zeen, and the newest Zhauri must be close, probably helping the kids.

I didn't know what to do. Their voices disappeared as they fled, leaving me rooted to the spot in shock, alone.

I could drop down and risk running into more Escalis, or the Zhauri, apparently. Or I could turn straight around and *definitely* run into the Escalis still trying to get through the marble doors.

I leapt down to the staircase and climbed the glass-flecked steps as quietly as possible, trying to keep from being sick as I began to pass rooms occupied by Escali bodies, bludgeoned, scorched, and riddled with holes full of grey dust. Some of them had no markings at all to reveal the natures of their demise, but not a single Human kid lay among them.

I reached a long stretch with no more signs of fighting, probably meaning I'd taken a different path than the escapees, and continued hiking upward wherever I could.

Young shouts and screams resonated faintly above me and I bolted toward them, but before I ever reached the kids, the tunnel before me forked. The voices echoed from the right, but I could see daylight to my left. An Escali woman spotted me from behind, and before she could accuse me of killing her king, I bolted left to get away from her, towards the freedom of the outside.

CHAPTER TWENTY FOUR

bby landed haphazardly in a field of cotton-corn, where the tall, dense stalks hid her from a large group of mages circling a great commotion. She made herself invisible, blocked her thoughts, shaded her presence, masked the loud thudding of her heart, and headed straight toward the frightened yelps and snarls she could hear from Vack.

The cotton-corn caught on her white dress as she dashed out of the field and heard Prince Avalask shouting, "I'm not shading her! If you can't see her, it's because she's hiding herself!"

Ebby was the fourth Epic in the clearing around a cave mouth, with the fathers squared off and Sir Avery holding Vack in a one armed vise. Vack kicked his feet out, hissed, writhed, and then whimpered when Sir Avery tightened his hold on him, crushing Vack against his chest.

"I'm ready to end this," Sir Avery spat at Vack's father. "I can't go another day wondering what you're doing to her, not knowing if she's even alive. Give her back, or say goodbye to your own!"

Prince Avalask yelled, "You know I never did anything to her!" and Ebby reached her mind out to Vack.

I'm right here, she whispered.

Terror flooded into her as she brushed against Vack's mind, unlike anything she'd ever felt from him. Every bit of him grabbed her presence and held tightly, crying *help me help me help me,* as though his soul was trying to jump right out of his body to escape Sir Avery.

"DON'T YOU DARE!" Prince Avalask shouted as a short rope appeared in Sir Avery's hand, and he wrapped it around Vack's neck to slowly begin strangling him. The end.

"YOU TELL HIM GOODBYE!" Sir Avery screamed, spit flying from his lips. "It will be more of a farewell than you gave me and my daughter!"

"Avery!" the Escali Epic took a shaky step forward with his arms held apart, as though surrendering. "Don't do this. Please." Silence fell over the field as Vack's struggling grew weaker and he locked pleading eyes with his father as he tried to gasp for air. "You know he's all I have."

Ebby panicked and reached her mind out to Prince Avalask. *Just tell me what to do and I'll do it!*

As soon as he felt her presence, he jerked around to look at her, then reappeared beside her and snatched her up.

Ebby screamed as her feet left the ground and she became visible. The arm around her waist felt strangely protective, but Prince Avalask also wrapped a glowing hand around her neck and shouted, "Is this what you want? We'll just kill them both here and now? Let's be done with this!"

Ebby flung her terrified feelings of betrayal at Prince Avalask, *I was trying to help you!*

He didn't respond with worded thoughts, but Ebby felt Prince Avalask's full reassurance she wouldn't be hurt, no matter what happened to Vack. And she knew him well enough to believe it.

Sir Avery said, "We'll trade. An Epic for an Epic." He released the rope from around Vack's neck and let his feet touch the ground.

As Vack bent forward to cough and gasp, Sir Avery wrenched his hands behind his back and fused the rope around his wrists so he still couldn't go anywhere.

The person Ebby wanted most appeared from the depths of the Escali caves with a mob of kids she recognized behind him. "Ratuan!" she shrieked, struggling to break free from Prince Avalask. Ratuan saw her and breathlessly mouthed *Ebby?* He was so close!

Ratuan obviously couldn't run at Prince Avalask, so he ran at Vack instead and launched a fist into Vack's stomach. Ebby yelped too as Vack doubled over, still held up by Sir Avery, and Ratuan used his elbow to strike Vack across the face. "Tell your father to let her go!" Ratuan shouted at Vack who was bleeding from nose and mouth. Vack hissed at Ratuan and twisted sharply to kick Ratuan in the jaw with a blow that threw Ratuan to the ground.

Prince Avalask flicked a palm through the air to fling Ratuan all the way back into the trees, his hands and eyes taking on a brilliant glow as Sir Avery shot raw crackling power at him. The Epic kept a tight hold on Ebby, but turned so she was behind him, and he could battle Sir Avery with one hand. Sir Avery dropped Vack so he could channel magic through both palms, and he threw fire and lightning at Prince Avalask, shouting, "If you want to trade, do it now!"

Ebby heard Prince Avalask's deep voice in her mind, *This may be the last time I see you. Grow up to be different, Ebby.*

Prince Avalask leapt into the air, leaving Ebby behind, and Sir Avery took his place in less than a second. Her father knelt immediately in front of her with wide, terrified eyes, his arms held passively apart. "Ebby?" he said frantically, as though afraid she might not recognize him.

Ebby quickly took in his brown eyes with just a hint of muted blue in the middle, and saw the deep lines of worry permanently creased around them. He *did* care about her. She wanted to say something in return, but broke into tears instead and ran into his open arms. Ebby expected a sense of comfort to envelop her as he wrapped them tightly around her shoulders, but it just felt like the hug of a stranger. "It's alright," he said softly, and Ebby could feel his chest rise as he took a deep breath. "It's over."

Ebby couldn't help knowing nothing was over. Her nightmare of a life was just beginning. Sobs wracked her entire body, and as she gulped air, she realized how unfamiliar he smelled. Like mud, rain, and destruction.

She turned her head to make sure Vack and Prince Avalask were gone, but an entire tree had wrapped its thick limbs around Prince Avalask, and two mages in white cloaks fought him, one taking hold of his arms while the other dug his fingertips into the Epic's skull. Ebby couldn't tell what the two women with outstretched hands were doing to Vack, but he was struggling just to get to his feet with nobody touching him.

"No," Ebby breathed, but when she tried to pull away from Sir Avery, he kept his tight hold on her.

"I want Avalask alive," Sir Avery shouted to the mages, and Ebby looked back into his eyes just long enough to see they were hard and determined. Vack was going to die.

"No!" Ebby screamed, trying to break free from his grip on her shoulders.

"Ebby!" he commanded, and she could feel forcefully calming thoughts at the edge of her mind. "You're safe. Just calm down."

"Ratuan!" she shrieked, seeing her best friend halfway between her and Vack. He had a knife in his hand. He could help. "Help me!" Ebby cried, fighting against Sir Avery with every limb, every thought. "Ratuan, help!"

Ratuan's hazel eyes met hers. "Hang on," he said in reassurance, giving her an encouraging smile before he flipped around and ran at Vack.

"NOOO!" Ebby screamed after him, but Sir Avery pulled her cheek against his chest so she couldn't see.

"Don't watch. It'll be over quickly."

"It can't be over!" Ebby brought green skinfire to her hands and took him by surprise as she tried to set him aflame. She ghosted herself back through his arms and met his eyes again to lunge mentally at him. Sir Avery recoiled, giving her just enough time to shield herself and sprint away from him, toward Vack and Ratuan.

"Ratuan! Don't do it!" Ebby felt all her magic leave her body and realized why Vack hadn't been able to stand. The women had taken magic from the air around him.

And she was too late.

Vack lay shuddering on the ground with his tied hands pressed into the dirt beneath him. Ratuan crouched over Vack, digging his knife further into Vack's chest as he whispered something to the young Escali about to die.

Ebby couldn't even breathe, let alone say anything. She just found herself standing in a dull stupor, gaping at Ratuan and Vack on the ground until Ratuan stood.

"Ebbs?" Ratuan said, extending his arms to her. "I can't believe it. It's finally over."

Something about Vack's blood on Ratuan's hands snapped Ebby back to reality, and she ran straight past her best friend, ducking beneath his arms to kneel next to Vack.

"Ebby, what are you doing?" Ratuan asked. "This is *Vack*. The one who—"

"I know who he is!" Ebby screamed. "I told you I didn't want anything to happen to him! Vack?" She set her hands on his vicious face and tried to look for any sign of life.

291

Vack's eyes fluttered, but he didn't seem to hear her until he whispered, "Tear-salt."

Ebby snorted an irrational laugh at the fact he would die with an insult on his lips. Then, in his you-are-so-stupid tone, he breathed, "Get the knife out."

Pulling the knife out wouldn't help, especially without any magic in the air, but Ebby wasn't about to deny him anything. She clenched her teeth together and ripped the knife back out, upset by the fact Vack barely flinched.

Prince Avalask was screaming, snarling, and crying out, and Sir Avery appeared next to the mages to help subdue him.

Ebby was nothing without magic, so she ran at one of the women keeping her disabled and rammed her shoulder into the woman's stomach. "Stop it!" she cried, hitting the mage three times before Ratuan grabbed Ebby's fists to hold her back. "No, we need magic!" Ebby shouted at Ratuan as he pulled her away from Vack. She stumbled over her feet as Ratuan tried to drag her and she tried to hold her ground.

"ALLIE!" Prince Avalask's voice cut through the chaos. "GET VACK! THE MAGES NEXT TO VACK!"

Allie had just sprinted out of the cave, and Ebby could see her frantically taking in the situation as Sir Avery shouted, "Tally! Come help us with Avalask!"

The choice was hers.

CHAPTER TWENTY FIVE

burst into the cool daylight and the worst decision of my life, all in the same stride. Kit had his hands extended over Prince Avalask, who was struggling to free himself from the grasp of a thick tree limb, and the Zhauri mind mage had two hands around the Epic's head as he thrashed. They also had half a mob around them, just in case.

"ALLIE!" Prince Avalask couldn't even look at me with the mind mage overpowering him, but he bellowed, "GET VACK! THE MAGES NEXT TO VACK!"

Vack lay possibly dead on the ground, and Ebby was screaming, crying, and clawing against Ratuan to get to the Epic who was supposed to be her enemy.

Sir Avery also shouted, "Tally!" and my entire world froze as he demanded I help subdue Prince Avalask.

I had always known I would have to pick between Human and Escali, but I had no idea so much would be on the line when I had to decide. I could feel Liz's eyes on me, wondering why I was even hesitating. On the one hand, I could stay with Liz, continue to live my life in the Dragona, and train with the friends I loved.

But the cost of such luxury would be letting Prince Avalask's son die. Ebby would grow up under Sir Avery's vengeful guidance, traumatized and unopposed, and Sir Avery *would* end the Escalis under those circumstances.

I brought crackling white light into my hands and eyes, which would be more than just conventionally destructive, and looked at Liz for the last time as her sister. I don't know how she guessed, but based on the shock and anger spreading across her face, she knew what I was about to do.

I broke my gaze away and dashed toward the kids, bolting white destruction toward the women keeping Vack incapacitated.

My power should have knocked them both off their feet, but the blinding destruction fizzled into soft grey smoke before it ever reached them.

I swore at myself for not realizing they'd taken the magic out of the air. I had just announced my intentions with an assault that was less than useless.

An uneasy silence swept through everybody who knew me, as though they were trying to understand what they had just witnessed. And the last person to join the stunned group was Archie, who emerged from the cave just in time to *not* know what was going on. My hands glowed brightly, itching to release a more effective flash of energy, and I knew with a gut wrenching certainty who my first target had to be.

I flung my fingers wide and shot a thick flash of lightning at Archie, nearly enough to knock him over despite the shield he instinctually threw between us. I threw my next bolt at Iquis, and it grazed his left shoulder. Prince Avalask gasped in relief as Iquis stumbled back a step, but Kit still wasn't letting him move. My next bolt of destruction ripped through the air on its way to Kit, but he threw himself to the ground and Sir Avery appeared between us to fire an equally aggressive lightning stream back toward me — the same as mine, but *black*.

294

I dropped one knee straight to the ground and launched white lightning at the terrifying bolt of magic that dimmed the entire clearing, except where mine still lit the grass. There was no flash of light, no fire, and no sound as the black and white collided and disappeared, which was more terrifying than a blinding clash of magic. Sir Avery's magic absolutely swallowed mine into nothingness, and the noiseless point of collision crept terrifyingly toward me.

I shot every bit of power I could muster into the silent black bolt of oblivion, and feelings of terror shook my core as my retaliation did nothing.

I had to keep up my stream of destruction and somehow make it stronger or more effective if I wanted to live.

Or...

I flung myself backward into the magic-free bubble around the Epic kids. Sir Avery's bolt of black destruction fizzled and faded into nothing at the barrier, but I also found myself in sudden shock, like I'd been doused in icy water. My body seized up and stopped functioning as Sir Avery dashed back to help Kit and Iquis. I barely kept my feet beneath me and struggled to gasp a breath, cursing the Escali magic that usually strengthened my veins but crippled me now.

It was like I had stepped into a different world, where nobody could reach me unless they chose to run and tackle me, but where I was useless and vulnerable. I forced my fingers to bend, and feeling spread slowly back into my limbs as I desperately coaxed each joint back into working condition. I wouldn't be able to take down either of the women I needed to, but Ratuan might be small enough to grab before I collapsed.

"Allie!" Ebby cried as Ratuan prevented her running to me and she flung her shoulders violently to shake him. "Help me! I know what I want. I need your help!"

295

I stumbled forward, and knowing I was going to fall, I lunged ahead and slung my arms around Ratuan's shoulders, bringing myself, him, and Ebby to the ground in a heap.

"What are you doing?" Ratuan shouted as I latched onto his arms with a sluggish grip, but one that could bend metal.

Ebby squirmed away from Ratuan and got quickly to her feet, her small white dress now bearing red and green stains on the shoulders and around the middle.

And then she froze.

"Ebby!" I shouted. She could *not* back out of this. Not with all I had just given up.

Ebby set her frightened eyes on me, and I realized she was just looking for a hand to hold. She was afraid to act on her own. "Go, go, go, *GO!*" I shouted as Ratuan kicked me and jabbed his elbow into my ribs.

Ebby turned and fled, and Ratuan screamed, "NO! What are you doing?" He thrashed with nearly enough intensity to knock me over as I got his hands pinned into the grass.

"She's alright," I told him quickly, feeling like nothing more than dead, exhausted weight.

"Get off!" Ratuan screamed, working one of his hands free to dig his nails into my arm. He looked up at me with more hate in his eyes than a young face should be able to hold.

"Ratuan—"

"No, don't let her go!" he cried. "Please, I can't lose her again."

I wasn't about to let him up, but his desperation tore at me because it was so sincere. Ratuan truly wanted her back because he loved her.

"Ratuan, listen," I demanded, but my next words were cut short as a rock the width of my foot sailed through the air and hit one of the women in the temple, knocking her unconscious.

"Shanking life!" the other mage swore as a slightly larger stone slammed into her shoulder. I could see Ebby outside the magic-free bubble, levitating another rock up from the ground to fling it toward the mage, which convinced me she was smarter than I'd ever given her credit for. Magic had nothing to do with the momentum of an already-moving stone, and the woman had to leap back to avoid the next one. Ebby sliced both arms dramatically through the air, and I let Ratuan wriggle away as I realized she'd severed the trunk of a now leaning maple tree.

Ratuan bolted straight for her as the tree picked up speed and careened toward the ground, splitting the air between Vack and the still-conscious mage. It was going to crash onto both of them. I made one frantic leap toward Vack and landed on him, ducking my head against his face and throwing my arms over us as soft leaves turned into piercing twigs and branches. My scream turned into a shriek as the largest boughs crashed beside us, leaving us in one piece, but pinned under the weight of the tangled foliage.

A sharp splinter jabbed into my lower back, and I felt a new flood of panic beneath the suffocating mass of leaves. I wanted to thrash until I could pull myself from beneath it, but I couldn't bear injuring Vack any further.

"You'd better be alive, you little brat," I half growled and half cried as I tried to get a look at Vack's face in the dim green light. "Do you feel that?" I shook him slightly as strength filled my limbs again but did nothing to dull the pain of being crushed. "There's magic again. You can heal yourself and get out of here. Come *on.*"

Small hands reached in to grab Vack beneath the shoulders, and Ebby cried, "Don't you dare die!" She must have performed a competitive dive to reach us through the leaves.

She also apparently had the strength of a bear to wrench Vack out into the daylight, giving me just enough wiggle room to twist and pull myself out after them. Ebby escaped the sea of leaves with

Vack in her arms just as Ratuan circled back around the tree and spotted her.

"Get out of here!" I shouted.

Ebby had tears streaming down her face and said, "What about you?"

"You don't owe me anything. JUMP!"

"What are you doing?" Ratuan screamed as he darted toward her and the limp form of Vack hanging in her arms. "Wait, Ebby! Wait!"

Ebby shifted Vack's weight to get a better hold on him, and in the second before Ratuan reached her, she leapt into the air and vanished.

Ratuan froze and whispered, "Don't leave me."

He stared at the space where empty air had replaced Ebby, and he turned slowly to me as I wrenched my last foot out of the snarl of branches. His eyes brimmed with tears of devastation.

I dashed back, even though he hadn't taken a single step toward me, and I gasped sharply as the gash along my lower back cried in agony. I reached both hands back, feeling the warm and slightly sticky indicator of blood, and I caught Liz's eye right before I fled. She looked more furious than sad, and my already broken heart shattered. I might never see her again.

Prince Avalask threw Kit to the ground, and Sir Avery grabbed Prince Avalask with a snarl to keep him from jumping. Archie widened his eyes to beg me to go, and I took a quick breath before turning my back on them all, dashing into the field of tall cotton-corn stalks.

"She is RIGHT THERE!" Sir Avery shouted as I heard the fierce growls of Prince Avalask fighting back. "I don't want excuses. Burn the field down if you have to! Get the other Zhauri and their dogs! Bring her back before she finds a way to hide!"

I was already running full speed when Prince Avalask hurled his thoughts to me. *Keep running! You're better off dead than with the Zhauri.*

I could hear the unmistakable instruction to kill myself if I had to.

Without a hope of rescuing him, I ducked my head and shoved the massive stalks out of my way, knowing I'd have both men and dogs on my trail in seconds, if not an Epic. A broil of fear, guilt, and despair threatened to overwhelm me and drag me to the ground in a fit of sobs, but I had to distance myself from those things — be Archie, not me. And I found it surprisingly easy, maybe since my life depended on it.

I pulled myself into a deep sense of calm where my breaths were quick, but also deep and controlled, and I focused on nothing but the ocean of distance I wanted between us. There was nothing else to fret over. Just run and breathe. Run, breathe, and *think*.

I knew exactly which mages the Dragona had. Terry could jump and move people quickly, but Sir Avery was the only one who could track with magic, and he was busy. I couldn't hunker down and hide in the field because the Zhauri's dogs would lead them straight to me.

So I turned sharply toward the trees, noticing thick grey smoke rising in several places around the field. They were trying to flush me out, which meant they must have already established lookouts to see where I'd emerge. What hope did I have to get out unseen?

I parted the tall stalks in front of me, coming to a lengthy field edge where the farmer had stopped planting seeds. I dropped flat to my stomach and pulled myself toward the safety of the forest, looking both ways to see if I had been noticed. There was, in fact, a man stationed to keep watch over this stretch, but he looked the other way, and enough distance lay between us that when he turned back, he didn't notice me lying between the ferns and fallen branches.

I waited until he turned his head again and then dragged myself forward a few cubits more. He faced me again and I froze, weirdly amused by how easy a game this was to learn, and how quickly it would be over.

As soon as he turned away again, I bolted into the trees unseen.

Ok. Calm, calm, calm. Distance, distance, nothing mattered more than distance. *Think.*

I could handle dogs — I had an entire forest in front of me to lose them. The worst part was that I didn't know how long my head start would be. So I made a mad, weaving dash through the trees for two solid minutes, then found a gnarled old oak with limbs I could easily climb, and ran in a straight line east for two minutes more. I turned around and perfectly retraced my steps until I reached the knotted oak again, my heart stopping as I heard approaching voices.

I leapt, hooked my arms around the rough bark and scrambled to pull the rest of myself up, obtaining several scratches along my arms and below my knees as the injury near my spine cried out. I reached up to the next limb and paid no attention to the leafy twigs digging into my hands and clinging to my hair. I did, however, still myself as the voices came closer.

I held my breath, hoping they wouldn't look up. People so rarely did.

"I'd never met her, had you?" a man's faint voice reached me through the trees, though he was nearly drowned out by a small bird who suddenly decided to burst into the solo of her life.

"No, but I've seen her around. The Dragona shanking loved her. I just can't imagine what she was thinking."

I missed the next part of what was said over the chirping bird, and I made several gestures for her to muzzle it.

300

The next piece I heard was, "That little sister of hers is getting something with her scent so the Zhauri and their dogs—" but the soloist flitted to a branch right next to me and I swatted at her as she continued chittering.

The searchers never actually came into my view, but I felt a new rush of energy in my limbs as their voices faded into nothing and the bird flew away indignantly, performing her encore in the next tree over. Liz was helping the Zhauri find me. After all we'd been through... Maybe she was being forced. Or maybe she thought I was somehow innocent and just needed to come back to prove it.

I knew the reasons didn't matter, so I promised myself I could dwell and be tortured by them later. Right now I needed to get out of this mess, and out of this stretch of forest.

I forced myself to count to thirty to make sure those searchers were well enough away, but I only made it to twenty-one before deeming it safe to move. I took careful, measured steps away from the trunk, pushing through leaves and twigs as the branches of my oak tangled with the boughs of another. I pressed forward until I could grab a sturdy limb of the next tree, and I made it to the next trunk with my eyes closed and my mouth full of leaves.

I stayed up in the tree limbs as I distanced myself from my eastbound scent trail, aware I probably had more twigs protruding from my head than hair by now. I had been exiled for roughly five minutes and already looked like a wild animal.

I laughed softly to myself, marveling at how many weird things I could think about when my life was in horrible danger. Maybe I was just in these situations too often.

I climbed into the inner branches of a third tree right as loud yapping filled the forest behind me. It sounded like three or four dogs, and only five minutes away. Three minutes if they didn't have to drag their owners behind them.

I leapt to the ground and began my exhausted jog west. Whoever was hunting me would come to the end of my false eastbound trail and spend the next few hours trying to figure out how I'd vanished. Hopefully. It still didn't hurt to put some distance between us.

Now that I was finally beginning to wear out, all the feelings I had thrown haphazardly into a box began leaking at an alarming rate. *What had I just done?*

I could never go home again, never see Liz's smile or hear another of her warnings to stay safe. I could never even show my face in a Human city, for fear they'd recognize me.

And Archie... Everyone knew how close we were — I may have just put him on the line for treason too.

And what had I even gained for all of this? I wasn't sure Vack had survived, and if my luck held out, Ebby would probably come crawling home to her father in the next hour with Prince Avalask out of the way. I may have given up everything for nothing at all.

But did I regret it?

No. Not for a second.

I could have followed Sir Avery's directions. I could have shocked the life out of Prince Avalask while his son lay bleeding to death, or even just stayed still and done nothing at all... but I would have looked back every day for the rest of my life and regretted it.

So as much as my current situation sucked, I refused to regret my choice. The right choice.

I couldn't say I felt good, but maybe a little less hysteric. I listened to the excited barks of dogs in the distance, then came to a stop as it dawned on me... They weren't so distant. We were travelling away from each other — I shouldn't be able to hear them.

I strained my ears and realized they were getting louder, heading west, as though they'd found my current trail. I stopped myself half way through whispering "What the..."

Those dogs must have been able to shanking fly! Unless...

Unless they had incredibly experienced owners who knew how to spot a back-traced trail. I was so stupid. How could I have underestimated the Zhauri like this?

I couldn't lay another false trail with the dogs this close, but there were a hundred different streams that wound west on their way to the lake. Running water was as good as any faked trail.

I checked the moss on the nearest tree trunk, glanced up at the sun, and then booked it north so I'd be sure to cross one of them. A rushing creek came into view just as excited braying filled the forest behind me. Three minutes from me? Two?

I pulled a knife from my side, sawed off the ends of my hair, and flung them in the water so they would float and collect along the banks further down. I never saw if the trick worked though, because I was already running upstream, splashing noisily but leaving no scent trail to follow.

As soon as I found a rocky patch where I wouldn't leave glaring footprints, I leapt from the water and headed north again until I hit the next rivulet and jumped back in to dash downstream, toward the lake. This *had* to buy me a few minutes of extra time.

An excited chorus of howls startled me because they sounded like they were already at the second creek, the one I was still running in. *No way.* They were figuring me out faster than I could stay ahead of them. I couldn't even fathom how, but I could still beat them to the lake if we made this a race of speed instead of wits. I wasn't winning the wits race.

I jumped back onto dry land as the barking came closer and bolted away like the hunted prey I was. I was slowed by a patch of thick grasses that grew up to my shoulders, but I tore through them and ducked under the limbs of a leaning maple before jumping over a small tangle of wild strawberries.

303

I reached the final slope, which tapered down to the lake, and tried to remember where exactly we had been on the shore last year when Archie had dragged me under. It was right here. I was almost sure of it.

I picked up speed as I flew down the hill and the dogs burst from the tall grasses. Black with white paws, grey with a black face, stark white, and brown with white patches – they were the Zhauri dogs.

I reached the water's edge in a panic. This was a horrible idea. I could barely swim to save my life. Horrible, horrible, horrible —

I picked up a rock the size of my head and dove into the water. The drenching cold enveloped me instantly, muting the dog's barks as if I'd stuffed pillows over my ears.

I needed to sink, but that didn't keep me from panicking as the lake darkened, thickened, and compressed around me. I've never been fond of water, or the dark, but nothing is more terrifying than the two combined.

In a flash of anxiety, I realized the cave entrance could truly be anywhere, and I'd been a fool to think I'd be able to just *find* it in the black watery cliffs. I dropped the stone and lashed out with my arms and legs, trying to get back to the surface to take my chances with somebody I could fight. This lake was just a slow death waiting to happen.

I was too far down, and not an accomplished enough swimmer. I screamed a silent, distraught cry without opening my mouth, savoring the last air my lungs would ever taste. I kicked my legs, but the more I struggled, the more I just needed air. My last hot breath was beginning to feel toxic.

At least a minute had passed underwater. I looked desperately for anything resembling a cave as I fought toward the surface, but another half-minute passed, and I couldn't hold my breath one second longer.

I tried to just let half of it out, but my lungs inhaled immediately on reflex and filled with water.

I coughed violently, expelling every bubble I'd kept inside of me, and that's when my will to survive finally woke with an image clearer than reality. It was the perfect recollection from last year when Archie had dragged me into the underwater tunnel. It wasn't far. Just a little further down and a little to my left.

I was so close, but I was drowning. There was nothing but water in my lungs and nose, and the tears in my eyes flowed straight into the murky lake as I thrashed.

My mind, my soul, it all just began to drift as though I was falling asleep. It didn't even make sense to fight — there was nobody left to return to, nothing left of the life I used to know. But there was still Archie. If I went to sleep here, I would never see him again, never laugh with him again, and if he was sentenced for being a traitor, I wouldn't be there to help him.

"NO!" I shrieked into the water, waking myself just a little as my hands lit in panic, illuminating the whole area. I grabbed handfuls of slimy underwater weeds and pulled myself into the cave, kicking my legs harder than I'd ever pushed them.

And I don't actually remember coming out into the air, but I must have, because I remember vomiting water onto the stones of a cave I had been to once before. I crawled on my hands and knees before collapsing among the wet rocks, heaving water from my body as I choked. I treasured the taste of sweet air making its way into my lungs once more, and I hugged my sides as I broke into deep, uncontrollable coughing.

I was happy to be alive, but sickened with grief because I'd just destroyed everything that mattered. Nobody to return to, no place to call home, and I might have just bought Archie a ten thousand year sentence.

CHAPTER TWENTY SIX

bby had absolutely no destination in mind when she jumped, and some demented part of her subconscious hurled her back into the Obsidian Tower. She dropped Vack's body as her knees slammed into the frame of her bed and Vack skidded to a stop on the glass floor.

Ebby shrieked and crumpled as the pain in her legs crippled her, turning the world momentarily black. And before her sight even returned, she used her hands and elbows to pull herself across the ground to where she knew Vack had settled.

"Don't be dead. Please don't be dead," she cried as the world of sight returned but Vack still hadn't moved. He lay on his side, just slightly curled in on himself, and Ebby put both hands on his face but still couldn't sense a single thought in his mind. He was still warm, and that was a good sign, wasn't it?

Ebby grabbed his limp arm and held her thumb to his wrist to feel for a pulse. There was nothing. She quickly grabbed his other wrist, *just in case,* but it held no more life than the first. She pressed a thumb to her own wrist and found that she, in fact, was dead too. She must be doing it wrong.

A small pool of Vack's blood crept toward her across the glass, and she wrenched his shirt up so she could press her hands to the wound to heal it. Vack just couldn't be dead. He couldn't.

Her entire body sagged, and she whispered, "I'm sorry," as the hole in his chest disappeared, but he still didn't move. She wished she'd spent more time reading Karissa's book, or that she had one of the Tallies here to help.

Ebby wouldn't mind dying here with Vack. She gave in to hopeless sobs and lamented for the millionth time that the world had been cursed with her for an Epic. It might just be her now. She might be free to destroy anything she wanted without Vack in her way.

But she wasn't going to. She would be more like Allie. Make her own decisions. Do what she thought was right, no matter the consequences.

The door squeaked open, and Ebby felt more panic fill the air.

"NO!" Jalia sprinted and collapsed beside them, grabbing Vack's hand as Mir stood frozen in the doorway, too startled to move. "Vack?"

Vack's hand twisted quickly to grab Jalia's, jerking her closer.

Ebby was caught mid-sob and didn't even have the strength to scream at the realization that Vack wasn't dead.

Mir crept cautiously closer while Jalia squeezed Vack's hand and stared sightlessly ahead. Her eyes were still swollen and red, and Ebby could feel understanding in Jalia, as though Vack was reliving the past twenty minutes to her. "He's not dead," she said, finally looking up at Ebby. "This is how he mourns."

Ebby choked on a laugh as Vack lay completely unaware. For all the times he'd mocked her for crying, it was sort of hilarious that he handled his own sadness by putting himself in a coma.

"Can you see Prince Avalask?" Jalia asked her. "Is he alright?"

"What happened?" Mir asked. Sparing no gruesome details, Jalia began to explain what Ratuan and Sir Avery had done to Vack, and Ebby reached to find Prince Avalask so she wouldn't throw up.

"I can't... I can't find him," Ebby said, trying not to pass out from overwhelming guilt.

"You think he's dead?" Jalia asked.

"I don't know," Ebby said. "I can see the Dincaran kids still coming out of the tunnels, and there are mages, but... he's gone."

"That's better than finding his body," Jalia said. "The Dragona is probably using mages to shade him, which means he's alive."

Ebby felt her shoulders sink with a tiny bit of relief. What would she do without Jalia?

"When will Vack wake up?" Ebby asked.

"He's awake," Jalia said, rubbing a hand across Vack's shoulders in an unexpected gesture of affection. "He can hear you."

Vack opened his eyes, but he didn't look at anybody and didn't move. He'd never been shy about how much he loved his father, and he'd never looked so broken or weak.

Ebby didn't want him to face this kind of hurt. "We can trade me for your father," Ebby said. Vack shifted his gaze up to her and blinked slowly.

"Don't do that," Mir said, his eyes narrowed with worry. "It's not a good trade."

"He's right," Jalia said, flicking her attention from Mir to Ebby. "Strategically, they'd be taking three steps backward if they traded Prince Avalask for you." Ebby knew she wasn't extremely loved or wanted, but it hurt to hear how much she *wasn't* worth. Jalia said, "Don't misunderstand me. Your father will try to convince Vack to make a trade, but he won't let Prince Avalask go once he has you. That's when they'll kill him."

Mir nodded and said, "It's their dream to have Sir Avery unopposed. They'll never give that up."

"They'll kill my father if we give her back," Vack muttered to the glass floor. "And they'll kill him if we don't give her back. Sir Avery's going to kill me the second he finds me. He's going to kill you guys if he finds you. Without my father, we all end up dead." He finally moved the hand that wasn't holding Jalia's, but it was just so he could put his thumbnail between his teeth.

Vack closed his eyes again, and Jalia said, "Sir Avery *will* kill you if you keep moping like this." She still had a comforting hand on his shoulders as she said it, as though simply stating a fact. "Yes, we're at a disadvantage, but we still have leverage. We have Ebby, for one."

Ebby hugged her stomach. "You'd be surprised how little I can do."

"You're eleven. There's time to get better," Jalia said. "But you do matter. With you here, we can make our own threats to keep Vack's father alive. With you here, we have two Epics. Those are advantages." Jalia looked down at Vack, who seemed a little more alert now. "We can probably convince everybody that Vack is dead, and Vack's Uncle Savaul is about to become king. He'll help us with whatever we need."

Ebby released something between a laugh and a sob, and shook her head. "You have got to be kidding. Savaul?"

"I'm not," Jalia said. "Savaul hates Humans, Ebby, I mean really hates them, but he cares what happens to his own people. He is going to make a great leader, and he'll help us. We have more leverage here than we need."

Mir nodded in agreement with Jalia, then added, "You both have to get strong enough to fight."

"Wait," Ebby said as her heart began to race again. "Who decided I was going to fight for you? I'm still Human. I never did join your side."

309

"We're not asking you to," Jalia said. "We're just asking that you *not* let Sir Avery burn our entire race to the ground."

Vack finally pushed himself up to sit, and then he, Mir, and Jalia fixed their eyes on Ebby, as though their lives might actually be in her hands.

"What do you need me to do?" she asked, feeling a hope in their thoughts that was hard to resist. Nobody was trying to manipulate her — they really just needed her.

Jalia glanced around the group and said, "We need you and Vack to get stronger so you can't be brought down by a few mages, or one angry Epic. We could get you there with enough hard work, but it means you can't see your father, and you probably won't be able to see Ratuan. Not for a while."

"I'm alright with that," Ebby whispered, unable to look anywhere but at her hands. She felt so embarrassed for how long she had spent pining for Ratuan and hoping Sir Avery could rescue them all. Now thinking about them brought heartbreak instead of hope. Sir Avery's name had become the image of an Epic holding Vack off the ground, strangling him in front of his own father.

Ratuan's name was the sight of her best friend running toward Vack even though Ebby was screaming for help. She had no doubt Ratuan loved her, but there was something else he loved more. Maybe it was vengeance, or maybe it was the fame and power that would come with killing an Epic, but it would be a massive mistake to pretend it wasn't there. More tears gathered in her eyes because she couldn't bear to live without him.

Vack grabbed Ebby's hand, startling her because she rarely saw his hands without gloves, and had never actually *touched* one. His thoughts were a jumble of confusion like her own, needing to be sorted and confronted. Vack was nearly paralyzed with fear, but he was somehow sharing in her worries too, taking just a bit of the

310

burden from her. He felt broken beyond repair, but also sorry for Ebby and all she had seen in her own father and best friend.

I know how much it will hurt to give them up, he said in one coherent thought meant for her. The rest of his mind was a wordless question, begging to know if she would help them. He desperately hoped she'd say yes, but reserved a certain amount of terror in case she wanted to return home. Vack's fears all ran together like mixing paint colors, painting a panicked mess of how much it would hurt to die, worrying that he might not be able to hide, and the terror that he might have to watch his friends and father die before him.

And for once, he didn't try to hide it behind a brave face and a snarl.

If I stay with you, my own family will get hurt, Ebby thought, glancing at his hazy green eyes. Vack felt too awkward to meet her gaze, but his thoughts said he understood perfectly.

I promise, he thought back to her, *I won't let anything bad happen to them. You and I can call our own truce. I will owe you more than I can ever repay.*

Ebby couldn't possibly say no when Vack was so desperate.

Where would we even go? she asked.

Jalia wants to go north. She doesn't think anyone will find us up there, and she's read enough books about magic that she thinks she can train us.

Ebby laughed softly and thought back, *If anyone could, it would be her.*

And she notices things that neither of us see. I think we'll be safer if she's with us.

What about Mir? Ebby wondered.

Vack looked up at his dark haired friend and asked, "If we leave, do you want to come?"

Mir glanced behind himself as though to make sure nobody was listening, and he hesitated. "I'll go wherever you want me," Mir said, radiating guilt for not immediately choosing to stay at Vack's side, "but... I don't want to leave my birds."

"You could be just as useful to us here," Jalia said, flicking her gaze from Mir to Vack to make sure he approved. "We'll need somebody to pass messages to Vack's uncle, and we'll need somebody to relay news to us so we can stay low."

"So, we're really going to do this?" Vack asked. "We're really going to run and hide?"

"Yes," Jalia said fearlessly. "But first we need to make sure all your remaining family members are safe. And then we're going to convince the world you're dead."

CHAPTER TWENTY SEVEN

Something about the smell of cedar trees has always made me think of warmth and safety, even on the worst of days. I lay on my back, looking at the freckles of blue sky shining through needles and mosses overhead, my dripping hair beginning to dry in the soft breeze with a hint of curl in the ends. The ancient trunks reached skyward all around me like towering monuments, and I was just a small thing among them, my life almost meaningless.

It had taken me ages to crawl out of the cave below, and I hadn't made it far.

My limbs lay sprawled out to every side of me, never wanting to move again. My stomach had constricted so tightly, I probably never needed to eat again. Two hundred shards of my heart were still plastered throughout my chest, all independently trying to beat and keep me alive, and all independently causing pain.

As much as I was tempted to play dead, I kept a small trickle of dialogue running through my head, recounting every horrific thing the day had thrust upon me. I wanted to feel every ache, and every stab of fear and sadness. Not because I wanted to punish myself, but because I had earned these bruises. I deserved to lie here and feel miserable, pouring alcohol on my wounds until the pain was blinding, but knowing they'd heal better later.

I smiled inwardly because I doubted anyone else did this to themselves. I was one of a kind, and probably a shanking lunatic. But these feelings of sadness weren't going anywhere. If I pushed them into the recesses of my mind, they would just come back later, so why not face them now?

And in facing them, there were other things I could think about. When I thought of Liz's face, I could feel threads of hope and plans coming together, like promises I would be able to see her again. The thought of Archie became a prayer that he wasn't being blamed for my actions. I felt another great stab of fear concerning Prince Avalask. At best, I could hope they'd keep him as a hostage to lure Vack out. I didn't want to fathom the worst.

Vack found me hours later, lying on my side with my head tucked toward my knees in anguish. At least one good thing had come from my sacrifice. He'd lived.

"Ebby hasn't gone back to her father yet, has she?" I asked, my voice scratchy, but flat.

"No," Vack replied. "Not yet." Vack watched me with a look that might just be pity as I lay unmoving. "What... are you doing?" he asked.

I just shrugged in response, the movement causing twigs and needles to scratch the side of my face.

Vack glanced around the trees where the mosses dangled nearly to the ground and bit through a few fingernails, tearing them mindlessly away. "You look like you prefer to be left alone."

"Stay a second," I finally said, my voice sounding worn and weak as I pushed myself up, brushing off the dirt that clung to my arms. "Can you tell me where the other Tallies are? And just, that they made it out alright?"

314

Vack narrowed his eyes and my heart sank as he said, "I can't just look through every soul on the continent, searching for half-Human and half-Escali blood. I can only track people I know."

"You know Archie," I said. "Your cousin?"

Vack nodded, his face void of emotion. "He's… alive. He's back at the Dragona…"

"And Ebby spent a little time with Karissa and Robbiel, reading through a book they gave her," I said, clenching my fists to keep my fingers from shaking. "She could help you find them."

"She and I will look."

I nodded silent thanks and then rubbed at my sore back where my skin had already knit itself together, the blood already washed away in the lake. I wanted to ask about Vack's father, but he must still be with the Zhauri.

I glanced up at his empty expression and asked, "Vack… are you going to be alright?"

Vack said nothing, but tilted his head and stared shamelessly at me.

And that was the moment I noticed a shift in the way he looked at me, like we were on the same team, facing the same nightmare.

"Ebby told me how you helped her," Vack said. "I want to know why."

The question took me by surprise. "Why what? Why I helped her save you?"

"You don't even know me," Vack said. "I wouldn't have done the same for you."

"Comforting," I replied, letting a smile through my misery. "I don't know you, but… I know this sounds dumb, but I believe in you." Vack kept his face impassively still, which is the only reason I was able to continue. "You couldn't have died today, not with how much influence you have. You might be the key to everything

315

ending well. And... even if you weren't, you didn't deserve to be murdered."

I could recognize guilt from a mile away, and Vack was suffering a serious case of it. "I don't regret it," I said. "I'll never regret doing a thing I think was right."

"Even when *this* is the consequence?" he asked, waving a hand around to the forest. I wasn't sure if he was worried for me, or worried his life might end up in equivalent disaster.

"It's better to live by the callings that define you than a comfortable lie. And it could be worse," I said. "I could be dead."

I sort of meant it as a joke, but the words sounded profoundly serious.

Ebby appeared in a stumble beside him, grabbing his arm to keep from crashing entirely, and Vack took an uncomfortable step back from her as she gained her footing.

"Hi, Allie," Ebby said softly, as though afraid I may crumble. She looked up at Vack. "It's done. It looks just like you, and Jalia's on her way to tell your uncles."

"What's done?" I asked.

"Vack's... body. We're convincing everybody he's dead," Ebby said.

"And then I'm going to take the Humans by surprise to get my father back," Vack said. He glanced back at Ebby and said, "You know the Tallies better than I do. Can you find any of them?"

Ebby opened her mouth without words and Vack said, "If you know them, I can find them."

I watched them lock eyes with each other, and it occurred to me *just* how much they must trust each other. They were willingly sharing thoughts, one of the most vulnerable things anyone can do. And they were working together. If Prince Avalask could be here to see this, I suspect he might have cried.

316

Vack was the first to glance at the ground. "They're nowhere," he said.

I laughed a scoffing, furious laugh, then said, "Look harder."

"Ebby remembers your friends clearly. There's nothing left of them to find."

"Wait," Ebby said, glancing at Vack again. "There's the one who threw you on the ground."

Vack didn't look particularly pleased to recall the moment, but said, "Ok. I see him. He's running."

"He's being chased?" I asked.

"Not by anyone I can see," Vack said, frowning at the trees.

"Jump me out there," I said quickly, knowing Vack wouldn't be able to see the Zhauri if Zeen accompanied them. "One of you, I don't care who. Get me out there."

Vack held out a hand to me and muttered, "Don't ever let Ebby jump you anywhere."

Ebby shot Vack a reproachful look before I grabbed his hand, and we leapt and reappeared on a grassy hillside dotted with piles of sparkling white stones like the ruins of an ancient city.

"Shanking life!" Emery shouted, skidding to a stop in front of us as flames jumped into his palms. "All darkness is only shadow!"

I scrambled for the right words before repeating in a fumble, "For... unless light has ceased to exist, it is merely an obstacle away."

He squinted hard at me before finally looking convinced. "Are you alright? Are any of our other friends with you?"

I shook my head and asked, "Are you being chased?"

"Chased? No. This is our emergency meetup. I'd hoped to find everyone else already here."

He snapped his head to look at the trees, and I heard the same whistling that had grabbed his attention. It was the duskflyer song, and Archie's favorite stanza.

The tone was warm like Archie's, but too warm. And the timing... Some of the notes were too quick, making them feel like jovial embellishments. It was the same song, and beautifully whistled, but it just didn't capture the beauty of sadness.

Silently as I could, I pulled my short swords from my side. "It's not Archie," I whispered.

"No," Emery said slowly. "It's Corliss."

"You're sure?"

He nodded and shouted, "Corliss! All darkness is only shadow!"

Vack watched silently as she dashed out of the trees, grabbing me and Emery in a tight embrace.

Corliss turned wide eyes to Emery. "Celesta's already here. Where's everyone else?"

Emery threw his hands up. "No one knows!" He kicked at the closest white stone with nearly enough force to break his foot. "We didn't know we were being blamed for Izfazara's death until a couple Escalis tried to murder Robbiel right in the hallway. We grabbed a few things and slipped out through the back crevices, and we had *everybody* together at that point except Nessava."

"Where was she?" I whispered.

Emery shook his head violently. "We'd hoped to find her outside, but we didn't. Karissa panicked and vanished on us to run back inside, and Robbiel, being the lovesick idiot he is, ran back in after Karissa."

I wanted to ask if he knew anything further, but he'd clearly come straight here. "Have either of you heard anything?" Emery asked.

Corliss shook her head, and my voice cracked as I said, "Vack and Ebby looked for Robbiel and Karissa. They... can't find them."

Emery balled his hands into fists and his face turned a furious shade of red as Corliss' jaw fell open. "And Nessava?" she asked, looking at Vack in desperation.

Vack shook his head uncomfortably. "I don't think she made it either. It's possible we're just missing her, since we only saw her once with the rest of you..." Vack trailed off and I looked straight at Corliss.

"Have you seen Archie?" I asked breathlessly.

Corliss took a moment to collect herself. "He's alright. He wanted to come, but he's under lock and key right now and can't get out of the Dragona."

"They've locked him up?"

"No, not in the Everarc Cave or anything," Corliss said. "Just stuck in his room. After you ran, he went straight to Sir Avery to plead for your life and his. He's a quick talker, and I think he saved you both."

"And then Sir Avery vouched for him to the rest of the Dragona?" I asked. "Because that's the only way they're going to believe he wasn't in league with me."

"That's what it sounds like," Corliss said, shaking her head slowly. "But Sir Avery owns him now. Archie's agreed to serve the Epic's every whim, and it's your life that's being threatened if he screws up."

I sighed and pressed a palm to my forehead.

"I have more bad news too," she said as her eyes settled on Vack. "This... effort to get Ebby back isn't over. Sir Avery's declared that if she isn't home by tomorrow, they're executing Prince Avalask."

Vack clenched his jaw and stopped breathing, and I grabbed his shoulder.

"*They can't,*" I said, even though we all knew they very well could.

Corliss shrugged sadly. "They're putting together an Eclipsival scale celebration in Glaria right now because everything is suddenly right in the Human world. Izfazara's dead, they suspect Vack might be dead, and they've got Prince Avalask in a dungeon

319

somewhere... The Dincaran kids are safely home, and fourteen ships are about to arrive from Tekada with our returners and some sort of weapon. They say it's going to lead to the downfall of the Escalis entirely."

I felt my jaw fall open at all that news laid out so casually. "Ratuan knew the timing when he planned the escape," Corliss said. "He knew when the survivors from the Tekadan massacre would be landing, and he planned it so the kids would get back just in time. He made himself a hero, and they're going to let him execute Prince Avalask at the end."

I could feel Vack beginning to shake, and he leapt into the air without warning, leaving the three of us alone in the sunshine.

"We have to get him out," I said.

"*How?*" Corliss asked, a hint of desperation in her voice. "You can't show your face at the Dragona, and Archie can't leave his room without a five man guard. Emery will be killed the moment somebody sees his arm spikes, and I'm supposed to do what? Kick down Prince Avalask's cell door and carry him to safety?"

I fell silent, and Emery still had his teeth gritted tightly.

"We only have until tomorrow?" I asked.

Corliss nodded and said, "Even if we could convince Ebby to come home..."

She shook her head slowly, and I agreed with her hesitation. Even if Ebby came home, nobody would release Prince Avalask. We all knew that.

Emery finally unclenched his jaw to say, "Let's all do some thinking on what we want to do, and then we'll regroup."

Corliss nodded, but grabbed his arm as he turned to leave.

"Look," she said. "Before you go running into the woods to kill a bunch of things, can you just promise to come back by dark?" Emery glared mutinously, and Corliss said, "It's not fair to make us worry all night about you too."

320

Emery looked out at the trees before muttering, "I'll come back before dark."

"Thanks," Corliss replied.

He strode away from us, seemingly in control, although I doubted his calm would last once he was in the trees.

"He's like you," Corliss said, watching him go. "He gets in his moods, and all you can really do is let him cool off."

"Have you always been the group mom?" I asked, not sure why I hadn't puzzled this out before. She knew everyone too well, and knew how to keep the group from disintegrating.

"Yes," she replied. "The group mom of a slowly shrinking family." Her eyes grew distant, watching Emery go. "We just keep getting smaller and smaller."

Celesta had always been a mystery to me. She was always working on something, and when Corliss pulled one of the sparkling white stones out of the ground to reveal a set of dirt stairs, we found Celesta in the dark room below, packing the dirt walls into perfectly angled corners.

"I heard everything you said. You don't have to repeat it," she said, running a tool down one corner crease, smoothing out the dirt she'd turned to mud. "I know it's hard to say." She didn't look upset about the fact she'd lost at least two more friends, most likely three. She didn't even look bothered.

I glanced at Corliss, who simply shook her head to tell me to leave it alone.

"There's a second level below this one," Corliss said, pulling a torch down to show me another set of dirt stairs, leading deeper. The basement, for lack of a better term, had eleven bedrolls laid around the edges.

"There used to be eleven of us?" I asked.

"Twelve, actually," Corliss said, and a distant sadness dulled her eyes as she looked around the empty sleeping pads. "That one's yours," she said, pointing to the corner nearest the staircase. I didn't even hesitate before flopping onto it, feeling twice my weight under the exhaustion of life.

Even though I'd spent all my daylight hours replaying Liz's horrified stare, the sight of Ratuan stabbing Vack, Ebby screaming, Prince Avalask's pleas to run for my life... Despite facing it all during the day, the dreams hit me even more vividly at night with their own small variations. Ratuan sank his dagger through Vack's eyes instead of into his chest. My legs refused to move as the entire clearing looked at me in shock, and when I finally gathered enough sense to run, my limbs were sluggish and barely moved at all. The Zhauri's dogs caught up to me in the forest and sank their teeth into my hands, dragging me to the ground in a frantic struggle for my life as I realized the death hound approached, his eyes glowing red and metal plating growing down his chest.

He clamped his jaws around my throat as I screamed, ripping me open and waking me with my hands scrabbling to pull him off. I wasn't actually screaming, but whimpering like a coward, breathing like I'd just sprinted five miles, and I'd clawed at my own chest and neck hard enough to leave a series of raised marks.

I'd never scratched myself like this. I pulled my sweaty hair out of my eyes and ran my fingertips over the red welts, knowing they'd heal soon, unlike Liz's. Was she having nightmares like *this*? All the time? I would have been sleeping in her room every night if I'd known.

I shook my head and swallowed, hearing whispering from the upstairs level.

322

"His brother is about to be killed," Corliss said softly. "Assuming he even has them, I think he'd let them go if we could tell him where Prince Avalask is."

I caught up quickly, but I wasn't sure if negotiating with Sav could end in anything but murder. He just hated us too much.

"Our odds of speaking with him and leaving alive are *way* too low, considering the fact Karissa, Nessava, and Robbiel are probably already dead," Emery replied.

"We can't assume they're dead and leave them," Corliss hissed. "Karissa would never do that to you."

"We're not leaving them. There just has to be a better way to find them than *asking*. Approaching Sav right now would be suicide."

I shook the tingle of sleep from my arms and climbed the stairs to crouch next to them, making a triangle of conversation without so much as a *good morning*.

"Aside from getting our friends back, Sav might also be our only hope of saving Prince Avalask," I said. "We have to tell him what's happening."

Emery rolled his eyes up to the ceiling and said, "Even if he doesn't have our throats torn out on the spot, he's not going to let any of us walk out of there."

"I'm on the fence," Corliss said. "Because yes, he's vicious and he hates us, but he does have honor. If we're trying to give him information about Prince Avalask, he might be proud enough to let us walk away. He'll threaten us, and send people after us, but I think he'd at least give us a head start."

"Oh, how generous," Emery said.

"Let him send them," I replied. "The three of us are more fight-worthy than anyone. Who in their right mind is going to stand in the way of lightning, fire, and the ability to collapse the caves around us?"

Emery and Corliss exchanged a quick, smirking glance.

"I'm going," I said, determined. "You two can either stay here or come with me. But it'll eat me alive if Prince Avalask is killed and we didn't do anything to stop it."

My face grew redder as I realized I was somehow amusing them. "I told you she hasn't changed," Corliss told Emery. I was growing more irritated with the both of them.

"So the real question is," Emery said slowly, in contemplation, "do we let her go running off on her own, *because we both know she will*, or do we help plan and go with her?"

I looked at them both and then shifted onto my knees so I could hunch forward and treat the floor like a map. "I don't want to blaze our way through a mass of Escalis if we don't have to," I said, packing a line of loose dirt together, "but we do have to acknowledge that the three of us weren't built for stealth."

"Especially not Corliss," Emery said, looking much more like his mischievous self as he relaxed into a more comfortable position on the floor. "She sometimes can't control when she bursts into song and dance."

Corliss said, "It makes for an excellent distraction though. The people love me." She nodded very seriously, and said, "If we can incorporate that into the plan, I'm in."

We planned and we plotted, and I eventually excused myself, needing to get outside and use the environment because I hadn't done so since waking. I climbed up the dirt-packed stairs and pushed the entrance stone out of my way, pulling myself into the blinding sunshine without thinking to check my surroundings.

"Hi Allie." The greeting nearly made me pee myself.

"Ebby?" I gasped, clutching at my heart. Her white dress sparkled without a single stain remaining. "What are you doing here?"

"I'm sorry," she said, looking at the ground. "I didn't mean to startle you. I just... I need to talk to you, and so I waited out here."

I took a deep breath, knowing there was no reason to be upset with her. "It's fine," I said. I crouched to her level, nearly sitting on my heels to get her to look at me. "What's happening? Are you alright?"

Ebby nodded and I set a hand on her shoulder. "What's going on?"

"I... I was listening to you talking earlier, about going to Savaul to see if he had your friends. And so I did it for you."

She glanced carefully into my eyes, as though afraid I would scold her.

"You looked for my friends?" She shook her head and I felt my eyes widen. "You mean you went and spoke to Sav for us?"

"Yes. Jalia came with me. And I'm an Epic. I wasn't really in any danger."

She looked ready to cry until I squeezed her shoulder and said, "That was really, *really* brave of you."

Ebby's face lit up, like my approval was all she needed. "I wanted to find out where your friends are," she said. "But Savaul doesn't know. He's put a ransom out for anybody who can kill a Tally, but nobody's brought back a body yet."

Incredible relief washed over me, even though we weren't a single step closer to finding them. "Thank you for telling me."

Ebby beamed, then looked back at her feet, suddenly shy once more. "I... need you to help me too," Ebby said, grabbing at her dress to twist it nervously in her hands. "Vack told me what's about to happen in Glaria."

I waited with uncharacteristic patience as she gathered her words. "Savaul's also heard about the weapon coming in with the survivors, but he doesn't know what it is. He wants me to get out

325

and wreck the ship carrying it before anybody knows what's happening."

"You don't have to do anything Savaul says," I told her. "I'm sure he threatened you, but you're the Epic. He has nothing to hold over you."

"He didn't threaten me," she said, "but they're going to kill Prince Avalask as part of the celebration. Savaul thinks he can save him if I can distract Sir Avery out on the ships."

I groaned and knelt fully down as my calves began to tingle from crouching too long.

"Prince Avalask can't die," she whispered, and I nodded my agreement.

"We'll help you," I said. "I'm just not really sure how."

"Just be there, please," she said. "I was hoping you could just blend into the crowd and be there in case we need you."

I opened my mouth to explain that I couldn't show my face among the Humans, but Ebby cut me off. "I can change what you look like. I can make your hair dark, or your eyes bright blue." She looked me over and said, "I can even make you fat. Whatever you want."

I snorted a short laugh and rubbed my dark brown eyes, imagining them like the summer sky.

"It won't last more than a few hours," she said. "We'd actually have to do it right before you went in. Can you meet me outside Glaria?"

"Glaria is a *long* walk from here," I said, making one more pass over my tired eyes.

"I could jump you over there," she said. "I'm just... not great at jumping."

"That's fine," I said, giving her a kind smile as I stood up, adding a couple fidgety steps to the motion. "I'll talk to Emery and Corliss and make sure they're willing to come too. First though, I am so sorry, but I *really* have to pee."

Ebby giggled at that and I messed up her wispy hair before dashing toward the trees.

Convincing Emery and Corliss to come with me took about a sentence and a half of explanation. Emery wanted to see Archie in person to make sure he was alright. Corliss was believed to be Human and perfectly welcome there. Celesta said nothing and we didn't ask her to come.

Ebby came back for us, and that girl was not kidding. She shouldn't be allowed to jump to save her life.

She nervously took my hand and I jumped with her, reappearing in the air above a massive twisting oak with Ebby nowhere in sight. I screamed and flailed my limbs as I fell into the sharp branches of the bare tree, breaking through several limbs before hitting one that I could grip in a screeching halt. I rubbed my back and left shoulder and came away with more blood on my hands before wincing and lowering myself to the ground.

Ebby found me with a look of pure terror in her eyes as Emery hunched over next to her to laugh at my sorry state.

"I'm sorry," Ebby said, looking ready to cry again. "I told you I'm not—"

I found myself laughing as well, because she was right. She'd warned me. "It's fine," I said, because the damage was already nearly healed. No permanent harm done.

I was a little jealous though, to see Corliss land perfectly on her feet beside Ebby a few minutes later.

"Looks like somebody's third-time lucky," I muttered as Corliss gave me a pose like *ta-da!*

CHAPTER TWENTY EIGHT

bby made sure nobody could use magic to track me before she leapt away, and I promised Emery and Corliss I would be alright if they went down to the celebration without me. I'd join them as soon as Ebby came back to disguise me.

I imagined my feet were feathers as I brushed silently through the forest, knowing I had to be back in a few hours to meet Ebby, but not worrying much about it. I imagined that no tree, no rock, no leaf would ever know I'd passed by. I was a whisper. I was a tendril of smoke among the forest, easily ignored and even sooner forgotten.

I don't mean to say I was sneaking around Glaria. The forest recognizes mischief. The *world* will shout your name across the ridge-tops when you try to sneak. What I was doing was moving with the grace of the unhurried, which is something I can't remember doing... ever.

A sea of leaves pattered softly above me as a deep-woods breeze brushed through them. Wisps of hair drifted up around my shoulders and I closed my eyes, taking a deep breath of the ocean air as a soft whistle carried past on the wind.

I'd only caught the faintest hint of it, so I waited in peaceful patience until a second whisper of song echoed through the trees.

I took great care to appreciate where I was stepping and what I was passing as I approached it, and I began to hear an undertone of beautiful darkness — the shrill hum of contemplation that made the hair on my arms prickle.

I knew it was Archie's whistling, even though I could hardly stand to believe I might be so lucky.

The beautiful song disappeared, but I moved toward the silence, suspicious of why he would be so conveniently close. The ground sloped away from me, into a deep valley with a tiny creek snaking back and forth through the bottom, and Flak glided from the trees to land on my shoulder.

I braced for the grip of her talons, but she took me by surprise when she bit my ear and tried to rip it off the side of my head.

"What do you think you're doing?" I hissed at her, shoving her off. She flew to a nearby limb and muttered an angry screech at me as I started moving again. "Flak, it's him," I whispered to her. "I know it's him."

She hissed at me, and I bared my teeth to hiss back. I could understand that this felt a little trap-like, but it was Archie's whistle. If he was being forced to lure me in, he would change the tone or do something to tip me off. "I'll be careful," I whispered, trying to appease Flak even though she was a shanking bird.

I was the epitome of careful as I heard the sad duskflyer whistle once more. I crept close until I saw Archie, sitting beside a slow trickle of a creek, leaning back against a mossy maple trunk. And I watched him for fifteen minutes more to make sure nothing was amiss, even though I wanted to run straight to him.

He threw a rock into the little rivulet, and I circled painstakingly around behind him, watching, listening, and smelling for signs of anybody else nearby. I knew in my gut that this was too good to be true, but I was so close, and I truly didn't sense anybody else as I crept toward him.

"Archie?" I whispered, standing so he could see me.

He looked straight at me with a mix of confusion and shock, massive grey circles of exhaustion around his eyes.

"Allie? What are you doing here?"

Archie looked entirely torn, like he wasn't sure if he should look relieved to see me, or if somebody was testing him with an illusion and he needed to pretend to hate me.

"I can hear you ten miles away when you whistle like that." I held my hands far from my swords to show I meant no harm.

"How do I know it's really you?" he asked.

"All darkness is only shadow," I said, slipping a smile into the end.

He gave me a sigh of relief and said, "You don't know how glad I am to see you."

I abandoned caution to dash toward him, and when Archie threw his arms around me I melted into the warmth of him. "I didn't know what to do when you turned on me," he said. "Where did you go? Do you know if Ebby's alright?"

"She's fine," I said. I felt a strong shudder run through him, so I held on just a little longer, taking in his warmth and the comforting hint of autumn spices. "I've seen her, and she's alright."

"Where is she?" he asked.

"I'm not sure. I only saw her for a short minute."

"Where have you been?" he asked.

"Nowhere special. I just went—" I hesitated as Archie jerked, flinching back from me. "I was going to visit Tolnath Raka, but then I heard about the celebration in Glaria and came this way."

I waited in anticipation for Archie to answer me, and I felt my heartrate increase as he said, "Oh. Nowhere else?"

Tolnath raka wasn't a person, but a question in Escalira — *Are you alright?* And if Archie didn't understand that, then the arms wrapped around my shoulders weren't his, and I really had just stepped into a trap.

I felt the sudden urge to bolt away, but I also had a chance to clear his name by lingering. "I'm sorry I never told you what I was doing," I said, taking a step back to meet his gaze. "I've known the Escalis for a very long time, and I just didn't think you'd understand."

He looked so normal, just... his eyes were one degree more studious than caring, like this was an interrogation. I knew for certain Sir Avery didn't need deception to get what he wanted, and who else could do this to him, except maybe Iquis?

"I should go before anybody comes to check on you," I said.

"Just stay with me a couple more minutes," Archie said with a disarming smile. "We'll be fine. Nobody knows I'm out here."

The smile would have nearly fooled me, but then he set a hand on my arm. I couldn't mistake it for a caring gesture because it was too tight. He was ready to grab and hold me.

I frantically deliberated. Was somebody trying to catch me, or were they just trying to get information?

I set a hand softly on Archie's and played the game. "I'm sorry I betrayed you," I said, letting remorse fill my words. "I just couldn't let Prince Avalask's son die. I know he's an Escali, but he's a kid first. I don't think I deserve to be hated and hunted for sparing the life of a child."

"You let our Epic go," he said quietly.

"Oh wake up. You saw her jump, Archie. She was not whisked away by monsters. She made her own decision to grab Vack and leave." I added a muttered, "About shanking time too."

"You must have some idea where she's gone," Archie said.

I snorted a laugh. "You really think she consults me with those things?"

"Where were you when you saw her?" he asked, his second hand snaking up to join the first in a double handed grip.

My stomach made an uncomfortable flip, and I gasped, "Did you hear that?" whipping around to peer through the silent forest.

"I didn't hear anything," Archie replied as I jerked the other way.

I hadn't heard anything either, but said, "No, I'm sure there's something here."

I twisted my arm to pull away, but his grip only tightened. I looked straight at Archie and said in my darkest voice, "Let go of me."

Archie narrowed his blue eyes with a smirk, like I was being ridiculous. "Allie, there's nothing out here."

"Let. Go." I tried to electrify my hands and eyes, but something in my brain rejected that Archie was a danger. So in the same way his shield no longer blocked me, my magic didn't rush into my hands to shock him.

I glanced at his white knuckles and knew I couldn't break his grip.

So I lunged forward and bit him instead.

Archie gasped as I sank my teeth into his bicep, clamping my jaw and shaking my head viciously.

With all my weight in my right heel, I stomped on his foot and made to dash away just as he grabbed a tangled handful of my hair and yanked me back.

I jerked around with a snarl and flung my full weight at him, crashing us both into the needled branches of a young sapling. Archie was still stronger than me, but this version of him wasn't as fast. So while he used my hair as leverage to get an arm wrapped around my neck, I wrapped one of mine around his neck as well. I leapt from the ground to twist my legs around his waist, clinging like a sea-star in a rough tide as my whole face turned red. Archie struggled to stay on his feet and support both our weight while I had my right arm around his neck and used my left to punch him in the jaw, once, twice, three times —

Archie flung himself to the ground, turning so I would slam onto the dusty forest floor first. He landed on his side, on me, knocking me breathless though neither of us broke our tight embrace around the other's neck. I brought a knee up and tried to twist for a groin shot, but Archie maneuvered to keep my legs pinned beneath his.

I was furious. I should have lightning in my hands right now, shanking life! What good was this power?

I writhed angrily beneath him, and he pried my arm off his neck, getting control of my wrists through the struggle. "Who are you?" I barked up at him, close enough to spit in his face. "What do you think you're doing?"

"We're waiting for the Zhauri," he replied, glancing around us. My heart froze, but still no lightning in my hands.

"What's the matter? Can't get me back to Glaria by yourself?"

"Not the issue," he replied, breathing hard, but sounding calm. "The Zhauri will convince you to tell us where Ebby is. *Then* we can head down to Glaria for the celebration. It sounds like you're going to be an honored guest, actually."

I flung myself to either side and struggled harder to free my limbs, but couldn't. Where was my Archie?

"You think the Zhauri can break me? Make me tell them where Ebby is?" I sneered up at him, teeth bared, ready to bite the first piece of flesh in reach. "My mind's as sharp as a razor-willow. Sir Avery can't even get me to confess what I've eaten for breakfast." I struggled again, then added, "And he's the best mind mage on the continent."

Archie looked down and considered me while every nerve in my head prayed, *take the bait, take the bait.* I just had to get him off me.

333

Whoever was controlling him bit the hook I'd cast. A vicious consciousness stabbed into my mind from every angle, like pokers straight from the fire, and I clamped my eyes closed, gritted my teeth tightly, and set a thunderstorm loose in my head, trying to shock the violating thoughts to death. The ensuing battle rivaled the assault on Dincara, just on a much smaller battle field. Sharp tendrils of control stabbed into every crevice that made me who I was, and I bit back at every one of them with a vicious will to fight.

My thunderous dreamscape was interrupted by something happening outside. My entire body was being moved, and I had to use every bit of my core will to split my focus. I waged a war of minds and lightning on one front, and on the other I focused on the feeling of being dragged up to my knees.

"Allie! Come on, don't let him win."

I couldn't focus enough to see what was in front of me, but I could feel Archie close, frantic.

He pulled me up to my feet and I stuttered, "He's—"

Another flash of blinding agony constricted my words, so tight that I could feel my brain shrinking and getting weaker under the pressure as my knees collapsed. Archie was the only thing holding me up, and I could hear him, not another word of what he was saying, but I could hear *him*, and I pulled together another defensive front around my shrieking thoughts.

I couldn't win here. There had to be something I could do in the real world.

I finally forced my eyes open and saw Archie at an uncomfortable angle, holding my left arm around his shoulders to keep me somewhat standing. He locked eyes with me and I gasped, "He's got to be close." Nobody could be this powerful from a distance. This mage made Sir Avery's mind powers feel like parlor tricks.

I wanted Archie to drop me and find the attacker, and I think he understood, but a small corner of my mind gave way as I was distracted. It felt like a quarter of my thoughts had been deadened and numbed, and I was suddenly only three quarters as strong.

With all my focus, I built a mental wall around my remaining self and felt my body crumple to the ground on the outside.

The destruction tearing through my mind was suddenly dulled and then turned to a light tingle. I finally felt my legs again and regained awareness of the forest around me as I stumbled to my feet, hearing a scuffle further into the woods.

I staggered toward the commotion just as Archie threw a man back into a tree. Short with sparse sandy hair and two eyes that didn't match in shape or size, it was Iquis.

My beautiful, sweet, deranged falcon dove down to claw the Zhauri's eyes out, and Archie ran at me and grabbed my shoulders. "You have to get out of here!"

"Come with me," I said, taking hold of his arm while he kept his feet planted.

"You know I want to," he said, leaving a hand on my shoulder, using the other to push the hair back from my eyes, "but I'm the only reason Sir Avery isn't killing you. I have to stay." Iquis' angry screams mixed with the screams of my angry bird.

"I'll be alright, Allie. It's better this way." He dashed forward to place a hurried kiss on my cheek. "This isn't goodbye. I'll find you."

Iquis threw Flak to the ground, and blinding pain raged through my head once more, ending the conversation.

I steeled my mind a second time and I stabbed back, unleashing more bolts of internal lightning. I bit down a scream before the assault ceased again, and I forced my watering eyes open. Archie had pulled Iquis' own bow off his side and was dragging him to the ground in an attempt to strangle him with the string of it. Iquis had turned his attack back to Archie, who still managed to shout, "Get out of here!"

I stumbled to my feet and scrambled off into the trees, whipping my head around to see that Flak had disappeared. Nobody was pursuing me. The woods were empty of sounds and souls to make them.

WHAT ARE YOU DOING? I screamed at myself, filled to the brink with confused panic as the instincts that usually saved me shrieked for me to turn around. Archie was a part of me. I knew he wanted me to get myself to safety, but I absolutely wouldn't be whole if something happened to him. I wasn't safe if he was taking the wrath of the Zhauri for me, and I wanted to scream my frustration as indecision tore me in two different directions.

CHAPTER TWENTY NINE

I had to escape, or I'd be tortured and probably given ten thousand years.

But I had to go back, because even though Archie said he'd be fine, he could very well end up with the same.

I skidded to a stop in the pine needles and turned around, sick with the thought of anything happening to him.

A grey snow-dog with black around the eyes stalked toward me with raised hackles, and I spotted the cloak of a large Zhauri brother behind it, the new one with the blond hair and thick beard, who apparently had Archie's power. I pulled my short swords from my side and stood my ground, knowing his dog would chase me down if I tried to flee.

I flicked my gaze to either side, expecting to be surrounded by white cloaks, but this was the only one, and he set a hand on his dog's neck with a quiet shushing.

"*Dauer?*" another man called through the trees. "*Lakta zhur.*"

"*Zhur dana,*" this one called back, watching me closely as I kept my blades up and ready.

He was no taller than me, and when he took a step, I countered with a skittish step back.

He smiled and said, "I told him I'd be there in a minute. It's just you and me until one of us causes a problem."

I stayed silent but for my hammering heart, taking another step back from him as he tried to close the space between us.

His dog left his side and began to stalk a circle around me. "I've heard about you," he said, watching with amusement.

"Seems you have me at a disadvantage then," I replied, ready to amuse him if that could buy me time. "You're the Zhauri brother I know the least about."

He set his hands playfully on his chest and said, "My brothers call me Dauer. I'm the youngest and newest member, the one who hasn't quite acquired the taste for torture, you may be pleased to know."

I narrowed my eyes and asked, "You sure you're one of the Zhauri?"

"Pretty sure. Just don't have the stomach for it yet. I've been told it becomes more enjoyable in time."

I swallowed hard. "And what have you heard about me?"

"They say you're the girl who can beat any man in a fight."

"What of it?" I asked softly, hoping this was going where I suspected.

"Well, you've got me curious. I've never met a girl who could bring a drop of sweat to my brow."

I peered behind him, knowing there were at least two more Zhauri brothers, not far from us. "It's not a fair fight if your friends can hear us and run to save you."

"They're brothers," he corrected. "Perhaps further into the trees then?" He gestured openly to the dense woods behind me. I held my breath, scarcely able to believe this luck. I could break his shield. I knew I could.

"What happens if I win?"

"You can go of course. I'll be dead at that point."

338

"And if you win?" I asked, already retreating back from where the other Zhauri could hear.

"Like I said, I'm not big on torture. So if I win, you're agreeing to give me everything I want, including our little Epic's location."

I narrowed my eyes dangerously.

"Or I can leave you to my brothers back there," he said, "and they will break you, I promise. It's your choice."

I turned around to walk with the most impressive display of confidence I'd ever faked. I looked frequently to either side, craning my head far enough to make sure Dauer wasn't too close and that his dog had returned to his side.

My gift would work this time. I was in serious danger, and every bit of me knew it. It had to work.

I waited until I was absolutely positive the remaining Zhauri couldn't hear us, and then I whipped around with hands full of destruction and shot a crackling bolt toward him.

His dog made a mad dash toward me as my lightning collided with a shield like Archie's, shimmering blue rather than gold.

But it wasn't breaking.

I shocked his dog before she leapt at me, and Dauer howled in outrage, throwing a shield in front of her as she yelped and crashed into the ground. He darted toward me, and I prepared for the fight of my life before realizing he was catching his dog, crouching to lower her instead of letting her crumple into a heap.

A hoarse, distressed scream echoed from my right, and I froze in terror, positive it was Archie's.

Dauer leaned over to kiss his dog on the forehead before stepping over her.

"That's my friend?" I pointed toward the next pained cry, frantic because I couldn't run to him until I'd dealt with this one.

"Yes. I think you're aware that my brothers don't share my squeamish stomach."

339

I shot another bolt of crackling destruction at Dauer, knocking him off balance before he regained his footing.

"You can't do this!" I hissed. "My actions had nothing to do with him!"

"Maybe not, but he sure came in useful for finding you."

My words turned into exasperation. "*Why* are you even here? I'm not worth your time!"

"You dear, sweet girl," Dauer said, making the hair on my neck prickle furiously, "there's a large bag of gold back at the Dragona that makes you worth our time. It would seem Ratuan took more than just lives on his way out of the Escali capital. So for several reasons now, you're going to tell us where our little Epic is hiding, and then we're to bring you to the celebration in Glaria."

I blew air through my lips in a jeering laugh. "You think *I* know where she is?"

He raised one eyebrow and said, "I guess we're about to find out, aren't we?"

Dauer would have been taunting me if the tone of his voice wasn't so... conversational. Playful, almost. Like we were old friends, and I posed him no danger.

I blasted him with my most powerful bolt of destruction yet, and he held his hands out to brace his shield. "I was thinking we might do this without magic!" he called over the explosive sounds of collision.

"I'm sure you'd like that, wouldn't you?" I retorted, digging my toes into the earth as the sheer force of my lightning pushed me backward.

Dauer said, "Have it your way."

He wound both hands back and flung each at me, one and two, like he was throwing invisible rocks.

Two solid brick walls slammed into me with a faint blue shimmer, one and two, and I found myself suddenly flat on my back, gazing at the sky above. *He could throw his shanking shield.*

The breath had been knocked from my lungs, and I gasped to get it back as I rolled strenuously back to my feet, my brain unseated and reeling. It was a miracle I didn't have blood pouring from both nostrils.

"Alright, changed my mind," I wheezed. "No magic. No need to… disadvantage you."

Dauer laughed as I regained my bearing. He was an overconfident fool, and I ran straight at him, probably before I should have.

Dauer kept his large sword in a defendable position right up until I reached him, and I struck twice with my blades, then spun for a surprise third. I was intent on making contact with any part of him, but he was *much* faster than I'd predicted and had such disciplined form that he blocked all three of my shots. Still, surprise lit his eyes as he realized that between the two of us, I was faster.

I twirled my right sword around his blade and stuck his tip into the ground, pinning it in place as I struck for the kill with my unopposed left blade. Dauer ducked and punched me in the gut, knocking the wind from my chest for the second time and grabbing my arm before I could hit him.

I twisted my left arm, trying to get my blade close enough to slice into him, but he cut me off by twisting the other direction entirely.

Oh shanking life, he was strong.

I could feel bones popping as pain shot from my wrist to my elbow and I yelped in panic, knowing it was close to breaking.

I lunged to bite his hand, startling him enough to loosen his grip, and then I led with a sharp blow from my shoulder, knocking into Dauer with enough force that we both crashed to the ground. I kept my momentum to roll away and quickly back to my feet, just barely escaping his grabbing hands, and then I crouched to take advantage even though my entire left arm cried and protested the movement.

I tried to slice through him on his way to get up, mainly using my right arm, but he dropped back to the ground with a laugh and avoided my swipe. I tried to stab him while he was down, but he knocked my blades away in a loud clang that reverberated through my hands. Dauer surprised me with a sudden jump that put him back on his feet, grinning as he went on the offensive. I was able to block his rapid strikes and throw in a few attacks of my own, trying to learn his habits even though he seemed to change his style with each shot.

Dauer flung his blade sharply left in a complicated twist that blocked my right sword and knocked the left blade straight from my numb hand. I was left with only one — a weapon that was significantly shorter than his, but rather than try to retrieve the first one, I darted to the side and blocked his next strike as he dashed after me. I had to use several ingenious parries against his longer blade, but I was able to keep him from hitting me.

He was going to destroy me if I couldn't pull off a stroke of brilliance, but I already had it planned. I needed to get Dauer close to the first blade I'd dropped without him noticing, and I could do that.

I darted in and out between trees as I dodged his attacks in something of a warped circle. I was eventually very close to the foliage where I had dropped my blade when I dove for the ground and knocked Dauer's legs out from under him. His instincts were quick and he broke his fall by throwing his hands out, but he actually managed to grab me with his legs as he hit the ground.

Dauer let go of his weapon to curl around and snatch my clothes before I could scramble away from him, and from there he dragged me closer until he had his giant hands around mine and I couldn't possibly maneuver my sword to harm him.

I couldn't lose to him like this, so close to my dropped left blade, so close to having an advantage. Dauer used brute strength to twist my wrists until I shrieked and dropped my second sword, and as he snatched my fallen weapon, I had a split second to grab a handful of dusty leaves and fling them in his eyes.

If Dauer was perfect, he would have grabbed me and dealt with his blindness later, but I caught a lucky break as he flung a hand to his face, giving me just enough slack to squirm free and scramble over to the first blade I'd dropped. In the split second Dauer used to claw the dust from his eyes, I slid the weapon up the back of my jerkin and into the waist of my pants.

I jumped to pull myself onto the branch above me as Dauer got his eyes open and his feet back beneath him, out of breath and angry. He thought I was disarmed and attempting to flee, so he dropped his sword before leaping to grab my sandaled feet with two hands — and I let him.

I just wasn't prepared for the pain of my torso hitting the branch as he attempted to drag me to the ground. Clinging tightly to the limb, I was just about to lose the blade on my back, so I made the riskiest move of my life, let go of the tree, drew the sword as I fell, and swung it at his undefended chest before I slammed onto the ground.

And it worked.

I sliced right through the front of Dauer's gray and silver tunic, and he exhaled an echoing shriek as it bit through fabric and flesh. The impact of the forest floor rattled my brain before I saw a red stain seeping across a wide arc of his chest, and I regained my footing.

I snatched Dauer's larger blade off the ground before staggering back from him, leaving him disarmed and bleeding as my head spun and my entire left arm still throbbed. He remained standing and clutched at his chest for a frantic moment. It likely wouldn't kill him unless I gave him a few more to match it, and though I was incredibly tempted to do so, I hesitated.

"Dauer?" another of the five called. They'd heard him shout.

Zeen tore through the trees to see his brother bleeding while I held the offending blade in my hands.

"What have you done?" Zeen shot me a look of wide-eyed fury, and then he whistled four short chirps to send his dog running at me as Maverick arrived in disbelief and circled behind. I crouched with Dauer's sword extended, ready to impale the brown dog with white paws and patches, but it recognized the weapon for what it was and pulled up short.

I felt a rope thrown around my neck from behind and I twisted to confront Zeen with a snarl, but the dog leapt and bit my weapon arm and Maverick crashed into me as well. The two men and vicious beast slammed me into a tree, and within three seconds had pulled my hands behind me, around the thick trunk, and tied them together.

In the time they'd taken to secure me, Dauer had remained on his feet, stripping his cloak from his shoulders as his breathing grew deeper and more strained. Zeen and Maverick stepped to his side, and with practiced efficiency they each grabbed a side of his tunic to rip it over his head and reveal a muscular chest with a giant gaping slash, nearly reaching both his shoulders.

They were speaking their own fluid language, and I didn't understand a word but for Dauer's name being spoken as they lowered him gently to the ground on his back. Kit appeared as well and said something unintelligible to the others. They responded in kind, and he glared at me before taking off toward where I'd heard Archie's screams.

I couldn't hear Archie anymore. What had they done?

344

I tugged at my wrists and rubbed the backs of my arms raw as I struggled against the tree. I was out of rescuers. I was out of options, and nearly out of hope.

I could stay calm in the midst of a fight, but now I was helpless. I had to keep a steady stream of encouragement running through my head to keep from hyperventilating. Sweat was already beading up all over my body as my stomach cramped and the urge to flee screamed through every part of me.

This couldn't be happening.

The two tending to Dauer had pulled first aid supplies from their packs and were going about the task like it was routine. Like they'd had a thousand practice runs of exactly this, and could bandage him in two minutes and take a nap afterward. They spoke in low, serious voices until Dauer said something that made Maverick and Zeen chuckle. The two glanced at me before they sank back into their task, conversing in a language I couldn't begin to interpret.

I tried not to watch, but they were the only things moving, and if I didn't keep myself distracted from the terror racing through my veins, I was going to throw up. Of course I was afraid for myself, but I also hadn't heard Archie in several minutes and couldn't handle wondering if that was a good thing or the worst thing imaginable. He had to be ok. I couldn't go on if he wasn't.

The two on either side of Dauer finished patching him up, got to their feet, and began to build a fire without further acknowledging me. Dauer tried to sit up, and Maverick responded by pushing him roughly back down with a booted foot. I didn't know what *Ika va tnouagh* meant, but the tone made it sound like *Stay down. You know better.*

Maverick said nothing further as he and Zeen gathered sticks and logs, and Zeen knelt to light the pile. Flames licked up to engulf the twigs, and just as I began to wonder why they needed a fire in the middle of a warm day, a strict voice in my head demanded I not think about it.

Do not feed the fires of fear, it said. *Discipline governs the embers and the flames.*

I wasn't sure if I'd just thought that up now, or if it was a memory from my past, but I repeated it over and over. *Do not feed the fires of fear. Do not feed the fires of fear.* It didn't make me any less afraid, but the mere repetition of something so flat and simple was better than running through a hundred imagined scenarios for how the day would end.

"Water?" Kit's thickly accented voice startled me from behind. I distinctly remembered the dark glare he'd given me no more than twenty minutes ago, and I shook my head quickly, despite an incredibly hoarse throat.

He unstopped the water skin and took a drink to show me he hadn't poisoned the thing, then held it out a second time. I shook my head again, and he shrugged and joined the other two at the fire, conversing once more in their fluid, melodic language. It seemed much too soft and... pretty for them, but such is the irony of life, I suppose.

Dauer finally sat up and inspected the bandaged strips across his chest without anyone scolding him, and I felt drops of sweat join together and trickle down my back as he turned his focus to me. I tried to keep a strong front and glare back at him, but it only lasted until he said something to Kit, who sniggered and responded in kind. I found my eyes on the ground with my teeth gritted like the torture had already started. Dauer got to his feet, and I closed my eyes so I didn't have to watch him approach me. I was too close to a panic attack.

I couldn't help hearing his footsteps though, and I felt his weight on the ground as he came toe to toe.

Fierce trembling rattled my tied hands as the reality of my situation sank in and I opened my eyes again, keeping them on the ground. Was this the part where I started begging? I was too distraught to even try.

Dauer leaned very close as I tried to push myself further back from him. "First things first. You fight dirty, you live dirty," he said. I didn't realize he had a handful of dirt and leaves until he threw it into my eyes, and I yelped, flinching back as far as I could.

I shook my head viciously as tears welled into my vision and I tried to blink the dust away.

"This, you earned fairly," he glanced toward his bandaged gash, "which makes you very rare indeed."

"You cheated," I said, dust still scratching my eyes, mixing with tears to make gritty mud as desperation made my voice shake. "You and I had a deal if I won."

"You hesitated. You knew you had to kill me to win, and you didn't," he said with an indifferent shrug. "Don't feel too badly. I didn't get what I wanted either."

"Untie me, and we can go back at it," I said, laughing because it was the only thing I could do other than cry with hopeless self-pity.

"Funny enough, I'm considering it," he said.

I smiled thanklessly at the ground. I knew he was toying with me, that the suggestion was a cruel game, and I would be a stupid, desperate girl if I clung to it.

I was a lot of things, desperate certainly one of them, but not stupid.

"Do it then," I said. "And if I can kill you, your brothers let me and my friend walk away from here."

Dauer's smile turned cruel, and I knew I'd just asked too much. "Please," I added quickly. "He's important to me. I... need to know where he is."

347

He leaned in closer and said, "Don't mistake me for a kind man. That, I am not. I simply have an appreciation for beautiful things. It saddens me to see them broken."

I huffed a snort of disbelief, because that had to be the dumbest thing I'd ever heard. "You misunderstand me," Dauer said, unashamed. "I've seen the most beautiful woman in the world, and you are not her." I squinted in disgust to let him know *just* how much this conversation pleased me. "You are attractive the way a meal attracts the starving, or water brings the thirsty. I find myself bored with endless money and a world that cowers before me, trying to please me. You are different and interesting." I studied his face, not sure if he was serious, and not sure if this was going to get me off the hook or not.

I swallowed lightly and said, "You should have been a poet."

"Who says I'm not?" His voice sounded playful again, like he'd forgotten I was tied to a tree.

I opened my mouth to speak, closed it again, then asked, "Can you untie me now?"

He grinned at the question, but turned and walked away rather than answer.

The rest of the Zhauri utterly ignored me, leaving me to suffer anticipation in silence. They knew what they were doing. Fear is its own form of torture, but as I blinked and shook my head to get the scratchy dirt from my eyes, I couldn't lessen my sense of terror.

They spoke in their own language and began unpacking the outer pockets of their bags. I closed my eyes the second I heard the clang of metal instruments being withdrawn. I didn't need to know what they were. I didn't want to guess.

CHAPTER THIRTY

An argument erupted from the trees. I couldn't hear the words, but they sounded deep and angry. Kit emerged back into the camp, shouting loudly in his language, followed closely by a disinterested Dauer, and behind him — Sir Avery.

I slouched forward and took a deep breath as Sir Avery glanced my way.

Sir Avery spoke in Icilic, then switched to Human and repeated for me, "I was just telling them I'm quite sure Ratuan knows Ebby's location is a mystery to you. He just wanted the Zhauri to teach you a lesson. I have a different deal for you though, if you'd like to get out of here."

I closed my eyes for a moment of disbelief, then opened them again and said, "I'm up for pretty much anything."

The hint of a frightening smile crossed his face before he said, "I'm sure you've heard we're having a celebration tonight. I need somebody who can translate Escalira for us."

I watched him, knowing that wasn't the whole of it. He could translate anything I could translate. "And I get to walk free afterward?" I asked, because I'd rather be anywhere but here.

"If I'm satisfied by your performance, yes."

"Alright," I said, feeling the ties around my hands vanish. I massaged my rope-burned wrists as Sir Avery moved closer and I stepped instinctively back. "The party is a few hours off. You can come with me now, unless you'd rather stay here, of course."

I twitched a corner of my mouth, attempting to look just a little amused by the joke. "I'll come with you," I said, adding, "Where's Archie?" in a whisper as he approached further.

"I saw to him. He's fine."

I worried that we might have very different definitions of fine, but before I could question him further, Kit shoved Dauer back with more shouted accusations. Dauer clutched his chest in pain as Maverick stepped quickly between them with hushed words, and Kit angrily backed off.

Sir Avery set a hand on my shoulder, and the woods were replaced by an unadorned stone tunnel of the Dragona, the entrance to the Everarc Cave beneath me. "Walk down, and lock yourself in," Sir Avery said as I glanced around. "If you cause a hint of trouble, I'll have you wishing I'd left you with the Zhauri."

"Understood," I replied, stepping into the cave where the shock left me breathless and chilled.

"I'll come and get you when the festivities begin," Sir Avery said as I entered a dank cell, smelling of aged straw and neglect.

I clicked the door closed to total darkness around me, suddenly afraid of being left entirely alone. "I thought Sav was supposed to get Ebby back to you. What happened to that?" I called into the empty darkness.

I heard a faint chuckle from above. "Savaul's interests had nothing to do with Ebby," Sir Avery replied. Silence fell, and I thought he might have disappeared before he added, "Actually, I should thank you. I didn't think Savaul would have anything to offer me, but an introduction to Izfazara was quite sufficient."

I sank down against the wall, reminded suddenly of my list of tally marks and the side that read *Deaths That Were My Fault*.

Sir Avery gave a hearty laugh. "Thank you for giving me his letter. Without you, I never would have gotten past Izfazara's interaction spell."

Maybe I shouldn't complain about lying in a pile of hay — some horses, cows, and sheep don't even get such luxury. I'm sure prisoners have lived in worse accommodations than my tiny cell, and for much longer periods of time. I wasn't shackled to a wall, and I wasn't being tortured... Well, not by anybody else. I was my own worst torturer, allowing fear to consume me, sadness to wad me up in a little ball, and anger to pour off me in toxic waves.

I felt drained and exhausted, and I wasn't sure if it was because there was no magic, or if I'd worn myself down in a fit of worry. But finally the pitch black of the cell sank in and I began to feel hollow. A few hours with no light is enough to make you question your safety. A few hours more leaves you with a gnawing fear, knowing that a rat could be a hand's length from your face. A few hours later, and you find yourself making noises, just to make sure sound still exists.

I also felt like I might be starving. I couldn't remember the last time I'd eaten a meal.

Careful footsteps began to echo around the cave, and I noticed the very faint outline of my hand appearing. Somebody was bringing light.

I wiggled my fingers and savored the sight after so many hours of gripping them together to make sure they were still present. Then the light grew stronger, so bright that I could make out the pale fleshy color of my skin.

My door creaked open, and I nearly had to throw an arm over my eyes as a burning torch cast flickering shadows across the walls. I squinted and forced myself to look at Tarace, who was wearing a look of hardened pity.

"I thought I adequately warned you," Tarace said. "I thought you would have run, knowing the punishment for treason."

"I *did* run," I muttered, folding my arms to look strong as a tight lump rose into my throat and my stomach growled angrily. "But I'm not here to get ten thousand years. Sir Avery wants me to translate for him. I'm walking free afterward."

Tarace stared at me, his face blank. "That's what he told you?"

"Yes."

I thought I saw a flash of irritation in his eyes before he said, "Ten thousand year survivors are always released after their sentence. They're left in the woods to wander until they die."

I closed my eyes for a moment.

Of course Sir Avery would let me go, after an eternity of loneliness, and after I was no more than a walking corpse.

"I'll see to it you get a trial first," Tarace said. "We won't be skipping that, even if you are a traitor."

"A traitor?" I repeated, nearly laughing because I didn't know how else to react. "*You're* the one who told Sir Avery I'd come to talk to you," I said, rising to my feet. "*You're* the one who chose to attack the Escalis when they were willing to negotiate, and now they've got a brutal king coming into power. You killed the one who was willing to negotiate!" I said, unable to suppress a manic laugh any longer. "I had us two steps from ending this entire war, Tarace. You knew that. And you. Betrayed. *Me.*"

I locked my eyes to his, because for as long as he lived, I wanted those words to haunt him.

Tarace didn't flinch, and he didn't look away from me either. He shrugged one pack strap off his shoulder, and I felt my knees shake

352

in a panic as he pulled it open. I had no way to defend myself here, in the cave without magic.

"If anyone brings you soup later, I would advise you not to eat it," he said, removing a small loaf of bread and holding it out to me. I hesitated, because my mouth watered at the sight of something edible, but I also knew he might yank it back at the last moment. I reached forward and closed my fingers cautiously around the food, left speechless as he released it to me.

Taking the bread burned my pride, and I couldn't even keep eye contact with him because I had just acknowledged that he had power, and that I was helpless. The feeling made me want to cry. I didn't look at him, and I didn't thank him.

"I know you were trying to help," he told me. "And I wish you had gotten away. Everything would be easier if you had just gotten away."

I picked mindlessly at the bread in my hands.

"Everything could have been over by now," I said, my voice choked to a whisper. "Why didn't you just take Prince Avalask's deal? You said you wanted the same thing we wanted."

"The peace we spoke of wouldn't have lasted. If Prince Avalask kept Ebby, in five years the Escalis would have three strong Epics against our one. That would mean the end of Sir Avery and every Human life on this continent."

"You are an idiot, Tarace," I mumbled, knowing I shouldn't be goading him. "That's not what Prince Avalask was trying to do. If you knew the first thing about him, you would know he wasn't trying to play you."

He sighed and said, "I did try. I did approach the other major city leaders, but we couldn't come to an agreement. I'm not Anna, I can't just make people listen. And without everybody on board for a truce, we had to take the alternative. Which you have to admit, went pretty well in our favor."

"Sounds like Izfazara's dead," I said.

"And Prince Avalask's son," Tarace said. I kept my face blank. "It's amazing what Ratuan did down in those Escali caves. He singlehandedly tipped the balance of power across the continent. Last week, we were crippled to the point of nearly needing to surrender. Now we've got the upper hand."

"That Ratuan. Quite the saint."

"You're going to see him at the ceremony. We're celebrating him and reuniting the Dincaran kids with their parents coming back from Tekada."

"And then executing Prince Avalask," I finished bitterly. "And what do they need me for? To translate his last words?"

"I'm not sure," Tarace said. "I honestly think Ratuan has other plans for you up there. Have you seen the stage in Glaria before?"

"I've heard it referred to as the sky stage."

"Be careful. It's very high above the ground, and Ratuan *really* doesn't like you."

I nodded and said, "I'll consider myself warned."

CHAPTER THIRTY ONE

"She can't be dead!" Ebby's voice startled the surrounding birds into silence.

"I've looked, you've looked, and she's nowhere," Vack said, crossing his arms tightly across his chest. "She's nowhere."

"Somebody could be shading her," Ebby said, her chin beginning to quiver. "Maybe the Humans caught her and they're just keeping us from seeing her."

Vack fell silent, turning to look over their ridge where Glaria lay spread next to the ocean. The city was *huge*, with giant towers in the middle, miles of docks extending into the water, and buildings sprawling so far along the coastline, the Epics couldn't possibly see the whole city in one glance.

Jalia was the one who said, "We can figure out what happened to Allie later. Right now is about Prince Avalask."

Ebby threw her hands over her face and tried to keep from crying. Jalia was right, but guilt and horror were twisting their way into Ebby's vision in the form of tears. Allie. The girl who'd been there to help her for as long as she could remember, the girl who inspired her, and told her to think for herself... Vack would be dead right now if not for her. Ebby would be back in the arms of Sir Avery and Ratuan.

355

"Get it together, both of you," Jalia said, making Vack scowl at the suggestion he wasn't already together. "What's happening in Glaria?"

"Nothing yet," Vack said, still gazing out over the massive city. "They're still setting up... Wait. I see my father. Come here." He held a hand to each of them in a hurry. Ebby and Jalia each grabbed him, and Vack showed them the top of the most prominent tower in the city — though not quite the tallest — where everybody below could see.

"Tell him we're here," Jalia said.

"I'm trying," Vack replied, looking anxious. "They've done something to him. He can't hear me."

"Let me see," Jalia said. Ebby caught a glimpse of Jalia squeezing Vack's hand, and Vack gave her the ability to control where he looked. Ebby had no idea they could even do that.

Jalia's thoughts absolutely fascinated Ebby as she scoped out the entire area around Prince Avalask. Jalia felt the emotions in the air, observed the architecture, examined the curtains along the back of the platform, and ran through every reason Prince Avalask might be there, narrowing them to the most probable.

"They call it the sky stage," Ebby said softly. "Look how it towers over the city so everyone can see, and then look at that huge open space beneath, where everyone's gathering."

"There's no question it's a stage," Jalia replied shortly.

"But it's also a trap," Vack said, pointing out the two women concealed on either side of the stage. "All five Zhauri are waiting on the staircase, and those women are the ones who took the magic out of the air when..."

Vack left his sentence hanging, and who could blame him? Ebby and Jalia knew the event to which he was referring.

356

"Look who else!" Jalia exclaimed. Prince Avalask was hidden from sight on the left of the stage, and on the right, Sir Avery was speaking to none other than —

"I knew she was alive!" Ebby said.

"Listen to them," Vack said, and the girls fell silent to focus.

"See the archers in the towers above us?" Sir Avery pointed out the two closest turrets to Allie. "If you or Avalask make a wrong move, you're both dead. Get it?"

"Got it," Allie replied, looking fiercely irritated, but not afraid.

Vack groaned. "There's no *way* to get them out of there."

"All we have to do is get Sir Avery away," Jalia said. "So focus on wrecking whatever's out on those ships, and trust that your Uncle Savaul can do the rest."

Ebby let go of Vack's hand to gaze at the ship Savaul had warned her about. It was the very last one coming into the harbor, the largest of the fleet but with the least people, and it seemed to no longer be moving.

The others were packed full of the non-mage survivors from the Dincaran battle, all of whom were beyond eager to see dry land and welcoming faces. They must already know the Dincaran kids awaited them, because the joy and relief in the air were incredible to witness. Overwhelming, actually.

"Ebby?" Vack caught her attention. "It's started. Ratuan's up on the stage."

Ratuan's name felt like an arrow through her heart. "Ok," she said, returning her thoughts to the ships instead. She couldn't stand to see him, and tortured minutes passed while Ebby watched the ships and Vack and Jalia watched the tower.

"Ebby," Jalia said, piercing her with her intensive stare. "The trap up there is for you. They're trying to lure you onto the stage."

Ebby's shoulders sank. "What?" she whispered.

Vack also broke his trance to look up at her. "Ratuan knows about your *nobody hurts my friends* complex. That's why Allie and my father are up there."

"You think he means to hurt them?" Ebby asked, already knowing the answer. Ratuan would do anything to get her back.

Vack and Jalia each grabbed her hands to show her what they were watching, making them a tight triangle of silence.

Ebby could see tremors wracking Ratuan's knees as he stood at the back of the stage, watching a wildly expressive mage named Shadar speak. Shadar had the gift of projecting his voice as far as the wind could carry, and happened to be the most beloved storyteller in the world.

"To all the heroes from the battle in Dincara last year, this celebration has been put together in your honor. We welcome you home with our sincerest condolences and eternal gratitude for all you've done for Humanity." His arm gestures were so wide that the furthest citizen in Glaria could see them, and his deeply respectful voice portrayed emotion as well as any facial expression.

His words echoed over the entire city and across the ocean, saying, "As you step off those ships and rejoin us, it is my pleasure to announce that we have incredible news with which to greet your return. First and foremost, we've killed King Izfazara, who's ruled the Escalis for nearly thirty years."

A huge wave of cheers swept through the crowds, and Shadar leapt playfully aside to gesture attention toward Ratuan. "Join me in commending a young man named Ratuan for his bravery, for rallying an army of children to rise up and destroy the Escalis from the inside!" Ratuan beamed and absorbed the infectious energy of the following cheer. "To all those parents returning from Tekada, you deserve to be proud of your children, more than you could ever imagine. Let's get another cheer for the reuniting of all those families, split up and sent across the world, only to return to each other once more!"

Cheers, whistles, and screams of pure joy erupted as, right on cue, Eric and Steph found their parents among the returners and ran to them among the wild applause of everybody watching. Everybody laughed and cried, and joy filled the air around them, infectious beyond all measure. And Ebby could sense that every second of it was planned.

"This is what it's all about, folks!" Shadar shouted. "We have on our hands nothing short of a miracle, and one brought to us by the bravery and leadership of this young man."

Ratuan gave a humble smile in response to the next wild cheers and said, "I just planned the thing. That's all."

The whole continent laughed as Sir Avery amplified Ratuan's voice to echo over them as well. Ebby heard Vack growl beside her, "That manipulative little—"

Ebby refocused to hear Ratuan telling the crowds, "I'd also like everybody to meet our guests of honor."

The white cloaked Zhauri pushed Prince Avalask onto the stage from the left, and then Allie from the right. Allie's hands were free, but Prince Avalask's were quickly bolted to the floor in strong chains.

"There's no way," Vack repeated, hands shaking.

"Those mages are positioned to take all the magic out of the stage area," Jalia said, her brows furrowed with a daring idea. "We can't rescue your father, but we might be able to save Allie."

A moment of silence fell across the confused crowd, followed by shouted threats and hate for the two villains, despite the fact that hardly anybody knew Allie. Allie and Prince Avalask glanced at each other and then hardened their gazes, watching over the ocean skyline like they couldn't hear the crowds below.

The angry rants turned back into excited screams as Sir Avery joined Ratuan on the stage, a smirk on his face at the attention and love of so many.

"Sorry to cut in," Sir Avery said, "The exciting part is happening sooner than we expected."

Sir Avery raised both hands to the sky and Ebby's stomach dropped as he called the very clouds down into a dark pillar above the city. Savaul's face appeared around the pillar so every person, from the harbor to the forest, could clearly see him and hear his voice booming over the top of them. His words were morose and hateful, and spoken in Escalira, meaningless to the crowds who didn't understand.

Chapter Thirty Two

My entire body stiffened as Sir Avery moved behind me and set a hand on my shoulder. I blocked my mind on instinct, but he wasn't attempting to break into it.

"Your turn," he whispered in my ear.

My breath caught in my throat. Too many people. Too many.

I felt like I was about to be lit on fire. I couldn't move, couldn't speak—

"I am going to count to five, and if you're not translating, I'm killing Archie."

I craned my head back to hiss, "You are a rat—" startled to hear my voice echo across the entire city.

Sir Avery raised his eyebrows at me and whispered, "Three, four—"

"Alright, listen up former friends," I shouted, hearing my voice carry like a thousand copies of myself shouting from the mountaintops. "This," I waved both arms up to the pillar of clouds as my heart slammed against my chest, "is Savaul, the younger brother of Prince Avalask, and the one who is taking over for Izfazara. I would lecture you about what a mistake it was to kill the former king, but whatever. Carry on celebrating your—"

I gritted my teeth as Sir Avery tightened his fingers on my shoulder with unnatural strength.

"Doesn't sound like we've missed much," I went on, almost without pause, but the grip didn't loosen. "He's just finished explaining about the brutal slaughter of their king by the Human kids, to whom they'd shown mercy. Now he's telling them that they need to band together as the fighters they are to get Prince Avalask back."

I glanced at Prince Avalask's impassive face as Sir Avery hissed, "Word for word."

I scowled and wanted to explain just how difficult it was to translate between two *completely* different sentence structures, but saved my breath and gave it my best shot. I waited until the end of each sentence to hastily translate into Human, which made me miss half of the next thing Savaul said.

"He's saying... that the... *soul* of the royal family was broken yesterday, and can never again be whole... Time is no... There's not time to waste. Every man and woman needs to come together to rescue Prince Avalask.... Because..."

I heard the words *"Drathna ol nirza dthek Vack,"* and jerked my head to see Prince Avalask, whose jaw had fallen ajar.

"Say it," Sir Avery said, sounding positively giddy behind me.

"He... he says Vack was killed in the escape," I said, my own soul falling apart as I watched Prince Avalask's expression turn to mortal horror. "The Escalis' new Epic has been killed before he was able to... pass down his gift. So Prince Avalask is the last Epic they'll ever have."

Savaul's furious voice faded and the clouds over the city dispersed back into the sky. I gaped at Prince Avalask and watched him fall slowly, silently to his knees as that news sank in. He hunched forward but couldn't bring his hands around to cover his face as despair saturated his eyes.

"*No.*" He whispered to the ground, but his breaking voice carried over the entirety of the city as well, amplified for all to hear. I turned to Ratuan in utter disgust. This was sick beyond measure.

Ratuan sneered back at me and whispered, "It gets better."

Prince Avalask shook his head in disbelief before finally breaking down in front of the masses. "He can't... Avery?" Prince Avalask looked up from his knees. "Let me see him. Please, just let me hold him one last time. My Vack... My..." He let his head fall and said, "You have everything you want. Just let me hold my little boy."

The Epic dissolved into breathless sobs, and I felt hot tears spill onto my cheeks, wishing I could rush to him, whisper that Vack was alive... *something.*

Ratuan said, "By the time the night is over, the Escalis will have lost two Epics and a king. We've regained a thousand potential mages, and you haven't even seen yet what's being unloaded from one of the Tekadan ships. The only thing we were supposed to come away with, and *didn't,* was Sir Avery's daughter. She was also held captive with us down in the Escali pits. She would have made it out with us if not for *her* betrayal."

Ratuan pointed a dooming finger at me and I heard shouting out at the harbor. I mainly heard the word *traitor,* and saw that Ratuan's cohorts, Eric and Steph, were the ones riling the crowd. Their parents seemed just as eager to watch me burn, and joined their kids, adding their own suggestions of *ten thousand years* and *throw her off the stage.*

My heart leapt into my throat as I realized kids all over the city were beginning to chant *ten thousand, ten thousand,* and Ratuan shot me a glance that said, *you should never have messed with me.* He was still their ring leader, and those kids soon had the entire city either chanting with them or shouting their general hatred for me.

Holy shanking life.

Sir Avery laughed behind me and said, "Sounds pretty unanimous. You can't argue with a crowd like that."

My heart shrank as I realized this might actually happen. I'd be better off dead than living ten thousand years of nothing. *So much better off.*

I looked at the edge of the stage in terror, not sure if I dared. Would they stop me?

"What do you say then?" Ratuan asked Sir Avery, his voice still carrying through the city. "We can have our execution, give the traitor the Time she deserves, and end the evening with the treasure we've brought back from Tekada?"

Joyful cheers rose across Glaria, echoing through the alley ways and out over the ocean, until Tarace burst onto the stage in outrage. The cheering got louder until they realized what he was saying.

"This isn't how we do things!" he shouted, and somebody finally amplified his voice so everyone could hear. "You don't get to destroy due process for thrills and jollies. This is *not* how we run trials!"

"These seem like pretty extenuating circumstances," Sir Avery replied with a casual shrug and a grin. The crowd just grew restless now, not sure if they should be cheering, or shouting, or possibly *thinking*. "I'll be the first to admit we need a leader on this continent who can make that decision though. It's about time we declared independence from King Kelian and established our own ruler. And what better time than tonight, when we're all gathered?"

I got the feeling that the crowd below us was just waiting for something to be said to which they could applaud, because they cheered raucously, so loud that I barely heard a violent crash on the stairs behind the stage.

A shriek was accompanied by shouted orders and the clang of metal on metal.

364

Sir Avery dashed back toward the stairs and disappeared, and as soon as he was gone, Ebby landed in his place, much to my horrified shock. She nearly startled Ratuan out of his skin as she walked straight up to him and set a hand on each of his shoulders, gaze dead-set on his.

"Nobody hurts my friends."

"Ebby?" he replied, utterly breathless.

More shouting echoed from the archers above us and I felt the sudden, icy shock of magic disappearing from the air. Ebby had to be insane to have fallen for this. She was nothing without magic.

Ratuan grabbed her hands and whispered desperately to her, but I couldn't make out his words without my Tally hearing.

Sir Avery reappeared on the staircase, and at the sight of Ebby, he jerked his eyes up to the archers in either tower and shouted, "We've got her! Shoot Avalask!"

I glanced up just long enough to see both archers' arrows trained on Prince Avalask. I couldn't let Prince Avalask die, and knowing that I'd rather be dead myself than suffer Time, my next course of action was clear.

I forced my deadened legs to propel me forward, and I tackled Prince Avalask out of the way, shrieking as one of the arrows meant for him sliced into my shoulder. It wouldn't kill me, but death couldn't possibly hurt like this blade tearing through my flesh, leaving a deep, bleeding stripe in its wake.

I clamped a hand over my bleeding left shoulder, seething through gritted teeth as Prince Avalask ducked back from me. "Allie!" he said, his voice hoarse with despair and his cloudy eyes tinted red. "You can't stop them, but you can stop Ratuan. Don't let him get his hands on Ebby!"

I looked over to see Ratuan's face half a breath from Ebby's, looking straight into her eyes and speaking quickly. And Ebby had frozen to absorb his every word.

365

"Hurry," Prince Avalask said. "I'll be fine."

I understood what he wanted and agreed that it needed to be done, so I stumbled toward the kids and grabbed Ratuan around the neck and waist, using every muscle in my body to jerk him off the ground, back from Ebby.

I flung Ratuan toward the edge of the stage and he barely skidded to a panicked stop instead of falling over the side to his death. I ran straight to him and lowered a shoulder as Ebby screamed, and Ratuan grabbed me as I slammed into him without any of my usual agility or control. He used my momentum to shove me off the side, and I kept my hold on him and dragged him over with me.

Our feet left the stage and Ratuan clawed hatefully at me as I tried to push him off for the fall. Ebby's shriek echoed across the city just before she leapt after us.

The ground was a staggering distance away, but within seconds, it was terrifyingly close and Ebby latched onto us screaming, "I can't jump two! I can't do two!"

Ratuan shouted, "Let her fall," and for once in her life, Ebby didn't listen to him and kept her hold on us both.

We were seconds from the ground, and I gripped Ebby's hand as terror flooded through me at the thought of dying here and now.

An instinctual rush of magic filled my hands and jumped into Ebby's, not to shock her, but to somehow give her the power for an incredible feat. And right before we slammed into the screaming crowd beneath us, the ground disappeared and was replaced with ocean waves.

The three of us plummeted straight into the harbor with all the speed of the hundred cubit fall. I screamed as the momentum tore at the gaping wound on my shoulder, ripping it apart with stinging ocean water.

I'd expelled almost all the breath in my lungs, and twisted around frantically to see that Ebby and Ratuan had vanished. All I could make out through the murky dark was the underside of a giant ship with several ropes securing it to the bottom of the ocean, like they'd dropped nearly ten anchors.

I kicked my legs to head for the surface, but shrieked again as a strong hand wrapped around my ankle. I had no breath left, and twisted violently as somebody dragged me further into the water.

My attacker had something that looked like a giant, upside down ceramic pot that she threw over my head, and I struggled harder until I realized it was full of air.

I immediately began coughing, and the Escali woman who'd grabbed me got uncomfortably close to poke her head up into the air pocket as well, wiping her eyes as I turned my head to the side to cough and cry from the sheer pain.

"Who are you?" she demanded, making me gasp as she grabbed me by the neck. She leaned even closer to smell me as I clutched weakly at her hands on my throat and avoided her dark, storm-cloud eyes. "What are you doing down here, Tally?"

"Just trying to help," I said, gasping a manic laugh because that was all I ever tried to do. "And bleeding."

I winced as she released my throat in concern. "Are you the one who's supposed to be up on the ship?" she asked. "We've kept it from reaching shore. You weren't our girl on the inside, were you?"

"What? No, not me," I replied. "What's up there?"

She shook her head, and I could see something like fear behind her menacing frown. "We just know it's going to make the Humans stronger if it reaches shore."

A different, smaller hand grabbed mine tightly, startling me in a gasp. I immediately dunked my head into the water to see, hoping Ebby had found me, but I only saw the dark, short outline of Vack as he pushed off from the ocean floor.

Vack and I landed on dry ground in a loud splash of water, and I crumpled into the dirt before taking in the sight of two other girls. Ebby looked like a drowned cat in her drenched white dress. The second was a dry Escali girl with braided hair, helping Ebby tug her dress off over her head.

Vack swiped a hand over his dripping arms, and every droplet of water clinging to him exploded into mist, leaving him completely dry. He did the same to his legs and torso as I watched the girls in utter confusion. They got Ebby's dress off, leaving her in the white slip of clothing beneath, and then handed the dress to Vack, who shook it once in another explosion of water droplets. Now that it was dry, the Escali girl started helping him put it on.

"Are you alright?" Ebby asked me. I frowned at her, then held an open palm toward Vack as he pulled the dress over his head, my question of *am I hallucinating* made pretty clear.

"Everybody thinks Vack's dead," Ebby said. "He's going out to destroy whatever's on that ship, but we're making him look like me in case he's seen."

The Escali girl was telling Vack softly, "Ebby will be watching. All you have to do is find it, destroy it, and get out. You're going to be fine."

Vack gritted his teeth with his eyes staring into nothing, and his hands shook fiercely. His brave face was impressive under this much pressure.

Vack clenched his fingers tightly as Ebby moved closer to put her hands on his face. Feature by feature, she changed everything about him. His hair became long, wispy, and lighter than mine. His eyes turned blue. His face softened until it looked innocent and kind, and he looked more like Ebby than the drenched girl in front of him with her hair in a knotted mess.

"Am I ready?" he asked, sounding eerily still like himself.

Ebby nodded, and Vack took one last look at the Escali girl, who'd watched the process with joyful fascination. She grabbed Vack to hug him, put her lips next to his ear, and whispered, "Go wreck them."

CHAPTER THIRTY THREE

Ebby sank to the ground and crossed her legs, focusing on some distant thing as Vack leapt into the air and the Escali girl settled studious, dark eyes on me.

"What's your name?" I asked her.

"Jalia," she replied, nodding to my shoulder. "How bad does it hurt?"

"It's pretty bad." I reached to my now-gaping wound, lurching back from the sting of my own touch. Then I rolled dramatically onto my side and heaved a sigh using all the breath in my lungs. "Oh, how I wish somebody nearby had the power to heal injuries…"

Ebby snapped her eyes toward me, startled. "I'm sorry," she said, glancing quickly at the bleeding sight. "I got distracted watching Vack. Here. I can help."

Ebby moved to set her fingers gingerly on the cut, and I took a shuddered breath as the sharp pain subsided to a dull throb.

"Our attention needs to be on Vack," Jalia said, sitting expectantly next to Ebby to grab her free hand.

"It'll keep getting better," Ebby told me with a friendly smile, using her free hand to grab mine as well.

I felt a fumble of thoughts mix with mine as I tried to lower my mental defenses in a hurry, and then Ebby allowed the three of us to watch Vack with more than just sight. She could hear what he was hearing, feel what he felt, and see everything around him.

Vack was invisible in the dim depths of a ship very different from the one on which I'd hidden last year. This one smelled like unfinished, roughly cut wood and was stacked floor to ceiling with boxes. The shape and size of each container made them look like coffins, like the whole ship was a floating graveyard.

Vack crept around the stacks, looking for anything significant, thinking back to Ebby, *These are all I see.*

Get one of them open, I thought loudly. Ebby winced at the enormous thought rumbling through her. Vack's teeth rattled fearfully as two people passed by him, checking for anything amiss among the stacked rows.

Come on, we need to know what's in them, I thought, careful to think it a little more quietly.

Vack pulled his courage together and leapt onto one of the giant stacks. He climbed up fourteen boxes to the top, barely an arm's length from the ceiling, and studied the wooden surface in front of him.

Look at this, Vack said, peering at the Human words burned into the light wood, beneath the starred crest of Kelian.

'A Reminder that Magic is Banned on Tekada. Long Live King Kelian.'

Apprehension prickled the hairs on my neck, and it was incredibly strange to feel the same jittery wariness cloud Vack's ability to think.

He looked over the frame again, found four latches around the exterior, and lifted each one before pulling the wooden face off the top.

I gasped as shock flooded through Vack at the sight of a dead Human body, and he dropped the wooden top to the floor in an unforgivably loud clatter. *A Reminder that Magic is Banned on Tekada.* One of our murdered mages.

Every muscle in Vack's body seized up, and I worried he might lose his grip on the stack and fall to the floor himself.

Vack? It's ok. It can't hurt you. I tried to calm him, but he'd frozen in utter terror. He stayed thankfully invisible as three pairs of lookouts converged around the commotion.

"What happened?"

"No idea. One of the lids fell off."

"What the..."

Vack. You have to climb down, Jalia thought to him, remaining the calmest of us. *Climb down and get away from them.*

And then set everything on fire, I added quickly. Ebby glanced at me, and I explained, *I don't know why they're bringing a ship full of the dead back, but if something about this ship is going to give Humans an advantage, then we do NOT want it reaching the shore.*

I could feel an added element of fear enter Vack's mind, imagining an army of dead rising up, and I repeated, *Get away from them, and start setting things on fire.*

One of the men on patrol leapt onto the same pile Vack had climbed, pulling himself to the top to investigate. Vack used the noise the man was making to mask his own steps as he climbed back down, leapt off, and retreated from the attention.

A voice carried down from above deck. "Something's wrong. The wind is blowing, and we're not moving."

Vack had found an abandoned walkway between the stacks of the dead, but froze in place. Jalia thought rather firmly, *Get it together, Vack. You're wasting time on childish fears.*

That, above all else, brought flame to Vack's hands, and Jalia added for good measure, *If you don't get Sir Avery's attention, he's never going to leave your father's side.*

Vack shot a stream of blue flames at the nearest stack of coffins, and then he spun and threw another flame-burst at the pile behind him. Vack pulled white destruction like mine into his hands and began punching loud, explosive holes through the outer hull of the ship, reducing the planks into millions of splinters wherever his power struck.

Ebby broke her focus away from him to check on Sir Avery, and Vack's ruckus certainly hadn't gone unseen. The older Epic had his eyes on the harbor, but his jaw remained set in a firm line. Prince Avalask hadn't risen from his knees, still crippled by the belief that he'd lost his world, and Sir Avery didn't look eager to leave his side.

Vack, he's not falling for it, Ebby thought to him.

What more do you want me to do? Vack retorted.

A bolt of lightning shot down from the sky, struck the mast, and scorched several massive cracks through the ship's wooden frame, adding sparks to the fires.

Fire! More fire! I thought to him, and Vack raised more flames from the floor, torching more columns of coffins as frantic shouting around him and above deck added to the roar.

Vack punched several holes in the floor to reveal a level of wooden boxes below, and he leapt down to land precariously on another tall pile of coffins. He set fire to the rows around him, coercing the flames to spread quickly through the lower level of the ship as the air grew heated, smoky, and difficult to breathe.

Ebby had her attention split between Vack and Sir Avery, and Sir Avery looked very pointedly behind himself at the Zhauri and said, "It's bait. I'll stay here. Go get her."

Sir Avery waved an arm, and all five brothers disappeared from the sky stage.

Vack! Get off the ship! I shouted into his mind.

Vack replied *I'm —*

But his response was drowned by his mind's equivalent of an earsplitting scream.

Ebby, Jalia, and I all jerked in surprise as vicious agony tore through Vack, and he crumpled atop the coffins, suddenly visible to anyone who wanted to see.

"It's Sir Avery's daughter!"

The men on the middle deck gathered around the hole in the floor as smoke poured up through it.

"Don't hurt her!" another sailor shouted to the Zhauri descending into the flaming mess.

"I'm not hurting her," Iquis called back, his voice tinny and unnerving. He was a filthy liar. Ebby, Jalia, and I could feel the blinding pain ripping Vack apart, so brutally intense that he couldn't even utter a cry of distress. He had been reduced to a pile of shudders on the stack of boxes as his mind was tortured, murdered, and brought back to life to be tortured further.

One of the crew above gathered enough courage to leap through the scorched hold in the floor and land on the same pile Vack had collapsed atop. He grabbed the little girl he thought was Ebby, pushed the hair back from her face, and said, "You're alright. I've got you."

To make everything worse, the entire ship was beginning to tip sideways.

"Which one has our weapon?" Kit shouted at the crew.

"Down below!" the man holding Vack shouted, pointing to one of the flaming stacks, coughing as smoke filled his lungs. "It's already on fire."

Vack's thoughts were purely screams and cries at this point, and I couldn't handle it. The entire ship was tipping, and the man holding Vack was beginning to panic as a row of the caskets next to them toppled over, each box weighing enough to cause them serious harm if their stack fell too.

374

"Ebby." I let go of her hand. "Get me in there."

Ebby froze in horror and her jaw fell open. "Stay invisible, drop me in behind that mind mage, and get out. I can help."

Ebby stood with me, grabbed my hand, and jumped.

I landed with unexplainable forward momentum, crashing straight into Iquis from behind with no hint of grace. I brought lightning into my hands, dug my nails as deep into his neck as they would bite, and attempted to shock the evil right out of him — all within an arm's length of his brothers.

Iquis screamed and crumpled to the ground as a row of coffins clattered down beside us and a massive chunk of the floor collapsed, falling to the lower level in a loud series of thuds and crashes. Vack regained control of himself just as his row tipped and fell, but the other Zhauri drew their blades in outrage, and I never saw what became of Vack. I shot lightning at Maverick, but Dauer leapt to his defense and threw a shimmering blue shield between us.

The floor became so slanted that I could barely stand as one of the men next to the fiery pit exclaimed, "We can't let her burn!"

Dauer lunged after me, and I bolted away as Maverick turned to Kit, giving him one simple, calm instruction.

"Break it."

I prayed Maverick didn't mean me, but I dashed behind a row of coffins in a rash attempt to distance myself anyway.

I tried to take short breaths, but began to cough as burning smoke coated my throat and lungs, and Dauer darted after me. I turned around with lightning in my hands and he pulled up short as I shot a powerful bolt of destruction at him, which hit his shield and pushed him back a few skidded steps.

A deep crack resonated across the ocean, like the cracking of a thousand-year-old tree trunk, and more burning caskets fell behind me, sliding across the floor as the ship began to capsize, one of them bursting open to expel a dead woman's body.

"You ready?" Dauer asked, seeming to take absolute joy from whatever was coming. The pile next to me was leaning, and I had to lurch back toward Dauer as it toppled over. The floor split beneath me, and I stumbled straight into him to keep from falling through to the fiery lower level.

I elbowed him sharply in the side as he caught me, but he just yanked me off to the side as the split in the floor widened with another earsplitting crack.

I jerked myself free of him and leapt across another growing fracture, back toward the other Zhauri, my only route away from Dauer. I stopped in pure shock as I saw Kit ahead, his hands glowing with purpled black. He was moving them slowly apart, a look of deep, strenuous concentration on his face, and I realized what he was doing. He was breaking the entire shanking ship in *half*.

A giant gaping fissure broke through the ceiling above us in a deafening roar, and the hull below the lowest level splintered apart as well, allowing water to rush in and quench the flames. The entire ship was solidly pulled into two halves, and I couldn't even figure out what was keeping either side standing.

Maverick stood directly in front of Kit, watching with calm intensity before telling him, "Drop it."

The dark bearded brother dropped his hands and both halves of the ship simultaneously fell to the left and the right in a whoosh of air, crashing into the ocean in a massive explosion of seawater.

I wanted to scream, but held my breath instead as water crashed in over me. Every coffin from the lower stacks sprang up to rush for the surface, and I threw my hands over my head for protection as they swarmed by, battering me along the way.

I clawed my way to the surface as well and took a great gasp of air, grabbing one of the closed caskets as somebody exclaimed, "Didn't you at least mark which one it was?!"

"Of course we did! We painted red over the words."

The weapon wasn't the dead themselves, but it was inside one of the countless coffins now dotting the ocean surface. I knew I could swim back to land unnoticed among all the wreckage, but I didn't want them to get their hands on whatever it was. I looked at the face of the coffin I'd grabbed, but the burned *Long Live King Kelian* didn't look red by any means.

"I found it!" shouted a woman near the border of the wreckage.

"Hold on, we're coming!"

I looked frantically around to see that the other swimmers were about the same distance from her as I was, but swimming was my most severe weakness. I'd never reach her first.

I pulled my knees onto the coffin to which I clung and recklessly leapt to my feet as it wobbled beneath me. I didn't have time to hesitate, but leapt to the next wooden box floating in the water, and then quickly to the next until I was essentially running across the tops.

I threw a bolt of lightning at Maverick before he even saw me, and kept going. I was two boxes away from the woman and could see the red paint across the words on the coffin when an arm lurched up from the water and tripped me. I stumbled and fell into the water, twisting to see my attacker, struck with the fear he might be one of the dead.

But it was shanking Ratuan, pulling me underwater as he clawed to get his hands around my throat.

I had my knife still in my sandal-laces, but Ratuan was both Human and young, so I wrapped an arm around his neck and strangled the life out of him instead as he thrashed and clawed at me. Easy prey.

At the top of the tower, I had been ready to shove him over the edge and kill him. But now I felt torn by the fact that the kid I was killing didn't have any hope of escaping me and was panicking in my crushing grasp. He was a child. I should be protecting him, not killing him.

I let go as Ratuan fell limp in my arms and somebody grabbed me from behind, shoving me underwater as I twisted around to grapple with him for the upper hand as well.

But this was Kit.

He had one arm around my neck and a hand holding the back of my head so I couldn't pull my face back above the surface. I had no idea how to fight in the water, and had already lost most of the air in my lungs, so I resorted to the age old trick of bringing lightning to my hands. I grabbed the arm around my neck and unleashed a deadly stream of destruction that sizzled through him.

Something was wrong though. I couldn't make it stop. It was something about the water, the lightning just kept flowing from my hands, lighting up the ocean around me, long after he'd released my throat and ceased moving at all.

I breached the surface but began to panic as the stream of destruction continued, growing continually weaker as I grew infinitely more tired. *Oh shanking life,* I didn't know this would happen. I would never have used my power in the water if I'd known, and all I wanted to do was take the decision back.

I sputtered and gasped for breath as the lightning in my hands dwindled into a dull glow and I clung to the nearest floating coffin, right on the verge of passing out.

All the other swimmers converged around the coffin with red paint, except Dauer who came straight for me.

He unlatched the nearest coffin and dumped the body of the man into the water, where he floated facedown to my absolute horror. I growled at Dauer as he grabbed the coffin edge to capsize

378

the box and fill it with water, scooping it beneath me before I realized what he was doing. The box leveled out, still floating with me inside, and Dauer grabbed the wooden lid as I threw my arms up to keep him from clamping it over me.

"Don't you dare!" I shrieked as my will to fight finally refilled my limbs and I tried to shove the lid away.

He already had one side wedged down, and I lunged forward to grab two handfuls of his thick hair, snaking my torso out of the box so he couldn't shut me in.

"What do you think you're doing?" I hissed. The heavy lid came to rest on my head and shoulders as he pried my hands out of his hair, shoving them back into the box with the rest of me.

I was nowhere near ready to give up, and already had one of my legs halfway out of the coffin when he lifted the lid and brought it heavily down on my skull, dazing me with the sudden urge to curl into a ball and vomit.

"I'm looking forward to the chase of a lifetime with you." Dauer snapped something cold and metallic around my wrist before pushing my every limb into the box and snapping the top down to encase me in utter darkness. I groaned and pulled my hands over my face, trying to regain my good sense when I just felt sick and dizzy.

His muffled voice carried through the sealed wood. "Make it worth my while."

The bottom of the coffin was filled with freezing seawater, and I pushed my drenched, tangled hair from my eyes, taking a panicked breath in the confined space. Things were happening all around me, but the lid above was stuck in place, and no matter how hard I pushed and kicked, I was wearing myself out to the tune of no progress. I tried to bring lightning to my hands and got nothing.

Ok. Still yourself and think.

379

I fell still, closed my eyes, and then withdrew the hunting knife I kept between the laces on my sandal. Taking one more deep breath, I wedged it into the tight space where lid met coffin. I couldn't get the opening to budge until I gripped the knife handle with two hands and used my whole upper body to splinter straight through the wood, just barely prying open a peephole between the latches.

I pressed my face close to my only source of light as the casket tipped forward and water gushed in through the opening. I moved my weight to the other side of the box to tip it back upright, and carefully leaned back to look out, mindful to keep the thing balanced.

I heard desperate voices saying, "It doesn't look like the fire got through."

"Well hurry up and get it open!"

"Out *here?*"

"Yes, out here. We have to check on her."

I squinted and watched as much as I could see, considering there were several other coffins bobbing between mine and the excitement.

The rescuers pried the lid off and I barely caught a glimpse of the red paint on the front before a very loud and panicked gasp rang from the opened coffin, and a woman with fiery orange hair bolted upright.

Well, shanking life.

This *would* make the Humans stronger.

They hadn't brought back a weapon, but a leader — one everybody would follow and listen to.

And her name was Anna.

CHAPTER THIRTY FOUR

My box tipped too far forward and water poured in through the hole again, so I dislodged my knife and returned it to my leg as I lay my head back in the drenching cold.

Even if Savaul hadn't killed Anna like he claimed, she would have been killed in the massacre of our mages on Tekada. I had no idea how someone had snuck her onto the ship and gotten her across the ocean, but it was no wonder they'd gone through the effort.

That was their final treat to end tonight's celebration, the knowledge that Anna would be able to unite the Human cities in a way nobody else could. She was well known, feared, respected, fierce — the leader Humanity desperately wanted and needed.

I wrung my hands together, trying to warm them with my breath as I caught a severe case of the shivers. There was no way to get warm with cold water caressing half of me. I curled my knees into my chest and hugged them as I resigned to ride this out. The ocean around me had fallen silent but for the waves knocking against my box. I'd been abandoned.

The adrenaline in my veins eventually turned to cold, slow-moving mud, and my fears of dying were replaced by fears of living. Because assuming I escaped this container alive, it would

381

just be to run from the Zhauri and their sudden fascination chasing me. There was nothing to go back to. The Escalis wanted me dead, and the Humans wanted worse.

Hours passed, and the only victory I had, alone in the dark, was that I refused to hate myself, even though I was incredibly, *incredibly* tempted to.

Why do we, as people, do that to ourselves? Why, when the world has turned on us, do we want to tear our hair out and scream at ourselves that we deserve everything handed to us?

I hated that temptation, and so I stomped on it by confronting every decision I'd made since saving Vack. I didn't regret a single one. I hated their outcomes. I hated where I was and what I had to look forward to, but there was triumph in knowing I hadn't lost sight of myself. My sense of self was all I had to cling to anymore.

That, and the tight metal band Dauer had clamped around my wrist before locking me in here.

I tried to slide it off my hand, but it was too small, and I couldn't feel a single crease in the metal where I could pry it back open. I toyed with it over the next hours, knowing I couldn't fall asleep with all the cold water pooled up around my head.

I was exhausted. So incredibly tired, and I did drift off at one point, only to startle myself awake, choking on the salty water with tears in my eyes.

After a day or two of drifting, my coffin began to tumble, and the spinning momentum tossed me around until the box finally settled to the sound of sand scratching the exterior, upside down. I wedged my knife into the opening to let the water drain out, but instead of gaining a fiery will to crack the lid open and flee to safety, I hugged my knees once more and drifted to sleep.

Of course my dreams were filled with coffins, and dead bodies, and Zhauri patrolling among them as I tried to pull the lids off. I got them off, one by one, to find Karissa inside, then Robbiel, then Nessava, Corliss, Emery, Celesta, and eventually, in a panicked stupor, I pulled off the coffin lid with Archie inside.

I woke with tears streaming down my still damp face, landing in my still dripping hair, and I shivered as I remembered how cold the world was. Closing my eyes, I rubbed at the fresh new welts I'd just clawed into my neck, and then began planning my next move.

Muffled voices reached me from outside just before my whole box was flipped over. I tumbled over inside but remained still, leaving my eyes closed for precious seconds longer.

The lid above me was pried off and I heard a sympathetic sigh.

"Can't believe Kelian did this," a girl above me said.

"I know. You can go if you want. Digging the graves might be easier than pulling them off the beach."

"No, I'm fine," she replied as two hands reached under my arms to lift me out. "I just think I might hate Kelian more than the Escalis."

"Gret... This one is warm."

"What do you mean?"

"I mean, she's freezing cold. But she's alive."

"*What?* How? The trip across the ocean — never mind! Let's get her up to the house."

The man and woman lifted and carried me all the way up to their home, and I didn't protest or even stir.

I was only vaguely aware of them bringing me inside. I heard the girl shooing her husband, or whoever he was away, and then warmth. I was warm again.

Chapter Thirty Five

The pile of coffins Vack had collapsed atop was tipping over. He was seconds from a long fall into a mess of flames and heavy tumbling boxes when the torture in his head became suddenly bearable.

Vack gritted his teeth against the pain still searing his mind, and he grabbed the man beside him before jumping them both off the ship.

He landed on the sandy beach with the man still at his side, then keeled over and pressed his hands to his skull as the agony of his attacker still throbbed through his head. Vack had never felt anything like it.

Ebby and Jalia watched from the ridgetop as the man knelt next to Vack, asking if he was alright, and looking around frantically to find somebody to help. He had a kind face, and still thought it was Sir Avery's daughter who'd curled in on herself in the sand. He took one glance toward Glaria before reaching his arms under Vack to lift and carry him.

Jalia growled protectively and then took off, sprinting toward the beach. Ebby watched her for a shocked second before turning invisible and jumping down to the beach as well. The man carrying Vack nearly panicked as he spotted Jalia running at him.

He set the little girl in the sand and drew a blade from his side, shocked by the appearance of such a young Escali, but also more than ready to kill her.

Jalia stopped short of reaching Vack and hissed at the man, crouched low like she was ready to spring at him, blade in his hand or not.

Ebby snuck behind him and pressed her fingers to the man's back, willing with everything she had for him to fall asleep.

He crumpled into the sand, and Jalia leapt over him to get to Vack, grabbing his hands and whispering, "I can help you. Let me help."

Jalia whispered more to him, and Ebby turned her attention back to Glaria to make sure they weren't being pursued.

The celebration had been disrupted by the commotion in the harbor as an entire ship was violently destroyed, but Sir Avery had never left Prince Avalask's side, and Prince Avalask was still alive on the stage.

Ebby watched fearfully around them as Vack opened his eyes, and Ebby noticed Jalia sharing in his headache, taking on some of the throbbing suffering so it would be more bearable. The two were staring hard at each other, and Ebby wrapped her hands around her lonely self, wishing she had somebody like Jalia in her own life. Ratuan would do this for her if she was ever in pain…

She had only told Ratuan two things before he tried to convince her to stay with him. *Nobody hurts my friends* and *if anything happens to Prince Avalask, you'll never see me again.*

In hindsight, she should have included Allie's safety in the ultimatum, but she was sort of proud she'd stood up to Ratuan at all. Ok, so she hadn't done it perfectly.

Ebby watched Glaria as they brought a woman with bright orange hair onto the stage to the amazement and vast excitement of the crowds beneath them.

Everybody on the continent had heard of Anna, and Ebby watched as Anna told the crowds of the horrors on Tekada, and she swore on her life they would never again take orders from King Kelian, or send him valuables, or refer to their continent as Kelianland.

Ebby watched the celebration until the very end, but Ratuan never reappeared on the stage, and no further acknowledgement was given to Prince Avalask. Maybe it was because of her threat. Maybe they had never planned to kill the Epic. She didn't know.

Jalia and Vack were still on the ground. The suffering shared between them was subsiding, but they hadn't taken their eyes off each other.

The man Vack had brought back with him still slept soundly as well, and finally, after the celebration had ended, after Ebby had scanned the ocean, and after she was certain Ratuan was safely back on dry land, she whispered, "I can't find Allie."

"Maybe we should stop pronouncing people dead, just because we can't find them," Jalia replied, making Vack smile at her. His hair had finally turned black again, his nose and chin had sharpened, and his eyes had regained their hazy green tint. "It's also about time we left. You two *have* to get stronger."

"We'll never be stronger than those Zhauri," Ebby said, hating that even *Vack* had been helpless against them.

"I know you won't," Jalia said, "but they only have five powers. You and Vack have all of them, and you're both brave. Fights aren't won on strength alone."

Ebby raised her eyebrows, surprised to hear her name anywhere near the word *brave*.

"You also have wicked intelligence on your side," Jalia said, tapping her own temple with a grin, looking at Vack.

"The Zhauri have no idea what's coming," Vack agreed with a smirk. The two of them finally sat up and released their hands to rub the sand off their faces.

"And Vack," Jalia said, giving him a stern look, "give Ebby her dress back. You look ridiculous."

Ebby laughed softly to herself as Vack scowled and got to his feet, looking ridiculous indeed.

Chapter Thirty Six

I woke up in front of a roaring fire, beneath three wool blankets, wearing soft clothes that weren't mine. My knife had been brought along and left on the hearth beside me, and I reached for it on instinct.

"You won't need that here," the girl said from behind me.

I twisted and winced as my joints protested. She was the only other person in the small, one room cabin, and didn't look more than a year older than myself, dressed in plain grey clothes with her mud-colored hair hanging freely behind her shoulders. I hesitated and then set the knife back down, knowing she could have already harmed me if that was her intention.

"We found you on the beach," she said with a soft smile. "You looked like a wreck, in more ways than one."

She held a crackled porcelain cup down to me with the warm, spicy scent of autumn tea inside, just a small chip missing from the side of it.

"Thank you," I said, quickly wiping my eyes at the familiar smell.

"You can call me Gret," she said, interlacing her fingers in a loose grip as she knelt close to me. "I'm pretty sure your name is Allie, isn't it?"

I felt blood race into my cheeks as I glanced at the door behind her.

"I recognized you when we pulled you off the sand," she said while I kicked the blankets away and stood slowly. My bones creaked with every small movement, and I moved to where my clothes had been hung on a wooden rack. They'd apparently dried ages ago, leaving me to wonder how long I'd slept. Gret stayed seated, her hands still folded. "Nobody knows you're here," she said.

I finished tugging off the soft shirt that wasn't mine and donned my own before I stopped to consider her.

"You have no reason to trust me," I said softly, muffling a small cough at the vibration in my throat.

I quickly overcame the discomfort that came with undressing my lower half and set to getting my full outfit back on.

"I don't trust you," she said. "But even the worst villains from the stories won't kill somebody who's rescued them. And I'm curious to know about you."

I set my hands on my hips, wishing I had my short swords hanging from either side, feeling bare without them. I hadn't held my blades since battling Dauer. "I'm exactly what they say. I'm the reason we didn't get our Epic back," I said with a pitiful excuse for a shrug.

"But why?" she asked, her voice breaking like I'd personally tried to hurt her. "You knew we could all die without her."

"She didn't want to come back," I said with a hopeless laugh. I knew Gret wouldn't be able to understand any of this, so I don't know why I went on. "Everybody will say she's brainwashed, but she's just been shown the other side of the conflict. And she knows she's powerful enough to tip the future. She's trying to make sure she tips it the right way."

Gret watched me with something like... sympathy? Empathy? Like she believed me, at least believed that I wasn't trying to watch the world crumble, but thought I was misguided.

"I should go," I said, stepping back toward her to grab my knife off the mantle.

"Gret?" her husband thrust the door open with a toddler in one arm. I was surprised to see a child, because he also looked no older than me. "We should have left her down there," he said, throwing the door shut, pulling the drapes closed over the one window next to it. "There's a falcon circling above the house. They're coming to get her."

"What color falcon?" I asked quickly, moving to the window to peek out and see a still, mossy forest.

"I don't know," he replied, looking furious as the little boy in his arms screwed up his face like he was about to cry. "Who have you brought upon us?"

"I don't know either," I said as the kid fought to get down and then stumbled in a fuss to Gret, who picked him up again. "I'm sorry," I said, glancing between them. "I'll go. Thank you, and... I'm so sorry."

Brum brum brum brum, rattled the entire small cabin and I felt like I'd choked on ice. How could this be happening? This new little family might end up dead, and all because they'd tried to help me?

"You have one minute to open this door before you all burn!"

I dug my palms into my tired eyes and said, "You're all going to be fine. I know who it is."

The father made to stop me as I moved to unlatch the door, and I looked straight at him. "You both just saved me. I'm not about to let someone hurt you."

Hesitation lit his eyes, because he'd *probably* just seen a massive crowd chanting to give me ten thousand years for being a traitor.

"Let her open it," Gret said.

I could see she didn't fully believe me either, but just enough to give it a shot.

I pulled the door open to see Emery with flames in his hands, looking ready to fight his way inside, and surprised to see me at the door.

"All darkness is only shadow," he said immediately.

I gave him a short laugh in response and said, "I'm sure light exists somewhere, but I have *no* idea how to get to it."

Emery studied me with a frown, then shrugged and said, "Good enough for me. You ready?"

I nodded and looked back at Gret, mouthing the words, "Thank you," one last time before turning to leave.

They both still looked frightened, so I pulled the door shut behind me and extended a hand so Flak could land on it. I held her up and butted my forehead against hers, as was our tradition. "Thanks for taking care of me," I whispered, taking off into the trees with Emery as Flak leapt up to my shoulder for the ride.

Emery glanced at me and asked, "You alright?"

"Yeah," I replied, and that was good enough for us both.

"Do you know how the celebration in Glaria ended?" he asked.

"No. Fill me in."

We trekked through the woods, distancing ourselves from Glaria as quickly as we could.

"Prince Avalask?" I asked.

"Still alive."

"Anna?"

"Going back to the Dragona for a little while to make it a school again before she steps up to run the continent."

"Ratuan? Vack? Ebby?" I wrung my hands together.

"Don't know, don't know, don't know."

391

I watched the ground carefully as I trod across the last of the autumn leaves that hadn't yet disintegrated, and swallowed hard.

"Archie?"

"We're on our way to see him right now."

"We're *what*?" My voice jumped two octaves and Emery threw a hand over his ear.

"Don't do that!" he said. "I wasn't even going to tell you until we got there. I don't want to listen to your love-blubbering the whole way."

I kicked him hard in the shins and he scowled back at me.

"I don't love-blubber," I said under my breath.

"Good. Puts you about ten steps ahead of Archie then."

A wide grin spread across my face, and when Emery frowned in disgust, I bared my teeth and hissed at him.

We didn't say anything else for the rest of the trip, but I somehow felt that we'd become closer friends that afternoon. Funny how these things work.

We found Archie sitting on a log next to Ebby, who was once more in her pretty white dress without stains or burns. He spoke with the smile of a storyteller, and Ebby had her hands folded politely in her lap, watching with doe eyes.

"We've arrived," Emery called to them, and Archie leapt to his feet immediately.

He didn't run to me. Actually, he looked rather like I frightened him. Or perhaps he just feared I would remember the last time I'd run to him, when he'd tackled me to the ground for the Zhauri.

So I marched straight up to him, watching him grow more skittish with every step, and then I threw my arms around his middle and pressed my face into his shoulder.

He took a sharp breath and said, "I am so sorry," wrapping his arms around mine. "It was Iquis, Allie. He kept convincing me I was alone, and safe, and that's the only reason I was whistling—"

"Could you stay here forever?" I asked. Archie laughed hopelessly and I smiled too.

"I wish I could. I just came to make sure you were alright. And then Ebby was trying to tell me you were dead—"

"I can't track you anymore!" Ebby said, as I finally let go of Archie. "What are you doing that's stopping me?"

"This is new," Archie said, reaching to grab the gold band around my wrist. I let him take my hand and Ebby moved closer to squint at it.

"I think that's it," she said, frowning. "Why have you never put it on before now?"

"One of the Zhauri slapped it on me, out in the water," I said. "Dauer, the new one."

"Why?" Archie asked, holding it up to look for any sort of clasp.

I was pretty sure I knew why. "They want to be the ones to track me down," I said.

Archie sighed and said, "*Somebody* is going to pay handsomely to send the Zhauri after you when nobody else can find you." I nodded hesitantly, but Archie sensed there was more to it. "And they know you'll be the most difficult hunt of their lives. They're looking forward to the challenge."

His eyes asked, *am I right?*

"Yeah, I think they're more interested in the fun," I said, folding my arms uncomfortably at the thought of Dauer in particular. "I was thinking with everything going on… that maybe you would stay with me instead of going back to the Dragona."

Archie's shoulders sank. "You know I want to," he said. "I always want to see you, but I have to be there to placate Sir Avery, and… I have to face reality at some point, Allie. If I don't get away from you now, I'm going to lose you, and I can't go through it again."

Emery leapt to his feet and said, "That's my cue to leave. Archie, it was good seeing you."

He retreated to the safety of the woods as Ebby asked me, "Are all boys allergic to emotions?"

I let a small chuckle escape. "It's almost scarier when they're not."

She took a deep breath of acceptance and then said, "I'll leave too then. You'll see me again soon."

"Thanks, Ebby," I said as she leapt into the air and disappeared.

I looked at Archie, and he watched me sadly before pulling a pack off his back.

"I brought you this," he said with a halfhearted smile. "I got back to your room and swiped everything valuable. Your old journal was in my room, and I found your list of tally marks. I put a pen in there for you too."

"Thank you," I said. I reached for him, but grabbed his hands and let the bag fall. Archie held my hands loosely, hanging at our sides.

"How's Liz?" I asked, knowing the answer was going to hurt.

Archie just shook his head and said, "Not well. She's lost everyone who mattered. I thought she'd collapse and need help, and I could be there for her, but it's gone the other way. She's become independent, and angry." He frowned at the ground. "Sir Avery told the whole Dragona that she and I are innocent, but people won't talk to us. And she won't talk to me. I don't know how to help her."

"I'll find a way to meet with her," I said, ready to start planning before seeing Archie's eyes firmly on mine.

"Don't. Trust me, she's not feeling particularly forgiving."

"But she needs me. She's… always needed me." I gritted my teeth and stared beyond him at nothing. Archie had warned me I might lose her. It had always been a risk, but I'd never expected to *actually* be in this position, not being needed anymore.

"You take care of Ebby, and I'll take care of Liz," he said. "You know I consider your sister family too."

"Yeah, family," I said with a bitter scoff. "I found out Sav is the reason Izfazara was killed. He betrayed him to Sir Avery."

"Really?" Archie asked, straightening in disbelief.

"Why do you look surprised? It's Sav."

"Yeah, but Sav cares about his family. I mean wholeheartedly. Present company excluded, of course," Archie said with a short laugh. "He must have really thought giving the Dincaran kids back was a death sentence for the Escali race. For him to kill Izfazara… he must have thought that becoming king was the only way to save them."

I stared at him for a moment and asked, "Are we still talking about the same Sav?"

Archie gave me a smirk and said, "Yes. He's a killer and he's vengeful, but he's a living being too. Nobody likes losing the people they care about."

I knew exactly where this conversation was heading.

"Archie…" I squeezed his hands and tried to find the most delicate way to explain his idiocy. "If you walk away from me now, it *is* the same as losing me."

He shook his head. "No, it's different. I know Emery is… well, a jackass most of the time, but he'll keep you safe, and you guys can find the other Tallies. I can handle losing you like this, when I know you'll be ok. I can't handle watching you die."

"You don't know that would happen," I said. His jaw fell open and I added quickly, "I know being with you makes me a target, but I'm still safer with you than without."

395

And now Archie just looked thoroughly confused. "What did Sav tell you about me?"

"Just that... I mean, he told me what happened to his sister, your mother."

Frightful shock crept into his eyes, his posture, the way he clenched his fists. "He didn't tell you what killed her?"

"I know it was birth, Archie, but that doesn't make it your fault—"

Archie put a hand over his eyes and moaned, "I thought you knew." He dragged his palm across his face, and groaned again. "Oh shanking life, Allie. Yes, I'm the reason she died, but she *shouldn't* have. Prince Avalask was there, doing everything he could to keep her alive, along with the best doctors in the Escali world. She died because there's a curse on the royal family. Anyone we love dies. There are no exceptions."

Holy life.

Anyone *we* love?

I knew about the curse on the royal family, and I knew now that Archie was related to Sav, Gat, and Prince Avalask by blood. *How* had I not realized this was his real fear?

"I'm so sorry," he repeated. "I thought you knew." He made a few gestures with his hands like he was looking for words, but took a minute to find them. "I... have to get away from you. The world is going to figure out how much you matter to me, and I can't handle watching you die too."

Well *that* changed every argument I'd planned ahead of time.

"I thought that every woman *in* the royal family died," I said. "You haven't... married me or anything, that I know of." I tried to throw in a harmless smile, but Archie just had his hands gripped fretfully into his hair.

"Marriage has nothing to do with it. It's a curse on every woman the royal family loves. Sir Avery's father cast it after his own wife

396

was killed, and then Izfazara's wife fell ill and died about two weeks later. Izfazara's older sister was buried three days after that in a freak landslide, and his mother went missing and was found drowned. Sav's sister, Glidria, was captured the month after, and we all know how that turned out."

Archie shook his head with the sour memory and said, "Prince Avalask had to marry so he could have a son, even though his wife barely lived long enough to have Vack at all. When they found out Prince Avalask was having a boy, the royal family threw a party in Dekaron that lasted two weeks. If Vack had been born a girl, the Escalis' Epic bloodline would have ended."

I knew of one more family member. "And your sister?" I asked.

I held my breath, because we'd never really spoken of her. I'd never asked. Archie had never volunteered.

Archie shook his head and said, "She grabbed me and ran before anyone could kill me, and she lasted the longest of any of them. Eight years, raising me. I just... I remember that day so well. I remember waking up and she'd already gone out and trapped a rabbit to cook for breakfast. I remember thinking that morning how incredibly lucky I was, and how much I loved her."

"You have to be kidding," I said softly. "That's why you blame yourself? You think it was because you woke up that morning thinking you loved her?"

Archie chuckled darkly and said, "I wish that's all it was. But there's this plant, called devil's temptation. It's covered in sharp thorns that look like needles, every one of them filled with a horrible, slow poison."

I knew the bright orange plant he spoke of, but said nothing as Archie shrugged and his eyes grew distant. "You almost always see them," he said. "But we were being chased. One of Sav's tracking teams had found us, and when I saw one of them about to shoot, I shoved her out of the way. I didn't know they were trying to bring

397

her home alive, and I'll never forget the look on her face as she fell, and landed right in a patch of them. I… know it was an accident, but sometimes I just…"

I set my gaze on the ground and drove a wildflower into the dirt with the toe of my sandal as his breathless words became wordless breathing.

He finally went on, "I like to say it's Sav's fault she died, because we wouldn't have been running if not for him… but I'm the one who did it."

"I'm really sorry," I said. I wished I had a better knack for words so I could say something profound, or at least a little meaningful. I wanted him to know how sincerely I felt his pain and wanted to make it better.

He swallowed and said, "It was so long ago. I don't know why it still hurts like it does."

"Some wounds are always meant to sting," I said. I could feel sadness all the way from my heart to the cold cascade of dirt falling between my toes.

Archie slouched heavily against an old, bent maple trunk and leaned back until his head rested in the moss.

"I just can't do it again," he said, eyes staring into nothing. "Some people can just grieve and get it over with, but… some people have to count to a hundred thousand to avoid thinking at all. Some people can't move, can't function, and they learn to hold their breath for minutes so they don't have to feel the shakiness of each stuttered breath, reminding them how broken they are."

I opened my mouth to say I understood, but Archie shook his head like I just couldn't grasp what he meant. "There are people who cry, and there are people who lay beneath the same blanket for weeks without even being able to breathe through their nose. And everything hurts from shuddering for so long, and that constant sting behind your eyes turns into a throbbing headache that you just can't sleep off, no matter how hard you try."

Archie wrung his hands together. "And everything feels hopeless. It feels like everyone you see with a smile is faking it, and they're just expecting you to do the same."

I closed my mouth and bore the weight of those words in silence. I wanted to wrap my arms around him and tell him how sorry I was, but I knew he'd move away from me. Such was the nature of our relationship. Such was all it could ever be.

So I looked in his eyes instead, the most beautiful blue I'd ever known, beneath the golden hair he'd inherited through no fault of his own.

"Archie... No matter where we are, or how bad things get, you never have to pretend you're happy for me."

He gave me a grateful smile. "I know you've never wanted that. It's just... you and Emery and Robbiel and Karissa all worried over me and took care of me while I was grieving... You did every single thing friends could possibly do, but I couldn't pull myself together. When I laughed with you though, I could see relief in your eyes, and I realized I had the ability to make all of *you* feel better. It took a while, but I learned to wear a smile all the time, and... Maybe none of it was real, but sometimes it doesn't matter if it's real or not. I don't hurt when I'm laughing."

Archie drew a deep breath and let it slowly escape through his teeth while I watched him.

"And then I came to the Dragona last year to bail you out of trouble, and... something changed. You and I were sparring on the table tops in the Wreck, and you kicked me down onto one of the chairs, and I remember laughing so hard... I'd forgotten what that felt like, and I suddenly realized I was walking back to my room with a smile on my face and nobody around to pretend for."

He shrugged and clasped his hands. "I started to feel like… there was sunshine inside of me, I guess. It sounds stupid, but that's the best way I can describe it. And over the past months, other things have changed too. I actually got mad at you when you almost killed us both. I haven't felt anger in… well a long time. And I haven't…" Archie hesitated and clenched his fingers together uncomfortably. "I haven't… cried in my sleep in years either. I can't believe that started again. I mean, it has been *years*."

He shook his head and looked at the ground like he had to pretend I was somewhere else to speak of the matter. "It's like you're bringing back all the feelings I worked so hard to numb, and I don't know if I like them, or if I want them… And I don't think I do, because I can't stay with you. And just having to think about that hurts."

Words slowly made their way back to me after escaping into space. "You could," I said, clearing my throat as my voice broke. "You could stay with me." I held a hand out so he could easily take it. "I understand the danger. I still think you're worth it."

Archie took a hesitant step toward me, wide eyes on my open palm, torn by an unwinnable decision.

"If I take your hand, then where do we go? We'll run away, stay best friends, and I'll tell myself every day that I don't love you? Try to trick the fate that's killed every other girl the royal family has ever loved?"

Archie pressed a hand to the back of mine, closed my fist, and pushed the invitation back to me. I knew we were parting ways, so I wrapped my other hand around his and held his warmth close for the last time in a long time.

I looked up and said, "I owe you something."

I kissed him quickly on the cheek, then pulled him into a tight hug. Archie laughed and said, "I'm going to miss you."

"I'll miss you too," I said as he squeezed me back with the strength of a Tally and the sincerity of a best friend. "Take care of Liz for me," I said.

"I will, and you take care of Ebby," he said. "Keep yourself safe, and wherever you go, Allie… make sure it's somewhere I can't find you."

I lowered my eyebrows, still pressed against him as a deep sigh filled his chest. I clarified, "You're worried somebody will use you to get to me?"

"The Zhauri already used me to catch you," Archie said. "And they… know everything about you now, and about me. I told them everything."

I tightened my arms around him, knowing he wouldn't have revealed our secrets willingly. I couldn't even guess how they'd hurt him, and I asked softly, "Are you alright?"

"Yeah, I'm fine," he brushed the question off, sounding entirely casual. Only the tightening of his fingers on my back suggested otherwise. "I'm pretty sure the Zhauri will head back north now, and Sir Avery's going to be less psychotic about finding Ebby, now that Vack's dead and Prince Avalask captured."

I nodded slowly. "I know things won't be great for you at the Dragona," I said, "but will you do what you can to protect him? Prince Avalask?"

Archie sighed and set his chin on my forehead. "Of course I will. Corliss and I will keep a good watch on the Dragona, and you and Emery can get out to find the other Tallies. We'll make the most of this."

My shoulders slouched at the daunting tasks, but I didn't want to ruin my last moments with Archie by worrying over them. I glanced past him, looking for two large sticks among the foliage, and when I spotted them, I leapt suddenly away.

"One last time, before you leave?" I asked, tossing one to him, which he caught on reflex before a smile spread across his face.

"You sure you want to part in disgrace?" he asked.

I pushed my knee into my weapon in several places to test its durability as he peeled the bark off his.

"I don't know how much disgrace I'll be leaving in," I said. "Emery tells me you're terrible."

Archie flipped his stick and caught it as he laughed, then he dashed forward to swing at me, and I deflected his strong blow before spinning to hit back.

Amid a series of predictable strikes and parries, I said, "I'll get rid of this curse too, Archie. It's on my list of things to do."

Archie shook his head and said, "You may not be aware of this, but Sir Avery hates you."

I laughed through my nose and then sniffled back in loudly. "I'll find a different way to get rid of it."

Archie lowered a shoulder and ran straight into me, regardless of the hard hit I gave him for his recklessness. He grabbed his own stick in two places and used it to pin mine against the tree, above my head. We both stopped for a moment, unbearably close.

"I believe you," Archie said, his eyes bright as they always were when he smiled. "You just let me know the minute it's gone, because I want…" he stopped and rethought his words. "I want to be with you. We'll just leave it at that for now."

I smiled devilishly and closed my eyes to forever remember the hint of autumn spices in the pleasantly cool air. "You'll be the first to know."

EPILOGUE

Ratuan wandered through the massive cavern they called the Wreck and played the part of the hero being thanked for his cleverness and bravery — over, and over, *and over* again. How could *nobody* come up with a unique form of thanks? How many times did he need to hear how brave and clever and brave and brave and clever and brave he was? Inspirational too — how could he forget how many people he'd inspired with his clever bravery?

Ratuan smiled with just the perfect amount of humility to be likeable, but not so much as to appear weak and lucky to have pulled off his feat — and he was doing it for the hundredth time of the night when he spotted a girl near the Travelling Baking Show who wiped the smile right off his face.

The way she held herself was a huge hint, and her purposeful steps as she began walking were a dead giveaway, but it was the shape of her face and her large brown eyes that made her Allie's sister. They were ringed with exhaustion beneath smooth dark hair, and she glanced in either direction as she hurried from the massive cavern.

A feeling of rage stirred through Ratuan, reddening his face as he imagined stringing her up right here and now, in front of everybody, to pay for her sister's crimes. That would make him feel better. Allie deserved to feel the pain he felt. She deserved all of it plus ten thousand times more for taking his Ebby from him, and he would sleep with pleasure tonight knowing he'd crushed something that mattered to her.

Ratuan excused himself from the latest young girl who'd burst into tears and proclaimed her loyalty to him, and followed Allie's sister as she slipped into the side tunnels. He moved quickly enough to keep her in sight despite her long strides, and though she hadn't turned around to look at him, she was moving with such hurry that she must know she was being pursued.

She rounded a corner at a near trot, and when Ratuan rounded the same corner he saw the tail end of her dark hair as she sprinted around the next curve.

Allie's mirror image had legs as long as Ratuan's and the incentive of fear to make her quick, but Ratuan had grown up as the fastest kid in Tabriel Vale. He was going to catch her.

Twice he had to stop and listen to which way she'd run, but she'd chosen speed over stealth, so her footsteps echoed noisily.

The caves opened up to a huge stone room in front of him where her footsteps finally ceased echoing, and Ratuan slowed and stopped in awe. It was a library. He'd heard stories of libraries and almost never believed them, but here it was. Eight long book shelves stretched toward the ceiling far above, and Ratuan hadn't realized that such a multitude of books existed. Didn't people ever run out of things to write about?

The shelves lay to his left, but on his right was a beautiful work of art, whispering secrets to be deciphered. Thousands of thin lines had been etched into the massive wall to make a map of the whole Dragona with hundreds of labels stretching around the caverns and corridors like a massive, intricate snowflake. *Ice Mage Wing Two, Combat Cavern One, Weaponry Store Seven, Defensive Training Six,*

If Ratuan had to order the things he loved most in the world, number one would without any doubt be Ebby. But secondly, he always felt a thrill of excitement at the thought of running his fingers over a well-drawn map — a real-world chess board. He could stare at them for hours, making plans, anticipating the moves of everyone else, and finding the surest way to win. Number three would be the beauty of watching Ebby make maps. She was so artistically gifted, and when he found her, that was all he ever wanted to do — watch her paint, and draw, and make maps to her heart's content.

He nearly forgot he'd chased somebody here and had to tear himself away from the wall with the promise that he'd be back to marvel at it later.

A faint flutter echoed around the room, like a page falling from a high shelf as he moved closer. Something about that map had calmed him, and taking in the aged scent of so many books, all filled with incredible knowledge and power, brought him to his senses.

He was Ratuan — the brave, the clever. Hurting this girl would make him feel better for how long? An hour? A day? But it was the same as sacrificing a piece from his set. He shouldn't be trying to destroy her. He needed to find a way to use her.

Ratuan kept his breathing even, ready for her to jump at him with each shelf he passed, until he came to the very last one, behind which was the cave wall. He cautiously peeked around and saw her.

"I didn't know, Ratuan." She had found a metal beam the length of his arm to brandish defensively, and Ratuan heard shaky fear in her voice, but she wasn't quiet. She wasn't weak, or cowering away from him. "Sir Avery has already been in my mind and vouched

406

for me and Archie. We didn't know she was going to do this. I'm sorry. I would have done something to stop her."

Upon assessing everything about her, Ratuan changed his expression to one of shock.

"I'm sorry if I startled you," he said, motioning to her two handed grip on the metal bar. "I followed you because I wanted to meet you and make sure you were ok. I don't know your name."

She hesitated and looked him up and down, but her eyes kept coming back to his, watching where he was looking. This girl clearly had a mind between her two ears, and he liked that.

"It's Liz," she said, not loosening her grip in the slightest.

"I'm sorry to hear about your sister, Liz. It sounds like she hurt you more than any of us."

Liz responded with a short bark of a laugh and then shook her head bitterly.

Ratuan moved closer and couldn't help noticing several deep scratches at the base of her neck. "Your sister didn't… give you those, did she?" he asked, using the perfect level of concern.

Liz set a hand hesitantly on her neck and surprised him by saying, "I guess she sort of did."

Ratuan held his own chin up to show her the deep bruises inflicted in the waters outside Glaria. "She gave me these too."

Liz's shoulders sank, and she lowered her metal beam to the ground. If her slouched posture could speak, it would be saying a mix of *I am so sorry,* and *I wish I knew how to make all of this go away.*

Ratuan had to fight to keep a smile from tugging at the corner of his mouth, because she wasn't the kind of broken that would render her useless, but just the right amount, the kind he could fix. He knew his strengths. It would take time, but Ratuan could make her trust him — of this he was sure.

"If there's anything I can ever do for you, please just tell me," Ratuan said, looking into her dark eyes that looked so similar to

Allie's, fighting down the urge to claw them out. "I just wanted to meet you, and tell you that I'm sorry, and that I'm not mad at you. I'm here to help."

THE END

THIS BOOK FUNDED BY KICKSTARTER

(And 154 backers)

Dean & Wendy
  Fewkes
Amy Fewkes
Ian Showalter
Evelyn Taylor-Nelson
Sam Peilow
Sheila "Maestra"
  Stuhlsatz
Edge Rods LLC
Gerald P. McDaniel
Jen Stiles
Jordy Weee
Jd Bute
Lisa B. Martin
Kirsten Bell
Darcy Burns-Jelcz
Maria Scaramella
Sue Boucher
Genevieve Showalter
Lexi Rosenbach
Tyene McDaniel
Ashley Falter
Brian Jaynes
McKenna Sheldon
Karissa & Robbie Neal
Jenn Donner
Tressa Holcombe
Lindsay MacKay
Anders Ytterdahl
Dan Neal
Corie Burck

Cody Baker
Jordan Wall
Nadia Lustig Frye
Laurel Gray
Jon Misiak
Iain Donoghue
Nicole Hall
Kat Steinberg
Shenandoah
  Hallstrom
Susan Red Thunder
Niki A. Kmetz
Dar Gacayan
Hannah Richard
Ashleigh Nicole
  DeBuse
Aubrey Hansen
Benessa
Atthis Arts, LLC
Amber Monroe
Cassie
Michelle Neal
Nichole Silveira
Kelsey Bickmore
Erica Baker
Scott Early
David Mortman
Matthew DeHaan
Nathan Youmans
Benjamin Ellefson
Chad Bowden

Janice Emery
Homeless Joe
Lisa Womack
Kayleigh Bostain
Evan Burns
Tiffany Eller
J.J. Petersen
Laura Adams
Ada Taylor
Lindsey Richmond
Dale Groff
Cody Wheeler
Sarala Ghanta
Asal Moradi
Michael Graves
S.
Suzie Moon
Klancy Shriver
Mary Ellen Bowers
Darian
Nina Venables
Lorie Dye
Chyna L. Wagoner
Brandy Jo Grampp
Lizeth Rodriguez
Sandra
Unity Lucore
Alexandra Lucas
Yuliya LEonidova
Kathryn Reed
Cody

Tatiana Schwiering
Kaitlyn Hort
Pennye Deal
Kathryn Lucore
Nico Morales
Mackenzie Greene
CF
Patricia M Pollock
Jonna Davis
Amanda McChesney
Matthew Johnson
Ellen Boucher
Maegan Murray
Sara Privatt
Paige Hause
Laura
Olya Kravchuk
Gerald Mickelsen
Neal Adams
Brandon Michael
  Williams
Ren Bettencourt
Noelle Salazar

Stuart Pollock
Sarah Ann Richards
James LaFave
Susan Sperling
Jill Gibson
Scott Freisthler
Kayla
Jody Shriver
Jarrod Swanson
Kyle Schmidt
Molly Wakeling
Madison Keezer
Brian Davidson
Adam Randall
Tina Fewkes
Chelsea
Mikayla Pena
Brody Gandy
Brynnan Fink
Darren Fitzgerald
Kari Burkett
Alissa Maley
Julia Jakubowski

Casee Callaghan
Rob Steinberger
Stephen Heston
Colleen McInnis
Caleb Palmquist
Shawna Rexroat
Dan Spindler
Shell Adams
Casey Melnrick
Jorge Antonio
  Jimenez
SW Addict
Kyle & Amy Tanton
Zee Sa
Dana Bolen
Travis Deal
Janessa Darr
Holly Holmquist
Alyssa White
Luu Le
Wesley Steward

Pronunciation Guide

However you pronounce these names in your head is perfectly acceptable, but for the sake of resolving those inevitable arguments, here's how I imagine a few of the harder ones.

Dauer – Dow-er

Dincara – Din-car-uh

Dragona – Druh-go-nuh

Eme – Em-ay

Escali – Ess-caw-lee

Escalira – Ess-caw-lir-uh

Gataan – Gat-ay-an

Icilic – Iss-il-ick

Iquis – Ick-wiss

Izfazara – Iz-fuh-zar-uh

Jalia – Jall-ya

Nessava – Ness-uh-vuh

Ratuan – Rat-yue-awn

Savaul – Suh-vall

Shadar – Shuh-dar

Tarace – Tare-iss

Zhauri – Zhar-ee

ESCALI ALPHABET

A	E	I	O	U	Ah
(Stay)	(Free)	(High)	(Low)	(New)	(Cat)

Eh	Ih	Aw	Uh	Oo	Ow	Oy
(Bet)	(Bit)	(Dog)	(Dug)	(Book)	(Cow)	(Boy)

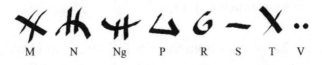

B	D	F	G	H	J	K	L

M	N	Ng	P	R	S	T	V

Th	Y	Z	Zh	Ch	Sh	W

About The Author

"I started writing this series at twelve years old, with a character named Allie who just never left me. It's been fourteen years now, and she still won't leave. "

The year is 2018, and I am in the middle of my Kickstarter campaign for Book III, A Deal For Three, as I sit down to write this new About The Author Section. WOW! It's been a crazy three years since my first printing of Secrets of The Tally, and I am ECSTATIC to have such amazing fans who love these books as much as I do.

The dream has always been to write full time, and I finally took the plunge about six months ago when I quit my day job and jumped on a train to travel the whole United States, working solely on my books. I've always been a fan of adventure (and a HUGE fan of train travel), and couldn't be happier with how the books have progressed in the past six months. I am so excited to be moving forward in the series, which will eventually be five books long, and hope you guys will check out Catching Epics and A Deal For Three. I'm sure Book IIII will be here before you know it. 😊

A Couple Thank Yous

As with book one, I owe quite a bit of my success to the people who have helped me along the way!

A big thank you to Robbie & Karissa Neal, Jordan Emery, Jessica Colvin, Laura Abbot, Caleb Palmquist, and Mom for being such wonderful proofreaders. I've now learned that the smallest typos can alter a book's meaning rather horrifically, so thanks for saving me from an unintentional nude scene, and an embarrassing jumble of letters where the cat stepped on the keyboard. (I'm kidding, I don't have a cat. I don't know what happened…)

154 Kickstarter backers brought wild success to the Catching Epics campaign, and Thomas and Cody Stoneham-Judge, once again, were instrumental in creating our opening Kickstarter video. We had just as much fun as last year, writing scripts, getting muddy, accidentally crashing a drone, and running into wildlife as we scouted for filming locations.

Ginger Anne London came back for round two, turning twenty pages of descriptions and examples into another masterpiece of cover-art, more beautiful than I imagined, and I couldn't be happier!

And as always, thank you to you, dear readers, for helping me survive as an independently published author. If you enjoyed Catching Epics, please leave a review, tell a friend, and pass the story on to someone who hasn't seen it.

Make sure you check out A Deal For Three, releasing early 2019!